The Gatekeeper of Night Spirits Vol Three

The Gatekeeper of Night Spirits, Volume 3

Miko ML

Published by Miko ML, 2024.

This is a work of fiction. Similarities to real people, places, or events are entirely coincidental.

THE GATEKEEPER OF NIGHT SPIRITS VOL THREE

First edition. October 20, 2024.

Copyright © 2024 Miko ML.

ISBN: 979-8227418609

Written by Miko ML.

Table of Contents

The Gatekeeper of Night Spirits Vol Three 1
Chapter 1 Bounty 2
Chapter 2 Many Questions 7
Chapter 3 Huang Shang and the Ghost Queen 12
Chapter 4 Monster 18
Chapter 5 Monster 2 23
Chapter 6 Drinking Party 28
Chapter 7 Mind Your Own Business 35
Chapter 8 Exposed 45
Chapter 9: Each with his own hidden agenda 52
Chapter 10: Nuwa Stone Appears 58
Chapter 11 Choice 64
Chapter 12: Killing 70
Chapter 13 Conditions of Alliance 77
Chapter 14 Eight Days Pass 1 83
Chapter 15 Eight Days Pass 2 90
Chapter 16 Eight Days Pass 3 97
Chapter 17 Eight Days Pass 4 102
Chapter 18 Changes in the Heavenly Gate 108
Chapter 19 Fight out 113
Chapter 20 Nuwa Fantasy 118
Chapter 21 In the Illusion 123
Chapter 22: The Dead End? 128
Chapter 23: The Great Disaster 133
Chapter 24 Good news, bad news 138
Chapter 25 Marriage 144
Chapter 26: The troublesome wedding 150
Chapter 27 Talks 155
Chapter 28: Decisive Battle with Lu Ping 160
Chapter 29 The First Battle 164
Chapter 30 Ancient Yin God Formation 169

Chapter 31 Keep Calm 174
Chapter 32: Draw... 178
Chapter 33: Retreating step by step............................... 183
Chapter 34 Appearance 188
Chapter 35 Night Exploration of Xingling 193
Chapter 36 Two corpses, fight! 198
Chapter 37 Coincidence.. 204
Chapter 38 Invited Breakfast.. 210
Chapter 39 Mysterious Power 215
Chapter 40: Fall of Stars.. 221
Chapter 41 Cooperation.. 226
Chapter 42 Safe and sound... 231
Chapter 43 Despair.. 236
Chapter 44 The Spirit of Meteorite................................ 241
Chapter 45 Secret Request for Help 246
Chapter 46 Zixuan's Request for Help........................... 251
Chapter 47 Welcome... 257
Chapter 48 The Battle of Babies..................................... 262
Chapter 49 The Battle of the Infant 2 269
Chapter 50 The Battle of Babies 3 273
Chapter 51 Weird Eyes.. 279
Chapter 52 Father and Heart.. 284
Chapter 53 Horrible Wail.. 289
Chapter 54 Xia Feng... 295
Chapter 55 Kiss.. 300
Chapter 56 Crisis Infiltrates.. 306
Chapter 57 Search 311
Chapter 58: Imprisonment.. 316
Chapter 59 Disaster in the Military Camp 321
Chapter 60: Life in Exchange for Brothers 326
Chapter 61 Where the Heart Falls 333
Chapter 62 Unknown 338
Chapter 63 Encounter... 344

Chapter 64 Let's Fight 354
Chapter 65 Steal 360
Chapter 66 Successful Forced Seizure 365
Chapter 67 Birth of a Child 370
Chapter 68 Touched 376
Chapter 69 The restless atmosphere 381
Chapter 70 Qin Feng's Change 388
Chapter 71 Heart Appears 394
Chapter 72 Welcoming Guests from All Directions 1 399
Chapter 73 Welcome guests from all sides 2 406
Chapter 74 Small Battle 411
Chapter 75 Acceleration 417
Chapter 76: Fight 423
Chapter 77 Fighting 2 428
Chapter 78 Fighting for Three 433
Chapter 79 Fighting for Four 437
Chapter 80 Fighting 5 443
Chapter 81 Fight for Six 448
Chapter 82 Husband and wife go to battle together 453
Chapter 83 The First Corpse King in History 458
Chapter 84: Extermination of the clan 463
Chapter 85 Battle 469
Chapter 86 Time Limit Expired 476
Chapter 87 Encounter 483
Chapter 88 Acting to Escape 489
Chapter 89 Transaction 495
Chapter 90: Fight Again 501
Chapter 91 The Power of Nuwa 507
Chapter 92: Fighting on their own 512
Chapter 93 I want you to submit 518
Chapter 94 Evolution 523
Chapter 95 Confrontation 528
Chapter 96 Tiansheng's Identity 533

Chapter 97 Tiansheng dances with Ganqi......................... 538
Chapter 98 Battle 543
Chapter 99 The Destruction of Dignity................................ 548
Chapter 100 The Passing of Life 553
Chapter 101 Black Hole 560
Chapter 102 Resentment... 565
Chapter 103: Xing Tian Reappears... 570
Chapter 104 Environment or Dream.................................... 575
Chapter 105 Sealed Energy... 580
Chapter 106 How can we be missing..................................... 585
Chapter 107 Ending 592

This episode continues the story of The Gatekeeper of Night Spirits Vol One and Two

Plot:

Xia Feng didn't say anything, but held the dagger horizontally, and then rushed up again, at a very fast speed. Ye Ye shook his head and ignored him, then dodged, pulled out Ye Yang, and blocked the dagger. He pushed hard and distanced himself from Xia Feng. How could Xia Feng give up? He rushed up again and kicked Ye Ye's head horizontally. Ye Ye squatted down slightly, and then lifted the Ye Yang in his hand up suddenly. Seeing this, Xia Feng immediately lowered the dagger and blocked the Ye Yang coming up. However, she was also blown away by the power attached to Ye Yang.

Chapter 1 Bounty

"Come again? It's been half a year! You still haven't killed me! In fact, I can't figure out why you saved me then?" Ye Ye said lightly on the top of Yemen Mountain.

In front of him was the assassin sent by Gu Zihao, Xia Feng.

Xia Feng didn't say anything, but held the dagger horizontally, and then rushed up again at a very fast speed. Ye Ye shook his head and ignored it, then dodged, pulled out Ye Yang, and blocked the dagger. He pushed hard again and distanced himself from Xia Feng. How could Xia Feng give up? He rushed up again and kicked Ye Ye's head sideways. Ye Ye squatted down slightly, and then raised the Ye Yang in his hand violently upwards. Seeing this, Xia Feng immediately lowered the dagger and blocked the upward Ye Yang. However, she was also blown away by the power attached to Ye Yang.

Suddenly, a silver thread invisible to the naked eye floated around Ye Ye, fluttering strangely. Then it slowly wrapped around Ye Ye's neck. A figure slowly walked out of the darkness, it turned out to be Sun Ye!

"I said, I will use your flesh and blood to treat the master!" After saying that, he pulled his hand violently, the silver thread wrapped around Ye Ye's neck tightened, and Ye Ye's head fell directly to the ground.

Huh... Suddenly Ye Ye stood up, holding the bed with his hands and breathing heavily.

That was all just a dream. Ye Ye shook his head, then got out of bed, picked up a water cup on the table, poured himself a glass of water, and drank it slowly.

"It's been too peaceful in the past six months! Not only the zodiac, but also the newly appeared star spirit is unusually peaceful! What happened? Forget it, don't think about it. It's good this way, giving Yemen time to develop!" Ye Ye muttered to himself lightly with a water cup in his hand.

Suddenly, a black shadow flashed past Ye Ye's back, silently. But Ye Ye noticed the wind brought by the figure when it flashed behind him! Her pupils immediately shrank into needles, and then she dodged a flying shuriken with her head. Then she immediately fell to the ground and rolled to the side!

'Pah'. The water cup in her hand also broke! Seeing this, the black shadow stopped hiding and appeared in front of Ye Ye. It was Xia Feng. She knew that if she didn't kill Ye Ye now, the guards would rush in soon and her plan would fail again.

So, she held the dagger in reverse, bent down, and bounced out like a cheetah. The dagger in her hand also slashed directly at Ye Ye's throat, but Ye Ye lay down directly and avoided the fatal blow.

Cai Feng's momentum was too fast, but she was as agile as a cat. She turned quickly in the air, kicked her feet on the wall, turned again, and stabbed Ye Ye with the dagger in her hand again, but Ye Ye couldn't dodge it.

With a click, Xia Feng's dagger was blocked again, but the person who blocked the dagger was not Ye Ye, but Ye Hen! Ye Hen appeared in Ye Ye's room without knowing when. Moreover, people kept coming to Ye Ye's room. The leader was the person Xia Feng feared the most - Huang Shang!

Seeing that the opportunity to kill Ye Ye had been lost, Xia Feng frowned, turned around, and disappeared!

In the past six months, Xia Feng had not given up on killing Ye Ye, and often carried out such assassinations! Fortunately, there were many masters in Yemen, and Xia Feng had no way to start.

This Xia Feng was also very stubborn. Even if she failed, she could escape and then find an opportunity to assassinate. Moreover, no one knew the details of this Xia Feng. His whole body was wrapped in black leather armor, and his face was also covered with a leather mask to cover the lower half of his face! Except for her eyes, her appearance could not be seen at all.

"Ye Zi, are you okay? She's here again?" Li Bin asked directly when he entered the door. Ye Ye nodded silently.

The zombie walked to the front and said to Ye Ye in a teasing tone: "I think she may have fallen in love with you! And you are so good to Li Yerui, she wants to kill you to vent her anger!"

"Okay, okay, it's not a big deal, I've been used to it for half a year! Let's go to bed!" Huang Shang said lightly with a lazy waist. After that, he walked out first.

Qin Minglei looked at Ye Ye and nodded, and left too! He still held the bottle in his hand, the bottle with the love poison! He was still blaming himself and still thinking about it!

After Qin Minglei left, everyone left Ye Ye's room. Ye Ye sighed, shrugged his shoulders and went to bed again. Huang Shang was right, they were used to it. They were used to Xia Feng's assassinations day after day! But anyone who has to experience a life-and-death assassination every two days or one day has to get used to it!

Nothing happened overnight.

Ye Ye was right, it was too quiet in the past six months! Quiet and weird!

Huang Dao no longer accepts any commissions, which is equivalent to closing himself off! No news can be heard from him at all! The newly established Xing Ling is also unusually quiet. Since its establishment, it has not had any confrontation with the Huang Dao League! It feels like it is developing silently. But it is true that this situation just gave Ye Men the opportunity to develop. Ye Men has developed very rapidly in the past six months, and there is a momentum to confront the old-school Huang Dao League and the Xing Ling with huge assets and countless people! It feels like a three-legged tripod!

And Ye Xincheng, who was in the reincarnation and did not wake up, also woke up. After waking up, he didn't speak, stayed in the room, didn't eat or drink, like a living dead!

"Hahahaha! Ye Ye! I didn't expect us to be famous! This Huang Dao League has not disappeared for half a year, and this move suddenly made such a big move!" Early in the morning, Li Bin rushed into Ye Ye's room with a piece of red paper in his hand. And his shouting attracted other people!

Ye Ye, who was sleeping soundly, was startled. He opened his eyes, looked at Li Bin and said calmly: "What are you arguing about so early in the morning? I was tossing and turning all night last night! You won't let me sleep?"

"Don't complain! Take a look at this first. This is what I saw when I went down the mountain to find my master today! You all come and see! We are all famous!" Li Bin ignored Ye Ye's complaints, sat directly on Ye Ye's bed, spread out the paper in his hand, and then said to the people who came in from the door.

Ye Ye and his friends looked over curiously, and then all laughed.

The paper Li Bin brought was a wanted order! There were portraits of Ye Ye and his friends on it! The bounties were 10,000 and 8,000 respectively! Ye Ye 10,000 and the rest 8,000! It said: The above people are all evil and crooked! Those who know the news will be rewarded, and those who kill them will be rewarded with their heads as evidence!

At the bottom of the wanted poster, there were two seals, one was the seal of the military, and the other was the seal of the Zodiac Alliance, a five-clawed dragon with a '◇' symbol behind it! It was indeed the symbol of the Zodiac Alliance!

"I didn't expect that there would be no news from the Zodiac Alliance for half a year. It turned out that they were colluding with the military? Now we are in trouble! The army will definitely not let us go!" The zombie said lightly.

Several people stopped talking immediately! Looking at the portrait on the wanted poster quietly, I guess this wanted poster issued by the military has been posted all over the country!

After a while, Ye Ye suddenly said: "Notify immediately and hold an emergency meeting immediately! I think the Zodiac Alliance should take action!" As soon as Ye Ye said this, a figure nodded slightly in the blind spot of his sight! If Ye Ye could see him, he would be surprised to find that he knew this person!

Chapter 2 Many Questions

Soon after, all the people with positions in Yemen arrived in the meeting room!

After looking around, Ye Ye took out the wanted poster with Ye Ye and others on it and said, "Huangdao League has been silent for half a year, and now it has made such a big move."

After looking at the wanted poster, the people below fell silent. Only the zombie and Yang Tianhai were as usual. The zombie said indifferently, "Don't you think it's weird?"

Ye Ye touched his chin and said, "It's really weird! Why don't you tell me what you think first?" Their meetings were not decided by one person, but by consultation! Whoever's opinion was beneficial would be listened to, but as the leader, Ye Ye naturally had the dominant power, of course, this dominant power was bound by the Ghost Queen and Huang Shang.

The zombie stood up and said nonchalantly: "The first strange thing is, why doesn't the military issue a wanted order or kill us themselves, but instead posts a wanted order and asks all the heroes in the world to kill us? The second strange thing is, why does Huang Dao only target you guys? Isn't that Xing Ling worthy of his attention? The third strange thing is, what have the Huang Dao League and Xing Ling Group been doing in the past six months? All of these are questions!" The zombie has regarded Ye Men as his home, and the people in Ye Men have also accepted him!

After listening to the zombie's analysis, everyone present fell into deep thought! The zombie was right, there are too many questions!

"No, I think it's not that the military doesn't want to send troops to suppress us! It's just that it's difficult to come forward for some reasons! But I'm not sure what the factors are! And! We must investigate what the Zodiac Alliance and the Star Spirit Group have been doing these days? Why are they so tolerant! And, what were they looking for in the Fuxi clan tomb half a year ago? Medicine King Pill? Who spread it? Why did they come out? Is it really the Zodiac Alliance?" Ye Ye spoke out his doubts.

Huang Shangcheng stretched his body lazily and said: "Who cares! Since the army doesn't come, then don't come. If one comes, kill one! If you want to know why they have been tolerant for half a year, then go and investigate! Why are you sitting here holding a meeting!"

The ghost queen smiled faintly: "That's right, Ye Ye, do whatever you want! Don't worry, with us here, Yemen is absolutely safe! Army? We have it too!" The army she mentioned is her people, the countless ghosts!

After the two said this, everyone's attention was focused on Ye Ye. Ye Ye looked thoughtful, and after a long time he said: "I have no clue at all! This is the only way! In a few days, I will go down the mountain, and then find a way to understand the situation outside, hoping to find out the purpose of the Huangdao League and the Xingling Group!" Ye Ye said, looking at the people sitting. Prepare to assign work.

Before Ye Ye could speak, the zombie said first: "Master Ye! I rarely call you like this! Please, let me go down the mountain with you! I'm almost suffocated!" Everyone laughed when they heard it. Indeed, in the past six months, Yemen has been almost isolated from the world! Life is very boring!

Ye Ye nodded and said: "How dare I not let you go? I said I would not restrict your freedom, and you have survived for the past six months!" Ye Ye's words were considered agreed!

"Okay, you discuss it, anyway, I can't go down! I want to go out, but now it's no longer necessary!" Huang Shang stood up and said, and after looking at the ghost queen, the tenderness in his eyes flashed!

After that, Huang Shang and the ghost queen left one after another! Ye Hen did not go down the mountain either, and also said goodbye now! Only Ye Ye, Qin Minglei, Li Bin, Yang Hengchao, Zou Shi, and Yang Tianhai were left. Ye Ye shrugged and said lightly: "Need I say more? Let's go together! However, Yang Hengchao, can you contact the people in the military through your previous network of relationships and get some information from them so that we can have some clues? Then Zou Shi, Yang Tianhai, you two should pay attention to the Xingling Group! We will divide the work!"

Zou Shi immediately objected after hearing this: "No, absolutely not! I won't go with him. If I go with him, I have to listen to his command!" After saying that, he suddenly felt a chill on his back. He turned his head and saw that Yang Tianhai had stood behind him without knowing when. He said coldly: "You don't have to listen to my command, just don't get separated from me and don't disrupt the plan! And our plan is to have no plan!" Zou Shi suddenly felt his breath choked and couldn't speak.

"Okay, that's it! We'll set off again after some time. During this time, we'll wait for news from you, Yang Hengchao! Remember, hurry up!" Ye Ye looked at Yang Hengchao and said seriously, after all, the only clue might come from him. "Then, let's go down the mountain to find Senior Shen Qing first! He might have news there too! We've been isolated from the outside world for too long!" After saying that, Ye Ye looked at the few people and sighed.

Yemen has been in a state of seclusion for the past six months. It has been developing internally! No news is allowed to leak out! However, the disadvantages brought about by this have only now been revealed.

"Master? Here is a letter for you!" Just as the few people finished discussing, a voice suddenly sounded outside the conference room.

"Letter? What letter? I shouldn't have many friends outside!" Ye Ye thought doubtfully, then walked out of the conference room and took a letter from a disciple outside the door!

The cover of the letter did not indicate who sent it, only Ye Ye's name on it!

Anonymous letter!

Ye Ye opened the letter and started reading it immediately. Several people gathered around curiously and read the letter.

The letter read: "Ye Ye, thank you for your help many years ago and for helping my father to transcend! Now, I know you are in trouble, so I come to greet you. If you have any difficulties, just come to me! At present, due to my relationship and opposition, the military has not sent any troops to suppress you, but I hope you can come up with a solution as soon as possible! After all, I can't hold on for too long! Have you changed after not seeing you for many years? I hope you can come to visit me soon."

The signature is, Zixuan!

"Zixuan? How could we forget him?" Ye Ye suddenly said loudly.

Li Bin frowned and asked in confusion: "Zixuan? Which Zixuan?"

Ye Ye immediately explained: "Remember when we came out of the well, we met an army?" Li Bin thought for a while, then suddenly realized: "It was General Zixuan who we helped to remove the corpse?!"

Ye Ye nodded and laughed and said: "It turned out that he helped the military not to send troops for the time being! We have to hurry up. You have all seen the content of the letter. He can only organize the troops temporarily! If the army really sends troops, then even if we are not afraid of Yemen, the losses will be heavy!" After that, Ye Ye called the disciple who had just delivered the letter and asked him to give the letter to Elder Yehen and the two guests.

After that, Ye Ye looked at the sky in confusion and sighed. Too many questions weighed on his heart, and he felt uncomfortable! But all this must be solved! He didn't know why he was doing it, but he knew that if he didn't do this, countless people would die because of him!

Chapter 3 Huang Shang and the Ghost Queen

The letter was quickly delivered to Ye Hen. After reading it, Ye Hen immediately sent it to Huang Shang.

After reading the letter, Huang Shang said calmly: "I have pursued and obtained the country and the beauty. What else do I want now?"

Ye Hen looked at Huang Shang and said worriedly: "Your Majesty...you...?" "It's okay, just sigh!" Huang Shang replied calmly, then sighed and continued: "Go and call her! After all, she is in charge of the troops in the Night Gate, and I have something to discuss with her."

Ye Hen agreed.

Soon, the Ghost Queen came to Huang Shang's side alone with a quiet step.

"What's the matter? Ye Hen said, you have something important to discuss with me?" The Ghost Queen asked as soon as she came. Huang Shang did not answer her, but took out the letter and handed it to the Ghost Queen.

After reading it, the Ghost Queen said calmly: "That's all? My people are enough!" Huang Shang sighed and said: "Huh... Zi Ruixin, a thousand years of loneliness, are you used to it?"

"Why are you talking about this suddenly?" The Ghost Queen asked in confusion.

Huang Shang did not answer her, but said to himself: "For a thousand years, I have gained everything, including the country, power, and beauty? Why do I still feel empty after a thousand years?"

"That's you... I am different. I am pursuing again now. I have to consider my people. I only know that Ye Ye will be a big tree, and my people will be protected under his shade! And, that... you also know it, right?" The Ghost Queen answered seriously. Huang Shang nodded: "Yes, I have contacted your king, but why is it him? You can stay in Yemen because of him, right?" The Ghost Queen said nothing and nodded silently.

Huang Shang saw it, but he didn't say anything. He walked to the side and looked at the teacup on the table and said, "The more bitter the tea is, the more aftertaste it will have. My thousand years is too sweet!" After that, his face suddenly became extremely serious and said, "Zi Ruixin! I'm really tired of the loneliness of a thousand years! Can you... ..."

"No... Absolutely not! My body and my soul belong to the king!" Before Huang Shang finished speaking, the ghost queen objected excitedly.

"Why... Your king has already given you to me, and your king can't come back! Do you really want to wait for him? He doesn't even know who he is, let alone that he is your king! How is it possible!" Huang Shang's emotions suddenly lost control.

"Huang Shang... I haven't given up waiting for a thousand years! What's more, now there is news about him! You said that the king has given me to you, but why didn't he tell me? I don't know, I only believe the facts in front of me! My king has appeared!" Zi Ruixin closed her eyes, not daring to look at Huang Shang's fiery eyes again, and said resolutely in her mouth.

Huang Shang suddenly collapsed, buried his head, and said coldly with his long hair covering his cheeks: "So what you mean is that I am dreaming? Then why are you avoiding me? Why?"

The Ghost Queen trembled, but laughed out loud: "Hahahaha, avoiding you? Why should I avoid you? We are in the Night Gate together, don't you know that men and women are not clear about teaching?"

"Hahahaha...Okay, okay! Well said! Just treat it as a dream! Humph, you are my only failure! I lost!" Huang Shang raised his head and said with a crazy look, and then turned and left.

The Ghost Queen looked at Huang Shang's departing back and said lightly: "I'm sorry, I really can't! The ghost clan cannot marry outside, otherwise you will be cursed!" After that, two lines of tears flowed down her cheeks, but Huang Shang could no longer see it!

Huang Shang and the Ghost Queen have always been a topic in the Night Gate! Everyone is guessing about them! Everyone understands what Huang Shang means to the Ghost Queen, but they can't understand it!

Moreover, in the underground cave, after Huang Shang's duel with the Ghost King, the Ghost King did explain that he had indeed handed the Ghost Queen to him! However, the Ghost Queen did not believe it, or she had been avoiding it!

After this day, Huang Shang and the Ghost Queen never met again, or Huang Shang did not show up! And Ye Ye and his friends were ready to go down the mountain. Now the only thing they were waiting for was the news brought back by Yang Hengchao.

And just yesterday, the walking corpses who had long been unable to bear the loneliness had already instigated Yang Tianhai to set off first. After all, their direction was the Star Spirit, and for their strength, there was nothing to worry about.

Huang Shang had been staying in the room alone and had not gone out. The funny thing was that the person living next door to him was Ye Xincheng who had also locked himself up!

There was a note in front of him, on which was written in regular script: "Ask what love is in the world, it only makes people live and die together!" Huang Shang had already fallen into it and could not extricate himself! Thousands of years of loneliness burst out in an instant when he met the Ghost Queen! Then it burned, a fire of love burned! However, it was completely extinguished by the Ghost Queen's resolute rejection. From extremely hot to extremely cold, the huge temperature difference cracked Huang Shang's heart, which he once thought was as solid as a rock!

When night fell, Huang Shang and Ye Xincheng were still sitting on the ground, looking at the ground! I don't know what they were thinking.

"Hey, no one brought water! I traveled day and night, and slept in the wind and rain!" Suddenly, a voice sounded at the gate of the Night Gate. It was Yang Hengchao who went down the mountain to find news.

When Ye Ye heard this voice, he immediately ran to the door, opened the door himself, and then brought a bowl of water: "The door is open, and the water is here. Tell me, what's going on?"

Yang Hengchao took the water, drank it in one gulp, and then walked directly inside, saying as he walked: "Let me sit down and talk!"

The crowd then walked into the Night Gate with him, and then all gathered in the meeting room.

Yang Hengchao took a few breaths, rested for a while, and said seriously: "Ye Ye, how many do you have?"

After hearing this, Ye Ye frowned and said in confusion: "What? What do you mean I have a few?" Yang Hengchao shook his head and continued to ask: "How many Nuwa stones do you have!"

Ye Ye immediately reached for the treasure bag and took out three Nuwa stones: "Just three!"

Yang Hengchao sighed: "Huh... this is the reason!"

"Hey, you also explain it clearly! What? I don't understand!" Li Bin was confused and didn't understand at all!

Yang Hengchao said seriously: "Huang Dao League wanted you for your Nuwa stone! As for how he knew you had Nuwa stone, I think you used it half a year ago when you fought Gu Weng! Huang Dao League knew about this thing in your hand, so they contacted the military. They didn't want the army to suppress us.! Instead, they hoped that they had a reasonable reason to kill us! Kill people and take stones!"

Ye Ye frowned when he heard it! Only he knew how powerful this Nuwa Stone was. This was the remnant left behind when Nuwa repaired the sky! But Ye Ye continued to ask: "Do you know what the Zodiac Alliance and the Star Spirit Group have been doing for half a year?"

"I've said it all, it's because of the Nuwa Stone! It seems to involve a huge thing, and no matter how hard you try, you can't find out about it! Even the special operations team doesn't know, they are a team specially formed to deal with supernatural things!" Yang Hengchao said.

Ye Ye nodded and thought, then looked at the three Nuwa Stones in his hand, and suddenly realized! It turned out that they were looking for the rest of the Nuwa Stones! After all, the power of this Nuwa Stone is too great, as we can see from the flames during the last decisive battle with Gu Weng!

"You, go! Nuwa Stone! It's not a trifle!" A voice suddenly sounded from behind them, and several people turned around, and it turned out to be Huang Shang who had been in a depressed state!

Huang Shang walked into the meeting room, looked at the ghost queen beside him, and then continued: "I know how powerful Nuwa Stone is! Thousands of years ago, I almost had my country destroyed by it! Fortunately, the user's power was insufficient, and the power of Nuwa Stone backfired and exploded!"

Hearing this, Ye Hen immediately reacted and said: "Are you talking about that person?" Huang Shang nodded! Then seeing the puzzled look of others, he continued: "At that time, Yemen had not been established! I founded the country not long ago! My national teacher at that time used means to collect Nuwa Stones, causing chaos, I was almost killed, and the army was vulnerable! It was just enough to destroy the country! In addition, there are five Nuwa Stones, not one! And the attributes are the five elements! After all, only the five elements can fill the gaps in the world!"

Hearing Huang Shang say this, several people were immediately surprised! It can destroy a country! That's unimaginable! No wonder the Zodiac Alliance and the Star Spirit Group have been forbearing to search!

"Let's set off as soon as possible! First, look for information about the Nuwa Stone! I have three here, one is from the Nuwa Tomb, and the other two are brought out from underground by the two of you!! There should be two more! We must get them before them!" Ye Ye said excitedly. But he didn't see the Ghost Queen's hesitant look!

Chapter 4 Monster

Knowing the power of Nuwa Stone, Ye Ye and the others did not dare to delay. The next day, he immediately left Yemen and went down the mountain.

After a brief moment of silence to say goodbye, the four of them embarked on their journey again.

"Are we just going to go on like this without any purpose?" The one who spoke was Qin Minglei, who had always been very cold.

After hearing this, Ye Ye shook his head and said: "No, don't worry. Have you forgotten the destination we didn't reach last time? We should be able to get what we want there." This sentence shocked everyone in their dreams, and several people heard it. Immediately he realized that the direction Ye Ye was heading was actually the headquarters of the Zodiac Alliance.

However, they did not go to the headquarters of the Zodiac Alliance last time. Instead, they left when Ye Ye was poisoned. This time, he wanted to go to the headquarters of the Zodiac League again and find out where the news came from.

"But, won't the Zodiac Alliance change its headquarters? I already knew about it last time. Aren't you afraid that we will cause trouble again? Although we are not very good, at least making trouble is okay." Li Bin asked, touching his chin after hearing this.

Ye Ye's eyes suddenly became excited and said: "No, they will not. First, they did not take us seriously. The Zodiac League has always had eyes on the top of its head! Second, it is also the key. I think they must be there to protect us. Something, or because of something, they can't or are reluctant to leave!" Ye Ye talked eloquently, and he guessed correctly that there was indeed a reason why Huang Daomeng couldn't move, or it was the reason why Gu Zihao couldn't leave! It was the paradise that his room led to!

This paradise is very strange. It seems to have always existed. It is full of aura and is suitable for meditation and practice. What's even weirder is that the paradise is actually underground! And, the sun is shining! Gu Zihao has been studying it for many years and still doesn't know what it is. All I know is that the secret here must be huge and must be well kept! Maybe one day the secret will suddenly reveal its truth, or be solved by him!

When Ye Ye said this, several people immediately understood, but they couldn't figure out what would make the world's richest and capable people capable of fighting against the army. , will stay there because of something. They don't know that actually all this is just because of Gu Zihao!

While they were talking, they had already arrived in Ningxia.

This time, several people did not choose to enter the Zodiac Alliance's sphere of influence more low-key. After all, now, they are not only subject to

He is wanted, and he doesn't know what the Zodiac Alliance is thinking now, so it's better to keep a low profile!

However, a few people chose the woods again, but when they reached the place where they had a decisive battle with Gu Weng, they immediately retreated and looked for another way. They did not expect that the last decisive battle place, It has become a highly poisonous place that no one can approach. Even Yang Hengchao, who has the most abnormal poison resistance among the few people, can't stand the poison! Several people had to find other ways! But what is very strange is that several people have been within the scope of the Zodiac Alliance for a long time, but they have not been attacked by any disciples of the Zodiac Alliance, nor have they seen any safe places. It feels as if the Zodiac Alliance has suddenly disappeared from the world. The few people who were harmed wanted to find a disciple of the Zodiac Alliance to ask questions, but there was no way.

However, when they saw a group of disciples from the Lingmu Sect of the Zodiac Alliance walking towards the interior in a panic, they believed that the Zodiac Alliance had not disappeared, but was holding back!

"Don't they want to kill us? Aren't they talking about killing people and seizing stones?" Yang Hengchao said boringly as he saw the Yellow Dao League ignoring them. Li Bin also played with his fingers and yawned with a bored look on his face and said: "Oh, I must be secretly fighting with the Star Spirits. Yes, they fought for the Nuwa Stone. In the end, no one was completely defeated. Now I have to so!"

After listening to Li Bin's words, Ye Ye thought about the group of Lingmu Sect disciples who had just entered in a panic, and his mind suddenly started thinking: Lingmu Sect generally does not act alone, why are they so panicked? Why haven't they taken action after we've been in for so long? Did they really confront the protoss and fail?

Ye Ye looked at him and rubbed his aching head. This is the sequelae left after poisoning. Every time you think about something, it will hurt if you think about it for a long time. The more you think about it, the more painful it will be, but your thoughts will become clearer!

However, the few people could not stop and slowly followed the group of Lingmumen disciples. Soon after, they arrived at the headquarters of the Zodiac Alliance.

Several people were immediately surprised. Rather than being a sect, the Zodiac Alliance was clearly a huge castle, or a castle that transformed the entire mountain!

The outermost part of the Zodiac Alliance is a thick city wall, which is more than ten meters high and two or three meters thick. Even if it is bombarded with artillery shells, it may not be able to move! On the city wall, groups of patrolling disciples passed by from time to time. And there was a huge dent on the city wall, as if something had hit it hard. Looking inside, the entire mountain has been transformed, and there are tall houses everywhere! And the most eye-catching thing is the wide road in the middle, winding up, with eight houses of different shapes on the way! Then at the top, there is a huge courtyard. The courtyard is so tall that you can even see its tall walls from the bottom of the mountain!

After Ye Ye saw the construction of the Zodiac League, he was immediately surprised. This is the momentum of a big sect. Compared with the Zodiac League, Ye Men is really a kid! Not staying overnight strengthened Ye Ye's determination! It strengthened Ye Ye's determination to build Yemen well!

"Who can enter such a Zodiac Alliance?" Li Bin was also surprised and said as he looked at the tall city wall.

"You can't get in at all!" Yang Hengchao answered tacitly.

Ye Ye smiled, held his head with both hands, then walked aside and said, "Since you can't get in, then wait for the opportunity! You have to go in anyway, it's just time!" Despite this, Ye Ye said seriously in his heart I thought: "Why is the Zodiac Alliance so vigilant? Did something happen? Was the collision mark caused by something?"

"Roar..." Suddenly a huge roar came from behind Ye Ye and the others. After a breath, they quickly flashed out from behind them. They only saw a huge figure appear, and then suddenly It was installed on the city wall of the Zodiac League.

With a bang, it seemed like a huge earthquake had occurred! Dust covers the sky!

After the dust cleared, a few people could clearly see what the black shadow was! The black figure turned out to be a monster five or six meters tall, with horns on its head and green scales, like an enlarged version of a buffalo! Its horns are circling like a spiral, emitting a dark light, it must be poisonous! His scale armor was completely invulnerable, because when Ye Ye saw a group of people on the city wall, it was useless to use spells or firearms! Only when some of the heavy firearms hit the monster did clouds of sparks burst out! It's impossible to penetrate its scales!

The monster seemed to want to break through the city wall and kept crashing into the city wall. But it couldn't get up, and the disciples of the Zodiac Alliance above had been fighting back non-stop, and were not surprised at all. They seemed to be used to its appearance.

Suddenly, Ye Ye's eyes shrank into needles, because he saw a person appear on the city wall. That person was none other than the leader of the Zodiac Alliance, Gu Zihao!

"It turns out it's because of this!" Ye Ye thought with a smile, he already knew the reason for the Yellow Dao Alliance's forbearance!

Chapter 5 Monster 2

On the tall wall of the Huangdao League, Gu Zihao suddenly shouted loudly: "Everyone hold on, today I will definitely take back this evil beast!" The voice was so loud that Ye Ye and his companions who were not far from the wall could also hear it.

Ye Ye smiled. His guess was indeed correct. Huangdao was indeed because of this big guy, so Huangdao League did not dare to act easily, and even gathered all its strength to fight against this big guy!

"Haha, you can see it too, right? That's the reason! This big guy made Huangdao lose! Haha!" Ye Ye smiled and said calmly while watching the battle between humans and beasts on the Huangdao League side, as if he had nothing to do with it and was watching the fire from the other side.

Li Bin and his companions did not speak. They were completely shocked by the huge monster.

The monster kept ramming the tall wall, and its huge horns kept hitting the wall. Then it stood up with its two hooves and kicked the people of the Huangdao League on the wall with its upper hooves.

Although it couldn't go up, or he couldn't bring down the city wall, but its attack caused them great damage. People kept falling from the tower, and some were even kicked to death!

Suddenly, the monster became more violent. The attack became more fierce. Ye Ye looked at the city wall curiously, but suddenly found that Gu Zihao had a blue stone in his hand. Ye Ye looked carefully and found that the stone was familiar!

"Ghost Orb!" Qin Minglei suddenly frowned and said seriously.

That's right, the stone in Gu Zihao's hand was the half of the ghost bead of Gu Weng! That day, after Gu Weng exploded, several people thought that the ghost bead must have disappeared with the violent explosion! However, several people didn't expect that the ghost bead survived tenaciously and was found by Gu Zihao.

And the monster also had a great origin. His ancestor was said to be the green bull of Laojun! That day, after Qin Minglei and his men left with Ye Ye on their backs, the monster happened to come there. At that time, the poisonous fog there was not so fierce yet. He first discovered the ghost bead hidden in the soil, and was very excited! When he was about to monopolize it, Gu Zihao took the lead and took away half of the ghost bead!

The monster was so angry that it attacked the Huangdao League. But Ye Ye and his men didn't know this fact. They only knew that the current situation was very beneficial to their situation!

"Let's take advantage of the chaos and sneak in!" Ye Ye said lightly. Several people were also prepared.

However, a strange phenomenon suddenly appeared!

Gu Zihao's body suddenly bloomed with a faint green light, and then he suddenly jumped off the city wall and hung directly on the body of the monster.

His light was very special, and he looked full of vitality, and it felt like a vitality suddenly bloomed! After he jumped on the monster, he shook his hand and there were six swords! Then he began to attack the monster. The monster's body, which was originally invulnerable to swords and guns, was pierced by Gu Zihao, and bright red blood was scattered everywhere!

"Has he improved again in the past six months?" Ye Ye and his companions watched him stab the monster with ease, and suddenly felt that Gu Zihao's strength must have greatly improved! But Ye Ye suddenly thought that it was wrong. If his strength really improved greatly, then why didn't he come out earlier? He had to endure for the past six months!

As he was thinking, the monster suddenly moved violently. It kept jumping around, trying to throw Gu Zihao off it. But it was in vain, because Gu Zihao's sword had been deeply inserted into the monster's body and hung firmly on it.

In fact, the reason for all this was that Gu Zihao had hidden a Nuwa stone! A wood-based Nuwa stone. The green ox was originally an earth-based one. According to the five elements, earth overcomes wood. The Nuwa stone had already killed the green ox. In addition, the existence of the ghost treasure ghost bead could temporarily increase strength at the cost of life! ! That's why Qingniu looks vulnerable. Otherwise, with that layer of defense, there is no way to break through it!

"No, run!" Suddenly Li Bin shouted loudly, and the monster gave up the attack and rushed towards the four people. If they followed the route of the monster, one of its feet would definitely step on several people!

"Evil beast, don't even think about escaping! How can you use this thing?" Gu Zihao roared loudly, and then accelerated the attack in his hand! Finally, he jumped up, with eight swords in his hand.

"Eight swords, flash!" After saying that, Gu Zihao disappeared for a short time, and when he appeared, he was already in front of the monster! Then he slowly put away the sword, and the monster's head slowly slid down, and was killed instantly by Gu Zihao!

After Gu Zihao put away his sword, he put away the ghost bead in a black cloth bag, coughed up a mouthful of blood and said with a face as pale as gold paper: "Come on, clean up its body, its whole body is full of treasures~! My injury can finally get better!" After saying that, he began to stagger. Fortunately, Feng Yi suddenly appeared and hugged Gu Zihao to support him, so that he did not fall down!

"It turns out that his injury has not healed yet! Let's take advantage of now and sneak in!" Ye Ye suddenly said cunningly. After saying that, he followed the group of corpse collectors who walked towards the huge corpse of Qingniu, and then found a way to subdue four people. After changing their clothes, he followed into the Huangdao League surrounded by tall walls.

"Hey, you four, move this thing over!" Before the few people had time to happily sneak in, they were stopped by someone! They slowly turned around and saw a person pointing a knife at them. He should be the person in charge of the command!

The four people had no choice but to reluctantly pick up the things on the ground, and then slowly followed the crowd!

"Hey? Why haven't I seen you four before? What are your names?" The man just now asked in confusion when he saw that the four of them were unfamiliar.

"Oh, boss. We are new here! My cousin brought us in!" Ye Ye suddenly said in a dumbfounded manner. Playing dumb is not considered as pretending for Ye Ye, that is his old profession or original appearance.

"Oh? Who is your cousin?" the man asked unwillingly.

"Hey, my cousin is called 'Feng Yi,' and the four of us are his brothers. I am Feng Si, he is Feng San, this is Feng Er, and he is Feng Da!" Ye Ye continued to say stupidly.

"Oh? Really? Are you relatives of Feng Yi, the head of the Feng family? Oh, great! Come on, come on, take a rest, we will move!" The man changed his tone immediately after hearing it. He began to compliment.

"Hey, boss, what is the house on that road? It looks so beautiful! It goes up in a spiral! There are still eight houses!" Ye Ye pointed to the eight houses on the most conspicuous road and asked.

"Don't call me the boss, you are the boss. I hope you can say good things to Master Feng in the future! There? We can't go there. It's called 'Eight Heavens Pass'. It's a dead end for outsiders to enter! We don't have the strength to go in! But that's the only way up the mountain." The man rubbed his hands and said.

When Ye Ye and the other four heard it, they immediately looked at the road with fiery eyes! They had no choice but to go there, through the dead end called 'Eight Heavens Pass'!

Chapter 6 Drinking Party

"Okay, everyone, it's time to go. Let's not dawdle any longer. Let's finish our work first, then get some snacks and some wine. We must treat the relatives of Master Feng well." The leader didn't look like he was flattering, but rather a look of admiration and gratitude. The four people were confused.

But even if they didn't understand, they certainly wouldn't show it.

Ye Ye smiled and continued to play dumb and said, "Hey, okay! Brother, are you familiar with my cousin?" After saying that, he lifted a box on the ground. The box was very heavy because it was filled with the fragments of weapons on the tower just now. But Ye Ye seemed to lift it up effortlessly.

"Hey... Get up!" The leader shouted, picked up a box, and then said, "Haha, we are very lucky. We don't have to go out to deal with that thing! That's a deadly job! Haha, you said Master Feng! He is a good man. If it weren't for him, I think many of us wouldn't even have a meal!" At this time, there was no original flattery in his eyes.

Li Bin also came up and asked in confusion: "Oh? Brother? Why? Why do you have to eat when he is with you?"

The leader sighed and said, then tightened the box in his hand and said: "Don't call me brother or something, it's not intimate, just call me Lao Li. You don't know that Feng Yi, the head of the Feng sect, is really a good person! In fact, we are all refugees! And we are all refugees who were robbed by bandits and are about to starve to death. It was Feng Yi, the head of the Feng sect, who took us in and provided us with food and clothes..." Then he carried the box in his hand on his shoulder and continued "After providing us with food and clothing, they also found a way to transfer us to this castle to do odd jobs. Although the salary is fragmented, and we can rarely go out, and the management is very strict, at least we have a stable place to live, and the problem of food and clothing is solved. Master Feng can be said to be a god in our hearts! Although he is young, everyone here regards him as a god!"

"It turns out that they have such a story here. It seems that Feng Yi is not a bad person!" Ye Ye thought to himself, and then stopped talking. There were many of them, and they quickly moved all the things.

"Huh." Li Bin sat on the ground, wiped his forehead and said, "Ye Ye, are we here to do hard labor?" Ye Ye smiled and said, "Of course not, let's find out the situation there first. It seems that there is only one place to go up the mountain! The Nuwa Stone has appeared in Gu Zihao's hands. Find a way to get it!" As he said, Ye Ye and his friends looked at the houses on the only road leading to the top of the mountain.

"Come on, you've worked hard! Come, drink some water, and then we'll go eat! Today, Master Feng Yi will come to have dinner with us!" Old Li brought some water, then walked to Ye Ye and the others and said.

Ye Ye took the water and said, "Old Li, does Master Feng come here often?" Old Li also drank a sip of water and smacked his lips: "Not often, but every time he comes, he will drink with us and ask about our well-being."

"Then why do you act like you're flattering?" Li Bin asked curiously. Old Li sighed: "Hey, we don't want to, but we are just poor people. Do we have to act like we're familiar with Master

Feng? Where is his majesty in that case? Outside, we are all his subordinates and his slaves, but inside, we are all relatives of each other!" This sentence made the four people completely confused. What kind of person is Feng Yi? And why did he help Huang Daomeng to wipe out Yemen?

"Okay, okay, you four, now that you are under my command, you have to listen to me! Do you understand? You just came here and don't understand many things. You must not make mistakes! Let's go and have dinner first, and then I will tell you what to pay attention to." Seeing that the atmosphere was a little dull, Lao Li said with a smile.

Ye Ye nodded and said nothing. He looked at the winding mountain road and the eight tall houses on the mountain road.

"Don't look over there, that is our restricted area, you can't even look at it. If you anger the master inside, we will die miserably!" Lao Li saw the four people looking at the house on the mountain road, and suddenly panicked, and hurriedly pushed the four people away.

Not long after, in a remote house, Lao Li and many people sat together, eating and drinking, it was very lively.

At this time, Ye Ye was even more surprised, thinking in his heart: This is a big sect! There is an inner gate on the mountain, and there are indeed outer gates and some idle construction workers at the bottom of the mountain. So many buildings have been built to accommodate them. I really want to go up the mountain! Gu Zihao, the Nuwa Stone is really here with you!

"Hey, hey, hey, come on, drink! Don't be dazed. You are new here. Have a drink with everyone. There are too many people. I won't introduce you one by one. You will naturally know each other in the future! Come on, everyone, drink!" Seeing that the four people were not very sociable, Lao Li stood up and said loudly, attracting everyone's attention, letting them know that there were new people here, and suddenly everyone began to pay attention to them. They raised their glasses.

Soon, under the frequent toasts of this group of people, the four people also became familiar with the road and joked with everyone. After all, they all came from poverty and life and death, and there was no barrier between them!

"Ah, why are you so happy today? Do you have any wine and food for me!" When Ye Ye and his friends were happy, suddenly a voice that they absolutely didn't want to hear sounded outside the door!

As soon as the voice was over, a man came in from outside the door. That man was Feng Yi!

When Ye Ye and the other four saw Feng Yi coming in, they immediately took out their weapons quietly and hid them under the table. They continued to smile and buried their heads while drinking and eating. At this time, everyone's attention was on Feng Yi, and they did not see the movements of the hands of several people, but this small movement did not escape Feng Yi's attention, but he did not care and smiled gently.

Because Ye Ye and the other four were all buried, Feng Yi did not recognize them. He thought they were just spies or assassins who had sneaked in. For his strength, he didn't care at all.

"Master Feng, you are here, come on, come on, your wine and meat are definitely available!" Lao Li seemed to have more leadership skills and the ability to speak in front of everyone. When he saw Feng Yi coming in, he immediately left his position and walked to Feng Yi's side, welcoming Feng Yi to the table where they were sitting, and then blocked a seat in the middle for Feng Yi to sit down. Feng Yi didn't mind and sat down directly.

But in this case, Ye Ye and his friends felt uncomfortable, because Feng Yi happened to be sitting opposite them!

"Old Li, I've said it before, you can call me by my name in private, my name is Feng Yi, next time you call me like that, I'll punish you with three cups!" Old Li immediately laughed and said, "Hey, hey, look at my memory, but Master Feng, oh no, Feng Yi, you are our benefactor, it's not good for me to call you like that?"

"There's nothing wrong, we are all a family, you are my Feng Yi's relatives! Oh? New here?" Feng Yi cleverly turned the topic to Ye Ye and his friends.

"Oh, Feng Yi, they are new here, don't you know them? They said you are cousins!" Old Li said as he took a bite of the dish.

Ye Ye and his four friends felt bad when they heard it. They buried their heads, exchanged glances with each other, and then tightened their weapons. If Feng Yi directly pointed out that he didn't know them and wanted to recognize them, then they would have to rush out.

"The four of you raise your heads! We are all family, why are you so shy!" Feng Yi said with a smile while drinking, which also caused everyone to laugh! The huge house suddenly became noisy again.

"Raise your heads! Don't be embarrassed! We are all men!" Lao Li also joined in the fun. And the people around began to mock.

Ye Ye and the other four had no choice but to raise their heads hesitantly.

"Cousin." Ye Ye called helplessly. But he looked at Feng Yi, who was frowning at this moment, with a serious face. The laughter just now disappeared, and even became cold.

"They? Why are they here? I want to identify them and kill them? But there are so many people here, it's not a good influence!" Feng Yi thought in his heart. He didn't want to kill people in front of the people he rescued. "But why are they here? Forget it, observe first. In fact, they are not bad, but I..."

Seeing that Feng Yi didn't speak for a long time, and even became cold, the people around him immediately looked at Feng Yi in confusion. Ye Ye and his men also tightened their weapons.

Soon after, Qin Minglei could no longer bear it and was ready to stand up and fight his way out. But Ye Ye grabbed him and held up a glass of wine: "Cousin, don't you recognize us? You brought us in!" Ye Ye, who was careful just now, saw the hesitation in Feng Yi's eyes.

Feng Yi only reacted after hearing this, and then smiled quietly and thought: "Playing this trick? Then I'll play with you!" But he said: "Are you okay? Are you still adapting here? I'm sorry, everyone. You know, I'm an orphan, and they are my cousins, but when I saw them, I thought of my past days, and I couldn't help feeling sad, which caused what happened just now. I disturbed everyone's interest. I'll punish myself with three cups!" As he said, he picked up three bowls of wine and drank them. While drinking, he looked at Ye Ye and the other four with a playful look.

"Cousin, you don't need to say anything. We are living well now. Thank you, cousin!!! I will also drink with you. Come on, everyone!" Ye Ye deliberately emphasized the word "cousin" and mocked everyone to drink. After that, he picked up the wine and looked at Feng Yi.

After three rounds of drinking, everyone had to go to work tomorrow, so the drinking party ended unsatisfactorily! Ye Ye also followed Lao Li, who had a poor alcohol tolerance and walked unsteadily after drinking, to the resting place.

"Lao Li, you go back first. I want to reminisce with my cousins!" Suddenly, Feng Yi appeared in front of Ye Ye and others again. After calling Lao Li away first, Feng Yi smiled and said, "You should not be drunk, right? Don't mind if we go over there to talk? Master Ye and several hall masters!?"

Ye Ye smiled and watched Feng Yi walk in the direction he pointed. Qin Minglei, Li Bin and Yang Hengchao also tightened the weapons that had been hidden in their clothes, then looked at Feng Yi warily and followed behind Ye Ye.

Chapter 7 Mind Your Own Business

Soon after, under the leadership of Feng Yi, the four came to a secret place.

Feng Yi regained his indifferent look, looked at the four people coldly, shook his hand, shook out a sword and pointed it at the ground obliquely, and exuded a sword-like pressure.

"Master Feng, what kind of person are you?" Ye Ye was not afraid or worried. He believed that Feng Yi would not kill them, otherwise he must have pointed out that he did not know them at the drinking party just now, and with his reputation among the group, it should be no problem to besiege the four people! But he did not, so Ye Ye followed him out.

"Me? Humph, you don't care what kind of person you are. I only know that if I kill you now and offer your heads, I can learn the supreme realm of the Nine Swords." Feng Yi's face was expressionless.

Ye Ye didn't say anything, he looked at Feng Yi coldly and then looked at Feng Yi and said: "Can you do it?"

"Hmph, you try! I believe that if it's really you three, you must not be my opponent, right?" After saying that, he raised the sword, the tip of the sword pointed directly at Ye Ye's neck. Ye Ye was not afraid, but raised his neck: "Then come on, since you don't want to know why we are here!"

This sentence just hit Feng Yi's life point. Feng Yi frowned, shook out another sword with his left hand, and then combined the two swords to stab Ye Ye, the speed was extremely fast. Qin Minglei and the other two were also unable to rescue.

But Ye Ye didn't dodge, and looked at Feng Yi's sword indifferently. Without any sound, the sword stopped directly in front of Ye Ye's eyes. Ye Ye's bet was right. Feng Yi would not kill them!

"Aren't you afraid? If my sword goes one more point, it will pierce through your eyes and take your life!" Feng Yi said coldly.

Afraid, of course Ye Ye is afraid! Who can not be afraid of death? "Haha, what do you think? Do you think I would do something I'm not sure of?" Ye Ye stretched out a finger and said after putting the two swords aside.

"You won, now tell me, why did you come here?" Feng Yi put away his sword and stood with his hands behind his back.

"Nothing, we just came to take a look, no?" Ye Ye certainly would not tell the truth. Feng Yi frowned when he heard it: "Do you think this is a vegetable market? Come whenever you want?"

"Of course not, Feng Yi. I don't know what kind of person you are, but I think people who are willing to worry about those refugees should not be bad people!" Ye Ye said with a raised eyebrow.

Feng Yi laughed and looked at Ye Ye. After a long time, he said lightly: "Put away your weapons! I said, you won! I just want to tell you. People are not all bad, I am like this, and he is like this! If you know anything or see anything, don't mind it!" After that, he turned around and prepared to leave.

Him? Ye Ye thought about it with doubts, and immediately asked, "Who is he?"

"You will know who he is when you should know! Remember, stay out of other people's business." Feng Yi said and turned away.

After Feng Yi left, he left a lot of doubts to the four people! Although Ye Ye was talking just now, Feng Yi's pressure has been exerting this effect on Qin Minglei and the other two, and the three people are also quite hard.

But now Ye Ye's mind is all in what Feng Yi said just now "Idle business? What is idle business? Who is the 'he' he said? What exactly is the Huangdao League?" Ye Ye thought and shook his head. He really couldn't figure it out, thinking that for the Huangdao League, the six-month retreat of Yemen had cut off the news of the Huangdao League.

"Hey, you three, what are you doing here? Don't you know it's time for curfew? Go back quickly!" Suddenly, an arrogant figure came to mind behind the four people. The four people turned around and saw a patrolling team of Huangdao League disciples, one of whom shouted at them.

"Oh, oh, ok. We are new here and don't know the rules. Sorry! We will go back now." Ye Ye didn't want to reveal his whereabouts now, so he chose to be tactful. After speaking, he immediately walked back with his head down.

Ye Ye was easy to talk to, but Qin Minglei and his friends would not choose to give in. Although they left behind Ye Ye, they looked at the patrolling disciples with a very cold look. They were not ordinary people, and they immediately made the ordinary disciples sweat.

"Country bumpkin, what are you looking at? If you look again...if you look again, you will go to the cellar tomorrow!" Although the Huangdao League disciple was frightened by being looked at, he still had the courage to say it.

Qin Minglei and his friends no longer paid attention to him and turned around and left. The disciple who spoke just now was also a narrow-minded person. He secretly remembered Ye Ye and his friends: "Humph, you almost embarrassed me. You will have a hard time in the future!"

Ye Ye and his friends didn't expect that the unyielding Qin Minglei and his three friends would actually cause a disaster! For them and for the Huangdao League.

Night. But Ye Ye and the other four could no longer sleep. After all, there were too many things in their minds and too many questions.

On the second day, Ye Ye and the other four were woken up by Lao Li early in the morning and started working. It was not that Ye Ye and the other four did not want to go up the mountain now, but it was not advisable to go up the mountain blindly without exploring the situation clearly.

"Haha, did you sleep well last night? Remember, don't tell others about what happened between you and Master Feng! Remember?" Lao Li said with many instructions.

Ye Ye and the others nodded indifferently, indicating that they knew.

After a busy day, the night came again! Everyone gathered together to eat and drink again!

"Are you four used to it? It's okay, it will be fine slowly! Don't be too restrained. Now we are relatives back here! We are all family members!" Lao Li walked to Ye Ye with a glass of wine in his hand and said.

Ye Ye and the other four no longer restrained themselves and joked with the people around them.

After three rounds of drinking, everyone started to talk more.

"Do you know, Feng Yi, the past of Sect Leader Feng? I know!" Suddenly, a drunken voice sounded.

"Oh, Shi Lei. You started again! Although your stories are true, they have been told countless times! Forget it!" Old Li said disdainfully, and everyone around laughed.

"Alas, Old Li, we haven't heard it yet! What was Sect Leader Feng's past like! Brother Shi, can you tell me about it?" Ye Ye was shocked when he heard it!

"Did you see it? It's better to be new! Okay, okay, I'll tell you! You four listen carefully!" Shi Lei began to tell what he knew about Feng Yi's past.

"Master Feng was once the son of a wealthy family! His family was very rich! And it is said that his family was once the inheritor of a certain sect! It has been passed down from generation to generation..." Shi Lei drank a glass of wine, and then continued: "But when Master Feng was 20 years old, a huge accident happened! It changed his life... "It seemed that Shi Lei was lost in memories and did not speak for a long time.

Ye Ye could not wait and pushed him! Only to find that Shi Lei was already drunk!

"Oh, forget it, I will continue for you!" Lao Li Jian and the other four were very excited, sighed, stood up, and told the story of Feng Yi, who they were all familiar with.

Old Li said, sighed, took a sip of wine, "Master Feng's life is indeed hard, his family was once very wealthy. And they were supported by a very large sect at the time. But... there are unexpected changes in the world! It should have been not long after he got married that year, the sect that his family relied on was suddenly destroyed by the Huangdao League! Master Feng's family was also implicated and the whole clan was destroyed! Fortunately, Master Feng was out and drunk and did not return. When he returned to his original house, he saw the corpses all over the floor and burst into tears... Alas..." Old Li sighed and shook his head, " Because no one dared to help him, Master

Feng had to bury all 70 people in his family by himself, and then he began to listen to the murderer who exterminated the clan. Finally, he learned that all this was done by the Qiankun Dao Sect in the Yellow Dao! He also began to think of ways to fight against the Qiankun Dao Sect! But in the end, he found that the Qiankun Dao Sect was just a dog under the Yellow Dao League! Everything was done by Gu Zihao. That night, Master Feng sneaked into the Yellow Dao League and wanted to assassinate Gu Zihao, but he didn't expect that he was just a mortal! Naturally, he was not the opponent of the masters of the Yellow Dao League! Captured! "

When Lao Li said this, he clenched his fists and seemed very angry! After a long time, he continued: "But Gu Zihao didn't kill him, but left his name and taught him to use the sword, so that he could kill him and take revenge after he had the strength! Therefore, Master Feng was so willing to stay in the Yellow Dao League, in the headquarters of his murderer who exterminated the clan! Just to kill the enemy with his own hands! "After Lao Li finished speaking, everyone looked angry! "Master Feng is really a good man!! He used his talent and ability to slowly climb to his current position. Although he can't kill Gu Zihao, the leader of the Huangdao League, he has been working hard! Over the years, he has been using the advantages of his position to save many people! At least all of us here are!"

After listening to Lao Li's words, Ye Ye and the other four had to re-recognize Feng Yi! At this time, Ye Ye and the other four were hesitating in their minds whether Feng Yi was the Feng Yi who led the crowd to wipe out the Yemen, or the real man who endured for several years for the sake of the people and revenge!

"So that's the case, but has he never thought about destroying others for the sake of his own genocide? Is that a good idea?" Ye

Ye thought in his heart. Then he sighed and said, "So, my cousin has such an experience!"

"Okay, okay, you have finished listening to the story, everyone continue drinking! You don't have to go to work tomorrow. It is said that outsiders will enter tomorrow, and we servants cannot show up!" Seeing that the atmosphere was not good, Lao Li began to adjust the atmosphere.

Everyone got used to it and stopped sighing, and all started drinking.

"Ye Ye, do you think Feng Yi is really that good?" Li Bin whispered in Ye Ye's ear during the drinking party.

Ye Ye shook his head to indicate that he didn't know, and then said: "It's not clear now, but at least it is certain that there must be an indelible hatred between Feng Yi and Gu Zihao, and they will never stop until they die, but he doesn't have the ability to take revenge now, so he has to endure it!"

"It turns out that he is also a real man!" Yang Hengchao said lightly, which is what the four of them think of Feng Yi now.

"By the way, Lao Li just said that some outsiders will come tomorrow, maybe they will go up the mountain? Maybe that's our chance!" Ye Ye said.

Qin Minglei and the other four also nodded in agreement. "Then sneak in tomorrow?" Li Bin asked lightly.

Ye Ye nodded heavily: "What exactly is in those houses? Go up tomorrow! The specific method... We will act tomorrow depending on the situation!"

"By the way, Ye Zi, I want to ask you a question, why are we here?" Qin Minglei asked abruptly.

A question immediately stopped Ye Ye. After thinking for a long time, Ye Ye said lightly: "I don't know, I just saw the Nuwa stone in Gu Zihao's hand, and I couldn't help but want to come in! Maybe it's because I don't want the Nuwa stone to be controlled by others? After all, the power of the Nuwa stone is too strong. If someone uses it indiscriminately, the people of the world will suffer!" To be honest, Ye Ye didn't know why he chose to come in at the risk of his life! However, when he saw the Nuwa stone, he couldn't help but think that the Nuwa stone in Gu Zihao's hand seemed to be calling Ye Ye!

Qin Minglei and others had to nod. They said that they would follow Ye Ye's footsteps without regrets!

A drinking party was over again. Ye Ye and his four companions returned to the resting place. After a night's rest, they will wait for an opportunity to go up the mountain tomorrow.

On the second day, everyone was strictly guarded and could not leave the room. Even if they had to go to the toilet, they had to go under the care of one or two people. It can be seen that the people who came this time were valued by the Huangdao League!

"Uncle, I want to go to the toilet!" Ye Ye suddenly shouted loudly. The person who seemed to be the leader of the Huangdao League disciples who was guarding them looked at Ye Ye and muttered: "Country bumpkin, you two follow him!"

"Wait, I want to go too, uncle, please be kind! We have been together since we were young, and I can't poop if I leave my brother! Hehe!" Li Bin suddenly said, which immediately caused everyone to laugh. Ye Ye and his companions also forced themselves to hold back the urge to laugh.

"You country bumpkin, bumpkin! You two brothers really share the same difficulties! Go, have fun and come back!" The leader said disdainfully.

"Okay, okay, uncle, I will definitely poop clean once! I will never poop twice!" After that, Li Bin followed Ye Ye and left.

"Hahahaha... Li Bin, you are like this!" Yang Hengchao couldn't help laughing anymore!

The leader glared at Yang Hengchao and said, "Laugh, what are you laughing at? If you keep laughing, go to the cellar for me!" Yang Hengchao didn't want to cause any more trouble, so he forced himself to hold back his smile.

The leader cursed again, "Country bumpkin." Then he turned and walked to the door. He didn't see the murderous eyes of Qin Minglei and Yang Hengchao!

After a long time, Ye Ye and Li Bin didn't come back! The leader also remembered them and immediately said angrily, "Damn, country bumpkin, there are so many feces and urine! You two go and have a look again!" After that, he instructed the two disciples around him to find Ye Ye and Li Bin again.

"Boss, no need, they are back!" As he was speaking, the two disciples who had just gone out had returned, carrying Ye Ye and Li Bin on their backs.

"What happened to them?" the leader asked in confusion.

"Boss, they fainted from shitting!" a disciple answered in a muffled voice.

"Wake me up! Quick, wake me up! Haha, I have never seen anyone fainted from shitting in all these years!" the leader said with a smile.

"Boss, no need! They are already awake!" a disciple continued to answer in a muffled voice.

The leader's pupils suddenly shrank, and he felt something was wrong and asked hurriedly: "What did you two call me just now? Boss? My men didn't call me that! You are spies! Someone come! There is..." Before he finished speaking, a strong hand had already hit the back of his head! He instantly collapsed.

It was Qin Minglei!

The two disciples also raised their heads, it was Ye Ye and Li Bin! It turned out that Ye Ye and Li Bin had just gone out, subdued the disciples who were guarding the two, and then changed into their clothes!

"Quick, put on their clothes, let's go out and go up the mountain!" Ye Ye said hurriedly. Then he turned around and said to the people who were locked up with them: "Old Li, don't be afraid, cousin is in trouble, we are going to help! Everyone get rid of it! Take good care of these people!"

Soon after, the four of them changed their clothes! Then they walked out of the room in a swagger! Their goal was the winding mountain road!

Chapter 8 Exposed

Wearing the clothes of Huang Dao League disciples, the four of them quickly blended in.

Huang Dao League disciples were all on high alert at this moment, as if they were receiving a very important person. Moreover, there was a man wearing an iron mask and walking in front with a few people, who was Gu Zihao!

Who was this person, even Gu Zihao had to meet him in person?

Ye Ye and the other four quickly went up the mountain with the large group of people, but they were far away from the eight houses on the mountain road. Whenever they approached those houses, they would always take a detour, so that Ye Ye and the other four could not know what was in those houses. But they felt that every time they passed a house, there would always be something peeping from behind!

"Okay, all of you stay here and don't move!" Not long after, the group finally reached the top of the mountain, and the leader stopped them all and rectified them on the spot.

After that, Gu Zihao took the few people into the house on the top of the mountain!

"Wait for the opportunity, and then we sneak in! You must have seen it, right? Among the people that Gu Zihao met, there are actually people we know!" Ye Ye whispered.

Qin Minglei and the other two nodded, all puzzled. They were not wrong, there were really people they knew among the people that Gu Zihao met! That person was the fourth Xingling who led a large group of people to form the Xingling Group in the tomb of the Fuxi clan! The other few people were also his other brothers!

"Okay, everyone dispersed and returned to their respective camps! Then the ban will end, but the patrol mission must be strengthened!" The Huangdao League actually adopted military-style management, integrating the originally mixed sects into one army, which is not only easier to manage, but also strengthens the cooperation between the sects!

"Right now... we..."

"What are you going to do, return to the team immediately! Don't talk!" Ye Ye was ruthlessly stopped before he finished speaking! Ye Ye had no choice but to sigh at the place where Gu Zihao and others entered.

"It seems that we have to sneak in tonight!" Ye Ye thought in his heart, and then followed the group of military-like Huangdao League disciples and slowly walked towards the camp.

But they didn't expect that the Huangdao League's training of disciples has been completely militarized! They are collectively organized into classes, and each disciple is very familiar with the people around him! It can even be said that they know each other how many people there are and which ones they are.

"Fortunately, they have their own name tags and camp numbers on them, otherwise we really don't know what to do!" Li Bin said while holding the wooden tag in his hand.

This is also one of the ways of militarized management of the Huangdao League. They use each wooden tag to record the disciples' travel and all records!

"We are from the Sixth Battalion and the Thirty-Eight Mansions!" Walk slowly over, it should be over there. "Ye Ye and his four companions didn't know the layout here, so they had to search slowly.

Soon after, Ye Ye and his four companions stood at the door of the Thirty-Eight Mansions, and then pushed the door open.

After entering, the four did not speak, but buried their heads, walked straight to the empty bed, sat down, and deliberately threw the sign in a conspicuous place!

However, the four did not notice that from the moment they entered, the few people who were originally in the dormitory suddenly frowned, and then quietly touched their waists. They all had a small dagger on their waists! Moreover, while they were doing this, they were still communicating with each other.

However, even if several people did it flawlessly, the murderous aura could not be completely blocked. Qin Minglei, who was extremely sensitive to murderous aura, was the first to notice something wrong, then raised his head slightly, took a look, and immediately said softly: "It's exposed!"

Seeing that Qin Minglei noticed their actions, the disciples immediately shouted: "There is a spy, there is a spy! "The shout spread far away, and all the Huangdao League disciples around slowly surrounded him.

Qin Minglei frowned and stopped talking. He drew out the Night Gate's strange dagger and rushed forward, followed by Li Bin. The two cooperated extremely well. They were not ordinary people. Although those people cooperated well, their daggers had no effect on them at all. Although they could use spells to strengthen their abilities, they fell down before they finished the spells.

Ye Ye had no choice but to shake his head and shout: "We are not here to kill! But there is no way now. Let's escape quickly, otherwise we will be surrounded and we will die!"

After that, Ye Ye quickly looked around in this dormitory. This dormitory is a single-type dormitory with only one door and a skylight. Without hesitation, the four people immediately came out of the skylight and walked on the roofs of other dormitories.

"They are on the roof! Immediately line up, beehive! "Things got out of hand, and a man with a 'hundred' embroidered on his arm immediately stood up to command.

As soon as he finished speaking, the Huangdao League disciples, who were originally in a mess, immediately began to reorganize and were fine in an instant.

After the reorganization, they immediately changed into several rows, and the people holding paper talismans were immediately picked up by several strong men behind them and ran forward quickly. On their backs, they began to chant. Moreover, the speed of their chanting was also different, so that their long-range attacks did not stop like machine guns. The fire talismans in the hands of the first row flew out, and the ice talismans in the second row followed, followed by the third row, the fourth row... and then the first row again! Over and over again.

Ye Ye and his men were immediately disrupted by such an attack, so they had to let Qin Minglei and Yang Hengchao block the talismans from behind! Then the four of them kept running forward.

"Quick, it's in front, hold on! "After a long time, Ye Ye and his companions finally saw the house that Gu Zihao and his companions had entered today. Then they immediately quickened their pace!

'Pah' the four of them jumped off the roof and continued to run forward. Then they directly pushed open the gate of the yard! Then they closed it tightly!

There was no guard! The four of them actually came in directly!

"Everyone, go away quickly. They are courting death if they go in! Let's not disturb the leader's meeting. We will wait not far away!" A voice came from outside the door.

Ye Ye was panting heavily, and he was also wondering why there were no guards. Was it really Gu Zihao's confidence? But there was no way. The soldiers blocked the road behind him, and he would die if he retreated! In front, although the danger was unknown, at least it was safe now. The four of them had to continue forward!

After walking for a long time, the four of them found that there were no guards in this house! The four of them wandered around in the yard as if they were wandering around their own backyard!

"Hahahaha, everyone, how about this tea? I don't have the blessing to taste it! "As soon as they passed a rockery, they heard Gu Zihao's voice coming from a house.

"Haha, how can you not be blessed, Master Gu? This tea is yours, you can taste it every day!" Ye Ye and the others had never heard this man's voice before, it should be one of the seven brothers of Xingling.

"Alas, I promised someone something, I can't take off this headgear until this thing is completed!" Gu Zihao's voice showed helplessness!

The four people listened quietly to the gossip in the house.

"Master Gu, we have toured this courtyard and tasted tea! Isn't it time to talk about business? What do you want to give up the Nuwa Stone?" Suddenly, a voice sounded, aiming directly at the Nuwa Stone in Gu Zihao's hand!

"This... Boss Xing, don't be so direct!? I don't have any Nuwa Stone here! Who is hearing rumors? Affecting my reputation! Nuwa Stone is a treasure, I want to have it but I have no chance to find it! "Gu Zihao was doing Tai Chi!

"A few days ago, you used the Nuwa Stone, right?" It was still the voice of the boss Xing in Gu Zihao's mouth.

"Boss Xing, don't talk nonsense. I respect the rapid development of your star spirits, so I call you Boss Xing! Don't slander me!" Gu Zihao said angrily.

"Hmph, you are still pretending. The Nuwa Stone is on you now!" Boss Xing stood up and said aggressively. His six brothers also stood up, and the atmosphere suddenly became tense.

"Boss Xing, this is my Huangdao League! What do you want to do! I said I don't have it, so I don't have it!" Gu Zihao said lightly.

"Still pretending! Since I can't let you take it out and give it to me directly, then I will let you take it out and then rob it. Your Huangdao League is powerful! But my eight brothers didn't grow up eating porridge! "After saying that, he took out a small bag, which was embroidered with gold thread! No, to be precise, it was golden cicada silk! Golden cicada silk that can block all energy! It can be seen how precious and powerful the things inside are.

Boss Xing smiled disdainfully, then untied the golden cicada silk bag and took out a gray bead from it! As soon as the bead was taken out, it changed color instantly! The originally gray bead actually began to emit four colors of green, red, blue, and white! In addition, Gu Zihao's bag also emitted green light, which was the light of the wood-type Nuwa stone! In addition, the treasure bag on Ye Ye's waist outside the house also emitted red, blue, and white!

"Good you Gu Zihao, you are still hiding it now. It turns out that you have more than one Nuwa stone! You even have the heart of Nuwa stone!" Boss Xing saw that the originally gray bead emitted four colors, and immediately said angrily.

"No, I only have one here! Could it be... Feng Yi, Xia Feng, open the door! "Gu Zihao suddenly thought of something, and then shouted loudly, Feng Yi and Xia Feng suddenly appeared from the darkness, and then broke through the door directly.

Ye Ye and the other four were directly exposed to the eyes of Gu Zihao and the seven brothers of Xingling! In addition, the treasure bag on Ye Ye's waist

Chapter 9: Each with his own hidden agenda

Ye Ye looked at the people in the room in surprise, his heart pounding: "This is terrible!" Then he tried to hide the treasure bag, but even though the treasure bag had been stuffed into Ye Ye's clothes, the three-color brilliance continued to radiate.

After Feng Yi and Xia Feng broke through the door, they immediately flashed behind Ye Ye and the other four, blocking their escape route.

"Who was it? It turned out to be Master Ye! What day is today? The three masters are all gathered here! It's really a blessing for Gu!" After a brief surprise, Gu Zihao came back to his senses and said with a faint smile.

Suddenly, a burly man with a shocking scar on his head walked out from behind Gu Zihao. He looked at Ye Ye and the others, then looked at Ye Ye in confusion, and then asked: "Master Gu, is this what you said that no one else would know about our conversation this time? Do you have guests?" From the voice, it sounded like the 'Boss Xing' that Ye Ye had just heard in the house! His eyes stayed on the three-color light wrapped in Ye Ye's clothes.

Ye Ye and the other three watched their conversation quietly.

Gu Zihao suddenly smiled calmly, turned around, and said to Boss Xing: "Boss Xing, calm down first. Getting angry often is not good for your health when you are old. This 'guest' came uninvited! Moreover, after you know his identity, you will be surprised, or you will not be so angry, and your fourth brother also knows them!" After Gu Zihao finished speaking, he smiled lightly. Although his expression seemed so calm, his eyes never left the three-color light in Ye Ye's clothes. Hearing what Gu Zihao said, Boss Xing immediately said, "Xing Yu, do you know them?"

"Yes, I know them! Big brother, he is the leader of Yemen, Ye Ye! The people around him are the main people of Yemen, Qin Minglei, Li Bin and Yang Hengchao! I saw them in the tomb of Fuxi clan last time!" Xingling's fourth brother was originally called Xing Yu. When he heard Boss Xing's call, he immediately whispered everything to Boss Xing.

Ye Ye didn't get nervous for long. After a calm smile, he showed the treasure bag in his clothes, hung it around his waist, and then said, "Hello, two leaders! I am a small sect of Yemen. I came to visit Huangdao League this time. Boss Gu won't be so stingy, right?"

As soon as the treasure bag was revealed, the three-color brilliance became more eye-catching! Gu Zihao and Boss Xing immediately stared at the treasure bag!

Gu Zihao snorted coldly, walked out of the room and said: "Master Ye, how could it be? The Huangdao League is so broad, do you want to join it! No problem, as long as you say it, I promise to give you a high position! At least it is much stronger than your little master of the Night Gate, right?" Gu Zihao's words were full of negation!

"Not for the time being, Master Gu, I'm sorry! I just want to be a small master of the Night Gate now! Oh, by the way, I don't know if your injury has healed last time! We are young and don't know the strength of our hands, so you got hurt!" Ye Ye smiled, bowed slightly, and fought back.

"Hahahahahaha, it's true that heroes come from young! I didn't expect Master Ye to be so young and promising. I only heard of your great name before, but this time I saw it and it's really well-deserved! Master Gu, everyone is a guest, how do you treat guests like this?" When Ye Ye and Gu Zihao were confronting each other, Xing Lao Da suddenly led his six brothers out and said to Ye Ye. In his tone, it seemed that he was the master here, completely ignoring Gu Zihao!

Gu Zihao certainly understood what Boss Xing said, but he didn't care! After a faint smile, he said to Ye Ye: "Oh, Boss Xing is right, Master Ye, do you mind going in to talk?" Then he made a respectful appearance. Ye Ye looked at it, smiled disdainfully, followed Gu Zihao's invitation, and went directly into the room, followed by Qin Minglei and the other two. Although Ye Ye was very calm on the surface at this time, he was very nervous inside. He knew that if they really fought, they would die! So, he chose to retreat, survive, and think of a way out.

"Boss Xing, you also come in! Let's continue!" After seeing Ye Ye go in, Gu Zihao turned around and invited Boss Xing! Boss Xing accepted it, laughed loudly, and entered the room generously.

After several people went in, Gu Zihao entered the room, and then Feng Yi and Xia Feng walked in slowly, closed the door, and continued to disappear into the darkness! As long as Gu Zihao gave an order, they could jump out at any time and kill the enemy!

Ye Ye sat down, looked at the people present, then looked at Boss Xing and said, "Boss Xing, can you put your stone in first? The light in this room is bright enough and a bit dazzling!" Boss Xing laughed loudly after hearing this, and calmly put the stone in his hand that was shining with four colors into the golden cicada silk bag.

"Master Ye, I didn't expect that you also have one. I have one here, wood type! Why don't we take them out and show them to everyone?" Gu Zihao said. After saying that, seeing Boss Xing's nervous look, he continued, "Don't worry, although this is the Huangdao League, my place, but I will never rob it!"

Ye Ye smiled indifferently, thinking in his heart: "The stone milliliter of Boss Xing is strange, it actually detected the Nuwa stone in my treasure bag, and judging from the color, even the attributes are detected!" Thinking about it, he said, "Oh? What are you talking about? I just came in, I don't know what you are talking about."

Boss Xing smiled indifferently, waved his hand, and asked his brother to take a bag. The bag was also made of golden cicada silk. After taking the bag, Boss Xing smiled, then grabbed two beads from it and put them on the table!

It was two Nuwa stones, one golden and one gray. Judging from the color, the two Nuwa stones were the Nuwa stones of the gold and earth systems!

After that, Boss Xing said proudly: "Master Ye, you should have seen this thing, right? Everyone, don't hide it! Take it out! Don't try to hide or lie, the gray bead here can detect the Nuwa stone in your hand!" Boss Xing said this, but he thought in his heart: "When the five-element Nuwa stone and the wind-element Nuwa stone are all gathered, they will naturally combine together and become a complete Nuwa stone! After that..." His gray bead also has a great origin. It is said that when Nuwa repaired the sky, the Nuwa stone she used was not an ordinary stone, but a powerful stone that evolved after hundreds of millions of years. It was not called Nuwa stone at that time. It was discovered by Nuwa and was hastily used to repair the sky before it was named. Nuwa stone is the name left by humans for the stone after the sky was repaired. There are also accompanying organisms in general minerals, and Nuwa stone is no exception. Its accompanying organism is the gray bead in Boss Xing's hand now! It is called: Heart of Nuwa.

Gu Zihao frowned when he saw the two Nuwa stones that Boss Xing took out, and then he also took out the green wood-type Nuwa stone in his hand. Then he stared at Ye Ye and thought in his heart: "When the five-type Nuwa stones and the wind-type Nuwa stones are all gathered, they will naturally combine together and become a complete Nuwa stone! After that..." They each have their own plans!

It turns out that in addition to the ability to reach the sky, the Nuwa stone also has a huge secret! A secret that only a few people know.

Seeing that he could not continue to hide it, Ye Ye had to smile bitterly and untie the treasure bag, and then took out three long-treasured Nuwa stones!

After Ye Ye took out the Nuwa stones, six beads were placed abruptly on the table. Except for the strange color, there was nothing strange about them: "Okay? Are you talking about these beads?"

Boss Xing suddenly smiled, stood up immediately, untied the golden cicada silk bag just now, took out the Nuwa heart, and threw it into the air!

A strange phenomenon suddenly appeared!

The six Nuwa stones on the table suddenly emitted a strong light, which even illuminated the figures of Feng Yi and Xia Feng hiding in the dark. Then they shook violently. Seeing this, Ye Ye and Gu Zihao were anxious and shouted in their hearts that it was not good. They immediately wanted to grab the Nuwa stones in front of them, but those Nuwa stones suddenly flew towards the Nuwa Heart in the sky.

Seeing this, Boss Xing and his six brothers laughed triumphantly, and excitedly looked at the stones in the sky and unconsciously said a few words: "Ancestors, sacrifice..."

But Boss Xing, who was proud, and Ye Ye and Qin Minglei, who were surprised, did not see that Gu Zihao's anxious face suddenly showed a cunning smile!

Chapter 10: Nuwa Stone Appears

The five-element Nuwa Stone in the air slowly floated towards the Nuwa Heart under the wind power of the wind-element Nuwa Stone Heart. Then, under the dazzling light, they slowly merged together!

Ye Ye had never thought that Nuwa Stone was fused like this! Not only did he need the five-element Nuwa Stone, but he also needed a wind-element Nuwa Stone as a power element. In the end, he even needed the bead from Boss Xing just now as a guide!

In the room, everyone was staring at the Nuwa Stone in the air. Not long after, the light suddenly dissipated. Only a bead was left in the air, but it was divided into six colors. In addition to the original color of the non-element, there was also the color of the wind system. The most peculiar thing was that there was an extra "head" next to it, which was Boss Xing's Nuwa Heart just now. If you look closely, the wind-element Nuwa Stone Heart is in the center.

The complete Nuwa Stone that was fused together, or still incomplete, was just a fragment left behind when Nuwa repaired the sky billions of years ago. Although the Nuwa Stone was small, its power could not be underestimated. It was suspended in the air, as if waiting for its owner to take it.

When Ye Ye saw this scene, his pupils shrank and shrank directly into a needle shape. He said to Qin Minglei and the other two around him: "Opportunity, grab it!" Qin Minglei and the other two heard it and immediately moved to grab the Nuwa Stone in the air, but they were shocked to find that they could not move.

That's right, Ye Ye could not move. Not only Ye Ye, but even the seven brothers of Xingling could not move at all. It seemed that something was entangled with them tightly! Everyone struggled hard but could not break free, and the more they struggled, the tighter the thing was!

Through the reflection of light, several people saw that they were actually wrapped around a transparent silk thread! Following the silk thread, several people looked and saw that there was actually a person on the roof! It was the grandson of the thief sect!

At this time, Gu Zihao walked out slowly, laughing: "Hahaha, it turns out that it can really merge! Sorry, two masters! I will accept this Nuwa Stone on your behalf!"

"You want to trap us brothers with a little snow silk, you underestimate us too much, right? Master Gu!" Just as Gu Zihao was walking towards the Nuwa Stone floating in the air, a voice suddenly sounded, and the owner of the voice was Boss Xing.

Gu Zihao looked over in confusion when he heard it. Among the seven brothers of Xingling, three of them suddenly swelled up, as if they wanted to break the snow silk with brute force! Gu Zihao was startled and looked at Sun Ye on the beam. Sun Ye nodded confidently, indicating that there was no problem.

"It seems that they are quite confident? Xing Mu, Xing Yan, Xing Jin, the three of you show them!" Boss Xing seemed very confident, and looked at his three younger brothers' bodies slowly swelling up.

The snow silk was very resilient, and even if the three of them swelled up, they did not break it! However, the three of them suddenly roared loudly, and then their bodies suddenly grew drastically. Originally, the three of them were only about 1.8 meters tall, but suddenly expanded to about 2.5 meters, and all the muscles on their bodies were exposed. They stood in front of Ye Ye and the others, like three human tanks. The snow silk had even been deeply embedded in their muscles, but surprisingly, their muscles were not cut open.

"Hey..." Suddenly, Sun Ye on the beam roared, and then he twisted his fingers and took back the snow silk! Then he said to Gu Zihao: "Master, it's no good! If you hold on any longer, it will really break!" Sun Ye only had one snow silk. After taking it back, the seven brothers of Xingling and Ye Ye and the other four were also freed from the bondage of the snow silk.

"Damn it!" Gu Zihao roared in shock, and then said to Feng Yi, Xia Feng in the corner and Sun Ye on the beam: "Grab!" Then he shook out several swords in succession and rushed towards the Nuwa stone.

Of course, the seven Xinglings would not sit idly by. After becoming larger, Xingmu, Xingyan and Xingjin also jumped over. Ye Ye and the other four followed closely behind!

Sun Ye looked down from above, controlling the snow silk as flexibly as his fingers. His ten fingers moved like water waves, waving the snow silk to wrap the Nuwa stone first, and then pulled it up violently.

However, Qin Minglei's Night Gate strange dagger just arrived, but because he was afraid of damaging the Nuwa stone, he immediately changed the dagger from chopping to slapping, and directly slapped the Nuwa stone out of the entanglement of the snow silk, and the Nuwa stone also flew out. After all, the snow silk is silk, and it can't hold round objects too firmly.

The agile Xia Feng suddenly appeared in the direction where the Nuwa Stone was flying, and then stretched out her hand, trying to grab the Nuwa Stone, but it was unknown which of the three brothers of the Xing family who had grown bigger actually knocked Xia Feng away from her original position, and then grabbed the Nuwa Stone. But before he could be happy, Gu Zihao appeared in front of him again. Gu Zihao was holding a sword in his mouth at this time, which was the highest level of the Nine Swords Style! He couldn't express himself with the sword in his mouth, so he saw him stabbing the sword in his hand at a very fast speed. In a flash, the strong man of the Xing family actually let go of the Nuwa Stone that he had been holding tightly in his hand in pain. After that, Gu Zihao slapped the sword in his mouth, and the Nuwa Stone also flew to the position where Feng Yi was!

What a Nine Swords Style, it's not that the strong man of the Xing family wanted to let go of the Nuwa Stone in his hand, but that the Nine Swords Style was really terrifying. The skin that Sun Ye's snow silk couldn't cut just now was pierced by Gu Zihao's sword at this time!

Feng Yi looked calm. Seeing the Nuwa Stone flying towards him, he calmly shook out three swords and threw them in the direction of Ye Ye and the seven Xingling brothers, buying time for himself to grab the Nuwa Stone!

"Hey!" Seeing this, Boss Xing immediately shouted. The sound was as shocking as a bell, and it actually shook Feng Yi's mind out of the trance for a moment, so that he passed by the Nuwa Stone.

When Boss Xing did this, Yang Hengchao, who had been lurking nearby to watch the situation, saw the opportunity. He put on his gloves and ran towards the Nuwa Stone! He was about to grab the Nuwa Stone, but he was tripped. It was the snow silk controlled by Sun Ye! The Nuwa Stone also stopped temporarily and floated in the air again.

Seeing that the Nuwa Stone, which was about to be caught by Yang Hengchao, was lost again, the seven Xingling brothers immediately showed that there is strength in numbers. The seven of them immediately formed a formation, and Xing Yu had already transformed. The four giants provided cover on all sides, and the other four were in the middle. With the full cooperation of the seven people, they knocked Yang Hengchao away, and the others did not dare to approach them easily. They also quickly approached the Nuwa Stone.

But don't forget. One of the three giants among the seven Xingling brothers had been stabbed by Gu Zihao, and that was the gap in the defense! Gu Zihao also broke through from there, and it was another nine swords, but this time the direction of the attack was still the giant of the Xing family who was stabbed by him just now!

Suddenly, the originally perfect formation was disrupted in an instant! Gu Zihao also rushed towards the Nuwa Stone. But would Boss Xing give him a chance? Of course not! Boss Xing smiled evilly at this time. Suddenly, they all grew bigger and surrounded Gu Zihao in the middle! Iron fists kept banging Gu Zihao who was surrounded in the middle! Gu Zihao took all of them, but after the seven brothers of the Xing family became bigger, their power was geometrically enhanced! After seven people punched one by one, even Gu Zihao could not resist it!

But Gu Zihao was Gu Zihao after all, the leader of the Huangdao League! With so much combat experience, he immediately chose to fight back! He spun around, and the nine swords suddenly turned into a blade storm, which immediately blocked all the seven brothers of the Xing family! And he kept spinning there, blocking the way for anyone else who wanted to fight for the Nuwa Stone.

Seeing that he couldn't get close to the Nuwa Stone, the old man Xing had to stand there and roared angrily, and then he swung Yang Hengchao, who was closest to him, as if he was angry, and then rushed towards Gu Zihao's blade storm again, but still failed.

It was Yang Hengchao's bad luck! He was slapped directly by the old man Xing, smashing the door of the room, and the fragments fell to the ground! The sunlight outside the door also took the opportunity to shine in.

Seeing that they could not obtain the Nuwa Stone for the time being, Ye Ye and his companions immediately went to Yang Hengchao's side.

"Damn, I'm fine! That guy was so strong! Fortunately, I'm not made of flesh!" Yang Hengchao was helped up by Li Bin, and wiped the blood from the corner of his mouth with the back of his hand.

Suddenly, a new situation occurred at the Nuwa Stone! Lingbao has spirituality! As one of the Lingbao, the Nuwa Stone is no exception! When it saw the sunlight, it immediately flew out of the door on its own, at a very fast speed! When several people paid attention, it had already dived into the sunlight and disappeared!

Chapter 11 Choice

When everyone sighed inwardly at the direction where the Nuwa Stone flew, Xia Feng suddenly moved quietly! She was a girl who insisted on her own opinion. When Gu Zihao first ordered to kill Ye Ye, she had kept it in mind. Now the opportunity came again. Ye Ye and all the people were looking outside the door and did not notice her.

She dodged lightly and disappeared into the surrounding environment. When she appeared again, she had already jumped high behind Ye Ye, and the dagger in her hand flashed coldly. In her eyes, Ye Ye was already a corpse.

But Xia Feng's action was seen by someone. The person swung his body and kicked Xia Feng, who was attacking Ye Ye in the air, like a dragon's tail. The owner of the leg turned out to be Boss Xing.

Xia Feng in the air could not dodge, so she had to give up the attack and held the dagger horizontally to block the fierce kick. However, she was also kicked away by the force, and then hit the wall and collapsed.

Boss Xing's kick was not only powerful, but also perfectly timed, hitting Xia Feng hard!

This series of actions naturally awakened everyone from their indignation over the loss of the Nuwa Stone! Ye Ye looked at Boss Xing in surprise. He was no longer dull or very smart, so he naturally understood that it was Boss Xing who saved him just now! But he didn't understand why Boss Xing wanted to rescue him, but the current situation did not allow Ye Ye to think too much. Ye Ye and the other four immediately stood in formation and looked at Gu Zihao and others vigilantly.

"What do you mean? Sect Master Gu, do you really want to kill me?" Ye Ye, who had calmed down, looked at Gu Zihao and said.

After hearing this, Gu Zihao didn't have time to reprimand Xia Feng for her impulsiveness. He was about to speak to explain, but was interrupted by Boss Xing. Boss Xing shouted loudly: "Master Gu, since you didn't get the Nuwa Stone, do you want to kill us and prevent the truth of the Nuwa Stone from being revealed? Then you can go find the trace of the Nuwa Stone yourself?" After saying that, he rushed towards Gu Zihao and punched him with his iron fist.

Gu Zihao had to give up explaining temporarily and resisted hastily. He waved the sword in his hand into a sword curtain, blocking all the attacks of Boss Xing. Then he suddenly raised his head and threw the sword in his mouth out with inertia. The sword temporarily forced Boss Xing back, and he said: "Ye Ye, it's not like that! I didn't ask her to kill you, it was that child..." Before he finished speaking, Gu Zihao was entangled by Boss Xing again!

Boss Xing winked at his brothers, and all the seven Xingling brothers immediately surrounded him. The offensive was more fierce than when they surrounded him just now, and Gu Zihao couldn't resist it at all! Feng Yi rushed forward immediately upon seeing this, and the master and his disciple joined forces to barely hold them off.

"Master Ye, let's join forces! Gu Zihao wants to kill us! Don't you want to get the Nuwa Stone?" The seven brothers of the Xing family have strength in numbers. The eldest brother Xing pulled himself out and said this to Ye Ye, then threw himself into the battle again.

Ye Ye frowned, looked at the battle between the seven Xingling brothers and Gu Zihao's master and his disciple, and fully understood that even if Sun joined the battle, he would at most draw with the seven Xingling brothers. They had become the key to this battle, and whoever the four of them helped would win!

While Ye Ye was wandering, Feng Yi stabbed several times in succession, then took a step back, blocked the fist of one of the Xing brothers with three swords, and said to Ye Ye: "Ye Ye, have you forgotten? Forgot that I let you go a few days ago?"

When Boss Xing heard this, he felt something was wrong and immediately said: "Master Ye, I don't know your past, but it is true that they wanted to kill you just now, right? You can do this favor yourself!"

Ye Ye was immediately more embarrassed! Feng Yi is a good man, and he did let them go a few days ago. Although Boss Xing is not a clear person, it is true that he saved Ye Ye's life!

What should I do? Ye Ye was immediately embarrassed. Qin Minglei and the other two also kept watching Ye Ye. As long as Ye Ye made a decision, they would rush up!

But Ye Ye was still hesitating!

"Ye Ye!" Feng Yi shouted loudly to Ye Ye, motioning him to hurry up.

"Master Ye!" The seven brothers of Xing actually shouted at the same time, wanting him to help quickly.

In fact, Ye Ye already had the answer in his heart. What he couldn't know was how the other party would treat them after helping. Among the three forces here, the strength of the four of them could not catch up with others. If the other party killed them after helping, it would be more trouble than gain!

The battle between the seven Xingling brothers and Gu Zihao and others was in deep water, but no one could do anything to the other! And at this point, both sides had no way to retreat. If anyone retreated, they would face death! So they still attacked back and forth, it was so lively.

"Hey!" Suddenly, the seven Xingling brothers shouted at the same time, and everyone was stunned by the thunderous roar! Gu Zihao and the other two also showed a gap in attack! Seeing this, the seven Xingling brothers immediately rushed up and blasted the three with their iron fists! Gu Zihao and the other two were immediately hit and flew out. Then they hit the wall! The sword in Gu Zihao's hand also flew strangely towards Ye Ye. Ye Ye flashed, and the sword stuck straight into the ground. Ye Ye smiled slightly after seeing it. No one saw that a little bit of something slowly fell to the ground.

The wall was destroyed by the huge force, and dust flew all over the sky, blocking the view! The seven brothers of Xingling did not dare to attack again rashly, but looked at Ye and said at the same time: "Master Ye, human feelings are precious! See, Gu Zihao wants to drag you to be buried with him!"

Seeing that the battle stopped temporarily, Ye Ye stepped forward and looked at the seven people and said: "Who is Boss Xing?" A strong man walked out of the seven brothers of Xingling and said: "Master Ye, what's the matter? Have you decided to help me?" The voice sounded like Boss Xing.

It's not that Ye Ye doesn't know Boss Xing, but that the seven brothers of Xingling all look the same, and they look exactly the same after they grow bigger. Even the slight difference in height disappears! How can you tell them apart?

Ye Ye smiled and said, "Boss Xing, if I help you, will you destroy us?" Ye Ye asked such a question. After all, facing such a situation, survival is the most important thing!

Boss Xing laughed: "Haha, as long as you help me this time, we will join forces to kill Gu Zihao and make the Huangdao League leaderless. Then our Xingling will quickly destroy the Huangdao League, and then there will only be you, Yemen and my Xingling in this world. Why not?"

But after hearing this, Ye Ye frowned, his eyes suddenly became sharp and asked back: "After destroying the Huangdao League, it will be my Yemen, right?" Boss Xing smiled and said, "How is it possible? As long as you help me, we are allies! How can I destroy you? We develop and succeed at the same time! Not good?" Although he said this, Boss Xing thought in his heart: "Huh, kid, if I don't destroy you? If I don't destroy you, my plan will fail!"

After hearing this, Ye Ye laughed, then stretched out his left hand and slowly walked towards Boss Xing. Boss Xing also laughed triumphantly, then stretched out his hand and slowly walked towards Ye Ye!

"Huh, kid, you really believe it!" Boss Xing laughed, but thought so in his heart.

Could it be that Ye Ye really wanted to help Xing Ling and destroy the Huangdao League?

Of course not, when Ye Ye's hand and Boss Xing's hand were clasped together, Boss Xing suddenly felt a slight tingling pain, and immediately felt something was wrong. He wanted to let go of Ye Ye's hand, but suddenly found that he couldn't let go! Or rather, his entire left hand was unable to move!

Ye Ye smiled and said, "Haha, Phoenix Thorn! Sect Leader Gu, come out!" Ye Ye said, and took out a small needle-like object from his fingers, which was the sharp part of the Phoenix Thorn. . It was also that little thing that pierced Boss Xing's unbreakable skin defense, and then the toxin contained in it directly paralyzed Boss Xing's hand completely! Then he took out the broken Phoenix Thorn from his other hand.

"Hahaha! I knew that Master Ye would not help them!" Three people walked out from the dust of the collapsed wall. They were Gu Zihao and the other two who were just knocked away.

It turned out that Ye Ye's hesitation just now was completely pretended! Just now, Gu Zihao saw Ye Ye take out the Phoenix Thorn and was immediately worried, but he saw that there was no hesitation in Ye Ye's eyes when he stared at him, and he immediately understood, and then pretended to be knocked away, and then took the opportunity to throw a sword, but it was not stabbed at Ye Ye, but accurately inserted in front of Ye Ye. Ye Ye was also very smart. He secretly cut off the Phoenix Thorn with the sword thrown by Gu Zihao just now, and then did all that.

The situation suddenly became clear.

Chapter 12: Killing

Seeing this, Boss Xing immediately retreated to his brothers, looked at Ye Ye and Gu Zihao warily, and said: "Hmph, have you really decided? Small Yemen, it's just a matter of turning my hand if I want to destroy it." Indeed, Yemen is indeed a small sect in front of the old sect Huangdao League and the newly emerged Xingling with many masters.

Ye Ye and Gu Zihao ignored Boss Xing's words, and slowly approached the seven brothers of the Xing family, slowly forming an encirclement.

Boss Xing looked at the people who were slowly surrounding him warily, and then said to Feng Yi: "Feng Yi, right? How does it feel to be exterminated? Do you still want to stay by Gu Zihao's side and slowly take revenge? By the time you have taken revenge, I think your parents' bodies will have been cold!" Boss Xing is so good, he actually found out the origins of the people here, and then he actually instigated them.

Feng Yi frowned when he heard it, and looked at Boss Xing coldly. Gu Zihao thought about it and said with full momentum: "Don't spread rumors there! You must have known that this Nuwa stone can be fused, right? You came here to seize the fragments of Nuwa stone, right?"

"No, that's not entirely true! He must not have thought that I was here, and I have other fragments of Nuwa stone!" Ye Ye said with a smile.

"Haha, what a joke, what a joke! That's right, I just want to seize your Nuwa stone, and I do know that Nuwa stones can be fused together! You must know that, Gu Zihao?" Boss Xing laughed instead of getting angry and pushed the spearhead to Gu Zihao again.

Gu Zihao smiled, waved the eight swords and said, "How would I know?"

Boss Xing ignored Gu Zihao and said, "Sun Ye. You are here for the Medicine King Pill and to treat your master, right? It has been half a year since the Fuxi clan tomb. Didn't Gu Zihao give it to you? Aren't you afraid of being cheated? As far as I know, your master's life will not exceed one year, right?"

Sun Ye was silent when he heard it. Indeed, after staying in the Huangdao League for more than half a year, Gu Zihao did not find the Medicine King Pill for Sun Ye.

Gu Zihao saw that Sun Ye hesitated, and immediately said to Sun Ye: "Sun Ye, I will do what I promised you, as long as you believe me! Xingtian, don't confuse the public with lies! Die!" Gu Zihao saw that Boss Xing was slowly provoking, and he couldn't help but panic! He immediately waved his sword and went up. However, surprisingly, Sun Ye and Feng Yi were still hesitating and did not step forward.

Seeing this, Ye Ye knew that what Boss Xing said worked. He thought: If the Xing brothers kill Gu Zihao, then we will be in trouble! Thinking of this, Ye Ye kicked the hilt of the sword stuck in the ground with his foot. The sword was kicked directly to Boss Xing by Ye Ye, and Boss Xing dodged. But the sword was caught by Gu Zihao who rushed to Boss Xing from the other side, and the Nine Swords Style reappeared!

Seeing Gu Zihao catch the sword smoothly, Ye Ye and the other four also rushed up at the same time. They all knew that since they chose to help Gu Zihao, they must kill the seven brothers of the Xing family without mercy, otherwise they would only face death!

"Ye Ye, are you so heartless? Don't you want to think about who saved you just now? Why do you treat me like this?" Boss Xing was still unwilling to give up and continued.

Ye Ye smiled, took out a phoenix thorn, and said, "Yes, you saved me! But the grudge of that girl has nothing to do with the Huangdao League. It's my business that she killed me. When did I ask you to worry about it?" As he said that, he stabbed Boss Xing with the phoenix thorn.

Boss Xing was nervous when he saw the phoenix thorn in Ye Ye's hand. The arm that was stabbed by the sharp point of the phoenix thorn was still paralyzed and could not be used at all! He only had one hand now, so he had no choice but to dodge. But he didn't expect that Gu Zihao behind him had broken through the defense of his six brothers and rushed up. They knew that to capture the thief, the king should be captured first.

Boss Xing had no choice but to retreat forcefully, using his abnormal skin defense to resist the stabbing of Gu Zihao's nine swords. When he retreated to his brother's side, he was already covered with wounds! The Nine Swords Flow is indeed terrifying. However, he had no choice. If he didn't dodge, he would be stabbed by the phoenix thorn in Ye Ye's hand and paralyzed all over. Then he would not have the skin injuries like now!

"Hmph." Boss Xing snorted disdainfully, and the seven brothers formed a formation and rushed forward. Ye Ye and his men could not resist the seven humanoid tanks, so they had to get out of the way.

After breaking out of the encirclement, Boss Xing had to put his chance on Feng Yi and Sun Ye who were still hesitating:

"Feng Yi, Sun Ye, as long as you are willing to help me, I promise to do everything you want immediately! Sun Ye...ah" Boss Xing's words suddenly stopped before he finished speaking!

They, not just them, but even everyone ignored the existence of one person! That was Xia Feng, who was kicked away by Boss Xing and collapsed on the ground just now! She didn't know when she recovered, sneaked, and then seized the opportunity to stab Boss Xing's eyes with the dagger in her hand! And stabbed! The blood flowed down his cheek, making the already terrifying Boss Xing even more terrifying.

However, only a short part of the dagger was inserted into Boss Xing's eyes, and it was actually blocked outside. Xia Feng had no time to pull away, and was grabbed by Boss Xing, who then grabbed her neck fiercely!

"Die! Bitch!" Boss Xing lifted Xia Feng up fiercely, and no matter how Xia Feng struggled, it was useless.

However, he made the biggest mistake in the battle, which was to be distracted during the battle of life and death. Gu Zihao and Ye Ye rushed up at the same time.

The Phoenix Thorn in Ye Ye's hand first pierced Boss Xing's back, and then Ye Ye quickly took out a few more Phoenix Thorns and pierced other acupuncture points. In an instant, Boss Xing was paralyzed and couldn't move. All this happened in a flash, and even Gu Zihao was surprised at Ye Ye's speed and accuracy! But he didn't distract himself for too long. When he saw Boss Xing was paralyzed, he immediately combined the nine swords into one, and suddenly a force that seemed to pierce the sky came out from the sword, and then disappeared into Boss Xing's arm, without any sound, Boss Xing's hand was directly cut off. Xia Feng was also rescued, and then she disappeared directly into the surrounding environment.

"Brother!" All this happened too suddenly and quickly. The brothers of the Xing family had no time to react. When they reacted, Gu Zihao had already cut off the arm of the boss. They immediately made a move, but found that they could not move, because they were all wrapped in a silver thread that was almost invisible to the naked eye! It was Sun Ye! At the same time, Feng Yi also moved suddenly. He grabbed six swords in his hand and threw them at the six brothers of the Xing family. Every sword hit the vital point! It also temporarily stopped their momentum to rush forward!

It turned out that Feng Yi and Sun Ye had already thought it through. They had been waiting for an opportunity. When they saw that Ye Ye and the others had cooperated perfectly to seriously injure the boss, and the brothers of the Xing family were ready to rush up to help, the two of them burst out with a fierce surprise attack!

At this moment, on the other side, the tragedy of the boss Xing had not yet ended. After he broke his arm, he was still unable to move, but Ye Ye and Gu Zihao's moves were old and there was no time to change. Moreover, at this time, the boss Xing was flushed all over, and there was a faint sense of breaking through the restraints of the Phoenix Thorn Poison!

At this time, the attacks of Qin Minglei and others also arrived. Qin Minglei and Li Bin's strange daggers arrived at the same time, slashing the front and back of Boss Xing's neck respectively, and then cutting into the flesh with force, and the most fatal thing was indeed Yang Hengchao's iron fist!

Yang Hengchao was originally a freak, with a thousand pounds of strength, plus the superposition of his boxing gloves, he actually hit Boss Xing's head directly to one side, and surprisingly broke his spine! !

In fact, according to Boss Xing's defense, Yang Hengchao could not do all this at all, but don't forget that Boss Xing was completely bound and poisoned by the Phoenix Thorn Poison at this time, and his defense was at its weakest period. In addition, the strange daggers of the Night Gate in the hands of Qin Minglei and Li Bin were clamped on his neck and kept exerting force, which made Yang Hengchao's attack have such an effect.

However, the attack was not over yet. Xia Feng seemed to hold a grudge very much. After she disappeared into the darkness, she saw such an opportunity and appeared again. She stabbed Boss Xing's heart with the dagger in her hand. This time, the dagger seemed to have no resistance and stabbed Boss Xing's heart directly, leaving only the dagger handle outside! Dead!

After that, several people immediately dispersed.

"Brother... At this time, the brothers of the Xing family finally broke through the defense network organized by Feng Yi and Sun Ye and rushed to the front of Boss Xing. But it was too late!

Is it really too late?

Everyone present suddenly saw a scene they had never seen before. The body of Boss Xing, who was destined to die, disappeared, and then slowly turned into a gray bead under the gray light. The brothers of the Xing family immediately stepped forward, picked up the bead, and then the six of them stomped on the ground at the same time.

Suddenly, the floor was cracked, and the house shook violently and collapsed! Then the six of them immediately took the opportunity to escape from the house, and they did not choose a route, but directly broke through the wall and knocked down countless walls along the way. They quickly disappeared from Ye Ye and the others' sight.

Afterwards, the angry voices of the six of them echoed in the sky: "Yemen, Huangdaomeng, you wait for our angry revenge! When my brother is resurrected, your heads and bodies will be separated!"

Chapter 13 Conditions of Alliance

When Ye Ye and others recovered, they had lost the whereabouts of the Xing brothers.

"Hmph, just a trick, the little Xing Ling dares to be arrogant in front of the Huang Dao League. From today on, the Huang Dao League will start to hunt down the Xing Ling group, and they will not stop until they die! Feng Yi immediately passed the order down, and the whole mountain began to hunt down the seven Xing Ling brothers!" Gu Zihao said indifferently, looking at the direction they left.

Feng Yi took the order and left. Ye Ye slowly walked towards Gu Zihao and asked: "Master Gu, I want to destroy Xing Ling is not your personal business, right?" Gu Zihao turned his head and looked at Ye Ye with a puzzled look: "Oh? Master Ye? I didn't say I wanted to destroy Xing Ling!" He actually ran away without answering Ye Ye. The words revealed the meaning of turning against him.

"What do you mean, Master Gu?" Ye Ye smiled and said calmly.

"It doesn't matter! My huge Huangdao League has never been afraid of the Star Spirit, but Master Ye, you, Yemen, have to be careful. I heard that it was attacked last time. How is the reconstruction going now?" Gu Zihao seemed to have completely forgotten that he had just cooperated with Ye Ye to expel the seven brothers of the Xing family.

Ye Ye did not get angry. He pulled Qin Minglei and the other two who were about to lose their temper, and then said: "Master Gu, how about this, let's form an alliance? All the past accounts are written off." Ye Ye thought about it, and the situation forced him to choose to retreat.

"Alliance? Write off? Can the hatred of so many years be written off? Besides, I don't need an ally who is so weak that I have to protect him! Unless..." Things seem to be turning around.

Ye Ye was actually quite helpless. Indeed, in the situation just now, he made a choice, so he had to bear the consequences, but Yemen is not the opponent of any of the Huangdao League or the Star Spirit Group. Take the last time, for example, the Huangdao League only sent one sect to almost destroy the Yemen. Although the power of the spell was used, it was hard to guarantee that there would be other spells between them. Therefore, Ye Ye had to endure it and choose the Huangdao League to form an alliance, so that the growing Yemen could develop.

When Ye Ye heard Gu Zihao's words, he immediately understood the meaning and immediately said, "Oh? What's the matter?"

Gu Zihao laughed and said, "Haha, I think it's better to forget it. I think you four can't accomplish it at all!" His words were full of disdain, as if the people who drove away the foreign enemies with him just now were not Ye Ye and his four people. There was no way, he was the leader of the Huangdao League.

Ye Ye also laughed and said, "Haha, is that so? I don't think so. At the beginning, the four of us almost killed a person who was much stronger than us!" Ye Ye certainly would not choose to swallow his anger, he immediately fought back.

This time it was Gu Zihao's turn to be defeated. He laughed dryly and said with no change in his expression: "Hey, is that so?

Actually, it's nothing. You just need to arrive at this place by this time tomorrow!"

"So simple?" Li Bin said in surprise. "Simple? You sneaked in with my disciples last time, right? This time, you have to come up by yourself! Did you see the houses on the roadside when you came? There are a total of eight houses, each of which is connected by a secret passage. You must enter from that house and arrive here before the sun sets tomorrow! This is the condition of the alliance! Aren't you very powerful? Then let me see it!" After saying that, he turned around and left.

"Hey..." Ye Ye just shouted and was about to speak, but was interrupted by Gu Zihao. Gu Zihao waved his hand and said as he walked: "Go down the mountain quickly, time waits for no one!"

In fact, Gu Zihao's move was very vicious!

The Eight Heavenly Gates, that is, the eight houses on the mountain road, each of which has a person or a group of people who are seriously wronged. They were all captured by the Huangdao League with great effort! Their strength should not be underestimated. And Gu Zihao wanted to use them to get rid of Ye Ye and his men! In his heart, Ye Ye and his men were not strong enough to get through even one level.

If Ye Ye and his men succeed, he can get rid of another powerful ally. If he fails, he can just get rid of a big worry in his heart. Why not do it?

Ye Ye and his men didn't know all this. After a while of silence, Ye Ye said lightly: "Everyone, we have no time and no chance! Only by doing that, I think it will be extremely dangerous this time, you..." Before Ye Ye finished speaking, Li Bin interrupted him: "Ye Ye, don't say more, I said, your decision is our decision!"

Ye Ye looked at the three of them in surprise, and the three of them also looked at Ye Ye with a determined look. Ye Ye stopped being hypocritical, smiled, turned around and left, Qin Minglei and the other two followed him with a resolute step. What greeted them was the Eight Heavens Gate that everyone in the Huangdao League feared.

Many years later, when future generations mentioned that Ye Ye and his four men bravely broke through the Eight Heavens Gate, they had to succumb to them because they had accomplished something that ordinary people could never accomplish.

Of course, Ye Ye and his four men would not rashly break through the Eight Heavens Gate. After they went down the mountain, they first returned to the place where Lao Li lived at the foot of the mountain to discuss the plan for tomorrow's pass!

"We don't know anything about that place, what will happen? But when I passed by there today, I always felt that someone was watching me from behind, which made my spine cold. I guess the strength of the people there must be terrifying!" Li Bin said, recalling the feeling when he passed those houses today.

"Yes, I felt it too!" Yang Hengchao also said. "It turns out that I am not the only one who has that feeling!" Li Bin said in surprise after hearing what Yang Hengchao said.

"But, no matter what, we have to go in! And, if we don't go, then how can we get out? Now the Nuwa Stone is missing, we must find it." Ye Ye said helplessly. Indeed, they knew nothing about the Eight Heavens Gate!

When several people were at a loss, suddenly a paper ball was thrown in from the window. Ye Ye quickly picked up the paper ball, opened it and took a look, and was immediately surprised. After that, he immediately opened the door and rushed out. Qin

Minglei and others followed him in confusion. But he saw Ye Ye thoughtfully walked to the place where Lao Li and others were gathering, and Feng Yi was already drinking there.

Seeing Ye Ye and the other four coming, Feng Yi raised the wine glass in his hand and said hello to the four of them. After seeing Ye Ye, the corners of his mouth slightly raised, and then turned and left, leaving Qin Minglei and the other three with a confused look on their faces to continue following him.

After the four returned to the room, Ye Ye first closed the window and door, then took out the paper ball just now, unfolded it and placed it on the table. Qin Minglei and the other two immediately gathered around curiously to take a look. Soon, even Qin Minglei showed a very surprised expression.

"This thing was thrown in by Feng Yi! Now we know something about the Eight Days Pass!" Ye Ye laughed and said confidently.

It turned out that Feng Yi knew that the condition for Gu Zihao and Ye Ye to form an alliance was to break through the Eight Days Pass, so he took great pains to get the information of the people imprisoned in the Eight Days Pass, and then quietly gave it to Ye Ye.

"It turns out that the people imprisoned in the Eight Days Pass were once people who had committed great crimes! And each of them is either strong or has a monster IQ!" Li Bin said lightly after reading the note.

Ye Ye laughed, holding his head back and said in a relaxed manner: "Now all we lack is strength! Let's go to sleep, take one step at a time, after all, plans can't keep up with changes." After that, he turned around and lay on the bed!

But can Ye Ye really sleep? Of course not. Although Ye Ye said so, he was thinking about how to pass the customs tomorrow.

It was past midnight, and Ye Ye and the other three couldn't sleep. But Ye Ye had a plan for tomorrow's clearance in his mind.

Chapter 14 Eight Days Pass 1

Early in the morning of the second day, Ye Ye and his four companions came quietly to the foot of the mountain road without waking anyone. The guards at the foot of the mountain seemed to have not seen them and let them go directly.

"That feeling is coming again! It seems that someone is watching me somewhere!" As soon as he walked outside the first house, the feeling of being watched came again. Li Bin took a deep breath and said.

Ye Ye walked up and didn't say anything. At this time, he was very depressed. He felt that something was calling him, right here, in the "Eight Days Pass" of the Huangdao League, something was calling him. But he didn't know what it was.

Ye Ye didn't say anything, walked slowly to the door, and gently pushed open the seemingly heavy wooden door. He didn't use any force, but he pushed it open! It seemed that someone inside had kept the door open.

Without saying anything, the four people walked in directly.

After the four people went in, the door suddenly closed silently. Moreover, the four people found in confusion that there was no lock or door handle on the other side of the door! It's just a bare door!

This door was actually designed by the Huangdao League specifically to imprison those strong men! It can only be opened from the outside, and it can't be opened from the inside. In addition, the door looks thick, but everything else is very plain.

In fact, the material of this door is indeed impervious to water and fire. It is made of fine iron inside and wrapped with a layer of black wood outside. It is very solid. Otherwise, how can it imprison those strong men and warriors?

"You can't go out, Li Bin, fire." Ye Ye said lightly. Li Bin immediately took out the fireworks and prepared to light them.

But suddenly, before Li Bin could light the fireworks in his hand, the room suddenly became bright. The four people couldn't adapt to it and covered their eyes quickly.

"Haha, it's you? Kill you and you can go out! I thought someone was so capable, but it turned out to be just a group of little kids." Suddenly, a sound like iron scraping sounded.

When Ye Ye and his friends gradually became familiar with the light, a group of people had appeared in front of them. One of the old men leaned on his cane and looked at them and said, "You guys, hurry up and come up to die! I've been here for more than 30 years, and I can finally get out." Another man with a sturdy body and thick hair, who looked like a gorilla, and whose hair had completely covered his waist, said. There were several people behind them, all looking at them with disdain and helplessness.

This 'Eight Days Pass' is actually the prison of the Huangdao League! Here are the strong men and warriors who have gone against the Huangdao League or the Huangdao League after they wiped out other sects. The Huangdao League has imprisoned them for hundreds of years, or even countless years.

Take the old man and the sturdy man just now, both of them are extremely evil people for the Huangdao League, and their imprisonment periods are 150 and 90 years respectively!

Such a period of imprisonment can only keep people locked up until death! However, Gu Zihao has already informed them in advance: as long as one of them is killed, the ten-year sentence can be offset, and killing Ye Ye can offset fifty years!

Fifty years, two hundred springs, summers, autumns and winters! Who doesn't want it? Therefore, they were so excited when they saw Ye Ye and the other four coming in.

"Who are you?" Ye Ye said, fearless, taking a step forward.

"It doesn't matter who we are! What's important is that you all have to die!" The boss said indifferently. He didn't take Ye Ye and the other four seriously at all. After that, he nodded to the sturdy gorilla beside him, motioning him to go first. The people behind him immediately showed dissatisfaction, but they didn't dare to say anything. This old man has a high prestige among this group of people!

The 'gorilla' saw it and stepped forward and said loudly: "I haven't eaten human flesh for 30 years! Who of you is Ye Ye? Stand up, I like to eat tender meat!"

Ye Ye frowned and wondered in his heart: "How do they know who is the youngest among us? Could it be..." Thinking of it, he said indifferently: "How do they know who is the youngest among us? I think Gu Zihao just wants to kill us!" Everything was awakened by a sentence after entering!

Qin Minglei and the other four thought about it and understood it immediately! They were furious, but there was nothing they could do. They had already fallen into someone else's trap and couldn't get out.

"Calm down. Looking at his appearance, he must be a power type! Let's temporarily divide their group into three types. The old man should be a magician from the appearance, and the strong man seems to be a power type. The few people after him and the other two should not be good at power! Maybe they are speed or magicians! Only in this way can we have a chance!" Ye Ye analyzed calmly.

"Hey, have you finished discussing? I'm asking you a question. Who is Ye Ye?" The big man seemed impatient and shouted loudly at Ye Ye and the other four, and then clenched his fists and made a crackling sound.

Ye Ye glanced at him indifferently, ignored him and continued: "So, Li Bin, you go first! Remember, hold him back, and then look for an opportunity to make a fatal blow!" After hearing this, Li Bin drew out the strange dagger of Yemen and nodded. Then he stepped forward.

"Hey, what's that look in your eyes! Wait, I'll eat your heart!" He looked at Li Bin and continued, "You are Ye Ye? Haha, prepare to die!" After that, he rushed out like a human tank!

Li Bin quickly dodged and tried to keep a distance from him. He was always looking for a gap in this attack.

"Hey, fuck you, stop and let me kill you! Otherwise, I will eat you up. If you stop, I will consider leaving you a finger or something!" After a few rounds, the strong man seemed to be annoyed by Li Bin's dodging and roared.

Li Bin ignored him and continued to dodge the strong man's iron fist. The strong man was not fast, so he had to chase Li Bin and waved his iron fist.

However, suddenly something strange happened. Li Bin's right foot suddenly stumbled, and a small amount of dust appeared from Li Bin's leg, and then disappeared. Li Bin half-knelt on the ground, and the strong man's iron fist just arrived, knocking Li Bin out. He collapsed on the ground, not knowing what was going on.

"Hahahaha, you want to hide?" The strong man roared, then rushed up, jumped up, and stood on his elbows, ready to give Li Bin a fatal blow! However, Li Bin suddenly opened his eyes and rolled away from the strong man's flying elbow. The strong man's attack suddenly missed and hit the ground. The floor was actually broken by him, and the gravel flew all over!

Li Bin slowly stood up, frowning and panting desperately. It seems that the blow did cause him a lot of damage. Fortunately, he has a special physique and can recover quickly from the injury.

"Boy, I don't know if you are beaten or my fist has been rusty for thirty years without using it! Come again! I'll eat your meat!" The strong man laughed instead of being angry, and then pushed the hair that was originally covering his face back, revealing a terrifying face like a hell Shura!

His face was covered with scars, including knife wounds, burns, and even black flesh from poisoning! Moreover, his chin was also missing a corner, and his teeth were uneven, just like Shura. The way he laughed was even more terrifying: "Haha, kid, you are still young to fight me! What kind of battles did I not encounter thirty years ago?" Yes, he did experience all types of battles. He was the battle madman Huang Qin who was once a powerful man thirty years ago, a battle madman born for fighting! After experiencing countless battles in his life, his existence seemed to be born only to challenge more powerful people in the future. Once in a duel, he killed several sect leaders under the Huangdao League, and there were rumors that he was going to kill Huangdao League! So he was wanted by Gu Zihao, and finally it was reported that he was attacked to death by countless talismans. Unexpectedly, he was not dead, and appeared in the Huangdao League's "Eight Heavens Pass"!

Huang Qin smiled, and then continued to rush up. Li Bin wanted to hide, but his right foot was stabbed again and couldn't move! But Li Bin would not make the same mistake twice. He rolled on the ground and dodged the powerful fist.

Ye Ye and his companions saw Li Bin roll to the side and quickly stood up. Ye Ye shouted in the direction of the old man:

"You actually attacked!" That's right, they attacked. Ye Ye was puzzled when he saw Li Bin's malfunction for no reason. It was not until just now that he found out that there was a person standing behind the old man. It was that person who hit Li Bin's leg with a hidden weapon, which caused Li Bin to malfunction.

The old man laughed and said, "Haha, did I tell you about one-on-one? Haha! Li Chen, keep waiting for us to get out, and your hidden weapon skills can continue to flourish! Haha!" After the old man finished speaking, an unusually short man walked out from behind him. He was holding a few stones in his hands. It was he who hit Li Bin's feet with stones and then the stones bounced off. His hidden weapon skills are indeed exquisite. This man was also a famous person many years ago. He was Sun Ye's uncle. The South Pirates had been looking for him for years but couldn't find him. He was imprisoned in the Huangdao League.

"You..." Ye Ye and his companions were furious when they heard this. Qin Minglei and Yang Hengchao wanted to rush forward, but they were stopped by Ye Ye again. Ye Ye suppressed his anger and said, "If we go up to help together, do you have to go up together?"

"Hahahaha" the old man laughed, "Smart! Baby, you are really smart. We just want to see you dying. Haha! Resisting is useless. We can only watch our companions die one by one." This group of people have become perverted in years of imprisonment.

"What if we question and come forward and kill you together?" Ye Ye said coldly, unconsciously pulling out Ye Yang and holding him tightly.

The old man suddenly realized something and said, "Oh, yes! Why didn't I think of that? It seems that I am old! Thank you for reminding me!" After the old man finished speaking, he took out a piece of black paper from his body, and then chanted a spell, and then threw it out fiercely. The spell burned as soon as it landed, and a wall of fire immediately burned in front of Ye Ye and the others, blocking the way ahead: "You can't do it now! Haha, Huangqin, he is yours! Go ahead! You can eat the meat or all of it!"

After receiving the old man's order, Huangqin's attack became more fierce, and Li Bin barely avoided it. However, Li Chen still used stones to mess with him from behind, and Li Bin was unable to move again! He was hit by the iron fist several times and fell to the ground! And the strong man Huangqin used his flying elbow again, jumping from a high altitude, a fatal blow!

Chapter 15 Eight Days Pass 2

It happened in a flash. When Huang Qin jumped up and was about to hit Li Bin with his flying elbow, Li Bin's eyes suddenly became extremely sharp. He did not dodge, but stood up the strange dagger of Yemen, held it with both hands, and then saw the moment when Huang Qin fell, and stabbed the dagger straight out, and then turned his head sharply, avoiding the fatal blow that should have hit his head!

However, the dust and debris on the floor blocked everything that happened just now. No one saw it all, they all saw Huang Qin's flying elbow hit Li Bin, and Li Bin must die!

After the dust cleared, Huang Qin did not get up for a long time. The old man began to doubt and shouted loudly: "Hey, come back! Are you stupid?" But Huang Qin still did not respond.

"Don't shout, he's dead!" Suddenly a voice sounded from under Huang Qin, and it was Li Bin. As soon as the voice fell, Li Bin pushed away.

Then he slowly stood up. At this time, Li Bin's face was covered with blood, which slowly flowed down his cheeks. His hands were twisted in a strange way, and his arm bones had been deeply pierced, obviously broken!

Of course, the force of Huang Qin's flying elbow just now was more than a thousand pounds. Li Bin actually chose to raise the dagger with both hands and stab it. He must be injured. The blood on his face was indeed caused by Li Bin dodging Huang

Qin's flying elbow when it fell. The flying elbow hit the ground and the gravel that was stirred up bounced him.

Li Bin ignored the old man's surprise, but slowly staggered to the side of Ye Ye and others. He even ignored the burning flames directly, stepped on the flames to the side of Ye Ye and others, and then said lightly: "Leave it to you!" After that, he fell to the ground and couldn't get up. Yang Hengchao hurried forward to check, and after a long time he said lightly: "It's okay, the Undead King's physique is too magical, and his recovery ability is very strong. He is fine, but his arm bones, if not set in time, so that the bones touch each other and recover, otherwise his hand will be disabled!" After Yang Hengchao finished speaking, he looked at Ye Ye and said that he had no way!

Yang Hengchao grew up in medicine, was immune to all poisons, had extraordinary defense, grew up in medicine, and naturally understood medicine!

Ye Ye didn't speak, looking fiercely at the group of people in front of him. In fact, he didn't hate them, but felt that he had made a wrong judgment, blamed Gu Zihao for being too cunning, blamed himself for being too timid, and didn't believe in the strength of Yemen... It was his mistake that Li Bin was so seriously injured. They had never suffered such serious injuries since they came out of their hometown together! Thinking of this, Ye Ye held Ye Yang horizontally, slowly stood up, and walked forward, but was pulled by a strong hand behind him. Ye Ye turned back indifferently, and the owner of the hand was Qin Minglei!

Qin Minglei was so cold and frightening at this time. His eyes were red and his two long fangs were completely exposed: "Let... me go!" Qin Minglei said unclearly because of his fangs. He could stay awake even in the state of corpse king.

Ye Ye looked embarrassed and was about to refuse, but Qin Minglei suddenly roared violently. His eyes suddenly turned red. Suddenly, a faint red light appeared beside him. It was Qin Minglei's evil spirit and corpse spirit! Then, in the surprise of Ye Ye and Yang Hengchao, he slowly took a step forward. When he passed the flame, the flame went out! It couldn't stand the evil spirit and went out. The light flashed and disappeared. The group of people didn't pay attention at all. They just thought that Qin Minglei had something to force fire.

Qin Minglei slowly walked to the center of the field , stretched out a hand, pointed his index finger back and forth among the crowd, as if he was selecting an opponent! After that, his hand was designated at Li Chen who had just shot Li Bin with a stone.

Since Qin Minglei entered the Eight Heavens Gate, the murderous aura in his heart has been attracted by something, but he has been able to restrain himself. However, when he saw Li Bin being hit by Huang Qin's flying elbow, the murderous intent and anger in his heart surged, and the murderous aura was immediately attracted by the attraction, resulting in the current appearance. Fortunately, he has maintained the murderous state for a long time, so he has not been controlled by the evil spirit to become a machine that only knows how to kill!

"Humph, Li Chen, he chose you! Go kill him! Don't be as useless as Huang Qin's son of a bitch! "Seeing Qin Minglei choose Li Chen, several people behind Li Chen said immediately. Among them, friendship is shit, only survival is the most important thing. Everyone is being used.

Li Chen shrugged helplessly and walked out directly, holding a handful of stones in his hand!

"Hey, wait, use this!" The old man suddenly called Li Chen, and then handed Li Chen a silver sphere. This sphere is unique to the old man, or it can be said that it was invented by the old man. The old man used to be a cultivator who specialized in developing strange things. It was because of his research that the Huangdao League suffered a great loss, so he was imprisoned here for 150 years. And no one knows his name, because he has always been in his old man and refused to tell his real name.

When Li Chen saw the sphere, the corners of his mouth rose immediately, grabbed it, put it in a pocket on his waist, and then turned and walked to a place far away from Qin Minglei and said to Qin Minglei: "Since you want to die! Then I will fulfill your wish! "After saying that, a stone was suddenly thrown out, and the stone was extremely fast, hitting Qin Minglei's head directly. Suddenly, Qin Minglei's head was bleeding!

Qin Minglei roared angrily, and then rushed forward. The strange-shaped dagger of the Night Gate in his hand had become a real machete, and he wielded it vigorously, but he didn't expect that although Li Chen was short, his legs were very fast, and he dodged Qin Minglei's attack every time! And he even had time to take out his hands and shoot Qin Minglei with stones.

Qin Minglei's attacks failed repeatedly, and his mood suddenly became irritable. His mind lost a little again, and his murderous spirit became more external, and his mind gradually became unclear, but his attack became more fierce, and a strange-shaped dagger of the Night Gate was wielded, forcing Li Chen to retreat step by step.

Suddenly, the dagger in Qin Minglei's hand was thrown out violently, forcing Li Chen to retreat a few meters, and then Qin Minglei held his head in pain Howled. Li Chen, who had retreated four or five meters away, was happy. The current distance was just right for him, and his opponent didn't know why he stopped attacking. So he gathered the stones in his hand and shot them at Qin Minglei. When the stones in his hand were almost all shot, he once again performed his superb hidden weapon skills. He actually only used three stones and shot back and forth. The stones seemed to be tied with a rope in his hand. After being thrown out, they would bounce back, and his hands kept moving. The three stones shot out, bounced on the wall, bounced back, shot out again, and bounced back again! Qin Minglei kept holding his head and crying and howling. Li Chen's stones almost all hit his head, and blood flowed.

In fact, it was not that Qin Minglei did not attack or defend, but that he wanted to keep the trace of clarity in his heart. He did not want to be controlled by the evil spirit, so he fought back, but did not want to become someone else's target.

"Okay, stop playing! Solve it! So as not to cause trouble! "The old man suddenly said, and Li Chen grabbed the three stones as soon as he heard it, then took out three small silver balls, smiled, and shot them out fiercely.

The bead suddenly turned into a silver thread and flew towards Qin Minglei. After touching Qin Minglei, it suddenly exploded violently and turned into a hot stream that swallowed Qin Minglei.

The bead was developed by the old man, named Silver Thunder. After being thrown out, it will explode violently and burn violent silver flames, burning everything. Hence the name.

"Haha, I didn't expect that a good person would die without leaving any residue!" The old man seemed to be very confident in Silver Thunder and laughed arrogantly. But Ye Ye and Yang Hengchao didn't seem to be worried much, just looking at the flame lightly.

Suddenly, the flame dissipated, and the old man's laughter stopped abruptly. Because he saw that after the flame dissipated, Qin Minglei was still standing there safely, and the red light on his body flashed and disappeared.

"Am I seeing things? No! He should just have something on his body. "The old man was surprised to see all that, and suddenly remembered the power of light on a group of people. He couldn't help but get scared, but quickly rejected the idea and immediately yelled at Li Chen: "Quick, kill him! "

Li Chen did not see the red light, but was surprised that Qin Minglei could survive and be unscathed under the power of the silver thunder! But he continued to throw the silver thunder in his hand, and suddenly the silver flames rose and fell, swallowing the more than one meter range where Qin Minglei stood.

Li Chen's hand speed was very fast, and he soon finished shooting the silver thunder, but after the flames dissipated, Qin Minglei was still standing in front of him unscathed, and he immediately panicked.

Li Chen was actually just a lackey in the Eight Days Pass. The Eight Days Pass was actually a small society, where strength was the key, and the weak were naturally oppressed by the strong. Moreover, Li Chen had always been very confident in his shooting. He often boasted that even if he was not a match for others, at least he was not bad. However, he did not expect that his shooting skills had not killed the person in front of him for so long, and he also used the silver thunder given by the old man.

But he just didn't believe in his shooting skills. He took out the three stones again and performed the ejection recovery again.

"Roar. "Qin Minglei roared wildly, ignoring Li Chen. The red light on his body lit up as he was burned into pieces, and along with the fragments of clothes, there fell a glass bottle and a charred insect. It was the bottle containing Yin Lin's love poison.

"Roar!" Qin Minglei roared wildly again, looking up and two drops of deep red blood slowly flowed out of his eyes! The corpse king cried, and what he cried out was his heart blood.

"Stop, stop, don't force him anymore!" The old man saw some clues and immediately roared at Li Chen. But Li Chen, who was in a frenzy, did not listen to his words, but shot stones faster.

"Roar! "Qin Minglei slowly lowered his head, looked at Li Chen calmly, and then threw out the strange-shaped dagger of Yemen in his hand. The dagger flew towards Li Chen with a hint of red light, and the speed was even faster than the stone in Li Chen's hand.

Without any suspense, Li Chen was naturally pierced through the head by the dagger, and he was dead! After piercing Li Chen, the dagger did not stop but went straight out and stuck in the opposite wall, leaving only a short handle outside.

"Hurry, hurry up! We are no match for them! Let's go find help! "The old man finally saw the red light on Qin Minglei's body and immediately drove the crowd. There was no way because the two most powerful fighters around him were already dead, and the man opposite him had the aura he had always feared and the occasional light. That light was theirs to him! But they were...

Qin Minglei did not chase them, but stood there coldly. After they fled, he slowly squatted down, looked at the love Gu that had been burned to a charred black on the ground, and roared violently.

Chapter 16 Eight Days Pass 3

After the old man and his men fled, Ye Ye observed their escape route, but was surprised to find that they all ran straight into the wall and then disappeared. He was immediately confused, but he didn't wonder for too long, because the person they cared about was in front of them and they didn't know the situation.

"Don't rush over, he may be controlled by murderous aura now, let's go slowly!" Ye Ye said, holding Yang Hengchao who was about to go forward. Unexpectedly, his words were heard by Qin Minglei, who slowly stood up, then looked at Ye Ye and spoke, he said: "Ye Ye, I'm fine! Don't worry!" After that, he looked at the charred mother Gu in his hand again, his eyes filled with sadness.

Ye Ye and the others were relieved when they heard him say that: "Fortunately, the murderous aura didn't control him! Let's look at Li Bin first and see if there is any way to connect his bones!"

In fact, Qin Minglei was not uncontrolled, but was already controlled. Otherwise, how could he throw such a powerful dagger to kill Li Chen? However, just when the murderous aura controlled him, he happened to see the burnt mother love Gu on the ground, which pulled him back from his unconsciousness and regained control of his body. Otherwise, when the old man and the others ran away just now, he would have chased them.

"There is no way. We lack materials here. There is no way to connect his bones." Yang Hengchao looked at the injuries on Li Bin's hands and said in embarrassment.

After hearing this, Ye Ye was silent for a while! Qin Minglei came over at this time, and he didn't know when there were two more pieces of cloth in his hand. Judging from the fabric and color, it seemed to be the cloth on Li Chen's clothes just now. Ye Ye and the others saw him coming over and looked at him in confusion.

Qin Minglei calmly wrapped the mother Gu with cloth, and then threw another piece of cloth to Yang Hengchao before saying coldly: "My brother is not so fragile, just wrap him with this!"

"But if it is not done well, then Li Bin's hand will be useless!" Yang Hengchao said in embarrassment, but he had no choice but to take the cloth strip, and then slowly symmetrically tied Li Bin's arm bones, and then bandaged both arms with cloth strips, and then he picked up Li Bin and carried him on his back.

"Let's go! Let's keep going!" Ye Ye looked at Li Bin's injuries, and then looked at Qin Minglei's mental state, and blamed himself again. It was his children's mistakes in thinking and decision-making that led to the timidity of the two people! But there was no way, they had no way back, so they could only move forward.

As Ye Ye walked, he took out a piece of paper from his treasure bag. After unfolding it, he said in confusion: "According to Feng Yi's note, the opponent in this first level should only be the strong man Huang Qin. Why are there so many more! I think it must be Gu Zihao who notified them to deal with us, or even kill us! I'm sorry, it's me who made you do this!" Ye Ye clenched the dagger in his hand and continued: "But, no matter what, we have already come in, and we have no choice but to continue. Just now I saw them all crash into the wall and then disappeared. I guess that is the secret entrance to the next level." After saying that, Ye Ye turned around, but only saw Yang Hengchao looking at him with trusting eyes, while Qin Minglei walked to Huang Qin's body with a cloth bag wrapped in the mother Gu, pushed Huang Qin's body away, and then put the mother Gu in the small hole made by the fatal flying elbow that Li Bin had just avoided, and finally covered the mother Gu with the surrounding gravel, which was considered a simple grave. After doing all this, Qin Minglei said lightly: "I'm sorry, I shouldn't have brought you here selfishly! Yin Lin, you can stay here with peace of mind!" After saying that, he stood up and smiled at Ye Ye, revealing incomparable hatred in his eyes!

He didn't blame Ye Ye, he only blamed his own strength for not being strong enough, causing the entire Yin Lin tribe to be destroyed, and the murderer was unknown. He used to think that the murderer was Feng Yi's Shenxingmen, but he asked Feng Yi quietly, and Feng Yi said that he would not kill civilians for no reason. So he only blamed himself for not being strong enough to protect the people he loved!

The three of them quickly walked to the wall with Li Bin on their backs. Ye Ye touched the cold wall and said in confusion: "This wall is a real wall. How did they get in?" Yang Hengchao also touched the wall and was puzzled.

Qin Minglei smiled and said: "Since they got in, we can get in too." After that, he was able to crash into the wall directly, and Ye Ye and the others could not stop him at all.

But suddenly, Qin Minglei directly sank into the wall. Ye Ye and the others also followed Qin Minglei and crashed in.

That wall is actually just a trick, or a real trick. The wall is called the Wall of Life and Death. Only by hitting it hard can you pass through it. Otherwise, even if you break the wall, you can't reach your destination. The Wall of Life and Death was made by a supreme elder named Supreme Elder of the Huangdao League many years ago, using the supreme Taoism of the Five Elements of Qiankun and various materials, but after the elder died, the method of making the wall also disappeared.

After passing through the wall, Ye Ye and the other two appeared in a long corridor. Walking along the corridor, there was a long staircase at the end. After going up the stairs, Ye Ye and the others appeared in another room that was exactly the same as the previous room. The only difference was that there were different people in this room. It seemed that they went up one floor, and on this floor, Ye Ye's feeling of being called intensified.

"It's them!" After Ye Ye and the other four appeared, the old man's unpleasant voice sounded again, and this time he no longer looked arrogant, but was completely respectful. It seemed that he had found a helper.

"Oh?" The man in front of the old man looked at Ye Ye and the other three in confusion, and then said to the old man with disdain: "Thank you, old man. I thought I would die here! I didn't expect that I could still get out. The four of them, 140 years! I have been locked up for 20 years, and I still have 150 years to get out. I didn't expect that you reduced my time by 140 years! Now, you can go and die!" As soon as the voice fell, the old man immediately showed a horrified expression, and then begged: "Saiben, you can't do this! We are friends, right? How can you do this? Don't forget, if the people above know what happened to me, they will not let you go! You..." Before he finished speaking, his head had been crushed by a hand!

The owner of the hand was exactly the Saiben he mentioned. After crushing the old man's head, Saiben licked the red and white thing on his hand, and said with a stern face: "Don't you know that I hate nagging the most? You see it, right? Then die with him!" Saiben said, looking at the several people who came up with the old man. Those people immediately begged for mercy and shouted that they saw nothing. But only the dead can't speak, and they were all killed by Saiben.

Saiben, 20 years ago, was imprisoned in the Eight Days Pass. Before that, he was a murderer, and no one could figure out his personality! No one knows how strong he is, because almost everyone who knows is dead! He was imprisoned because he underestimated the enemy, and then he was ambushed and restricted. After that, he was caught, but he could never get out again.

After killing the old man and his group, Saiben arched his back, turned to the direction of Ye Ye and the other four, and said, "Next, it's you, right?" As he said that, he licked the red and white thing in his hand again!

And Ye Ye and the other four looked at Saiben killing them so easily, and immediately realized that this person was not at the same level as Li Chen and Huang Qin just now. Immediately alert, Yang Hengchao put Li Bin down, and then made a fighting posture.

Unexpectedly, Qin Minglei walked up again alone, looked at Saiben and said coldly: "Get out of the way, don't block me out, or you will die!" After that, the red light on Qin Minglei's body suddenly appeared! He could actually control the red light formed by the murderous aura.

Saiben looked at the red light on Qin Minglei's body and immediately put away his contempt: "Stand up!"

Chapter 17 Eight Days Pass 4

When Saiben said the words "Let's fight", Qin Minglei's eyes instantly turned red, his fangs were exposed, and a faint red glow appeared from time to time, just like a quasi-combat posture. Ye Ye and the others immediately carried Li Bin on their backs and quickly walked to the side. They knew that this battle must be extremely dangerous. If they stood too close, they might be hurt.

At this time, Qin Minglei's mind was infinitely clear. He knew what he was doing and was also surprised by the power in his body! His self-confidence suddenly soared. The only thing he wanted now was to break out of the Eight Days Pass and then take revenge on everything.

Saiben didn't have so many concerns. He had been silently paying attention to Qin Minglei's every move. In his heart, Qin Minglei was an opponent of the same level as him, and it was worth his best efforts!

I saw that his face slowly flushed, and then suddenly raised his head, and a pair of fangs grew out of his mouth, and then the claws on his hands gradually grew longer. His final posture was about to take shape.

Qin Minglei saw all this and suddenly saw an opportunity. He pointed his finger like a knife and chopped at Saiben's head. Unexpectedly, Saiben's transformation was just completed. He immediately crossed his hands into a cross shape, blocked Qin Minglei's knife, and immediately turned around and kicked Qin

Minglei's lower body fiercely. Qin Minglei had no choice but to put his hands away, then retreat slightly, block the flying kick with his palm, and then use the power of the leg to retreat.

Neither of them took advantage of this contact. After Saiben transformed, he immediately stood up, waving the claws in his hands, breaking through the air one after another. Qin Minglei had no sharp weapon in his hand to resist the claws, so he had to keep retreating.

"Hahahaha." Seeing Qin Minglei retreating continuously, Saiben laughed arrogantly and his movements became more fierce. Suddenly, the red light on Qin Minglei's body disappeared slightly, and then Qin Minglei felt that his power was concentrated in his hands.

Without hesitation, Qin Minglei stretched out his hands. His hands were like a dragon exploring the sea, grabbing Saiben's hands directly. After that, Qin Minglei suddenly turned around, pulled Saiben's hands and threw him over his shoulder.

Saiben was thrown out directly, but when he was about to fall to the ground, his feet suddenly bent, and he actually used the strength of his legs to ease the momentum of the over-shoulder throw, and then fell on the ground in a flash, grabbed Qin Minglei's hands, and then used his feet to support Qin Minglei's stomach, throwing Qin Minglei out!

How could Qin Minglei be thrown like this, especially Qin Minglei who was already completely in the state of corpse king.

In mid-air, Qin Minglei twisted his body suddenly, then stood firm, looking at Saiben coldly.

Ye Ye and Yang Hengchao were standing aside, clenching their fists tightly, and they were also shocked by the thrilling tremor just now. Neither of them noticed that Li Bin behind them suddenly moved...

"Roar." After a short rest, Qin Minglei rushed out first this time, punching repeatedly, leaving some fist shadows in the air! Saiben took all of them, and then quickly counterattacked. The claws also swung out quickly, and Qin Minglei retreated after facing the claws.

"Catch it." Suddenly, Yang Hengchao roared loudly, and then threw a strange dagger of the night gate at Qin Minglei. Qin Minglei caught the flying dagger with his backhand and immediately counterattacked. The two of them fought again. Qin Minglei had iron weapons, so he was naturally not afraid of the claws. The two of them fought back and forth, and neither of them could take advantage of the other for the time being.

But Ye Ye and Yang Hengchao were terrified. Several times they wanted to go up to help, but they were forced back by the claws. They had to anxiously watch Qin Minglei and Saiben fighting back and forth in an extremely thrilling way.

Suddenly, Qin Minglei punched Saiben with his free hand, and then took advantage of the opportunity when the iron fist hit Saiben and Saiben's vision was swaying to stab Saiben with the dagger in his hand. Unexpectedly, Saiben's instinctive reaction was very intense, and he instinctively used his claws to push away the fatal dagger.

Qin Minglei missed the first attack, and immediately repeated the same trick. His left fist continued to swing under the cover of the fierce attack of the dagger in his right hand, and Saiben retreated step by step.

But who would make the same mistake many times? Saiben suddenly roared violently, then retracted his claws, and swung his fists violently, with fist shadows flashing in the air. Qin Minglei was unable to defend himself.

Qin Minglei saw that Saiben was so violent, so he simply threw away the dagger in his hand, and the two of them actually punched each other in the middle of the field, and the muffled sound crackled.

Ye Ye and the other two became even more anxious, but they still couldn't help. They were too focused on the life-and-death battle on the field, and didn't see Li Bin behind them slowly crawling up.

At this time, Li Bin actually looked like a human and a ghost! His body was covered with black lines, two short fangs were exposed, the corners of his mouth were slightly raised, and then he walked silently. No one noticed him!

The life and death in the field was still going on, and Qin Minglei and Saiben's faces were completely swollen. Suddenly, Qin Minglei rushed up and hugged Saiben, and the sharp teeth in his mouth bit Saiben's neck directly! Suddenly, Saiben cried and wailed. Then he tilted his head and bit Qin Minglei's neck.

The two of them had completely lost their humanity, just like two wild beasts who only knew how to attack instinctively and fight only for flesh and blood!

The two of them hugged each other and bit each other, crying and wailing, angry roars, constantly coming out of their throats!

"Roar!" The two suddenly roared at the same time, pushing each other away at the same time, then blood dripped from the corners of their mouths, hunched their backs, and looked at each other with red eyes. Under them, a pool of blood slowly spread. It seems that the two were seriously injured.

Everyone is afraid of death, even if the two only have instincts. After all, fear of death is the first instinct! Therefore, the two dared not move forward easily. Just look at each other and roar threateningly.

A strange phenomenon suddenly occurred! No one noticed that a black shadow suddenly appeared behind Saiben. The black shadow jumped up directly, hugged Saiben's head with his hands, and then held it tightly! No matter how Saiben pulled and struggled, he couldn't get rid of him. That person was the mysterious Li Bin who suddenly woke up!

Li Bin was on Saiben's head, and then he hit Saiben's head with his elbows! Suddenly, the broken bone that was originally wrapped in cloth strips broke apart, and the broken arm bone stabbed straight at Saiben's eyes. Saiben had no time to struggle, and the bone passed through his eyes and died!

Li Bin seemed to have no pain, just quietly got off Saiben's body and laughed! At this time, Li Bin was actually covered with black lines, and then he looked at the bone broken from his arm indifferently, and then he lowered his head and looked at Saiben's body! There was fanaticism in his eyes!

The most surprising thing to Ye Ye and the other two happened! Li Bin actually started to gnaw on Saiben's body! Ye Ye and the others immediately stepped forward to pull him up.

Unexpectedly, Li Bin seemed to be possessed by evil spirits, desperately struggling to get away from Ye Ye and Yang Hengchao, and gnawed again. Seeing that Ye Ye and the others could not pull him up, they had to let him go!

Not long after, Li Bin suddenly stopped gnawing, and then stretched out his arms, looking like he was resting! Qin Minglei on the side fell down!

Entering the second level of the Eight Heavens Pass, Qin Minglei fell down, and Li Bin was unaware of the situation!

In fact, it was not that Li Bin was unaware of the situation, but the effect of the Corpse Demon Mother Stone in Li Bin's body played its original role. The effect of the Corpse Demon Mother Stone can be described in two words: immortality!

Just when only two of the four people had the ability to fight, a voice suddenly sounded from behind them: "You, follow me."

Chapter 18 Changes in the Heavenly Gate

At this time, only Ye Ye and Yang Hengchao were awake. When they heard the voice, they turned around and looked at the man behind them vigilantly.

"Don't be nervous, I'm just doing a deal with you." The man walked slowly towards Ye Ye and the others, his face full of calmness. Strangely, this man actually looked like a scholar, his face was unusually clean, and he was not as dirty and scary as those people he had just met.

Ye Ye did not ask who he was, but asked in confusion: "Deal? What deal?"

The man laughed, gentle and elegant, and seemed to be powerless, but Ye Ye and Yang Hengchao clearly felt a huge pressure constantly squeezing them. The man smiled and said: "Trade, of course, we trade with what you are worth trading with."

Ye Ye said with difficulty, holding on to the huge pressure: "You?" The man stopped laughing, his expression became serious, and said majestically: "That's right, we! In fact, let me tell you, this is the prison of the Huangdao League!" As soon as he said this, Ye Ye and the others were shocked!

The man ignored the two's surprise and continued, "We were all arrested by the Huangdao League under various excuses over the years! And the sentence is very long! When you came in, you must have discovered that you can't get out of here! There is actually a spell on the gate that can't be destroyed at all! Do you know how it feels to be imprisoned in here? Those days, we had to live in fear every day, and fall asleep in the blood and flesh of others every day. If you are not careful, maybe your head will be gone!" As the man spoke, his eyes suddenly became red and bloodthirsty, and a murderous aura that was dozens of times stronger than Qin Minglei emanated from him. This murderous aura was obviously generated through blood and flesh killing. He was right. When this prison was first built, the Huangdao League arrested many people. Those people had been imprisoned for a long time, and their hearts were naturally irritable. The killing began in this Huangdao League prison, the 'Eight Days Gate'.

Ye Ye and the others were even more surprised when they heard it, but they were suppressed by the murderous aura. They couldn't speak, and could only resist the murderous aura.

"Suck~! There are three ways of being a gentleman, and I am incapable of doing anything. A benevolent person is superior, a wise person is not confused, and a brave person is not afraid." This person is knowledgeable and knows how to use words to suppress his anger. He muttered this ancient sentence, and gradually the murderous aura disappeared.

The man then bowed slightly and said, "Excuse me!" Ye Ye felt that there was no suppression of murderous aura, but the pressure still existed, but at least it was much easier. Then he said lightly, "No, no! You continue!"

The man sighed and shrugged helplessly, then pulled out the fan from his waist, fanned it a few times and said, "After that, it became quiet here, and then I started to think of a way out! But there was no way, so I had to wait for death here!" Ye Ye and the others saw that the fan in his hand was made of pure iron.

"Wait to die? It turns out that Gu Zihao didn't want to kill us, but wanted to lock us up in here! Enjoy the pain of confinement! But why didn't Feng Yi tell us? Does he also want to lock us up?" Ye Ye was shocked and thought. In fact, Feng Yi didn't know all this at all, because Gu Zihao told everyone that only those who were threatening the Huangdao League were imprisoned inside, and they were guarding inside after being subdued.

During the conversation between the three people, no one noticed that Li Bin suddenly opened his eyes and looked at the scholar with a bloodthirsty light! Then he moved his arms and was able to move freely. Finally, he rushed towards the scholar, and Ye Ye and the others couldn't stop him in time.

Li Bin jumped up, bent his arms, and was in a posture of elbowing down, but suddenly two sharp bone spurs stretched out of his elbow! So if you look closely, you will find that the bone spur is actually the arm bone that was just broken!

The scholar didn't panic. Seeing Li Bin's elbow attack, he dodged, then used the iron fan to block the bone spur of Li Bin's other hand, and stepped on the Bagua Qiankun step to dodge Li Bin's violent attack.

"No more playing, follow me!" After saying that, he suddenly threw away the fan, and the fan turned to block Li Bin's vision. After the fan fell, the scholar's hand grabbed it again, and then swung it violently. The edge of the fan was extremely sharp and directly cut Li Bin's neck.

Li Bin did not feel any pain or bleeding, but smiled strangely and continued to rush forward, but was pulled by Yang Hengchao: "Li Bin, stop!" Li Bin was not clear at this moment, but he looked at Yang Hengchao in confusion and did not attack.

Ye Ye walked forward, looked at Li Bin and said: "Okay, Li Bin! Everything is fine!" Li Bin seemed to know Ye Ye. When he saw Ye Ye, he immediately revealed a look of hesitation in his eyes, then squatted down with his head in his arms, roared loudly in pain, and soon fainted.

"Okay, don't worry, this is normal! Take them two, let's go!" The scholar put away the fan, held it in his hand and said lightly.

The two looked at each other, then carried Li Bin on their backs and supported Yang Hengchao, following behind with wounds all over their bodies.

The scholar led Ye Ye and the other three inside, and stopped only when they passed through four walls. This was the sixth level. Qin Minglei also recovered a little, but still needed the support of the two.

"Okay, that's it, wait a minute!" After saying that, the scholar walked to the side with a serious face and stood still. And beside him, there were several people, all with serious faces, even standing there with a little fear and respect, as if waiting for someone.

When Ye Ye and the other two were confused, a majestic voice suddenly sounded: "Haha, three friends! I didn't discipline them strictly! I let my men be seduced by the Huang Dao League, and you got hurt!" Ye Ye looked in the direction of the voice, and an old man with white hair and a childlike face said with a smile. His voice sounded like a spring breeze, which improved Ye Ye and the other two's favorability towards him.

But Ye Ye was confused, and didn't speak, just smiled slightly. Yang Hengchao was the same. Only Li Bin looked at the old man in surprise, because he saw that the black air above the old man's head was as thick as the dark clouds covering the sun! He knew that it was murderous aura! How many lives would be needed to exchange for such a thick murderous aura!

"Yue Ziheng has already told you about the situation here, right? You all know who we are, right? Don't worry, we have no ill will towards you, we just want you to join us and go out together! To be honest, I have been here for eighty years, and I am one hundred and twenty years old this year!"

Eighty years! Ye Ye thought in surprise, and couldn't help but said: "I haven't been out for eighty years? Can I still go out?"

The old man smiled and said enthusiastically: "It couldn't be done in the past, or before yesterday, but today, or soon, it will be done!" When Ye Ye and the other two heard it, they were immediately confused.

The old man looked at Ye Ye and the other two kindly, then stood up and took out a bead from his clothes. The bead had six colors, and there was a gray stone on the bead that looked like a human head!

It turned out to be the Nuwa Stone that disappeared that day!

Chapter 19 Fight out

When the old man took out the Nuwa Stone, Ye Ye's call in his heart suddenly became more intense, and his eyes never left the Nuwa Stone!

How could it be in his hands? Ye Ye and his companions thought, and doubts suddenly arose in their hearts.

The old man seemed to see the doubts in their hearts, and after a faint smile, he slowly said: "This may really be the mercy of God, letting us get out of this ghost place!" After a pause, he continued: "Just yesterday, this bead suddenly rushed in by itself! Then it stayed in the center of this room. After I took it off, I found that this bead turned out to be the legendary Nuwa Stone! Haha, it's really God's help!" As he said, the old man laughed.

Ye Ye didn't say anything, he didn't even hear what the old man said, his attention was completely on this bead! This is the first time he has seen the Nuwa Stone so closely! It turns out that the Nuwa Stone is very beautiful. The six-color appearance, the center is a green heart, and the round outer circle has a gray stone like a small head, but it doesn't look weird, but looks more harmonious!

As the old man spoke, his face suddenly darkened, and he sighed and said, "But, we can't use it here! Until you came in, it actually emitted a faint glow just now! Maybe, we will see you when we go out!"

Ye Ye came back to his senses at this time, and said in surprise: "Can I take a look?" The old man didn't say anything, smiled kindly, and then handed it to him. He was not afraid of Ye Ye and the others making trouble! Because no one dared to make trouble here!

Ye Ye excitedly took the Nuwa Stone and observed it carefully. Ye Ye was very excited to observe the Nuwa Stone at such a close distance! He observed quietly, and suddenly he looked carefully at the Nuwa Stone Heart of the Wind System in the middle of the Nuwa Stone, and suddenly a hallucination swarmed in.

Monsters, demons, ghosts, dragons, immortals, Arhats, gods, goddesses... suddenly all appeared in front of Ye Ye's eyes, and then finally all turned into a violent spark and disappeared, leaving only a girl in white clothes!

Ye Ye was surprised when he saw the girl! He knew that girl! That girl was the girl who could only repeat one sentence every time he fainted!

When Ye Ye was immersed in the illusion, everyone who did not see the illusion saw a scene that they might never see in their lives.

The Nuwa Stone slowly floated up, and the seven-color halo illuminated the entire room, constantly blending and changing like a rainbow, and finally retracted into the bead like smoke. However, they all looked at the wonders in the sky and did not notice Ye Ye at all.

"Great, it turns out that you will be our savior!" The old man suddenly said excitedly, seeing Ye Ye's confused eyes, and then explained: "Just now, you made the Nuwa Stone reappear! We need your power! Please, take us out!"

Ye Ye didn't know what happened, he said casually: "But I don't know what power I have!" At this time, Ye Ye was still immersed in the illusion just now. He thought about it. If the demons and gods before were to prove that it was the prehistoric era, then who was that girl? Why did he appear in the illusion created by the Nuwa Stone?

But Ye Ye's thoughts were interrupted by the old man's words: "Please! Look at me, I'm already old! Do you know? How many lonely old people like me will die here? We also have our own homes, our own sons and wives. Even if we live to be two hundred years old, when we go home, will we hold our great-grandchildren and say I am your great-grandfather? Please, save us."

Ye Ye has a kind heart. Hearing this, he hesitated immediately. After thinking for a while, he said, "Tell me what to do!" Ye Ye and Yang Hengchao could not see the murderous aura covering the sky and the sun above the old man's head, but Qin Minglei saw it for real. He saw that although the old man looked amiable, the murderous aura above his head kept surging when he spoke. The old man could actually control such a huge murderous aura, and his strength was really unpredictable!

When the old man heard Ye Ye say this, he immediately smiled and bowed. Ye Ye hurried forward to pull him up, but he insisted on taking the luggage. Ye Ye had no choice but to let him go. After the bow, the old man said: "Benefactor, my name is Murong Di, they all call me Grandpa Murong, you can call me that too! We will tell you what to do, kid, don't worry! As long as you are willing to save us, we can give you anything!"

Ye Ye thought about it: I should call him Grandpa out of courtesy. After thinking about it, he nodded and said: "Okay! Then lend me this Nuwa Stone to observe it?" Murong Di smiled and nodded! Then he said: "Let Yue Ziheng take you to rest, your friend needs to be recuperated!"

After hearing this, Ye Ye and the other two did not hesitate and followed Yue Ziheng to another direction.

"Master Murong, do we really have to rely on them?" After Ye Ye and the other four disappeared from sight, a person on the right of Murong Di said respectfully.

Murong Die's face suddenly darkened and became extremely cold. Instantly, the air around him seemed to condense, as if his breath turned into ice: "Hmph, rely on them. Do you know that? If they use that thing, they will die! To open this place, they can only blow up the Nuwa Stone and then use the violent energy inside. Blow up this place. And you, can't go. I will use your lives to avenge the Huangdao League!" After saying that, Murong Die turned and walked into the darkness.

"Okay, I can finally rest!" After being taken to the resting place by Yue Ziheng, Ye Ye finally relaxed. But Qin Minglei stepped forward and asked: "Ye Ye, do you really think they can be trusted?" This sentence attracted the attention of Ye Ye and Yang Hengchao, and then he went on to tell the murderous aura that he saw on Murong Die's head.

Ye Ye and his friends understood that Yang Hengchao was very sensitive to murderous aura, and he could not lie. After hearing this, they immediately remembered.

"Ye Ye?" When several people were discussing, a voice suddenly sounded outside the door, and it sounded like Murong Di. He stepped forward and said, "What are you doing? It's so boring! Okay, you'll lead us in tomorrow! Have a good rest!" His words were gentle, but the murderous aura above his head was shaking violently like the wind blowing the clouds, which showed that he was very disgusted with pretending to be a good person. It even reached the point where he was about to get angry!

Ye Ye nodded without answering him, and Murong Di continued, "Then I won't bother you anymore, you have to lead us in tomorrow!"

Chapter 20 Nuwa Fantasy

Murong Die left Ye Ye and his companions on crutches. "Ye Ye, no matter what, be careful!" Qin Minglei said with concern. Ye Ye nodded, then took out the Nuwa Stone and continued to observe.

This is composed of the five-element Nuwa Stone plus the wind-element Nuwa Stone Heart and the Nuwa Heart, and a faint glow emanates from it. This Nuwa Stone is also very strange. It only emits a strange glow in Ye Ye's hands. In the hands of others, it suddenly becomes just a beautiful stone!

Ye Ye gradually lost himself in the faint glow and the slowly rotating wind power between the Nuwa Stone. As the night deepened, Qin Minglei and his companions fell asleep. But Ye Ye was still sitting there alone, quietly looking at the Nuwa Stone.

Suddenly, the originally faint glow of the Nuwa Stone suddenly became very intense, but it flashed and disappeared, and Ye Ye also collapsed after this glow and fell to the ground, without anyone seeing it.

After a while, Ye Ye opened his eyes, only to find himself in a completely different world, which was exactly the same as the pure white world he entered when he was unconscious.

"Since I'm here, I'll make the best of it!" Ye Ye said lightly, and simply sat down.

After a while, the white world suddenly began to distort, and then the white was covered by black, and finally slowly turned bright. Ye Ye saw something that surprised him.

He actually saw his own body! No, to be precise, it was his body lying on the ground and sleeping! And Qin Minglei and the other two were dozing off.

Ye Ye walked towards Qin Minglei and the other two in surprise, and then touched them, but found that his hand could not touch Qin Minglei, but went straight through!

Soul out of the body! That word emerged in Ye Ye's mind! Unexpectedly, observing the Nuwa Stone in this way, his soul actually left his body!

Ye Ye suddenly became curious, and he slowly tried to leave the range of his body and began to wander around here.

"Great, I can go anywhere! This soul is nothingness, anything can go through it!" Ye Ye muttered to himself. Then he slowly strolled here, anyway, there was still a lot of time.

"Master, is it really that way tomorrow?" Ye Ye, who was wandering, suddenly heard a voice. The voice sounded strange, and it should not belong to someone he knew.

"Well, that's right! When Ye Ye learns the method I taught him to use and opens the way out of here, we can get out!" The voice turned out to be Murong Di.

"But, Master, is it that simple?" Another voice said in confusion. Ye Ye knew there was a backstory when he heard it, and continued to listen.

"Humph, Meng Da, do you know that the power of the Nuwa Stone is the power of the sky, how can you really use it? Unless you are a nine-day god, it's almost the same! And, the method I taught Ye Ye to use was just to suddenly and completely trigger the power of the Nuwa Stone, and then break through the wall!" Murong Di said. It was extremely stiff and gentle.

"But, Master, if too much power is poured out at once, wouldn't it be..." Meng Da said worriedly.

Murong Die smiled: "Haha, Meng Da, you don't have to worry! I have a way to keep us safe! But, it's hard to say about Ye Ye! Alas, it's a pity for the Nuwa Stone! If I could live another hundred years, and have this Nuwa Stone again, I can dominate! But sometimes, choosing one thing will definitely lose another! Meng Da, be more open-minded! Don't be too childish! But you really need to learn, otherwise you wouldn't come in!" Murong Die said earnestly.

"So they want to kill me? Or use my life to open the way for them to be free!" After hearing this, Ye Ye's heart was disturbed, and his spirit suddenly swayed, stirring up gusts of cold wind.

"Who!" Murong Die actually felt the cold wind, so he roared, and then his momentum spread out violently. Ye Ye was immediately oppressed by the momentum. At this time, he was in the state of soul leaving his body. His soul was like a small boat sailing under the waves, and it was about to be destroyed!

"No, I can't die!" In the soul state, if the soul dissipates, the physical body will become a walking corpse, and then slowly die after losing its vitality. But Ye Ye's will to survive is quite strong. Deep in the sea of soul, Ye Ye roared loudly, "I can't die!"

After that, the Nuwa stone in Ye Ye's physical hand actually emitted brilliance, and Ye Ye's soul suddenly rose with infinite power, and immediately got rid of Murong Di's persecution of the monstrous murderous aura.

"Eh?" Murong Di naturally felt this energy, and immediately looked at the place where the power was emitted with a puzzled sound, but it was empty, and immediately said puzzledly: "Am I feeling wrong?"

At this time, Ye Ye mustered all his strength and kept passing through the wall. Although he had just escaped the persecution of Murong Di's murderous aura, he was still injured by the murderous aura! If he can't return to his body quickly, his soul will still dissipate.

At this time, Ye Ye realized the horror of Murong Di. If he were to compare him with Gu Zihao, Gu Zihao might not be his opponent!

Finally, Ye Ye finally saw his body. At this time, the corners of his mouth were bleeding. That was the blood of his heart, and it was the appearance of his soul after being damaged! Then he saw the Nuwa Stone in his hand emitting this faint light, and he suddenly understood that the power just now was the Nuwa Stone, and it was the Nuwa Stone that saved him!

Ye Ye didn't hesitate at all and immediately crashed into the body! But he didn't wake up immediately! Instead, he fell into the black illusion just now, and the black slowly twisted and turned white! Ye Ye was still waiting for this, he knew that he could get out after the white! And the soul has returned to the body, so there is no need to worry about the soul dying.

However, Ye Ye waited for a long time but didn't wait for the sign of going out. The white world has been a white world for a long time!

Ye Ye suddenly became impatient! At this moment, he really wanted to know if he was injured and how serious it was! The soul state can't understand the physical injuries at all. ◈

Ye Ye stood up and began to slowly explore in this white world. Just after taking two steps, the illusion suddenly began to twist. Ye Ye breathed a sigh of relief! However, after the twist, Ye Ye actually appeared in a valley!

In that valley, flowers flourished, birds sang, and flowers bloomed, looking like a warm spring! Extremely beautiful! Ye Ye looked around in surprise! Smelling the fresh fragrance of soil and flowers, Ye Ye gradually lost himself!

If Gu Zihao or Xia Feng, Feng Yi, saw this valley, they would definitely be surprised, because this valley is the valley that the secret passage in Gu Zihao's room leads to!

Chapter 21 In the Illusion

Ye Ye strolled in the valley, very relaxed, as if everything that happened just now was fake! And this place is real!

"Where is this place?" Ye Ye said to himself. Then he walked slowly on the grass.

Suddenly, a noise sounded, and Ye Ye was startled and immediately followed the sound. Then when he was close to the source of the sound, Ye Ye hid behind a tree and listened to the conversation there. Then he stretched his head to see the owner of the voice clearly, but found that his vision was completely blocked by the tall grass. I don't know when the tall grass grew out!

A female voice said with great resentment: "Are you still going to leave me?" Ye Ye's heart was broken when he heard the voice.

"That's right, I must go! If he is not destroyed, how can I live in secret and ignore the people of the world? Sorry, I'm going!" A boy spoke with a sonorous and powerful voice, with a resolute tone, as if he didn't hear the woman's resentful voice that could break people's hearts at all.

"All the people in the world, all the people! You are just for the people, don't you think about yourself? Don't you think about me? Don't you think about the child in my belly?" The woman's voice suddenly raised a little decibel and yelled hysterically.

"What did you say..." The man paused when he heard it, but then said again resolutely: "I have made up my mind! All the people are my everything! I'm sorry!"

"I'm sorry, I'm sorry! If sorry can make up for everything, then why bother to thank you? Can you play that song for me again? I want to hear you play it for the last time!" After hearing this, the woman complained again and said with pleading.

"You... okay!" After that, no one spoke. Soon after, a piano sound suddenly sounded. The sound of the piano was like jade beads falling on a plate, and like drizzling rain, as if expressing endless love!

However, the momentum suddenly changed, slowly becoming stronger. It seemed that the man had to go to the battlefield during the variation, and the woman begged hard, and the man had been on the battlefield for a long time! After that, it was like thousands of troops trampling on the ground, and it was like thunder roaring on the ground, roaring in the ears!

Ye Ye was immersed in the sound of the piano, and suddenly remembered what was said in the Yemen Corpse Suppression Technique: The great master of the piano, raised his hand to pluck the piano, and thousands of troops automatically retreated, this is the momentum!

When Ye Ye was immersed in it, the sound of the piano turned again. Ye Ye clearly felt a strong back coming from the sound of the piano, but the sadness revealed a kind of heroism! That feeling... That feeling is like the victory, the soldiers returned home, but the men died on the battlefield! The woman was tearful, pale and helpless accusing the sky...

Unconsciously, Ye Ye was also in tears!

"I'm leaving, this song is for you!" The man said as his voice gradually faded away. Leaving the woman crying alone.

"I'm waiting for you here! I will wait for you to come back! Always! Until you come back!" The woman shouted loudly after seeing the man walk away. This requires courage. When a woman shouts like this, she has entrusted her voice to the man!

Ye Ye wiped his tears, and suddenly felt dazed. Then he walked out unconsciously to see who the woman was!

However, when he walked out from behind the tree, he saw nothing! The tall grass was gone, and the woman was gone!

Ye Ye stood there in confusion! Recalling the fragment just now, he found it so real!

"Forget it, let's find a way out!" Ye Ye sighed, thinking about the song that the man played for the woman just now. He sighed in his heart and said, then turned and left, continuing to wander in this strange valley that he didn't know whether it was real or illusory.

Days passed, and Ye Ye stayed in this valley, eating wild fruits when hungry and drinking river water when thirsty. With the beautiful scenery, Ye Ye would not worry about loneliness for the time being.

However, he was worried in his heart, because he already knew Murong Di's conspiracy, and after so many days, he didn't know how Qin Minglei and the other two were doing! Murong Die's strength is terrifying. It is hard to guarantee that he will not kill the three people just for his unconsciousness!

The more Ye Ye thought about it, the more worried he became. Suddenly, the beautiful scenery around him was no longer beautiful. He was full of worry! Then he anxiously looked for a way out.

Not long after, he suddenly found a cave! However, the cave was blowing a biting cold wind, which made Ye Ye feel cold to the bone and could not get close at all. Ye Ye had to give up here and seek other ways out.

However, when Ye Ye finished exploring this valley, he found that there were no other caves and ways out, including the water, which Ye Ye had explored and found no way out.

"It seems that there is only that cave! But it is so cold, how can I get out? I don't know how they are!" Ye Ye said to himself worriedly. Then he had no choice but to do this. There was no way. The cold wind in the cave was indeed too fierce and could not be resisted at all.

When Ye Ye was in trouble, he suddenly felt a faint warmth in his arms! Ye Ye pulled open his clothes in confusion and saw that there was a stone inside. To be more precise, it was a stone called Nuwa Stone!

"It wasn't there when I took off my clothes and went into the water just now! Why did it suddenly appear?" Ye Ye said in confusion, but he laughed, because he knew that the attributes of Nuwa Stone happened to have wind, and he thought that the wind would not be able to hurt him again.

With a smile, Ye Ye slowly approached the cave with Nuwa Stone in his hand. Although he had Nuwa Stone in his hand, which came out of nowhere, he couldn't help but worry because the wind was too cold!

However, when Ye Ye walked into the range of the cold wind, he didn't feel any cold at all, but only felt a warm wind like spring breeze, which made people feel relaxed and happy.

So Ye Ye walked without hesitation and slowly walked into the depths of the cave! The deeper he went, the more clearly Ye Ye felt the violent wind. Not only did the wind blow hard and whistled past his ears, but the coldness in it even froze the surrounding stone walls!

Moreover, Ye Ye just saw with his own eyes that a frozen rock could not withstand the ravages of the cold wind and fell down, but was suddenly caught by the cold wind and instantly crushed into powder!

If Ye Ye had not possessed the Nuwa Stone, which had immunity and protection to various attributes, then Ye Ye would have died long ago!

The cave was not long, and Ye Ye quickly walked to the end. There was a small door at the end, and there was a stone tablet next to the door. The stone tablet read: This secret realm can only be entered by those who have the Nuwa Stone. Although other methods can enter, they cannot obtain the secret of this Farewell Valley!

There is also a signature after this paragraph, but it seems to have been killed by someone with a sharp weapon! Can't see clearly!

"It turns out that this Nuwa Stone can enter this valley, but this place is not real. I don't know where this valley is! What secret is mentioned above? Why didn't I see it?" After talking to himself, Ye Ye pushed open the door, and there was a white behind the door, and he was at a loss!

It was that pure white illusion again!

Ye Ye smiled and walked in! Then he sat down safely. Soon after, the white world twisted and turned black!

"Ye Ye... wake up! It's dawn! Murong Di is here!" Suddenly Li Bin's voice rang in Ye Ye's ears.

Ye Ye woke up in a daze, and then said, "How long have I slept?"

Li Bin said lightly, "Two days! No matter how I called you, you didn't wake up! That Murong Bo came several times! He's almost angry!"

Ye Ye frowned and thought about everything he encountered after his soul left his body! Sighing, they still had a hurdle to die!

Chapter 22: The Dead End?

Ye Ye frowned and recalled the real and illusory experience just now, then said: "Let's go!" Ye Ye had no choice, right! He didn't, Murong Di's strength was completely incomparable to them! They had no choice but to compromise! And then look forward to a miracle!

Ye Ye touched the Nuwa Stone in his arms, but felt that this Nuwa Stone might be the thing that took his life. He suddenly felt that the Nuwa Stone was extremely hot, as if it was going to burn through his chest.

Suddenly, the Nuwa Stone emitted a red light, like a blazing flame!

Ye Ye quickly took it out, and the Nuwa Stone continued to emit this red light. Li Bin curiously touched it, but before he touched it, he quickly withdrew his hand and said painfully: "It hurts!" His palm was spread out, and he was actually burned.

Looking at the injury on his hand, Li Bin asked curiously: "Ye Ye, how come you are fine holding it? Why am I burned before I even get close to it?"

Ye Ye shook his head to indicate that he didn't know!

"Why? Why do I feel it is so hot? If it is really so hot that it burns through my chest, it will emit high temperature? Why am I fine? Could it be..." Ye Ye suddenly thought that he was protected by the Nuwa Stone and was safe and sound in the illusion just now.

Then, Ye Ye's thoughts turned, and he imagined that the Nuwa Stone was as cold as ice, cold to the bone.

Sure enough, the Nuwa Stone immediately emitted a blue light, which was the light of the water system. Ice is also water, but it is just the solid side of water.

"Li Bin, try again! Touch it!" Ye Ye said to Li Bin with a smile. There is no other way, only to find Li Bin, because Li Bin's recovery ability has increased sharply since the last madness! And the most terrifying thing is that he can also transform autonomously like Qin Minglei. After he transformed, his whole body was covered with black lines, and there were two sharp bone spurs on his elbows, which can defend and attack! And the speed is several times faster. Maybe his defense is not the highest, but his recovery ability is the strongest!

Ordinary knife wounds heal immediately after being cut! However, the side effects are also terrible. The pain caused by the wound when it heals is dozens of times more than the original one! It is incomparable to ordinary people!

Li Bin shook his head helplessly and stretched out his hand hesitantly!

However, as soon as Li Bin's hand approached the blue light, a layer of white frost immediately formed on his hand! Li Bin felt the pain and took his hand back and said lightly: "It's cold, I can't get close to it at all. Just the light has frozen me!"

Ye Ye smiled, pulled the four people over and whispered: "I can control this Nuwa Stone!" A shocking statement!

Qin Minglei, Li Bin, and Yang Hengchao looked at him in surprise. Ye Ye didn't seem to understand what he meant! Ye Ye smiled and told his experience just now: "... That's it! Murong Di's strength is extremely terrifying! He should want me to take the Nuwa Stone, and then he will use the secret method to pour out the power of the Nuwa Stone, so as to blast a path! But he didn't think that I can control the energy of the Nuwa Stone! Or I can control it a little! But I think it's enough!" After Ye Ye finished speaking, Qin Minglei and others laughed. But they were more worried. They were worried about Murong Di's terror and that if he failed later, Ye Ye would die!

"Don't worry! Don't worry! I'm fine!" Ye Ye comforted everyone, and he already had an idea in his mind!

After a short rest, Murong Di came to them again.

"Friend Ye Ye, have you rested well? I came here two days ago and saw you sleeping. Is it because studying the Nuwa Stone made you too tired, so you rest like this!" Murong Di's voice was full of concern, and his kind look really made people relax their vigilance!

Ye Ye looked at Murong Die's kind face and caring words, and felt sick in his heart, but he said: "Thank you for your concern! I'm fine now!"

Murong Die laughed, and then touched Ye Ye's shoulder: "My friend, can you help us open the way out?" There was no flaw in Murong Die's tone.

Ye Ye had to smile and said: "Okay, but I don't know how to do it." "My friend, don't worry, I have a way to control the Nuwa Stone. You stand in the place I set, and then follow it!" Ye Ye listened, quietly squeezed the Nuwa Stone in his arms, and was extremely angry. He thought to himself, maybe that was the secret method to stimulate all the divine power in the Nuwa Stone. Will I die?

Ye Ye hesitated for a moment, then smiled and took the cloth strip full of words and diagrams: "Okay, we can go out!" After Ye Ye finished speaking, he became angry. And the Nuwa Stone in his arms became hot, as if to vent the anger in Ye Ye's chest! Ye Ye was nervous and quickly dispelled the anger in his heart.

He didn't want Murong Di to see anything now, otherwise they would be dead!

"Then watch first, my friend. I will send someone to call you after a while, and then we will go out! I won't disturb you! I will go to prepare first," Murong Di said with a smile, and then turned and left! Then when he walked to a place where Ye Ye and the others could not see, his expression immediately changed, and he said coldly: "Humph, thank you! Haha! When I go out, I will definitely pay tribute to you! Gu Zihao, you wait for my revengeful anger!" After speaking, his eyes were so cold that it was terrifying, and the black light on his body turned into flames, burning silently.

After Murong Di left, Ye Ye immediately unfolded the cloth strip and studied it immediately.

"Destroy life and death, establish destiny. Warm spring, red sun, strong wind, cold snow, spiritual wood, where the five spiritual brilliances are scattered..." Ye Ye read the words above. Just after reading two sentences, the Nuwa Stone floated out of Ye Ye's arms silently, and then emitted six-color brilliance. The energy emitted was very violent, as if to destroy everything.

Life and death are always opposites! Since the Nuwa Stone repaired the sky and maintained life, it must have a side that maintains death.

The cloth strip that Murong Di gave to Ye Ye just now did not record the formula for using the Nuwa Stone, but only the formula for quoting the power of the five elements of heaven and earth. Therefore, the originally short and smooth spell was so profound. . However, Murong Di added other sentences just because he was afraid that Ye Ye would recognize it.

However, that formula can completely trigger the five elements of the Nuwa Stone! The power contained in the Nuwa

Stone is so terrifying. If it pours out at once, it will cause an explosion, a violent explosion!

Ye Ye shook his head, put away the Nuwa Stone and continued to read. There were some diagrams on it. Ye Ye read on and found that it was just some sitting postures and French diagrams for attracting spirits. However, if the spell just now was used, the power of the five elements would be easier to draw out.

Murong Di was really thoughtful!

Ye Ye smiled and said nothing. The more he read, the clearer his thoughts became: Maybe this dead end will become my springboard!

Chapter 23: The Great Disaster

Time passed quickly, and Murong Di came to Ye Ye and his companions again.

"Friend Ye Ye, are you ready? Everything is up to you! Come on, come on, this way!" Murong Di continued to speak hypocritically.

Ye Ye smiled and said, "Well, OK! I already know what to do!" Ye Ye pretended to know nothing, but he was very serious. He knew what to do, but due to Murong Di's terrifying strength, he could not reveal any doubt or resistance.

Murong Di made way, and then pointed out the way for Ye Ye and his companions to pass.

After passing through a long corridor, they came across a cave with a simple stone staircase. They walked down the stone staircase. After a long time, Murong Di led Ye Ye and his companions to a huge room. The room was very huge, with eight pillars standing in the center, and the positions of the eight trigrams were exactly the positions. The eight pillars were very thick, flashing with cold light, like stars, and they would confuse people if they looked at them for a long time.

Everyone was waiting there. Murong Di looked at the group of people and smiled slightly.

"Friend Ye Ye, this is the pillar of this place, the star pillar. It can absorb spiritual energy and is the only place where we can break through! As long as we can break one of them, we can get out! But we can't break all of them, otherwise the mountain will collapse and we will be buried in it." Murong Di pointed at the eight pillars and said seriously.

During the time Murong Di was imprisoned, he had tried to break one of the pillars, but he couldn't leave any mark on it at all! It can be seen that this pillar is very hard!

Seeing that Ye Ye didn't speak, Murong Di took Ye Ye to a pillar and said, "This is the Kan position. After many years, I found that it is easiest to break through here! You start here! Be careful! You guys follow me, don't get hurt by mistake!" After Murong Di finished speaking, he took Qin Minglei and the other two away from Ye Ye.

After seeing Murong Di walk away, Ye Ye touched the stone pillar and said, "This pillar is amazing!" After speaking, he sighed helplessly and sat down. Put the cloth strip between your legs, arrange the movements and sitting posture according to what is written on it, and then recite the spell: Destroy life and death, establish destiny. Warm spring, red sun, strong wind, cold snow, spiritual wood, where the five spiritual brilliances are scattered, who knows that the human heart is as cold as the moon, the way out, the way to come, and the way to the future. The five forces combine to open the road to heaven! "

While reciting, the Nuwa Stone actually floated up, and then emitted a seven-color light, which was very dazzling! After that, Ye Ye stood up according to what was written on it, held the Nuwa Stone, and finally squeezed it hard! Then he shouted loudly: "The power of the five elements, break everything!"

Suddenly, a colorless light emanated, making it impossible for people to open their eyes. A huge force suddenly poured out, and the whole room suddenly became sticky and felt inconvenient to move.

"Everyone, disperse quickly! Go to the left hall!" Murong Di's voice suddenly sounded, and then led all the people to escape from the room!

"Great, I can finally get out! Hahaha! Ye Ye! I'm sorry for you! I will take over your Yemen and take good care of Dali for you. My revenge requires too many conditions! ", "Murong Di walked in front of the crowd, thinking with a horrified look.

At Ye Ye's place, Qin Minglei and the others did not leave. But they were already pressed to the ground by the force, unable to move.

Ye Ye, however, was in the light, and outsiders could not see the situation inside at all.

"Boom~!" Suddenly, a shocking sound emanated from Ye Ye, and at the same time, there was a wave! A colorless wave! A wave with a destructive force of a thousand pounds!

However, the wave did not radiate, but was instantly absorbed by the other seven pillars! It can actually absorb power! No wonder Murong Di could not destroy it!

"Okay! Everyone go back! The road should be open! "Murong Di was just fleeing from this dangerous place, but suddenly heard the violent explosion! He immediately led the group back!

When they returned to the eight-pillar room, they saw that there were only seven pillars in the room, and there was only a huge hole in the empty pillars! There should be a way out.

However, they did not see Ye Ye and the other four!

"Haha, they should have turned into ashes! It's a pity for the Nuwa Stone, but it's good to be able to get out!" Murong Di said with a smile, but he changed from the kindness just now, and was very gloomy! A murderous aura emanated from his body. He looked extremely ferocious!

"Come on, follow me! Get out! Let's get revenge! "Murong Di said, and jumped down first.

Are Ye Ye and his companions really dead?

No, at this time, Ye Ye and his companions had already left the Eight Heavens Gate. To be more precise, they left the scope of the Huangdao League through the hole they had just made!

They didn't expect that the hole could lead to the outside of the Huangdao League!

"It was too dangerous! Ye Ye, how are you okay?" Li Bin recalled the violent power just now and said with fear.

Ye Ye smiled and said lightly: "Because he won't hurt me! "At this time, Ye Ye's face was as white as jade, his eyes were clear, his forehead was smooth, his eyes were bright, and even his skin was as smooth as jade! He was like a god when he raised his hands.

It turned out that just now, after Ye Ye finished chanting the spell, the dazzling light drove away all the people! The spell can indeed trigger all the power of the Nuwa Stone, and then cause the energy in the space to be squeezed, causing an explosion! After that, Ye Ye was actually wrapped up by the power of the Nuwa Stone, so that he was not hurt in the explosion! Moreover, Ye Ye was extremely decisive. Before the explosion began, he actually moved to Qin Minglei and others, held their hands, and thought to himself: "Protect, protect!" Sure enough, the Nuwa Stone strangely protected Qin Minglei and others.

"The Nuwa Stone will not hurt me! And I can use it! It seems that I am its owner, but I don't know how to use it!" Ye Ye said with a smile.

Yang Hengchao looked behind him, and gradually more people appeared. He said worriedly: "Let's find a place to hide first, they are coming! "

Ye Ye listened, looked back, frowned, and hurried to the side of the road! Hiding in the woods!

"What a strong murderous aura!" When Murong Di and his companions passed by them, the murderous aura they exuded could almost break the sky!

Above their heads, a thick dark cloud was condensing! It seemed to indicate the coming disaster!

"In the future, the people of the world will suffer again!" After Murong Di and his companions left, Ye Ye looked at the mountain of the Huangdao League and said suddenly.

At this time in the Huangdao League, Gu Zihao naturally felt the sky-high divine power just now! Naturally, he was shocked, and then he immediately explored! Soon he found out that it came from the Eight Heavens Gate, and finally he was surprised to find that the Eight Heavens Gate was empty!

"The catastrophe is coming! I am a sinner!" After knowing all this, Gu Zihao hid in the valley leading to the secret room and said lightly.

The catastrophe is coming!

Chapter 24 Good news, bad news

Ye Ye and his companions escaped from the Eight Heavens Pass and learned of Gu Zihao's evil plan. After escaping, they quickly fled from the scope of the Huangdao League and returned to Yemen Mountain!

"Alas, in comparison! Our Yemen is much more shabby!" A few days later, Ye Ye and his companions returned to Yemen. Li Bin looked at Yemen Mountain and shook his head helplessly.

I have to admit that the construction of the Huangdao League is indeed well done! When Ye Ye heard Li Bin say this, the corners of his mouth rose confidently, and he said lightly: "We will be fine!" After that, he went up the mountain.

This time, Ye Ye and his companions were not stopped and walked directly into the meeting room! Before notifying everyone, Ye Hen had already hurried over to Ye Ye and the others: "Master, you are back? Are you okay?" Ye Ye naturally relaxed when he saw an acquaintance: "It's okay, aren't we back? By the way, why are you in such a hurry?"

After hearing this, Ye Hen frowned and said: "I heard that you are back and came to find you. There are three major events during this period!"

Seeing Ye Hen's serious expression, Ye Ye immediately asked: "What's the matter? What makes you so nervous?" Ye Hen sighed and said: "First, Elder Ye is gone! He left a letter!" After that, he took out an unopened letter from his clothes. Ye Ye took it, opened it, and read it.

"Huang Shang, Ye Ye, and all my fellow disciples in Yemen. I, Ye Xincheng, feel guilty towards our ancestors. For some trivial matters, I betrayed the sect, causing too many people to die. I deserve death! However, Ye Xincheng still has something else on his mind. After a long period of consideration, I decided to complete these things first. After that, I will definitely offer my head to sacrifice to our ancestors to make amends!"

The signature is Ye Xincheng. The words are vigorous and powerful, and it is indeed Ye Xincheng's handwriting.

After reading the letter, Ye Ye frowned and asked, "What about the other two things?"

Ye Hen frowned and asked back, "Master, when the crane and the clam fight, can the fisherman benefit? If the crane and the clam win, will the fisherman be in trouble?" Ye Ye asked puzzledly, "Why?"

"Just yesterday, the Xingling Group issued a war letter to the Huangdao League! A fight to the death! Xingling spread that the Huangdao League went back on its word and killed their eldest brother! And threatened that after destroying the Huangdao League, the next one would be Yemen!" Ye Ye knew the whole story, frowned and sighed helplessly and said, "There is no way, we have two choices, one is to retreat, but if Xingling can really capture the Huangdao League, then our small Yemen will be even more of a problem! So, we can only choose the second one, secretly help the Huangdao League, but while helping, we will destroy it!" Ye Ye said in a sonorous and powerful voice.

"Help and destroy at the same time! What do you mean?" Li Bin asked hurriedly in confusion. Ye Ye smiled and looked at Li Bin and said, "Yes, we will also join the war! However, the name of the war is to help the Huangdao League! For example..." Ye Ye thought for a while and said, "For example, in the encounter between Xingling and Huangdao League, we will watch the battle first, and then take action when both sides are injured and destroy them! Clean and neat! In the battlefield, the news must not be released! As long as we do it cleanly, who will know the news of this battle? They must think that the other party has wiped them out! This will not only allow us to conceal the truth, but also allow us to obtain spoils of war!" Ye Ye clenched his fists and his eyes flickered. ,

Everyone understood Ye Ye's explanation! The people present immediately looked at him with excited eyes. As long as Ye Ye gave an order, they could go into battle and kill the enemy now!

"Good! Well said! Never shrink back when it is time to make a decision! Ye Ye, you really have the spirit of an emperor!" Just when everyone was excited, a voice suddenly sounded from the door of the meeting room.

Everyone turned around and saw that it was Huang Shang and the Ghost Queen.

Huang Shang walked into the meeting room first, then held the Ghost Queen's hand, let him cross the threshold, and then the two walked to Ye Ye intimately.

Ye Ye, Qin Minglei, Li Bin and Yang Hengchao were stunned. Ye Hen smiled, changed his seriousness and said: "This is the third thing, they..." Before he finished speaking, Huang Shang interrupted him. Huang Shang smiled and said: "Haha, I will talk about my own things! The Ghost Queen and I are about to get married!"

"Ah!" Except for Ye Hen who already knew about this, everyone else screamed in surprise.

Ye Ye barely suppressed his surprise and asked awkwardly: "Then may I ask, when did you decide to be together?"

Huang Shang said, "Hehe, it was the seventh day after you left!" It turned out that after Huang Shang talked with the Ghost

Queen that day, the Ghost Queen couldn't escape the word love after thinking about it day and night. After seven days, she was finally distressed by Huang Shang's indifference, but then she was conquered by Huang Shang's strength!

"Godfather! Congratulations! Godmother~!" Li Bin and Qin Minglei, who had been without parents since childhood, regarded Huang Shang as their father from the bottom of their hearts. How could Li Bin be happy to see his father happy? After waking up from the surprise, Li Bin immediately shouted obediently. As a result, the ghost queen blushed for a while, and then she showed a little woman's posture and hit Huang Shang's chest and said: "See, it's all your fault! They all laughed at me!"

"How could it be? Who dares to laugh at you? Let me see?" Huang Shang looked at him, and was very happy in his heart. He hugged him and said with a big laugh. The ghost queen was immediately more embarrassed and hit Huang Shang's chest repeatedly, but Huang Shang laughed even more happily!

Ye Ye smiled when he saw Huang Shang and the ghost queen like this, but his heart was full of waves: It seems that the power of love is really huge, and it can turn a cold person into a soft one!

Thinking of this, a figure actually appeared in Ye Ye's heart, and then he smiled! Then he sighed helplessly, adjusted his sleeves, and walked away. He had to go see Li Yerui when he came back, the Li Yerui who became demented because of him!

Li Yerui's room was not far from the meeting room, and Ye Ye walked there quickly. As soon as he walked to the door of the room, he heard Li Yerui shouting loudly: "No, I don't want to eat! You want to kill me! No, I don't want it!" Ye Ye's heart ached, and he hurried in.

I saw a maid feeding Li Yerui, but Li Yerui hid in the corner of the cabinet and didn't come out.

Ye Ye saw it and immediately stepped forward and said to the maid: "You go down first, I'll come here!" Yes, Master! "The maid responded to Ye Ye and went down.

Ye Ye held the fragrant porridge, squatted down, scooped up a spoonful and blew it, then handed it to Li Yerui, and said in a gentle tone: "Ye Rui, be good! Come out to eat! I'm Brother Ye Ye! "Li Yerui looked at him with fear and confusion in his eyes and stopped making noise!

"Come on, Yerui, let Brother Ye Ye feed you! Come on, look, I'm Brother Ye Ye!" Ye Ye said, stretched out a hand, took Li Yerui's hand, and slowly brought her out.

As soon as she was pulled out of the corner of the cabinet, Li Yerui started to make trouble again: "You are not Brother Ye Ye! Don't kill me! Brother Ye, save me!" She roared and bit and kicked Ye Ye. Ye Ye did not dodge at all, and endured Li Yerui's bite.

After a long time, Li Yerui seemed tired, looking at Ye Ye with doubt and vigilance.

Ye Ye continued to smile, picked up the porridge that had been spilled in his hand, scooped up a spoonful and said gently: "Be good, eat! After eating, brother will take you out to bask in the sun! "

Li Yerui opened his mouth in confusion, then took a bite, and then seemed to be hungry! His eyes were very eager, but he didn't dare to ask for it!

Ye Ye smiled gently and fed all the porridge in his hand to Li Yerui! After eating, Li Yerui fell into a deep sleep!

Ye Ye carried her to the bed, then let her head rest on his legs, touched her soft hair, looked at Li Yerui's deep dark circles and said lightly: "I'm sorry..."

After a long time, Ye Ye came out of Li Yerui's room, and then told the maid to take good care of her! After that, he came to the meeting room again!

As expected, everyone else was waiting for him here!

"Ye Ye, you were not here just now! We discussed it and decided to get married first, and then face the war!" Seeing Ye Ye walk in, Huang Shang immediately said to Ye Ye.

Ye Ye smiled, nodded and said: "Then, let's start preparing today! Three days later, a lucky day! You two elders should get married on that day!"

"We have decided on that day!" Huang Shang said loudly and happily, and the Ghost Queen leaned against him like a little bird. Some women are like this. Before being conquered by a man, they are like an iceberg, but after being conquered, they will become a complete little woman! The Ghost Queen is also like this!

Chapter 25 Marriage

Hearing that the two of them were actually getting married, Ye Ye suddenly relaxed! But he couldn't help but think of the war between the Zodiac Alliance and the Star Spirit Group! Wouldn't the country intervene? This is really a problem! Moreover, if any of them seized the fruits of victory, it would be bad news for Yemen!

In fact, Ye Ye didn't know! The Zodiac Alliance and the Star Spirit Group almost controlled the power of the whole country! Therefore, private fighting is not a big deal! Even if they want, it is not impossible for them to move out the army to fight! Moreover, Yang Tianhai and the others don't know where they are now!

"Hey, Ye, what are you thinking about? Don't think so much! What is coming will come, right?" Yang Hengchao saw Ye Ye's sad face, so he walked up and punched Ye Ye and said.

Ye Ye smiled and indicated that he was fine: "It's okay, okay! We have to arrange this wedding well! This is the biggest happy event for Yemen recently!"

Yang Hengchao nodded and said: "But, how should we face it later? We have seen the strength of the Huangdao League! I'm afraid that the Star Spirit is not as easy to mess with as we look! And we don't know which side Murong Di and his group who were released from the Eight Heavens Pass have joined! But I guess they should have joined the Star Spirit, otherwise how could the Star Spirit so easily start a war against the Huangdao League?" Yang Hengchao spoke freely and expressed his views!

Ye Ye nodded and thought for a while, then said: "Well, I think so too! But, is that all we can do? Only guerrilla warfare, and then gain momentum in it!? But, it's easy to say! But it's harder than climbing to the sky to do it!" Ye Ye sighed and said helplessly

Yang Hengchao stepped forward and patted Ye Ye's shoulder and said: "It's okay! If the sky falls, the tall man will hold it up! Why do we have to seek the future? We can do well now! So, let's do a good job of Huang Shang and the Queen of Ghosts first!"

Ye Ye heard what Yang Hengchao said, looked at Yang Hengchao, and found that his eyes were full of sincerity! His eyes flickered: Indeed! Why do we chase the future? Let's do well in our present! After thinking about it, Ye Ye suddenly felt relieved.

"Okay! Let's start arranging the wedding in the next few days!" Ye Ye turned to everyone and said after being relieved.

Suddenly, everyone quieted down. They all waited for Ye Ye to arrange it!

"Ye Zi, I'll leave my wedding to you! I haven't been married for a thousand years! Hahaha!" Huang Shang suddenly said with a smile. But what he got was the ghost queen's claws grabbing the soft flesh on his waist! Huang Shang could only laugh dryly at everyone, and his expression was actually immature!

Yang Hengchao sighed again at the power of love, sighed and stood up and continued: "Well! No problem, leave it to me! According to custom, the woman cannot meet the man within these three days! Must go back to her parents' home, right? However, Ghost Queen, you are in a special situation, but you still can't escape the custom. You stay in the room for these three days! Don't come out! Until Huang Shang comes to pick you up!" Yang Hengchao said according to custom.

After hearing this, the Ghost Queen smiled and nodded and said: "Well, okay! No problem! Then I'll go now! But you always tell me which room it is? Otherwise, be careful that I go into the wrong room, and someone will..." The Ghost Queen said sourly.

Huang Shang was immediately more embarrassed, and hurriedly laughed dryly with his head down! Everyone also laughed.

Ye Ye smiled, then stopped smiling, and then said, "The quietest courtyard in the west will be your bridal chamber! By the way, find a few women to accompany you!" Ye Ye said, and led the Ghost Queen out of the door, leaving Huang Shang looking at the Ghost Queen's back eagerly.

Not long after, Ye Ye brought the Ghost Queen to the west wing! Then he called a few maids, and when he was about to leave, the Ghost Queen suddenly stopped him!

"Do you really want me to marry Huang Shang?" The Ghost Queen asked faintly. Ye Ye was puzzled and said strangely, "Me? Why don't I want it? This is the first big happy event of Yemen!"

The Ghost Queen sighed and looked more resentful. She looked at Ye Ye and continued, "But, are you really willing?" Ye Ye was even more puzzled. When he was about to answer, Ye Ye's eyes suddenly became chaotic, and he said lightly, "You go down first!" Ye Ye said and called the maid out. Then he said: "It's not that I am willing! But I am forced to do so! I'm sure you have guessed my current situation!" This is not Ye Ye, this is the Ghost King, the Ghost King who lives in the depths of Ye Ye's soul sea!

"But, but you know, I can only marry you, otherwise the other party will be unhappy!" The Ghost Queen didn't know what to do! He fell in love with Huang Shang, but he was worried about hurting Huang Shang!

'Ye Ye' raised his mouth slightly and said: "Unfortunate? How could it be unfortunate? Those are just messages left by the ancestors. For example, in my case, am I unfortunate? At least now it's just unknown whether it's a blessing or a disaster, right?" Ye Ye sighed after speaking, his tone full of helplessness.

The more the Ghost Queen listened, the more shocked she was, and hurriedly said: "King! No! How could you oppose the prophecy left by the ancestors?" The Ghost Queen's words were full of surprise!

The ghost king smiled and said lightly: "That's right! No need to say more! Go ahead! I won't say much, this body is not strong enough, I can only be out for so long. I just tell you that Ye Ye's future is not something you and I can think about!" After that, Ye Ye suddenly collapsed and fell on the table. The ghost queen was still in surprise and dazed.

Soon, Ye Ye woke up and rubbed his head and said: "What happened to me just now? Did you say anything just now?" Ye Ye's abruptness woke the ghost queen from her surprise, and then the ghost queen said: "No! I didn't say anything! Ye Ye, you may be too tired! You should rest more! Okay, go and arrange other things! I have nothing to do here! Haha, just waiting for him to marry me!" Although the ghost queen said very happily, Ye Ye always felt that the ghost queen was avoiding something. Without thinking too much, Ye Ye smiled and walked out of the room.

"King! I hope you are right! Otherwise, we will all be cursed! Not just me and Huang Shang, but everyone!" The Ghost Queen said lightly as Ye Ye left, her eyes full of uneasiness!

Three days passed quickly! The wedding was arranged slowly!

On this day, the entire Yemen Mountain was very lively. Although Yemen is a newly emerged old sect, the people who gave gifts almost lined up from the foot of the mountain to the inside of Yemen!

The atmosphere of joy spread throughout the Yemen Mountain!

"Hahahaha, everyone drink! I haven't enjoyed such a wedding! Drink with relatives and friends, and don't stop until you are drunk! Haha!" Huang Shang was very happy, and pulled the guests to drink again and again! Ye Ye and his friends couldn't stop him at all.

"Master Shen is here!" At this time, the messenger at the door suddenly shouted loudly. Ye Ye and his friends immediately stepped forward to greet him.

"Haha, congratulations!" Shen Qing had just entered the door and asked the servants to take the gifts to count, and then immediately congratulated Huang Shang who was walking over.

Huang Shang was very generous, pulling Shen Qing and holding a can of wine and said: "Let's celebrate together! So, just drink! Hahahaha" Shen Qing and his three disciples had no choice but to drink with Huang Shang aside!

Ye Ye and the other two looked at Huang Shang helplessly and shook their heads at the same time!

"You are the head of the Ye sect, right? Someone just said that if I send this thing up, I can get a reward!" Suddenly, a voice sounded from behind Ye Ye and the other four. Ye Ye turned around and saw a ragged man holding a red sandalwood box and said with a wretched face.

Li Bin frowned, quickly arranged a few coins, threw them to the man, and then took the box: "Go down the mountain quickly!"

The man took the money, counted it, and muttered: "It's better to have it than not to have it!" After that, he turned and left.

"What do you think it is! It's so mysterious, and the person who gave the gift didn't come by himself!" Li Bin said puzzledly while holding the box.

Ye Ye looked at the box worriedly and took everyone aside and said calmly: "Beware of fraud!"

When Li Bin heard it, he immediately put the box on the table and opened it carefully!

After the box was opened, a burst of fragrant cigarettes suddenly rose! But it didn't seem to be poisonous! After the cigarettes dispersed, Ye Ye and his friends gathered around and took a look, and were immediately shocked by what was in the box!

Chapter 26: The troublesome wedding

Ye Ye was startled when he saw the thing, but he quickly came to his senses, quickly closed the box and said with a frown: "Move to another place, hide it, don't attract other people's attention! This thing is not suitable to appear here! Then, notify them immediately! Something really big has happened!"

Li Bin nodded lightly, his heart was full of surprise! After a long time, he walked slowly in shock, looking for other people! After Ye Ye finished speaking, he picked up the box and left, going to the North Wing with the least people!

"Hey, Li Bin? What's wrong? Are you drunk? Why are you like this?" Yang Hengchao asked when he saw Li Bin's panic.

Li Bin swallowed his saliva and said lightly: "Help me notify others, be careful not to alarm the guests to the North Wing! Big thing! I haven't recovered yet!" Yang Hengchao heard Li Bin's tone and immediately felt that the matter must be very important, so he immediately looked for other people.

"Sorry... I have to leave for a moment!" After Yang Hengchao told Huang Shang about this, Huang Shang's eyes turned slightly, and he immediately felt that this must be unusual. He immediately said goodbye to his relatives and friends, and immediately rushed to the north wing with Li Bin and others!

In the north wing! It was very dark! Only Ye Ye was sitting there quietly, his face was terrified!

"Ye Ye, what's the matter! Why are you so urgent to ask us to come here! And come to this place where no one is!?" Huang Shang asked in confusion as soon as he and his friends arrived.

Ye Ye didn't say anything, but pointed to the box on the table! Indicating that they should look for themselves!

Huang Shang looked at it in confusion, then walked forward and slowly opened the box! The others also surrounded it curiously!

"This... How is this possible!" Ye Hen said in surprise when he saw what was in the box. After seeing it, Huang Shang's face suddenly became silent, just like Ye Ye, silent and terrifying!

The box actually contained the head of a walking corpse!

Seeing their surprised looks, Ye Ye stood up, frowned and said seriously: "Don't doubt it! This is true! The zombie... was killed!" Ye Ye said, his eyes became sharp. Although the zombie joined the Night Gate halfway and framed them before, since they entered the Night Gate, and after entering, the zombies gradually integrated into the Night Gate. How can we not be nervous when someone in the Night Gate is killed? Besides, the zombies are quite powerful! Who can kill the zombies like this?

Excessive surprise can also make people more sober, and Ye Ye's words immediately woke up everyone present.

"Now, you know why I am so surprised?" Li Bin said lightly, after so long, there is still a lot of fear in his expression!

Yang Hengchao nodded and said, "This is incredible! The zombies are all dead! And no one knows where Yang Tianhai is! Maybe..."

"No... Impossible! Yang Tianhai can't die! He is a punisher, he can't die! The question is how strong is the person who killed the zombie? Moreover, you can see the expression on the zombie's head, there is no expression of pain, which proves that he didn't struggle too much before his death! So it can be seen that the person can only sneak attack or kill him with one blow!" Ye Ye analyzed calmly!

"Well, let's take a long-term view on this matter. Let's bury the zombie first! After all, he is also a member of the Night Gate!" Ye Hen also woke up from his surprise and sighed.

Huang Shang nodded and touched his chin and said, "I agree with Ye Ye! But we do have to think long-term. Let's go out and greet the guests first. We can discuss it after the guests leave!"

Everyone nodded, and then temporarily placed the box with the head of the walking corpse on the table in the north wing as an offering. After the guests dispersed, they moved to the main incense room and accepted the offerings of the hall master level in the night gate!

"Haha, everyone, excuse me just now! Come on, let's continue drinking! Come on, everyone, have fun today!" After Huang Shang walked out of the north wing, he came to the guests again and accompanied them to drink.

Ye Ye and the others also suppressed the look of surprise or worry on their faces and smiled apologetically!

"Minglei, Li Bin, is there something wrong with you? Tell me!" Shen Mo saw that Li Bin and Qin Minglei looked wrong. Although he stood up, the three masters and apprentices of the Shen family were so good at judging people that they could see the abnormality in their eyes at a glance!

After hearing this, Li Bin smiled and said, "You misunderstood! We are just tired! How can we accompany so many guests? You two elders, enjoy yourselves! Minglei and I will go to accompany other guests first! We are family, you can do whatever you want!" Li Bin answered tactfully, and then pulled Qin Minglei away.

Shen Qing looked at the backs of the two people leaving, and said lightly: "There must be something big happening in

Yemen. After the guests have dispersed, let's also tell them what we know! After all, maybe the three of us will have to rely on Yemen to survive in the future!"

After speaking, Shen Mo sighed helplessly!

The wedding was quite grand. In addition to the dignitaries from all walks of life who were invited, there were also people who came to flatter Yemen after hearing the news.

The gifts piled up into a mountain. Although they could not be called natural treasures, there were a lot of pearls, gems, and various precious objects!

Crackling... Crackling! Suddenly, bursts of firecrackers sounded, attracting everyone's attention, and then a sharp voice shouted: "The bride is here!"

At this moment, the Ghost Queen Zi Ruixin was wearing a purple cheongsam, which fully highlighted her fiery but balanced figure. Her head was covered by a purple wedding cloth, but her hair was flying down, black and enviable. The Ghost Queen was led by a wedding woman and slowly walked towards the main hall!

"Hurry up, hurry up, go!" The guests saw the bride coming, but Huang Shang was still in dementia, so they all mocked Huang Shang and pushed him to the Ghost Queen who was standing at the door!

Huang Shang excitedly took the Ghost Queen's hand, and then led the Ghost Queen across the door and into the main hall.

Ye Hen, the master of ceremonies, also stood up at this moment, and after Huang Shang and the other two stood in position, he stood up and said loudly: "The newlyweds are here! First bow to heaven and earth!"

As soon as Ye Hen finished shouting, Huang Shang and the Queen of Ghosts immediately bowed deeply to the outside of the door.

"Second bow to relatives and friends!" Huang Shang and the Queen of Ghosts had no parents, so they didn't have to bow to their parents, so they had to choose to bow to relatives and friends.

Huang Shang and the Queen of Ghosts turned to their relatives and friends, and then bowed! Everyone cheered.

"Husband and wife bow to each other!" Ye Hen shouted with a long tone.

"Bow...Bow...Bow!" Hearing the husband and wife bow to each other, the relatives and friends began to play, and then Huang Shang and the other two bowed to each other in laughter!

"Enter the bridal chamber!" Ye Hen continued to shout, but the word "bridal chamber" was dragged out even longer!

Then, the matchmaker took Huang Shang and the Queen of Ghosts to the bridal chamber, and the guests and relatives followed to make trouble in the bridal chamber!

"It's finally almost over!" Ye Ye said in a low voice. Although this wedding was quite happy, Ye Men was not in the mood to face it now!

Chapter 27 Talks

After the bridal chamber was over, all the guests lost their temper and slowly dispersed in groups of three or four and went down the mountain! Only the three masters and disciples of the Shen family have not left!

"Minglei! Tell me honestly, what happened?" Shen Mo asked in a stern tone as the guests dispersed.

"Master, stop asking! It's better for you not to get involved in this matter!" Qin Minglei frowned and answered worriedly, but it seemed that this was not the answer she wanted. He continued: "Okay! Stop hiding it from me! If If it's really okay, you won't be frowning on this happy day!" He sighed and continued silently: "Actually, I know what you are worried about! Is it the heads?"

Hearing the word 'human head' popping out of Shen Mo's mouth, Ye Ye and the others suddenly became nervous. Ye Ye looked at Shen Mo seriously and said, "You also know about the box?"

Silence nodded and said: "Yes, we know that box! Because, we also received a box like that! And, there is a word inside! There is a word on the back of the head where the hair covers it." Silence said lightly. said.

"Who is that head? What are the words on it?" Ye Ye was shocked when he heard it and asked quickly.

"Night! There is only one word for night! So, we guessed that the clues would appear at the Night Gate! Unexpectedly, it really happened! That head is the head of Butler Mu! You don't know, right? Butler Mu's strength is extremely terrifying. I only saw it He exuded an aura once before, and I think that aura can be compared to that of Elder Ye Xincheng!"

"Uncle Mu? How is that possible! Uncle Mu never leaves Shen Yuan!" Qin Minglei suddenly shrank his pupils and said emotionally. After all, Qin Minglei was afraid of Butler Mu, but after all, Butler Mu had always been very kind to him since he entered the Shen family. good!

Shen Mo looked at Shen Qing and Shen Ling and said, "Oh! The blame lies here! How could a master be so easily cut off without resisting?" After saying that, Shen Mo pinched hard. Clenching fists, Butler Mu is his butler on the surface, but in fact they have been friends for many years!

After hearing this, Ye Ye thought for a while, then stood up and said: "We have analyzed that there are only two possibilities, sneak attack and forced killing! Only these two possibilities will cause a master to lose his life inadvertently or unable to resist! "

"Word! Ye Ye, word!" Li Bin suddenly said with enlightenment.

That's right, they haven't seen the writing on the walking corpse yet! Thinking of this, a group of people immediately ran towards the north wing, then took out the head of the walking corpse, turned aside the hair and saw that there were actually words on it!

"Flat?" Ye Ye looked at the word on the back of the zombie's head, it was the word "flat"!

Li Bin asked in confusion: "What do you mean?" Everyone shook their heads to indicate that they didn't know either.

Ye Ye thought for a while, put the zombie's head back on its head, and then said: "Okay, today's big day is really not the right time to do these things! I'm thinking about tomorrow! Everyone go and rest now! Senior Shen, you just stay here Let's stay in the night gate! It's safer for everyone." Ye Ye turned around and left. He said this not because he didn't want to think about this weird thing, but because he wanted to think about it quietly.

Thinking about the walking corpse and the cause of death of Butler Mu, thinking about the word "flat" on the back of the walking corpse's head, thinking about where Yang Hengchao is now...there are too many questions!

In Huang Shangyu's bridal chamber, the red candle burned silently. Huang Shang excitedly walked up to the Ghost Queen, gently took off the red hijab, and called out softly: "Madam!" The Ghost Queen nodded lightly and said nothing!

Huang Shang smiled and walked to the table, poured two glasses of wine, handed one to the ghost queen, and the two drank from it. When you pay homage to the church, you can even drink a glass of wine! The two became an official couple!

Huang Shang smiled, put his hand on the Ghost Queen's shoulder and said softly: "Madam, let's sleep peacefully!" After saying that, he pulled the Ghost Queen to the bed.

The ghost queen patted Huang Shang's hand gently and said with a frown: "I don't know why, but I suddenly have a strange feeling! It seems like something will happen to you tomorrow!"

Huang Shang said: "No! Who can do anything to me?" After saying that, he put out the candle with a wave of his hand. Not long after, a soft cry of pain rang out, and the whole room was filled with the breath of spring like spring mud!

The next day, Ye Ye got up very early, and then notified everyone to come to the meeting hall again! After everyone gathered, Ye Yecai said helplessly: "To be honest, I have been thinking about it all night, but there is still no result. I have called everyone here today to ask you if you have any opinions?"

Everyone shook their heads!

"No objections! Let's go according to the previous plan! I don't believe anyone can take off my head!" Huang Shang's happy voice suddenly sounded from the door of the chamber. Everyone turned around in response, Huang Shang walked to his seat and sat down and continued: "I heard about it! It's not a big deal! Now, the most worrying issue is how to face the war between the Zodiac Alliance and that star spirit! "Huang Shang looks so high-spirited after a long night of supper!

Ye Ye listened to Huang Shang's words and said, "But..." "Nothing but! Ye Ye, when did you become so indecisive? Now is the time for you to make a decision!" Ye Ye's worried words Before he could say anything, he was interrupted ruthlessly by Huang Shang!

Ye Ye could only nod and said: "Okay! But now we don't even know their whereabouts, how can we take action? After thinking about it, I realized that my guerrilla tactics were too naive! Moreover, Yang Tianhai is nowhere to be found now. Is it safe? Or not! I really don't know who our opponent will be!" Ye Ye thought about it all night and rejected his thoughts from the past few days!

Huang Shang smiled and said with contempt: "Since the opponent doesn't know who he is, then we should move forward, otherwise it will be easier for the opponent to sneak in and take us out one by one! Since we don't know his whereabouts, then we Let's make a temporary decision then! Yang Tianhai, the punisher doesn't have to worry at all!" Huang Shang answered Ye Ye's rebuttal word for word!

Ye Ye thought for a moment and said, "Yes! Why should I be afraid of potential opponents? What's more..." Ye Ye slowly revealed a shocking secret!

"Ah! Ye Ye! You...are you a human? No wonder, no wonder!" After hearing what Ye Ye said, everyone was very surprised and immediately regarded Ye Ye as a monster!

Ye Ye nodded and smiled: "So, we should wait for the Zodiac Alliance and the Star Spirits to take action before we take action!"

"There are no stars in the stars, no alliance in the zodiac, traveling around the world, why fear only one? Hahaha!" Suddenly a very arrogant poem entered the meeting hall!

"What an arrogant poem! Who can walk into the night gate so freely?" Ye Ye said with a frown.

While everyone was wondering, a tall and thin figure walked into the meeting hall!

Chapter 28: Decisive Battle with Lu Ping

Ye Ye saw the figure of that person and immediately said excitedly: "Yang Tianhai!?"

That person was Yang Tianhai. He walked in with a confident smile and looked around and said: "Where is the zombie? Hasn't come back yet? I won! Haha!"

When the zombie was mentioned, the atmosphere suddenly darkened. Yang Tianhai asked in confusion: "What's wrong? When I came in just now, didn't I see a happy word posted on the door? Is there a happy event? You should be happy, you...?"

The crowd didn't speak, and slowly made way, revealing the box containing the zombie's head. They didn't have time to bury the zombie or offer it to the Merit Pavilion.

Yang Tianhai looked at the box, frowned and said lightly: "Dead air!" After that, he walked to the box, slowly opened the box, and saw the zombie's head that would not rot, and a murderous aura suddenly surged out! His eyebrows were also frowned and he said: "Who did it?" The zombie and Yang Tianhai can be said to get along well or both cater to each other's preferences.

Several people didn't speak. Ye Ye walked up to him, closed the box and said, "Aren't you with him? Don't you know?"

Yang Tianhai shook his head silently: "We separated on the way back! We wanted to see who would return to Yemen first! So, we separated!"

Ye Ye sighed and didn't speak. He picked up the box, then went to the offering room, put the box at the bottom of the offering table, and then lit a stick of incense and inserted it into the incense burner: "The first person to die in Yemen!" There was no ceremony, no noise, and the corpse was enshrined on Yemen!

Several people watched Ye Ye silently and lit a stick of incense. After finishing everything, Ye Ye said: "The wine man has gone, now let's do our best now!"

Ye Hen nodded and said: "But, I don't even know where they will start now!"

"Lu Ping, their first battle will definitely be in Lu Ping!" Yang Tianhai suddenly said, then looked at the box with the zombie's head and said: "I have been in contact with the zombie during this period of time, and I have developed a deep relationship with him! I want to avenge him! The glory of punishment will shine on the whole earth again! On my way back, I heard about the decisive battle between the Zodiac Alliance and the Star Spirit, and if there is no accident, they will meet in Lu Ping and start the first encounter battle!" Then, Yang Tianhai told the news he got from this trip!

"You mean, Boss Xing said they will meet in Lu Ping?" Ye Ye said in surprise after hearing what Yang Tianhai said.

Yang Tianhai nodded and said, "Yes, that's what they called that man!" Suddenly, Ye Ye, Qin Minglei, Li Bin and Yang Hengchao fell silent. According to his experience, Boss Xing must die! But in Yang Tianhai's words, he was resurrected!

"No, there must be something strange! However, we can't care about it now. Let's go to Lu Ping immediately! Then take the opportunity to reap the benefits!" Ye Ye couldn't figure out what was going on, so he had to put it aside for the time being.

Yang Tianhai smiled, stood up and walked out of the room. "Where are you going? Not with us?" Li Bin asked.

Yang Tianhai turned around, revealing his bloodthirsty eyes that he didn't know when he became cold and said, "The walking corpse was killed while exploring the Star Spirit! It has something to do with the Star Spirit, so I'm going to take revenge!" After that, he turned and left!

"Be careful!" Ye Ye shouted at Yang Tianhai's back, but Yang Tianhai didn't look back, I don't know if he heard it!

After Yang Tianhai left again, Ye Ye and his men discussed the strategy without stopping! This action is different from the past. This time it is a war!

At this time, in a distant place, a group of people were setting up camp, and in the middle, a camp had been set up.

"Haha, this time we must eliminate the Huangdao League from the world!" Such a sentence suddenly came from the barracks. The voice sounded so familiar that it could really be Boss Xing!

Hearing Boss Xing say so, the brothers of the Xing family burst into laughter. Xing Yu, the fourth brother of Xing, said: "We can't die at all! The Huangdao League should not know yet! Moreover, this time we have..."

"Hahahahaha!" Hearing Xing Yu say this, the others laughed!

"Humph. That's all! But this body is not bad!" Just when several people were proud, a cold snort suddenly came from the darkness of the barracks, and the seven brothers of the Xing family laughed even more arrogantly! Then, a ball of red light lit up from the darkness! A gust of cold wind blew, and the air around suddenly became a little colder.

Boss Xing stopped laughing and said to the air: "Okay! You guys can find your body at will! But don't disrupt my plan, otherwise I will let you enjoy the taste of being imprisoned again!" After Boss Xing said this, the cold wind suddenly stopped. The red light in the dark corner also disappeared into the darkness again!

"Humph, has the Huangdao League taken action?" Boss Xing said. Xing Yu seemed to be more informed of the outside news and stood up again and said: "Brother, they have taken action. If we follow our speed, then we will meet in Lu Ping! Start the first encounter battle!"

When Boss Xing heard this, he laughed immediately: "Lu Ping! Haha! Lu Ping, the continent is flat!" It seems that he has full confidence in this war!

Chapter 29 The First Battle

At this time, the most powerful forces of the three parties gathered towards Lu Ping! Here, an extraordinary world war will unfold!

"Hmph! We must win this war! The destruction of Huangdao Mountain is a slap in our face! Hmph, after destroying the star spirit, I will naturally get it back from Yemen!" The Huangdao League has naturally taken action. The leader of the Huangdao League sat in the tent and said to several Huangdao generals under him.

Indeed, Murong Die used Ye Ye to pour out all the power of the Nuwa Stone and opened the Eight Heavens Gate, but Gu Zihao didn't know that it was the Nuwa Stone that was secretly causing trouble. After a long time of inquiry, he still had no clue, so he had to put all the blame on Yemen!

Just when Gu Zihao looked stern, a hand gently rested on his shoulder. The owner of the hand said: "Don't worry, it's just a Xiaoxiaoxiao star spirit! With our invincible trio here, what are you afraid of?" The voice turned out to be Ye Xincheng! He returned to the Huangdao League again!

"That's right, what are you worried about? Zihao, we are here!" A gentle female voice suddenly sounded. Gu Zihao turned around and said with a very gentle look: "Yes! But the lion uses all its strength to catch the rabbit. We can't underestimate the star spirit too much. A dog will jump over the wall when it is desperate!"

Ye Xincheng smiled, hugged the woman's slender waist and said: "Wanjun, you are right! But your body is important. You have just recovered from a serious illness and can't catch a cold! Let's go back first." The woman turned out to be Xia Wanjun? The Xia Wanjun buried in the tomb in the paradise leading to the secret room?

Xia Wanjun heard Ye Xincheng's voice and looked at Ye Xincheng with eyes as gentle as Daisy. The two of them ignored the presence of other people and hugged each other, just like a fairy couple!

"Everything is up to Xincheng!" Xia Wanjun said softly, and then leaned in Ye Xincheng's arms. After that, Ye Xincheng took Xia Wanjun away from the tent. After the two left, Gu Zihao's eyes returned to their cold and fierce look and said to everyone: "This time, Lu Ping encounters a battle, and we must win but not lose! You go and prepare! Go down!" Gu Zihao gave this order coldly, and everyone agreed and retreated one after another.

"Feng Yi, come out! During this period, you and Xia Feng should pay close attention to the whereabouts of Yemen! Remember, it's not assassination, it's tracking! Report to me at any time!" After everyone left, Gu Zihao stood with his hands behind his back and said to Xia Feng and Feng Yi who were hiding in the darkness behind him.

Xia Feng naturally obeyed Gu Zihao's words, but Feng Yi was very opinionated, so he frowned and asked: "Master, I don't know, how are you going to face it this time?"

Gu Zihao's brows suddenly turned into a "◇" shape when he heard it, but everyone could see his expression. He turned his head and looked at Feng Yi coldly. A three-foot cold sword appeared in his hand at some point, pointing directly at Feng Yi's neck. Feng Yi felt the cold air coming from the sword and was startled, and hurriedly looked at Gu Zihao without knowing it.

After a long time, Gu Zihao took back his sword, and then said coldly: "As for these things, you don't have to worry about them! I have my own ideas! Go!" After that, he looked at Xia Feng with a little more tenderness in his eyes: "Xia Feng, remember, you can't appear in front of Ye Xincheng, understand?" Xia Feng nodded silently, and then disappeared into the darkness, probably to find and track Ye Men's whereabouts according to Gu Zihao's order.

Feng Yi bowed slightly, and then slowly walked out of the tent.

After leaving the tent, Feng Yi suddenly touched the place where the sword was just held in fear, and then felt his hand slightly wet, and was suddenly shocked: "Such an unintentional sword energy hurt me. And from the movement of his shaking sword just now, I can't see clearly. Presumably, he has surpassed the original realm and reached a state of no one!" Feng Yi thought in his heart, and his fists were clenched at some point. While thinking, he walked out of the camp set up by the Huangdao League.

A few days later, on Lu Ping.

The masters of the two battlefields were already waiting for the attack signal! The two sides were only a few thousand meters apart!

Gu Zihao smiled, sat on a pure white horse without mixed hair, looked at the opposite Xingling with a simple military telescope, and raised his mouth with disdain. But suddenly, the Xingling army that had already assembled actually split a road from the middle, and the seven Xingling brothers slowly walked out from that road!

It seems that during this period of time, Xingling has trained the originally idle Jianghu people into an army with more military qualities!

And Gu Zihao's originally raised mouth corners froze the moment when Boss Xing and the seven brothers of the Xing family appeared: "How is it possible! Isn't he dead?" Gu Zihao was also shocked by Boss Xing's rebirth. However, he quickly came to his senses. After all, now is not the time to be shocked.

On the Xingling side, Boss Xing did not observe the movements of the Huangdao League, but waved his hand disdainfully and summoned a messenger. After receiving the order, the messenger trotted to the center of the field, and then walked to the front of the Huangdao League, unfolded a piece of beautifully made cloth paper and began to read: "Today on Luping, we will fight to the death with the Huangdao League. Considering that we once knew each other, I hope that the Huangdao League will not be stubborn and surrender immediately! Otherwise, we will kill you without mercy! Surrender, otherwise..." Before he finished speaking, the messenger's head had fallen to the ground, and on the ground, a Qingfeng sword was stuck in the ground, which must have been done by Gu Zihao!

The two sides will fight to the death, and the messenger will not be killed!

The behavior of the Huangdao League immediately angered the opposite Star Spirit Army!

Boss Xing frowned, raised a yellow military flag with his hand, and waved it twice. Suddenly, all the troops behind him dispersed, and then a group of people in yellow clothes stood up, holding knives in their right hands and shields in their left hands, and took the lead in walking slowly. After that, Boss Xing took out a red flag, separated a group of red-clad soldiers from the army, and followed the shield bearer.

After doing all this, Boss Xing smiled with a playful look in his eyes!

Gu Zihao looked at what Boss Xing did, wondering in his heart: "You want to attack with just these people? What's the plan? But since you want to die, I'll take it!" Because he didn't know what Boss Xing was doing, Gu Zihao didn't dare to give orders easily. He just raised his sword high and pointed it forward. The army behind him also spread out on a road. After a few breaths, there were suddenly bursts of violent horse hoof sounds!

It turned out to be cavalry! And they were cavalry wearing iron armor and even their horses were covered with iron armor! Those cavalry were wearing heavy armor and were extremely fast. It seemed that they were all BMWs! Fortunately, there were not many such cavalry, but even so, facing the lightly armored soldiers sent by the Protoss, it was already a nightmare!

When Boss Xing saw the cavalry appear, he looked a little panicked, but a gust of cold wind came from behind him, and he immediately smiled and stopped worrying!

In the center of the field, the soldiers of the Zodiac Alliance and the Star Spirit had already come into contact! The cavalry took the lead, wielding their long swords with great force, and rushed into the enemy group like a massacre! The shield soldiers and red army sent by the Star Spirit had no resistance at all!

Not far away, the bystanders or orioles of this battle stayed quietly aside, watching the beginning of this war! However, they did not notice that there was a black shadow behind them!

Chapter 30 Ancient Yin God Formation

At this time, the battle was still going on. The cavalry of the Huangdao League was really powerful. Although there were not many of them, they stabbed into the light soldiers of the Xingling like a sharp knife and started a massacre!

Ye Ye and his group, who were watching the battle not far away, watched the war quietly: "It turns out that cavalry has such great power on the battlefield!" Ye Ye looked at the cavalry rampaging on the battlefield and couldn't help but say it. But he saw that Boss Xing was sitting on the horse safely, and he didn't seem to be panicked by the light soldiers killed by the Huangdao League. Instead, when he saw that the light soldiers were almost slaughtered, he waved his hand and sent a bunch of light soldiers forward again! Ye Ye couldn't help but wonder: "What does he want to do?"

Boss Xing's move also puzzled Gu Zihao. He didn't give any orders. After thinking about it, he let the cavalry stay there, hoping to see the other party's intentions.

The heavy cavalry was slaughtering the light infantry. Not long after, the team of light infantry was slaughtered again. The army of the Huangdao League suddenly became more motivated and shouted: "Huangdao League, Huangdao League..."

The cavalry sent out galloped even more arrogantly, and it seemed that no one could defeat them!

But the Xingling side was very quiet, without low morale, and Boss Xing's eyes suddenly became very cunning, and he said: "It's over, hundreds of lives, in exchange for your entire army, it's worth it!" After that, he got off the horse, walked to the front, and took out an object from his clothes.

"Huh? What is he doing?" This question flashed in everyone's mind at the same time.

After getting off the horse, Boss Xing took out a stone slab from his clothes, and then put it on the ground, and then got back on the horse and shouted loudly: "Gu Zihao, goodbye!"

After he shouted, the entire Luping land became very quiet! A gust of wind blew up from nowhere! It rolled up some dust, and the horses under the cavalry suddenly became very uneasy, anxiously pacing on the spot.

Suddenly, several gusts of wind rose silently, and the dust suddenly covered the sky and surrounded the cavalry in the center.

"Not good! Retreat!" Gu Zihao saw this and realized that he had fallen into the trap of Boss Xing. He immediately ordered the cavalry to retreat and asked the drummer behind him to beat the drum.

Boom, boom, boom... The inspiring drum sounded in the empty air. But for a long time, the cavalry still did not appear from the dust. The wind became very violent. Gu Zihao had to order the troops to stay where they were and wait for the inexplicable wind to dissipate.

After a long time, the wind stopped. The cavalry fell down. If someone looked closely at this time, they would be surprised to find that the bloody corpses on the ground had become very dry, as if they were dried by the short strange wind just now!

The entire decisive battle site suddenly became very quiet, with only the heavy Breathing sound!

Gu Zihao frowned and looked at the position where the cavalry had just stood. Then he observed the surroundings and found that there was nothing strange. Then he thought of the action of Boss Xing getting off the horse just now. He suddenly thought that it was just the power of the spell. He smiled disdainfully, waved his chess again, and sent a team of people to continue moving forward. This team of people also has a great background. They are a mixture of various factions. Some of them rely on spells to strengthen their defense, and some rely on spells to attack and assist. This team is the elite team of the Zodiac Alliance, but judging from the number of people, it should be only a part of it.

This team of people is not fast, but suddenly a green light flashed through this team of people, and their speed suddenly increased by several percent, almost catching up with the speed of the cavalry just now, and rushed towards the Star Spirit. and go.

Up to now, the Zodiac Alliance and the Star Spirits have been attacking tentatively, and have not rushed forward to start a real battle!

Boss Xing looked at the people coming at a high speed from the opposite side, and did not speak. He shook his head, suddenly raised his hand high, and then put it down, pointing forward.

Just when the Zodiac Alliance's team arrived at the center of the field and was about to reach the firing range, something amazing happened!

Suddenly, a Star Spirit light infantryman with half of his head cut off jumped high, bit the neck of the Zodiac Alliance's sorcerer, and then exerted force to tear off most of the sorcerer's neck. After doing all this, the light soldier with only half of his head did not delay and pounced on other people again!

This mutation came so suddenly, No one reacted. By the time they reacted, the half-headed resurrected soldier had already killed the three spell soldiers! At this time, the spell soldiers united and used magic to kill the strangely resurrected light soldier who didn't know what he was!

However, before they could catch their breath, they suddenly heard a series of rustling sounds of clothes rubbing from all around them! They looked around in horror and found that the people who had just died had all resurrected! And, they all rushed towards them! The spell soldiers in fear had no time to fight back again, and they were all killed immediately!

Gu Zihao looked at the resurrected soldier gnawing at the spell soldiers one by one with a cold face, biting his fine teeth and squeezing out a sentence from between his teeth: "It turned out to be the Yin God Formation! "

Ye Ye looked at the sudden change below in amazement and said nothing, but everyone knew that relying on the Zodiac Alliance, even if more troops were invested, it would be a death sentence. This was obviously a bottomless pit that could not be fed!

Because they all saw that the cavalry and spell soldiers who were killed just now actually all stood up! And they lined up in a row, as if they were alive!

At this time, Gu Zihao woke up from his anger, looked at the front and said in horror: "Ancient, Yin Shen Formation! "

This ancient Yinshen formation is of great origin. It was created by Xing Tian in ancient times. It was by using this formation that the emperor was forced to retreat step by step. The greatest horror of this formation is that it can revive those who died in the formation and make them obey the words of the person who set up the formation. Unless the resurrected corpse is completely smashed, it will continue to attack everyone except the person who set up the formation! Moreover, the resurrected person, in addition to obeying commands, will also have the skills he had before his death!

For example, the resurrected spell soldiers actually went towards the Zodiac Alliance at this time, and they flashed a green light, a symbol of acceleration, and the cavalry team also got on the horse, and they were also blessed with acceleration, cooperating with the light soldiers and spell soldiers, and went towards the Zodiac Alliance troops!

This is simply an invincible formation! At the beginning, if the emperor had not possessed the Xuanyuan Sword and restrained the evil spirit, he would have killed Xing Tian, otherwise, the world would have fallen long ago!

"Why did this star spirit come to this formation! "Gu Zihao thought with fear in his heart, looking at the resurrected corpses rushing towards them, and immediately issued an order to retreat!

First update is here!!!

Chapter 31 Keep Calm

When the troops of the Huangdao League saw Gu Zihao issued the order to retreat, they immediately turned around and retreated without any hesitation, just like an army.

However, the resurrected corpses were blessed with acceleration, and their speed was extremely fast, especially the resurrected cavalry, which was even faster! In a few breaths, they caught up with the retreating Huangdao League troops and launched an attack.

The resurrected corpses were extremely strong. Every time they swung the sabers in their hands, they would chop down one person. Moreover, they still had the cooperation and horse skills they had in their lifetime, and they hid in an orderly manner from the retreat and cover attacks organized by the Huangdao League. After a few breaths, many people had died under the sabers. And behind the cavalry were the resurrected spell soldiers. They also reached the firepower points that the firepower could reach at a very fast speed, and used the talismans in their hands one after another. Suddenly, groups of fireballs, ice cones or curses and other attacks were overwhelming towards the Huangdao League members who were slightly behind and covering the retreat. The power of the spell is much greater than that of the saber. When the spell attacked, the people behind the Huangdao League fell down like wheat.

After Gu Zihao issued the order to retreat, he did not lead the retreat. He knew that if he took the lead, the morale would drop to a low point. He had to take the two soldiers around him and wait for the troops to retreat first! However, when the cavalry rushed into the crowd, he completely felt the power of the ancient Yin Shen formation. After a fight, the two soldiers around him fell under the saber, and because of his strong strength, he fired nine swords at the same time, beheading many cavalrymen, and each of them was broken into pieces by the sword energy and the extremely fast sword, and these resurrected corpses stopped the offensive. But he himself was surrounded by several cavalry resurrected corpses again. Although your resurrected corpses could not hurt him at all, they blocked his way. Afterwards, the overwhelming spells came towards him, unable to resist, and extremely embarrassed.

Finally, the Huangdao League finally retreated and sent out a signal of successful retreat. Seeing this, Gu Zihao hurriedly used his sword to pick up several powerful sabers, and then muttered: "Nine swords, dodge." After that, he disappeared. After that, he didn't even look at the group of cavalry resurrected corpses behind him, and walked away.

After he took a few steps, the group of cavalry resurrected corpses slowly broke apart. There were no more resurrected corpses, and there were only piles of minced meat on the ground!

However, Ye Ye and his group saw Gu Zihao's actions clearly in the dark, and they all sighed at Gu Zihao's strength! But when they saw that the Huangdao League member who was killed by the resurrected corpse was resurrected again, Ye Ye also quickly issued an order to retreat. How can you stay in a place of right and wrong for long?

After everyone dispersed, they didn't see that four huge faces appeared in the sky where the Huangdao League and the Star Spirits had just fought!

When retreating, Ye Ye's peripheral vision seemed to see something, but when he looked carefully, there was nothing around. He shook his head in confusion and left.

After Ye Ye and his group walked away, two people appeared in the darkness. They were Feng Yi and Xia Feng who were on a mission to follow Ye Ye's whereabouts!

"I didn't expect that your hiding skills were so poor, and you almost got exposed!" Xia Feng still said coldly, without seeing Feng Yi in her eyes.

Feng Yi almost got exposed just now, but fortunately Xia Feng used a hiding skill to help him avoid being discovered. Even if Xia Feng said that, Feng Yi couldn't say anything back. He just looked at the direction where Ye Ye and his group left and followed them.

A few hours later, after Ye Ye and his group retreated to a safe place, they discussed today's battle!

"What happened just now? Why did the dead suddenly come back to life?" After settling down, Ye Ye looked at the several consuls who came out together and asked.

Everyone shook their heads!

Ye Ye also shook his head helplessly and said: "If it's like this every time, how can we take advantage of the situation? If it keeps like this, then the Star Spirit will win! In the end, we are dead!" Ye Ye said sternly.

Ye Hen thought for a while and said: "Then let's choose to help the Zodiac Alliance? First, we will recover the disadvantage, and then the two sides will fight fairly again, so that we can have a chance to be the oriole." Everyone knows that the mantis stalks the cicada, and the oriole is behind!

Ye Ye had no choice but to nod.

On the Zodiac Alliance side, the morale was very low. Facing the almost invincible resurrected corpse, how could the morale of that army be high?

Gu Zihao stood in front of the generals with a stern face and said lightly: "Everyone, don't be like this! I don't believe that the Xingling formation can be moved! Everyone take a rest, retreat thirty miles tomorrow, and then wait for the attack again!" In Gu Zihao's mind, the general formation cannot be moved, and the larger the formation, the more difficult it is to arrange. The Xingling must have arranged it a long time in advance. Once it is out of the range of the formation, then the Huangdao League will win!

But is it like this? The morale of the Xingling organized by Boss Xing is not high, and it is dead. At this time, if someone approaches the Xingling army, they will be surprised to find that this group of people are like zombies. Although they do what people do, they are extremely rigid! Even the bending of their arms is like a machine!

But Boss Xing and the seven brothers of the Xing family are sitting in the camp. The atmosphere is extremely excited, which is completely opposite to the outside of the camp!

They laughed arrogantly, and behind Boss Xing, a gust of gloomy wind blew lightly.

Chapter 32: Draw

Facing the invincibility of the ancient Yin God Formation of Xingling, the Huangdao League chose to retreat, which was helpless! And for Yemen who wanted to be the yellow bird behind the scenes, they were also helpless. They saw the strength of Xingling and the retreat of Huangdao League. In order to balance the strength of both sides, they had to choose to help or secretly interfere and make trouble, so that the Huangdao League and Xingling could fight directly, and then after the war between the two sides, they would be the yellow bird behind the scenes and the fisherman.

But Ye Ye didn't know that all his actions had long been conveyed to Gu Zihao's ears, but he didn't care. In his mind, even if the small Yemen wanted to be the yellow bird behind the scenes, the fisherman didn't have that ability! So he just issued an order for Feng Yi and Xia Feng to continue tracking, and then continued to work on this war with Xingling!

"If we follow the current marching speed of Xingling, it will take about four days to arrive here! But why does Boss Xing let the army move so slowly? Isn't he afraid of insufficient food and grass? Or isn't he afraid of four days, I set a trap, and then fall into it?" In the meeting room, Gu Zihao said puzzledly with the reconnaissance record just sent by the scout.

After Gu Zihao finished speaking, everyone under him also shook their heads to indicate that they didn't know, and then an old man with a long beard stood up and said: "Alliance leader, maybe Xingling's victory in the last encounter made him underestimate the enemy! This is a good opportunity. Since Xingling has given us time, why don't we follow his arrangement of the formation and use it to get back the low morale last time!" The old man's origin is unknown. He had been sent by Gu Zihao to guard the gate of Batianguan before. Naturally, he is strong enough to guard Batianguan!

After listening to it, Gu Zihao thought for a while, nodded and said: "What you said is indeed possible! However, since Xing Ling dared to take such time out, he must have a killer move! What formation should be arranged?" There are many formations in the world. Gu Zihao has not studied the formations thoroughly, and he doesn't know what formation to use to face Xing Ling.

The old man pinched his beard, stepped out of his seat, and thought about it. After a long time, he smiled and said in the hot eyes of everyone: "Leader, if you don't mind that I am old and confused, you can leave this matter to me. How about it?"

Gu Zihao saw that there was a way but did not agree immediately, but said sternly: "I can leave it to you! But if I don't do it well..." The old man was also a shrewd person and naturally understood the hidden meaning of Gu Zihao's words. He immediately said slowly: "If I don't do it well or fail, I will come to apologize with my old head!" It seems that the old man is extremely confident in this formation!

"Okay! Then what formation do you want to use? What do you need, and how many people and horses?" Gu Zihao asked.

Old Wen smiled faintly and said with a rosy face: "What formation to use, please rest assured, it will not be bad! As for the objects and people, the requirements are not high. Only two hundred strong men are needed, and a few drops of their morning blood are taken. The objects only need top-grade jade!"

After listening to the old man's report of the formation, Gu Zihao thought about it and suddenly said excitedly: "Qin Weng is really insightful, this formation is OK! Although I don't know much about your formation, I know that the more blood you take, the better. Two hundred strong men's morning blood is definitely not enough! I will appoint one thousand strong men to take blood for you! But don't hurt their lives! You can control the manpower of each department! This matter must be done well! Otherwise..." Gu Zihao thought about it, and thought to himself that a formation would definitely be able to catch all the star spirits! Although he was confident in this formation, he still said harsh words in advance! After all, there is no joking in the army! Qin Weng smiled and said: "I will definitely live up to the expectations of the leader!" After speaking, he took the order and left. Gu Zihao dispersed the crowd, and then looked at their backs as they left. His expression suddenly became very cold and he said to himself: "Since you gave me time, don't blame me for being ruthless!"

"Oh, Brother Gu! Why are you like that again? So scary!" Gu Zihao continued to look cold after he finished speaking, but was unexpectedly seen by Xia Wanjun and Ye Xincheng who walked in. Xia Wanjun said coquettishly.

Gu Zihao immediately changed his expression to a gentle one and said to Ye Xincheng and Xia Wanjun: "You are here? Haha, in four days, you will watch the battle with me and see how I defeat Xingling!"

Ye Xincheng did not speak, but nodded lightly. At this time, he had changed his appearance, a scholar in a green shirt! But there was no fan in his hand! After hearing this, Xia Wanjun pulled Ye Xincheng's arm and said excitedly: "Okay! Brother Ye, let's go together! We haven't been on the battlefield to kill the enemy for a long time! Although I can't go this time, I can encourage you from the side!" Xia Wanjun was like a child.

Ye Xincheng and Gu Zihao laughed happily at the same time! Ye Xincheng thought to himself: After a thousand years, I finally experienced such a life again!

Four days passed in a flash! The star spirits slowly appeared, and the Huangdao League had already set up the formation the day before! Waiting for the star spirits to fall into the trap!

"Brother, this Huangdao League looks so confident, I'm afraid..." Xing Yu looked at Gu Zihao, Ye Xincheng and Xia Wanjun on the command platform in the distance with a telescope, drinking and talking as if no one was around, and couldn't help but say worriedly.

"Humph, it doesn't matter! Even if it's a trap? Let's see how we break the formation! Since they want us to go in, then we will go in! Fulfill their wish!" Boss Xing said confidently, and continued to lead the troops slowly forward!

In the dark, the soldiers of Yemen were still lying in ambush. However, they still looked at Gu Zihao and the other two drinking and talking freely on the command platform in confusion. Ye Ye said, "There must be a trick! Maybe, we don't need to take action!" Ye Ye saw that there was a trick, said to the people around him, and then gave the order to wait quietly!

"They are coming in! Hehe, let's start!" Qin Weng mixed in a group of people and then gave the order to charge!

Qin Weng was very satisfied with the formation he laid this time, and thought wildly in his heart: Hum, this formation is the Refining Yang Formation! Use the blood of the strong man in the morning, mix it with the top-grade jade, bury it in the ground, enter this formation, and you can restore your blood and qi, and even heal immediately without being injured! On the contrary, the local area can absorb the blood and essence to replenish it into this formation, and it can improve its own ability! It can even pour the supplemented blood and essence on one person at once, making him like a heavenly soldier and general descending to the earth, invincible! Moreover, the most terrifying thing is... Haha, unless your ancient Yin God formation can be moved, you will die!

Qin Weng thought slowly and confidently!

If this formation is in accordance with Qin Weng's idea, it is indeed invincible! But why is Boss Xing still so confident?

Boss Xing saw a group of people coming, raised his hand and ordered everyone behind him to stop marching, and then suddenly made way for a road from the troops behind him. From this road, the sound of horse hooves stomping on the ground suddenly came! It was the cavalry and those spell soldiers who were resurrected four days ago!

At this time, they have been blessed with acceleration, and they are thinking about the thousands of people led by Qin Weng! Go forward!

The two sides soon came into contact!

The Lianyang formation is indeed magical. It actually allowed the thousands of elite soldiers led by Qin Weng to resist the impact of the cavalry, and they only suffered minor injuries! But often, as soon as the blood appeared on the elite soldiers of the Zodiac Alliance, the ground flashed red, and the injuries healed immediately! And they became more vigorous! The battle with the resurrected corpse ended in a tie!

Gu Zihao, who was standing on the command platform, saw the fighting below and felt that victory was gradually approaching him. He couldn't help but smile confidently towards Boss Xing.

Gu Zihao's smile fell into Boss Xing's telescope. Boss Xing was not upset, but said more calmly: "Lian Yang? Haha"

Chapter 33: Retreating step by step

"Brother Zihao, you know I really don't like them fighting like that. I don't want to watch it!" Xia Wanjun looked at the fighting in the distance. Although she couldn't hear the sound of fighting from a distance, the scene she saw was too bloody. Xia Wanjun didn't like it very much!

Gu Zihao looked at Xia Wanjun caressingly, then looked at Ye Xincheng, and saw Ye Xincheng nodded to him before saying: "Okay, let's end it!" After that, he stood up, walked to the giant drum on the left side of the command platform, picked up the drumstick, and hammered it hard.

Bang bang bang... The exciting drum sounded.

Qin Weng was mixed in with thousands of people and commanded the Lianyang formation. When he heard the drum sound, he laughed immediately! Then he began to chant: "Lianyang refines the infinite, the infinite is nothing. Lianyang refines the universe, yin and yang are the limit! Lianyang, infinite life!" A long spell was chanted from Qin Weng's mouth. After that, the Lianyang formation, which involved a wide range of things, suddenly emitted an extremely hot light. The people who were illuminated couldn't open their eyes.

Suddenly, the red light penetrated into the bodies of all the members of the Huangdao League in the formation!

"Ah...ah!" Roars rang out, and the elite soldiers of the Huangdao League suddenly swelled up, with their muscles showing blocky shapes, just like soldiers from heaven descending to earth! Suddenly, the world seemed to be quiet. Even the resurrected corpses were stunned and unable to move!

Qin Weng actually used the ability of the Lianyang formation to gather yang, and evenly distributed the energy collected in the past few days to everyone, which would have such an effect!

"Lianyang Wuji Sheng, Sheng is infinite!" The loud voice of Qin Weng suddenly rang out in the quiet world! After the voice, the red light flashed again, and a group of red light appeared around each person. After a few breaths, the red light suddenly turned into a human form, and finally the light dissipated!

Shockingly! There was an extra person who looked exactly like him around each member of the Huangdao League! All of them had blocky muscles, which was obviously the result of absorbing the power of the Lianyang formation!

It turned out that the Lianyang formation had such an effect! This is the most terrifying part of the Lianyang formation. The Lianyang formation can actually copy the people in it! And it was a strengthened person!

After doing all this, Qin Weng suddenly softened, but a flash of blood-red light instantly restored his strength: "It's over! Go!" Qin Weng looked at the elite soldiers around him who were like gods descending from heaven, and said with a playful look in his eyes.

"Oh?" Boss Xing showed a surprised expression, but soon calmed down and said: "So that's it! Well, enough of the show, it's time to deal with you! Go!" After that, four black gloomy winds floated out from behind Boss Xing, and after the gloomy winds floated out, they disappeared into the air! But soon, their figures suddenly appeared around this huge battlefield. Boss Xing also dismounted, placed the stone slab on the ground again, got on the horse again, and finally issued an order for the resurrected corpse to attack with all his strength.

As soon as the order was given, the resurrected corpse suddenly burst out with its original power, instantly knocking down several unguarded elite soldiers of the Huangdao League around him, and then several resurrected cavalrymen immediately surrounded it and killed it! After that, the same trick was used again, and many elite soldiers were also killed!

However, the strengthened elite soldiers were very clear-headed and immediately fought back, fighting with the resurrected corpses. The entire battlefield suddenly became chaotic, with spells, attacks, and shouts coming one after another!

The strengthened elite soldiers were very strong, but the resurrected corpses had no sense of pain, and they could only be completely killed by dismembering them. Taking advantage of this advantage, many strengthened elite soldiers were killed.

However, Qin Weng had been controlling the formation. Every time an elite soldier fell, another elite soldier would be copied! It was really like they could not be killed! However, after the resurrected elite soldiers were killed, there were corpses on the ground! They would not disappear! Moreover, when the resurrected corpses' sabers chopped them, no blood would flow out, only a slight flash of red light. If the wounds were not serious, they would heal immediately. If the wounds were too serious, they would naturally not heal!

After a long time, many resurrected corpses in the field were decomposed, and a large number of copied elite soldiers were piled on the ground!

"The time has come, big brother, let's start?" Xing Yu said carefully, and the boss Xing nodded after listening. Seeing this,

Xing Yu raised the flag in his hand high, as if commanding something!

Qin Weng, who was mixed in the elite soldiers, looked at the fight between the replica elite soldiers and the resurrected corpses with disdain, and said lightly: "Hmph, you dare to be so presumptuous? Go to hell!" After that, he recited the spell again, and the replica soldiers increased again.

But suddenly, something strange happened.

A replica elite soldier who fell beside an elite soldier suddenly stood up, and looked at the elite soldier fiercely with the weapon in his hand. The elite soldier was caught off guard and was hit in the head by a sharp knife. Half of his head was lost and he fell down.

Not only that, all the fallen replica elite soldiers stood up and launched a crazy attack on the "kind" around them!

"Ancient Yin God Formation!" Qin Weng's confident smile suddenly froze, and he said tremblingly.

Gu Zihao, who was on the command platform, suddenly dropped the wine glass in his hand and said in shock: "Ancient Yin God Formation! How is it possible! It can be set up so quickly! That is a divine formation! I have been setting it up for four days!" As he spoke, Gu Zihao immediately ran to the drum again and hit the heavy drum, but the sound was very urgent, it was an order to retreat!

The sound of the drum spread thousands of miles, and Qin Weng naturally heard it. He continued to summon the replica soldiers, and then ran back with the elite soldiers of the real people around him.

But those resurrected corpses seemed to have a great hatred for them and kept chasing them. Qin Weng had no choice but to retreat quickly while continuing to summon the replica soldiers to block their way! However, those replica soldiers were copied from the real elite soldiers. This refining spirit was too magical. It could even copy the mood. At this moment, those elite soldiers were all terrified. How could they have the mood to fight! In this way, those replica soldiers also lost their fighting spirit and were quickly killed by those resurrected corpses, and then resurrected again. Suddenly, the number of resurrected corpses became terrifying!

The elite soldiers of the Huangdao League were defeated under the leadership of Qin Weng!

"Hahaha! Gu Zihao, thank you for your gift. Now my army has so many more! Hahaha!" Seeing that he had completely eaten the opponent's chess piece, Boss Xing was very happy and roared to Gu Zihao from a distance. Boss Xing's voice spread very far!

When the voice reached Gu Zihao's ears, Gu Zihao's face turned pale! He took two steps back, but fortunately Ye Xincheng supported him from behind so that he would not fall down.

Ye Xincheng looked at Gu Zihao like this, and hurriedly called Xia Wanjun to his side and said nervously: "It seems that we have no choice but to use that trick!"

"Retreat!" Ye Ye was in no mood to watch any more, and hurriedly issued an order to retreat and retreated to a safe place.

Chapter 34 Appearance

This ancient Yin Shen formation is invincible! It can even revive the elite soldiers of the Huang Dao League! Looking at the tens of thousands of resurrected corpses standing in front of him, Boss Xing couldn't help but laugh proudly: "Hahahaha, in ancient times, if the emperor hadn't used the Xuanyuan Sword to restrain this ancient Yin Shen formation, the world would have changed hands long ago. How could it be this turn? Humph, but the Xuanyuan Sword has disappeared. It's just a foolish dream for the Huang Dao League to defeat me!"

"Hahahaha, big brother, now we can defeat the Huang Dao League without that!" Xing Yu and several other brothers of the Xing family said at the same time.

Boss Xing listened more and more proudly and said: "Haha, how could they expect that my Yin Shen formation can move? Once Huang Dao is destroyed, the next one will be Yemen, and then the whole world! What is unfinished will be completed on us! Haha!"

Hahahahaha, the brothers of the Xing family immediately knew that they were even happier! Behind them, four gusts of Yin wind suddenly blew silently, making the chess pieces in the camp rustle.

The war was divided into three parties, the war between the Huangdao League and the Star Spirit. At present, it seems that the Star Spirit has an absolute advantage with an ancient Yin God formation, while the Huangdao League is losing ground.

On the other hand, Ye Ye has always chosen to keep calm and continue to observe the situation. For this war, the relatively weak Yemen can only choose to fish in troubled waters. However, when the people of Yemen saw that the Star Spirit was powerful, they immediately changed their strategy!

"I guess you all saw how powerful the Star Spirit was just now?" Ye Ye stood with his hands behind his back and asked the people in front of him.

Everyone was silent. Ye Ye sighed and continued, "There must be something treacherous in this Star Spirit! I want to go in and explore it! Yang Hengchao, what do you think?"

Yang Hengchao heard Ye Ye asking him, but did not answer. After thinking for a long time, he was about to speak, but someone beat him to it. It was Yang Tianhai: "That formation is called the Ancient Yin God Formation. It was used by Chi You in ancient times to fight against the emperor, but was finally broken by the Xuanyuan Sword!"

A shocking statement! Yang Tianhai's words shocked everyone! The Ancient Yin God Formation, just by hearing the name, you know that it is a formation passed down from ancient times! Terrible! However, if this was said by someone else, maybe everyone would not believe it, but this was said by Yang Tianhai, who is a punisher and has absorbed the memories of the punisher clan, so it is naturally credible!

After a long time, Ye Ye said solemnly again: "In this case, it must be extremely difficult for them to set up this formation! Why did Xing Ling take out this formation for the second time? We must find out the truth! We must not let Xing Ling destroy Huang Dao, otherwise, it will be Ye Men who will perish later!" After saying that, Ye Ye limped back and forth for two steps, and then continued: "We will set off at midnight today. We don't need too many people. Yang Hengchao; Li Bin, you two can go with me! Yang Tianhai, you stay behind in case of an emergency! Ye Hen, you meet us outside Xing Ling Camp!"

"But this trip is extremely dangerous! Can the three of us do it?" Li Bin said worriedly.

Ye Ye smiled and said helplessly: "We have to go even if we can't! Just sneak in and explore! There is no need for too many things, be careful, it should be fine!"

Seeing that Ye Ye had made up his mind, everyone didn't say anything more! They had to rest for the time being, wait for the arrival of night, and then act.

But no one saw that Yang Tianhai, who was behind the crowd, suddenly raised his mouth and showed a playful look in his eyes: "Hmph, it seems that it's time to meet old friends!"

"Huh? Yang Tianhai, what are you talking about?" Ye Hen, who was in front of Yang Tianhai, heard Yang Tianhai's mumbling and asked in confusion. Yang Tianhai smiled dumbly and said, "No, I was wondering why the ancient Yin God formation was so powerful. I really want to see it!" Ye Hen didn't say anything when he heard it, turned around and walked out. He didn't see the weirdness in Yang Tianhai's eyes when he turned around!

At the same time that Ye Men decided to explore Xingling at night, Huang Daomeng also made a decision!

"Xincheng, do we only have that trick?" Xia Wanjun asked worriedly. In this huge meeting room, there are only Gu Zihao, Ye Xincheng and Xia Wanjun, and they can talk freely.

Ye Xincheng touched Xia Wanjun's head lovingly and said helplessly: "That Yin God Formation is too powerful! Apart from that trick, we have no choice! However, everything depends on Zihao!" Ye Xincheng turned around and looked at Gu Zihao.

Gu Zihao sat on the chair without saying a word, with his fingers crossed in front of him. The iron mask covered his face. I don't know what he was thinking! Ye Xincheng and Xia Wanjun looked at him, waiting for his decision. The whole meeting room was unusually quiet!

After a long time, a long sigh suddenly came from under the iron mask. Gu Zihao supported the table with both hands, stood up and said: "Okay, we have no choice but to do that! I can't let the ancient Yin God Formation defeat us. That's our only chance!" After that, Gu Zihao did something that would surprise everyone except Ye Xincheng and Xia Wanjun.

He actually took out a dagger and stabbed it in the head, but it was not self-mutilation. The dagger stabbed directly into the gap of the mask. Then Gu Zihao roared, exerted force with his hands, and with a click, the mask split into two halves and fell to the ground. Only then could he see clearly that the inside of the mask was engraved with inscriptions, flashing with a faint light.

Ye Xincheng and Xia Wanjun also looked at Gu Zihao happily.

Gu Zihao slowly raised his head, then turned his long hair to one side, revealing his face!

Shock! Under that cold and terrifying mask, there was such a face hidden! A charming face, a face that men would envy and women would be jealous of! A handsome face that was almost like a demon!

"Suck!" Gu Zihao took a deep breath, and then said: "How long has it been? How long has it been since I breathed fresh air through the mask!"

"Zihao! Great! This time, we will definitely be able to break the formation!" Xia Wanjun said happily as she looked at Gu Zihao.

Gu Zihao shook his head and said, "It's impossible to break the formation! The ancient Yin God formation, even the emperor couldn't do anything to it, and it was the Xuanyuan Sword that finally restrained the formation. We can only contend with it! However, as long as we can contend with it, why should we fear the Star Spirit!" After saying that, Gu Zihao raised his hands in front of him and suddenly clenched them.

In an instant, a transparent air wave spread. This air wave did not hurt people, but kept passing until it reached Xing Boss, and then it stopped.

After Gu Zihao took off his mask, in addition to his charming face, he actually had such terrifying power! And the air wave that Gu Zihao spread just now was to demonstrate to Xing Boss!

"Oh? It seems that Gu Zihao has found a helper? Haha, but it's fine." Gu Zihao sent out the air wave for Xing Boss, and Xing Boss naturally felt it. Surprise flashed by, and he continued to squint his eyes to rest.

"What a powerful force!" This wave of energy started from the Huangdao League camp and spread thousands of miles away. The people of Yemen also naturally felt it, knowing that the Huangdao League had gained another powerful helper in this war. But they all doubted whether this master could compete with the ancient Yin Shen formation! Of course, they all believed in their hearts that the master could not! Although they didn't know that this strange force was their acquaintance!

Chapter 35 Night Exploration of Xingling

Night fell quickly, and Ye Ye and the other two were ready to explore Xingling at night.

The location where Yemen was stationed was not far from where Xingling was stationed, or to say, not far from the Zodiac Alliance and Xingling. In order to grasp the movements of both parties, Ye Ye decisively decided to choose the location between the Zodiac Alliance and Xingling.

At night, after wearing night clothes, Ye Ye and the other two set off.

Tonight, there was no moon, and the heavy dark clouds also obscured the starlight, giving people a solemn feeling, as if the dark clouds were condensed from the breath of death.

After a long time, the three of them came to the outside of Xingling Camp with the faint fire in their hands and blew out the lights.

"Okay, pay attention, first check the situation of the guards separately, and gather here after you hold an incense stick!" Ye Ye said in the weeds not far from Xingling Camp.

Qin Minglei and Li Bin did not speak, but nodded secretly and began to explore. After seeing them leave, Ye Ye pulled up the cloth covering his face and went to investigate.

Ye Ye ran outside the camp in the dark, crouched down, and then looked at the situation inside. He was immediately surprised: Why is it so dark? Resting so early? But even if they are resting, there should be a patrol team!

Ye Ye walked slowly to the camp gate with doubts in his heart, and suddenly he was even more surprised: Why is there no one guarding the camp gate? Go back and discuss with them first.

Thinking of this, Ye Ye continued to bend his waist and returned to the weeds.

Ye Ye returned to the weeds and waited for a long time before seeing Qin Minglei and Li Bin return. ,

Li Bin pulled off the cloth covering his face and said with a puzzled look: "No one! It's like a dead city!"

Qin Minglei nodded after hearing this, indicating that the situation he saw was the same as Li Bin's.

Ye Ye frowned and said, "Is this a trap? However, knowing that there are tigers in the mountains, we still go to the tiger mountains! I just checked the main gate, and there are no guards, not even patrolling soldiers! Let's go in through the main gate openly."

After that, the three of them did not communicate again. After a short rest, the three of them walked together and headed towards Xingling.

Sure enough, there was no one in Xingling! There were no guards at the door, no patrolling soldiers, and even the torch that was supposed to be lit was extinguished. Qin Minglei touched the torch and whispered, "It's cold, and there is no ashes! It looks like it has never been used!"

Ye Ye was even more confused after hearing this, and then walked into a tent casually.

The tent was unusually quiet, there was no deafening snoring, and even the breathing sound that should have been there was gone!

Ye Ye thought about it, took out the fire starter, blew it up, looked at the situation in the tent, and was immediately shocked. There were dozens of people standing in the barracks. They closed their eyes and stood there like that. It was very strange.

Qin Minglei and Li Bin saw Ye Ye getting angry, and they also walked into the tent. They were also frightened! Li Bin walked towards the standing people in confusion, and carefully touched his nose with his hand, and then said coldly: "Dead!"

"These should be resurrected corpses! But where are they?" Ye Ye said, and then walked out of the tent and entered the next tent, where there were still resurrected corpses standing.

The three of them did not give up, and continued to carefully explore the Star Spirit, but when they entered most of the tents, they gave up the exploration and said solemnly: "All are resurrected corpses! Is this their resurrected corpse camp?"

"No, no! Look there!" Ye Ye said, pointing to the tent in the middle, where a general flag was flying. Qin Minglei and Li Bin were not ordinary people, and their eyesight was also very good at night, so they looked over immediately. Li Bin said: "The general flag is here, so how can there be no soldiers?"

Ye Ye shook his head and said nothing.

Suddenly, a gust of cold wind blew, and the three people had goose bumps.

"Haha! This is the stone slab that the eldest brother treasured! With it, the world will be yours." A voice suddenly sounded softly from the tent of the commander that Ye Ye pointed to.

From the voice, Ye Ye and the other two knew who that person was, Xing Yu, Xing Lao Si!

The three of them moved over and eavesdropped on Xing Yu's words from the outside.

There was no one else in the commander's tent, only Xing Yu, who seemed to be holding something in his hand. Moreover, that thing emitted a faint blue light through the tent!

"Alas, it's a pity that this thing can't be carried for a long time at night. It's really unsafe. But who can steal it at night?" Xing Yu suddenly sighed, then gently opened a box, put the things in his hand into the box, locked it with the key, and walked out of the tent.

After seeing him walk away, Ye Ye and the other two secretly remembered the direction he walked, and then the three of them entered the tent.

In addition to a few tables and chairs, there was also a large gold-plated box in the tent. The three walked towards the box in the dark. Qin Minglei took out a thin wire from his clothes, twisted the head into a hook, and put it into the lock of the box, slowly hooking it.

"Click." The box opened. Qin Minglei was a disciple of a master of tomb robbing. How could a small lock be difficult for him?

Ye Ye opened the box, and the blue light emanated again, illuminating the entire tent.

After a brief surprise, Ye Ye picked up the things in the box. It turned out to be a stone slab! If Ye Ye and his team had carefully watched Boss Xing's actions during the day, they would have found that this stone slab was the one that Boss Xing took out and placed on the ground in the two battles!

The three puzzled people looked at the stone slab emitting a faint blue light, and they didn't know what it was.

"Take it away first, and talk later!" Ye Ye said decisively, then took the stone slab and prepared to rush out. They had to rush. The stone slab emitted a faint blue light. Even if all the Star Spirits were resurrected corpses, they didn't know whether they could move during the day. But Xing Yu had just gone out. If they alarmed the seven brothers, Ye Ye and the other two would have to lose their lives.

Without saying a word, the three rushed out immediately. However, they didn't see that there were four black gusts of wind behind them. The wind was extremely strange. In fact, they had already appeared when Ye Ye took the stone slab, but when Ye Ye and the other two rushed out, they suddenly disappeared.

Ye Ye and the other two, who were sprinting to escape as soon as possible, didn't know that all the resurrected corpses in every tent of the Star Spirit had opened their eyes! Red bloodthirsty eyes!

Chapter 36 Two corpses, fight!

When Ye Ye and the other two were thinking about quickly taking the mysterious slate away from the Xingling camp, none of them saw the four gusts of Yin wind following behind them, and the resurrected corpses with bloodthirsty eyes in each tent!

If any of them could get close to observe the situation after Boss Xing put the slate during the daytime battle, they would see the four gusts of Yin wind, which were the Yin winds that appeared on the battlefield but disappeared in a flash, and no one saw them!

Ye Ye and the other two were still running desperately. Suddenly, a hand stretched out from their left, and the hand actually broke through the tent and grabbed Qin Minglei's arm tightly. Qin Minglei was slightly startled, and without any hesitation, he immediately drew out his dagger and slashed at the arm fiercely. The arm was cut off, and the three continued to run.

But suddenly, all the tents in front of them shook violently, and Ye Ye and the other two had to stop and observe what was going to happen.

In those tents, countless arms suddenly tore through the cloth tents, shaking in the open, arms everywhere, looking very scary.

"Roar!" A series of inhuman roars sounded, and then the tents were torn apart, and countless resurrected corpses swarmed out. They had no weapons in their hands, so they raised their hands and grabbed Ye Ye and the other two. The three immediately took out their weapons and fought back. The three had seen such scenes, and even more terrifying scenes than this, so they could organize a better counterattack. In their minds now, those resurrected corpses were just thicker than the zombies controlled by Gu Weng at the beginning.

However, among the group of resurrected corpses, waves of light of different colors gradually flashed, and Ye Ye and the other two knew that it was the resurrected corpses of the spell casting auxiliary spells.

Gray, thick defense like mud, gold, sharp attack like metal, green, damaged recovery... and so on. More and more resurrected corpses were blessed by the auxiliary spells of the spell soldiers, and the three gradually couldn't bear it, so they had to form horns and rotate each other to defend. However, anyone knows that such a defense will not last long in this sea of corpses!

Because it is now dark, the four people can only see a range of no more than ten meters. If it were daytime, they would see four huge black human-shaped winds hovering above their heads. And all the resurrected corpses swarmed towards Ye Ye and the other two who seemed to be shrouded by the wind.

"Da Da Da Da..." Suddenly, a series of chaotic horse hoof sounds sounded from all around. Then in an instant, resurrected cavalry corpses rushed up from all around Ye Ye and the others.

The resurrected cavalry corpse was also very good. It controlled a resurrected horse and jumped high. Regardless of whether there were other resurrected corpses below, it jumped high, picked up the saber in its hand, and chopped Huashan with one move, heading towards Ye Ye and the other two.

This move was impossible for the three to resist. In a flash, the three made the same move. When the three saw the cavalry jumping up, they immediately squatted down and used the sharp weapons in their hands to cut off the legs of the resurrected corpses. After that, they rolled on the ground and avoided the fierce and deadly Huashan attacks from the resurrected cavalry corpses.

However, even though they avoided the attacks of the cavalry resurrected corpses, they were surrounded by the resurrected infantry, and the three of them were separated and could not form a horn to resist the attacks again. Suddenly, all three of them were injured. If this continued, they would still die soon, and their death would be even more miserable than before!

Although Ye Ye was injured, it was not serious. However, he did not care about the injuries. While he was barely resisting, he actually thought: "Why did these resurrected corpses move on their own without anyone controlling them? Is it because I took this stone tablet?" Thinking of this, Ye Ye touched the stone tablet in his chest.

Ye Ye didn't know that, in fact, this stone slab was the center of the ancient Yin God formation, and those human-shaped Yin Feng...

"Hiss." Ye Ye, who was distracted by thinking about things, was suddenly cut by the resurrected corpse with a small dagger on his arm. These resurrected corpses didn't know when they had taken up weapons. Suddenly, the attack power increased sharply!

Ye Ye and the other two set out at Yinshi, and now it is close to Maoshi. The sky is about to dawn. But the three of them are still barely resisting, and they are getting weaker and weaker! Gradually unable to resist.

"Roar!" Suddenly, a violent and angry roar sounded, and this roar even temporarily shocked all the resurrected corpses.

"Roar!" Another sound, but compared with the previous sound, this sound is a little sharper.

Ye Ye took the opportunity to turn his head and saw that the roar was actually from Li Bin and Qin Minglei. Qin Minglei, who had been resisting for a long time, was already covered with wounds and bleeding. And Li Bin actually had a wound that healed very slowly!

At this time, there was no resurrected corpse beside them. Qin Minglei, covered in blood, was as red as if he had just been reborn from the ashes, with a face full of anger, and his fangs stretched out long from his mouth, howling to the sky. Qin Minglei, on the contrary, was covered in black stripes, extremely weird, and actually echoed Qin Minglei's roar.

The two of them turned into corpses!

What was even more surprising was that their roars actually suppressed the resurrected corpses! Although it was only temporary. However, at least it gave Ye Ye time to react. Ye Ye didn't think much about it, and broke through several resurrected corpses in succession and arrived at Qin Minglei and Li Bin.

At this time, the scene was very quiet. The moon didn't know when to show up. Suddenly, a breeze blew, blowing Ye Ye's hair slightly. After the breeze, the resurrected corpse seemed to suddenly wake up and howled at the same time. There were so many resurrected corpses that they overwhelmed the pressure caused by Qin Minglei and the others!

"Pah!" Two consecutive horse hooves sounded, and a resurrected cavalry corpse suddenly jumped high, using the same trick again, and split Huashan with force.

Ye Ye turned around, but it was too late to dodge.

Li Bin's mouth corners suddenly rose slightly, and when the saber was about to chop them from above, he suddenly swung his fist and hit the resurrected cavalry corpse in the air. No, that's not right, it should be hitting the saber in the hand of the resurrected cavalry corpse.

With a "hum", the saber flew in response to the punch. , But Li Bin's attack did not end like this.

After Li Bin swung his right fist, his left fist was another fierce straight punch, hitting the horse chest under the resurrected cavalry corpse.

"Crack." A tooth-grinding fracture sound sounded, and Ye Ye looked carefully and saw that Li Bin's left arm bone had been broken and stabbed out of his hand. However, he shook his left hand as if nothing had happened. Extremely weird!

On the other hand, the resurrected cavalry corpse was actually knocked down from mid-air by Li Bin's punch. After falling to the ground, Qin Minglei took action, holding a strange-shaped dagger of the Night Gate in his hand, and danced vigorously. He did not give the resurrected cavalry corpse any chance, and had already dismembered it.

At this time, the sky was bright, and Qin Minglei and Li Bin, after doing all that, actually howled to the sky at the same time. It seemed to be a demonstration, and Ye Ye did not understand. In fact, the two of them howled because they sensed the four groups of Yin wind in the air!

The four groups of Yin wind in the sky were not small, and they were the components of the ancient Yin God Formation. How could they be so threatening by two people. Suddenly, they disappeared at the same time. Ye Ye looked up in confusion, and naturally did not see anything, only saw a sun about to rise in the east.

At this moment, the stone slab in Ye Ye's arms suddenly emitted a huge downward pulling force. Ye Ye could not hold it, and took out the stone slab and put it on the ground.

"Roar!" Ye Ye had just put down the stone slab, and those resurrected corpses actually howled again at the same time!

Chapter 37 Coincidence

As soon as the mysterious slate touched the ground, a faint blue light flashed and disappeared. Ye Ye was careful and saw the light emitted by the slate. He immediately squatted down and tried to pick up the slate. Unexpectedly, the slate was like embedded in the ground and could not be taken out!

Before Ye Ye could press the edge of the slate again, a resurrected corpse behind him had already grabbed the saber in the hand of the resurrected cavalry corpse that was just knocked away by Li Bin, and rushed towards Ye Ye fiercely. Seeing this, Ye Ye immediately rolled to the side, and the resurrected corpse's knife also chopped in vain.

"Ah!" Qin Minglei and Li Bin suddenly screamed violently again, and flattened their heads that were originally tilted up. Without saying a word, the two of them grabbed the weapons in their hands and rushed directly into the group of resurrected corpses.

Suddenly, the group of resurrected corpses became restless. Where Li Bin and Qin Minglei passed, broken arms and pieces of meat flew everywhere! However, the two of them did not have much time to dismember the endless resurrected corpses. Therefore, although they caused great damage to the resurrected corpses, it was not a big deal for the resurrected corpses that had no sense of pain. Even without their heads, they still rushed towards Qin Minglei and Li Bin.

"Huh" a gust of wind blew again for no reason. After the wind passed, the resurrected corpses actually gave up besieging Ye Ye and turned to Qin Minglei and Li Bin.

Ye Ye, who was temporarily proud of his safety, was immediately worried when he saw this situation. No matter how powerful Qin Minglei and Li Bin were, they could not withstand the siege of these endless resurrected corpses without pain!

But how could Ye Ye be immune? After a brief consideration, he took out a few phoenix thorns that had not been used for a long time from the treasure bag on his waist, and then rushed into the group of corpses.

The effect of the phoenix thorns was extremely terrifying. Ye Ye just stabbed the exposed parts of the resurrected corpses with the sharp part of the phoenix thorns, and the resurrected corpses immediately became immobile and could be cut and slaughtered! Soon, Ye Ye rushed to Li Bin and Qin Minglei. They formed a two-horn formation without knowing it was appropriate, and kept counterattacking and defending. It was completely contrary to the brave charge just now.

In fact, the terrifying thing about this ancient Yin Shen formation is that it resurrects all the creatures that died in the formation and is controlled by the controller. However, these resurrected corpses are resurrected based on soldiers. Even if there are many resurrected corpses strengthened by Lian Yang, they are ordinary people who are resurrected after strengthening. It is powerful. But there is no horror in ancient times.

In ancient times, the Yin Shen formation resurrected those ferocious monsters and powerful humans! How can this mere resurrection soldier be compared!

Even so, this Yin Shen formation is extremely terrifying and no one can break it!

And it is impossible for Ye Ye and the other two to rush out of this endless group of resurrected corpses with their meager strength! However, at this moment, these resurrected corpses are missing the controller, that is, the boss Xing! That's why they attacked blindly without any rules, which also gave Ye Ye and the other two a chance.

Ye Ye mixed in the group of corpses, and seemed to rely on the fact that the resurrected corpses would not attack him, so he used the Phoenix Thorn in his hand to pin down many resurrected corpses. It gave the three people a lot of breathing space.

"Buzz~" A metal collision sounded violently, and Ye Ye stopped his attack and looked at Qin Minglei and Li Bin. They were actually facing the copy elite soldiers who were strengthened by the Refining Yang Formation, copied, killed and resurrected (tragic fate!). Those strengthened soldiers had weapons in their hands and surrounded them in groups. Moreover, from behind these strong resurrected elite soldiers, countless fireballs, ice cones or fire talismans flew. It turned out that those resurrected spell soldiers started to attack after performing auxiliary.

The fireball and fire talisman were blind. After Ye Ye dodged a fire talisman, he ran to Qin Minglei and Li Bin without thinking, and stabbed those resurrected strengthened soldiers with the Phoenix Thorn in his hand. However, the Phoenix Thorn, which had always been invincible, failed for the first time!

Ye Ye clearly saw that the Phoenix Thorn had pierced the neck of the resurrection soldier, but a black line appeared on its neck. That was the poison of the Phoenix Thorn. The poison did not disperse, but accumulated in a small area where it was pierced.

Ye Ye did not know that those resurrection soldiers were copied from the Lianyang formation. They were bloodless and fleshless, but they were real and immune to all poisons.

After failing to hit the target, Ye Ye picked up the Phoenix Thorn again and stabbed the resurrection soldier, still in the same place, but the result was the same! The resurrection soldier was still full of energy, and the weapon in his hand was dancing vigorously.

Ye Ye had no choice but to put down the Phoenix Thorn, then drew out Ye Yang, combined it into a long sword, and attacked. Then he took advantage of the gap to look at Li Bin and Qin Minglei.

The two of them were no longer as brave as before. Although there was a bloodthirsty light in their eyes, a strong sense of fatigue became more and more obvious.

Suddenly, Li Bing roared violently and stopped attacking while defending. Instead, he jumped onto a resurrected corpse, and dark sharp bones had extended from his elbows.

After Li Bin jumped onto the resurrected corpse, he used the attack method that killed Saiben at that time. He stabbed the protruding sharp arm bones into the eyes of the resurrected corpse, and then opened his mouth wide and bit his head. The solid skull was bitten off directly, but Li Bin didn't even dislike it and ate it directly. He held the resurrected corpse on the ground, which was still struggling violently, with both hands. The scene was extremely bloody!

Although the resurrected corpse was bloodless and fleshless, Li Bin still ate it with relish. Soon, Li Bin seemed to be tired of the resurrected corpse that had been bitten to pieces under him, and then jumped onto another resurrected corpse and repeated the same trick!

Although there was a fatal hazard on the top of his head, the resurrected corpses had no fear nerves. In addition to attacking Li Bin who kept jumping and eating, the offensive against Qin Minglei was even more fierce!

Suddenly, Ye Ye felt a murderous aura appearing beside him. Looking back, it was Qin Minglei. He didn't know when the red and black corpse qi that appeared when he confronted Saiben at the Eight Heavens Gate appeared beside him. Murderous aura! A weapon of a resurrected and enhanced soldier chopped towards him, but was blocked by the murderous aura. Then the murderous aura slowly spread along the blade to the resurrected corpse, and the resurrected corpse was instantly wrapped in murderous aura.

Two breaths later, the murderous aura dissipated. The enhanced resurrected corpse was gone. But Qin Minglei became fierce again. It seemed that he absorbed the power of the enhanced resurrected corpse just now.

Not only Qin Minglei, but Li Bin, who had been constantly gnawing, also had the same situation. After Li Bin gnawed a lot of enhanced resurrected corpses, he became more ferocious. If you look closely at the wounds of Li Bin gnawing on those resurrected corpses, you will find that most of the parts Li Bin gnawed were the heart.

In fact, all this is not Li Bin. Qin Minglei and the two can absorb the power of others to restore themselves. All this is thanks to the Huangdao League!

These enhanced resurrected soldiers were copied from the enhanced soldiers or the enhanced soldiers themselves were resurrected by the ancient Yin God Formation after death. They absorbed the masculine blood collected by the Zodiac Alliance in the past few days. Even after death, they were immediately resurrected, and the extremely masculine and powerful masculine blood still remained in their chests. The two people who had transformed into corpses sensed the power contained in it, which caused the situation just now!

Chapter 38 Invited Breakfast

The sun slowly rose, and the sky in the east gradually became like a fish belly. The fiery red sun revealed half a shadow, illuminating the whole world. Very gentle.

However, it was still the same in Lu Ping. The breath of killing was transmitted crosswise.

Ye Ye looked at everything that had just happened, and his heart was very excited. His breathing was also very rapid, and his chest was up and down. Qin Minglei and Li Bin still stood there with their backs hunched, and a deterrent force deterred those thoughtless resurrected corpses.

However, in the Star Spirit Camp, which was originally slightly gentle under the sunlight, a breeze blew again. After the breeze, the resurrected corpses howled to the sky in unison, and then continued to attack.

Moreover, the attack became more fierce, and even Ye Ye, who had not attacked just now, was included in the attack range. The three of them were weak, and even if they were strong, they could not resist for too long.

Moreover, during the attack and counterattack, Ye Ye discovered that the Phoenix Thorn was useless against the resurrected copy elite soldiers, but it was very effective against other resurrected corpses! So, Ye Ye interspersed in the defense formation formed by Li Bin and Qin Minglei, bypassed the copy elite soldiers, and accurately stabbed the necks of other resurrected corpses with the Phoenix Thorn, paralyzing them.

Everyone knows that too many ants can kill an elephant. When the sun completely appeared above the horizon, the three of them were already tired. Qin Minglei and Li Bin used the same trick again, absorbing the blood essence of the copy resurrected elite soldiers again, and regaining their strength again. However, Ye Ye could not absorb it, and the Phoenix Thorn in his hand was no longer as accurate as before. He could only defend himself.

"No, I'm really dead this time!" Ye Ye took advantage of the gap and stood between Qin Minglei and Li Bin. He looked at the scene and couldn't help sighing in his heart. Suddenly, the hair on Ye Ye's forehead was blown by the breeze. Ye Ye, who was already sweating, suddenly shuddered and calmed down: "Right! That stone slab!" Ye Ye thought of the stone slab just now. It was that stone slab that caused the current situation.

"We must find the stone slab just now. Otherwise, Ye Hen and the others will come to rescue us after seeing that we haven't returned for so long, and then we will be completely destroyed! However, with so many resurrected corpses, we can't see where the stone slab on the ground will be." Ye Ye thought about it and couldn't help but worry.

Just when Ye Ye was worried, the resurrected corpses suddenly stopped, and the scene suddenly returned to silence. Ye Ye came back to his senses and saw that the resurrected corpses had all given up the attack and surrounded them, making it impossible to get through!

"Haha, who did I think it was! It turned out to be Master Ye! I don't know why you put my Xingling there?" A voice suddenly came from the sea of corpses. As soon as the voice fell, the sea of corpses in the west suddenly made way for a road, and seven people walked out of that road. It was the seven brothers of the Xing family. And the one who spoke was the dead Boss Xing!

Ye Ye was startled, looked around the surroundings, and said calmly: "It turned out to be Boss Xing, I wonder how he has been doing in the past six months?" Ye Ye looked very calm, but he was worried: "This Boss Xing is not dead, why?" The gap in strength made Ye Ye worried. He was not afraid, but he was afraid that the Yemen would be leaderless.

"Thank you for the greetings, Master Ye. I have been doing well in the past six months. What's the matter, Master Ye?" Boss Xing said with a fake smile. After saying that, he took something from Xing Yu's hand. Ye Ye looked at it carefully, and his pupils shrank into needles. That thing was the stone slab that Ye Ye wanted to find just now!

"Haha, Boss Xing, we are old friends, can't I visit you?" Ye Ye heard the murderous intention in Boss Xing's tone, and had to smile.

Hahahahahaha... The seven brothers of the Xing family laughed at the same time. "How can I not be happy that the head of the Night Sect actually visited me?" Boss Xing said with a smile. After saying that, he waved his hand, and all the resurrected corpses dispersed and started to work like ordinary soldiers. Not long after, the entire Xingling camp gradually began to see smoke rising from the cooking, just like the breakfast of an ordinary army.

Ye Ye looked at the resurrected corpses around him in surprise, and was amazed that those thoughtless resurrected corpses actually did what ordinary people did. He took a deep breath and said, "Excuse me! Now we have also seen the Xingling. If Boss Xing doesn't mind, the three of us will go first and visit next time." With that, Ye Ye wanted to leave.

"Oh? So you're leaving now? We are cooking breakfast in Xingling, why don't you stay and have a military meal before leaving?" Boss Xing said with a wicked smile.

After hearing this, Ye Ye raised his eyebrows and thought to himself: "This Boss Xing should have expected Ye Hen and the others to come and find us, and then destroy us all!" Although thinking this, he said: "Since Boss Xing has invited us like this, we would rather obey than respect! However, you can see that they are in their current state, it is not suitable for them to stay, let us go back and treat them!" Ye Ye's words were also very meaningful. On the one hand, he cleverly and decently refused Boss Xing's request to stay. On the other hand, Ye Ye guessed that Boss Xing saw the strength of Qin Minglei and the others, and let them know that even if something happened, once they fought hard, they would not let Boss Xing get any benefits.

Boss Xing frowned slightly, and continued to smile and said: "Don't worry, Master Ye, I still have military doctors in Xingling. If you don't mind, let my subordinates take a look at them, okay?" Boss Xing said again

Ye Ye had no choice but to say, "Okay, since Boss Xing invited us so sincerely, how can we not go? Right? Minglei, Li Bin?" Li Bin and the others couldn't hear him talking now, and Ye Ye said this deliberately for Boss Xing to hear.

"Roar!" But suddenly Qin Minglei and Li Bin roared at Boss Xing angrily. Seeing this, Ye Ye smiled and said, "Look, Boss Xing, how can you eat like this?"

"I don't mind, but does Sect Leader Ye mind that my Star Spirit is too small to accommodate a great god like you?" Boss Xing's words were slightly angry.

Ye Ye had no choice but to hold Qin Minglei and Li Bin and said, "Then let's go! Please lead the way!" Ye Ye said neither servile nor arrogant. He knew that if he refused again, Boss Xing would have a perfect reason to kill them! Strangely, Qin Minglei and the others, who were in a state of confusion, stopped moving and quietly let Ye Ye pull them away.

Boss Xing smiled in a heroic manner, walked to the side and raised his hand to point the way. After Ye Ye and the other two had passed by, he followed them with a smile on his face.

Following Boss Xing's instructions, Ye Ye and the other two walked into a tent. Unexpectedly, the tent had already been set up with food, and the food was smoking. It was hard to imagine that it was the food made by the resurrected corpses!

Chapter 39 Mysterious Power

"Why don't you try it? Do you think it's poisonous? Come on, let me try it first." Boss Xing said when he saw Ye Ye was still not moving his chopsticks. After that, he picked up the vegetables and started eating.

Seeing this, Ye Ye didn't hesitate to put off anything. He picked up the vegetables and started eating. However, out of the corner of his eye, he kept looking at Qin Minglei and Li Bin beside him. They were surprisingly quiet. Ye Ye took advantage of the gap between picking up the vegetables to watch. Looking at Qin Minglei, I found that the bloodthirsty red in their eyes had faded! He knew that they were about to return to their human form!

"You must get out before they change back, otherwise you will die!" The strength of Qin Minglei and Li Bin has become Ye Ye's only guarantee now. Thinking about it, Ye Ye picked up a glass of water on the table and said, "Boss Xing, I've eaten this meal, so I'll use this water instead of wine to thank Boss Xing for the hospitality!" After saying that, Ye Ye stood up and raised the cup, Looking at Boss Xing from a distance.

The elder Yuki picked up the cup and stood up. When his other brothers saw him standing up, they also stood up and picked up the cup. Boss Xing said, "Hahahaha, but Master Ye, you can leave, but they must stay." It turned out that Boss Xing's goal was actually Qin Minglei and Li Bin.

Presumably, he had just seen how powerful the two of them were, and he started to research, and wanted to keep the two of them for research.

When Ye Ye heard this, he was shocked and said, "Boss Xing, what does this mean?"

"It's not interesting. It's just about expelling guests and keeping guests. Leave those who should leave quickly, and you can't take away those who should stay!" Boss Xing's words suddenly became cold and stern, and Ye Ye's brows twitched.

Ye Ye stopped talking, sighed and took out a phoenix thorn and said, "Since Boss Xing thinks that the fish will die, will the fish break through the net?" After saying that, he threw the phoenix thorn in his hand violently, killing Boss Xing directly. . But he was caught by Boss Xing.

"Let's go!" Ye Ye said loudly when he saw the phoenix thorn attracting Boss Xing's attention. "Roar." Qin Minglei and Li Bin roared immediately, and then rushed out with Ye Ye.

However, the Yuki brothers could be fooled so easily. When they saw this, they immediately transformed into muscular men, and then rushed forward to block the three escaping people. But Boss Xing laughed and watched his brother chase Ye Ye and the others.

There was a flash of red light, and where the red light passed, the brothers of the Xing family stopped immediately, and cold sweat suddenly covered their entire backs. That red light turned out to be Qin Minglei's look. Those eyes full of bloodthirsty, murderous intent, and evil spirits actually intimidated the brothers of the Xing family.

A red light flashed past, and Qin Minglei suddenly collapsed, wailing feebly in his mouth, and his eyes were bleeding with bright red blood! It seemed like you had squandered all his strength just now. That's right, just now Qin Minglei hit all the energy together, and then fired it out from his eyes, intimidating the brothers of the Xing family!

"Hmph!" Mr. Xing suddenly snorted coldly, took out the slate from his arms, placed it on the ground, and then said: "Since it is not for your own use, then go die! You might as well be for my use after you die!" "Boss Xing activated the ancient Yin Shen Formation.

Suddenly, the four dark winds appeared in the sky, and then four dark clouds rose from all sides, covering the sky tightly. This ancient Yin Shen Formation is actually so powerful? Make the world change color!

"What's wrong!" Ye Ye dragged Qin Minglei, who could no longer stand, and said with a dark expression as he looked at the four dark clouds.

"Roar!" Li Bin blocked the knife coming from the left, and then roared violently, with black light emerging from his body. However, when he was roaring arrogantly, he was hit by a fire charm flying from behind, and his entire back was burned. He cried and screamed in pain while recovering.

Then, the resurrected corpses coming from all directions actually knew how to cooperate with each other, and they attacked blindly and without any moves, one by one, one by one. It was more difficult for the two to defend. However, although there were many resurrected corpses surrounding them, and their cooperation was extremely clever and tacit, not many attacked, and the two of them could barely resist.

Suddenly, Li Bin jumped up silently, trying to use the essence and blood of the replicating resurrected soldier, but he was dodged by it! Li Bin jumped up again, but was dodged again. He couldn't help but stood there and roared angrily.

All this fell in Ye Ye's eyes. Ye Ye looked doubtfully in the direction of the camp they just rushed out of. Boss Xing was sitting there leisurely, with the corners of his mouth raised slightly, but looking in their direction intently. However, Ye Ye was sure that Boss Xing was not looking at how he would die. But...yes, he is controlling those resurrected corpses!

The mindless resurrected corpse can only dodge and cooperate when under human control! However, it is extremely difficult to kill the powerful Boss Xing, and he is surrounded by corpses at this moment, which is perfect: Boss Xing's skill in leading troops, combined with the resurrected corpses that have no thoughts and only know how to obey the orders of the person setting up the formation.

Seeing this situation, Ye Ye suddenly had a playful look in his eyes, a playful look like a cat looking at a mouse, a look like a god looking down at a person, a look of control. Moreover, he slowly took out Yeyang and combined it slowly, as if he was not worried about the attacks of the resurrected corpses. Because every time a resurrected corpse tried to attack him, it was cut into pieces in strange ways.

As for Li Bin, Li Bin could no longer resist, so he suddenly released all his strength and released all the black light. The black lines on his body suddenly disappeared. When they appeared, they had already appeared on the bodies of the resurrected corpses. . The resurrected corpses stuck with black stripes suddenly stopped and lowered their heads. Li Bin stopped moving, and Li Bin also smiled and fell down. With this move, he overdrew his own strength! But the moment he fell, the resurrected corpses clinging to the black lines suddenly raised their heads, and their eyes turned completely black, reflecting a strange brilliance. Moreover, after they quickly cut the resurrected corpses around them into pieces, they immediately ran to Ye Ye to protect him.

This is also Li Bin's only killer move, black pattern control. He will shoot out the black lines on his body, and the black lines will find the target on their own, and then control the target. And this is also the only order Li Bin gave when he was in a coma: protect Ye Ye!

Ye Ye looked at Li Bin unconsciously and fell unconscious, then looked at the resurrected corpses with black stripes surrounding him to protect him, and two words popped out of his mouth: Boring!

After saying that, Ye Ye swung out Ye Yang, who had formed a long thin sword, and ruthlessly divided the resurrected corpses that surrounded and protected them, and ruthlessly divided Li Bin's good intentions!

After doing all that, Ye Ye stretched out his body again and said calmly: "I don't need the protection of the enemy! Let me protect you!" After saying that, Ye Ye picked up the unconscious Qin Minglei on the ground, and then let him After he rolled to Li Bin's side, he slowly walked over. Ye Yang slowly dragged it on the ground and found some sparks. There were endless resurrected corpses around him, but Ye Ye's expression was very calm.

At this moment, if the Ghost Queen were here, she would definitely be shouting. At this moment, Ye Ye and his king are so close. They both have endless fighting spirit and the courage to fear any challenge. However, while shouting, they will also be confused. Why did Ye Ye have a very soft energy in his body?

In fact, Ye Ye was not controlled by the Ghost King at this moment. He was also very surprised by his fighting spirit, courage and madness. However, he could not control his body, but he could control his body to make all actions. Those who had just attacked him The resurrected corpse was dismembered because of him. He used his strange power to dismember it at such a speed that it was difficult to see with the naked eye!

Ye Ye thought for a moment and suddenly knew something. He raised the corners of his mouth slightly, raised Ye Yang upright, and pointed at the boss who controlled these resurrected corpses from a distance, preparing to start the killing spree. However, he suddenly looked at the sky in confusion.

The sky, which was originally covered by four dark clouds, suddenly appeared with traces of strange brilliance. Seeing that brilliance, Ye Ye's expression suddenly froze.

Chapter 40: Fall of Stars

When the strange light appeared in the sky, Boss Xing, who was originally immersed in controlling the resurrected corpses, was awakened. He looked at the sky in surprise, his face as solemn as Ye Ye. As if facing a great enemy. However, he did not give the order to retreat, because he felt that the whole world was bound by a force, a feeling that no matter where he ran, he would be enveloped by that force.

Seeing that Boss Xing was awake, Ye Ye did not control the resurrected corpses anymore. They stood still without moving after losing their controllers. Ye Ye was too lazy to pay attention to them. He looked at the strange light in the sky that was getting stronger and stronger, buried his head, thought for a while, and then placed Qin Minglei and Li Bin tightly on the ground. After doing all this, he slowly folded Ye Yang into a shape that was easy to collect and pinned it on his waist. Finally, he continued to look at the sky vigilantly.

At this time, on the side of the Zodiac Alliance, Gu Zihao, Ye Xincheng and Xia Wanjun used the blood essence they had collected for a day to reactivate Lianyang. They sat cross-legged in the Lianyang formation. From their expressions, they were crying very hard. Ye Xincheng had even turned into a corpse, and the thick black corpse gas came out of his body. His body would crack from time to time, but it would be repaired by Lianyang in an instant.

However, above their heads, a strange cloud gathered, emitting a strange brilliance, which was exactly the same as the wisp of brilliance that appeared in Xingling. It turned out that they made it!

The sun slowly rose up, revealing its full appearance. The golden red sun brought warmth to the bleak battlefield, and made Gu Zihao and the other two who were sitting cross-legged on the ground look like gods.

Suddenly, the three of them stood up violently and roared to the sky. A wave of air, upside down, rushed straight to the cloud in the sky that was emitting brilliance, and quickly pushed it into the sky.

After the cloud emitting strange light disappeared from their sight, Gu Zihao said weakly: "Okay, success or failure depends on this one move." After that, Ye Xincheng and Xia Wanjun nodded at the same time, and then the three of them fell down and fainted.

On the side of Xingling, the sky, which was originally emitting only a little light, suddenly became stronger.

"Here it comes!" Ye Ye frowned and said lightly. Just after he finished speaking, a shining spherical object suddenly appeared in the sky with a long tail, smashing towards the Xingling camp.

In an instant, the spherical object reached the ground. In the violent roar, the object smashed a huge hole in the ground and directly crushed the resurrected corpses into dust! When the object hit the ground, the light in the sky disappeared instantly.

Boss Xing is knowledgeable and must have read a lot of classics. When he saw the thing with a long tail, he said in horror: "Starfall!" It turned out to be a meteorite! Could it be that Gu Zihao and the other two used their power to summon the meteorite? Surprise flashed by, and then he looked at the sky again, and saw that the light disappeared, and then he took a breath and said: "Fortunately, there is only one! Hmm? No..." Before Boss Xing finished speaking, the light in the sky that had disappeared suddenly became violent, and hundreds of meteorites with tails just now appeared in the sky! They smashed down madly with the intention of destruction, and the speed was very fast, and they were about to smash down.

It happened in a flash, Boss Xing was worthy of being the leader of an army and the leader of a gang. When he saw the meteorite in the sky, he immediately picked up the stone slab on the ground and hit the ground to make a huge pit that could accommodate him, and then he jumped in, and the brothers of the Xing family behind him also did the same. After seeing that his brothers had hidden in it, Boss Xing gave a world order.

He actually ordered all the resurrected corpses to press towards their pits, and suddenly, countless resurrected corpses rushed towards them, and in an instant, they piled up several meters high. Moreover, there were countless resurrected corpses trying to crush the pile of resurrected corpses. The pile of corpses was getting higher and higher.

He actually wanted to use the resurrected corpses as a meat shield to block the meteorites falling from the sky.

But Ye Ye did not make such a big move. He just lightly protected Qin Minglei and Li Bin under his body, looking extremely thin.

Boom... The first meteorite successfully touched the ground and hit the ground not far from the pile of resurrected corpses, decomposing many resurrected corpses and leaving a pit on the ground.

Boom... Boom... Boom... Meteorites kept hitting the ground, and the ground was hit with holes. Many of them hit directly on the pile of corpses, but because the pile of corpses was extremely high, they did not directly hurt Boss Xing and his men.

On Ye Ye's side, they were very lucky that no meteorites hit them within five meters, but their situation was also precarious.

Meteorites kept falling from the sky, and this devastating disaster ravaged the Xingling camp and within a ten-mile range. The three people who caused the disaster could no longer see the spectacular scene, as they were already unconscious. However, many people saw the magnificent scene.

On the Yemen side, they were thirty miles away from the Xingling camp and could not be affected at all, but they could see every meteorite hitting the ground carefully, and even feel the vibration of the ground when the meteorite hit the ground.

Each meteorite was like a god punishing the Xingling for its sins. But they were worried because their leader, Ye Ye, Qin Minglei, and Li Bin, had not come out of the Xingling yet. Fortunately, he ordered them not to rush to rescue them for the time being, otherwise, facing such a powerful force, they would be completely destroyed. However, they could only watch the disaster in horror and could do nothing.

Boom... Boom... Meteorites continued to fall, and there were still many resurrected corpses pressing on the Xing brothers, and Ye Ye and his team were still very lucky and none of them were hit.

The stars have been falling for a long time, and the number has become a few, and the power has also decreased sharply. It was not until there were no more meteorites falling in the sky that the people of Yemen breathed a sigh of relief, and Yehen also ordered to prepare to enter the Star Spirit Camp that was hit by meteorites and prepare for rescue.

However, before the people of Yemen had finished their reorganization, a huge force suddenly came from the sky! Everyone in Yemen looked at the sky blankly, hoping to see clearly what was there, but it was so heavy that they almost couldn't breathe.

It would be better if they didn't look at it, but they were even more frightened and couldn't breathe. In the sky, there was actually an extremely huge meteorite! It was breaking through the clouds, seemingly slowly, but actually falling quickly, and the range was actually the entire Star Spirit Camp! That huge camp that can accommodate tens of thousands of people!

Chapter 41 Cooperation

The huge meteorite fell slowly and quietly. At this time, in a valley far away from the battlefield, a person suddenly opened his eyes in surprise, looked at the distance in horror, and slowly shook out two words: "Disaster!" This person was Murong Di who had escaped from the Eight Heavens Pass.

After saying that, Murong Di quickly stood up and said, "It's time to go out and reap the benefits!" After saying that, he walked out of a secret room. Outside the secret room, the strong men who walked out of the Eight Heavens Pass were waiting at the door.

Murong Di quickly looked around and smiled, pointing to the direction of the battlefield and said, "Go harvest the fruits! Revenge, it's time to start!"

"Oh!!! Ah!..." As soon as Murong Di finished speaking, everyone in front of him cheered, and the sound was transmitted to the not very large valley.

At this time, in the Star Spirit Camp on the battlefield.

Because the meteorite was too huge and flew from the sky, it seemed to be very slow.

Boss Xing felt the huge pressure and became confused. He immediately dispersed all the resurrected corpses on top of him. Then he looked at the sky and his face suddenly became even uglier. The seven of them looked at the sky in amazement at the same time, their faces dull, as if they were frightened by the power of heaven and earth.

In fact, this huge meteorite was not made by Gu Zihao and his friends. It was a coincidence, or a semi-artificial coincidence.

Gu Zihao and his three friends used the huge power of Lian Yang to summon the falling stars to attack the star spirits, but they didn't expect that there happened to be a huge meteorite floating outside the sky, and it was just attracted by them. Therefore, such a disaster had already happened.

The meteorite was getting closer and closer. Ye Ye had already stood up, standing with his hands behind his back, looking at the sky. The huge pressure formed a light air pressure, and then floated around, blowing Ye Ye's hair. Ye Ye didn't speak, and there was a little helplessness in his eyes. Facing such a meteorite, no one could do anything!

Ye Ye raised his head and looked at Qin Minglei who was unconscious under him. Li Bin and the others said softly, "You are so kind. You can die without any pain, but it's hard for me to watch myself die like this."

"Hey! Ye Ye, come and help if you don't want to die! Quick!" Suddenly, Boss Xing roared. Ye Ye looked at him in confusion. Ye Ye didn't know what power could withstand this destructive meteorite! However, he still ran over doubtfully, but still looked at Qin Minglei and the others worriedly.

"Don't worry about the two of you. If you help, then we don't have to die!" Boss Xing's words were like a drowning man grabbing a life-saving straw. Ye Ye's originally indifferent eyes suddenly became fanatical: "What to do? Quick, we don't have much time!"

"Don't worry, there's still time! Xing Yu, go and carry Qin Minglei and the others over first." Boss Xing said nervously. In fact, he didn't know if there was enough time, but saying this at least gave himself psychological comfort. After he finished speaking, he counted the number of people and continued: "Just right, eleven people, if our blood and qi are strong enough, then it will be enough!"

"Blood and qi? What are you going to do?" Ye Ye asked.

Boss Xing looked at the huge meteorite in the sky, which affected dozens of miles. Even if they ran faster, they couldn't run more than ten miles between ten kinds of people, right? He sighed helplessly and said: "We can only hit our blood and qi in this ancient Yin God formation, and then forcibly combine the resurrected corpses. However, no one has done this before. I don't know what the consequences are. I'm not afraid. I don't know if Master Ye dares to bear the consequences?"

Ye Ye frowned, stared at Boss Xing and said: "What are the consequences?"

Boss Xing said: "I don't know, ask if you dare or not?"

Ye Ye didn't speak, but nodded. Agreed.

"Okay, you have courage." After speaking, he took out the stone slab, put it on the ground, and then took out a dagger, cut open the artery in his hand, and the blood flowed out desperately. After the stone slab came into contact with Boss Xing's blood, it emitted a blue halo and completely absorbed Boss Xing's blood. The other people in the Xing family did the same thing.

Ye Ye raised his eyebrows, took out Ye Yang and cut open the blood vessels to bleed, and then cut Qin Minglei and Li Bin's blood vessels to bleed.

After absorbing the blood of eleven people, the stone slab on the ground suddenly emitted a blue glow. Seeing this, Boss Xing stopped the blood on his hand and sat down immediately, his mind was all tied to controlling the Yin Shen formation.

"Roar!" Suddenly, all the resurrected corpses cried and screamed, and then all fell to the ground. Seeing this, Boss Xing was not anxious, but continued to control it. After a few breaths, the countless resurrected corpses that were left after being fainted by the stars suddenly fell to the ground.

"Blood, not enough blood!" Boss Xing suddenly roared, cut open the blood vessels again, and continued to bleed. His brothers also continued to bleed. Seeing this, Ye Ye also bleed again.

"Don't stop, don't stop until I tell you to!" Boss Xing's heart was divided into two, and he shouted while controlling the Yin Shen formation.

The blood of the eleven people kept pouring out, and all of it was absorbed by the small stone slab. The blue light became stronger and stronger.

"Boom!" Suddenly, a blue beam of light came out from the stone slab and broke through the sky.

However, the beam actually went straight through the meteorite and did not stop the meteorite from falling.

"Boss Xing!" Seeing that they had been pouring blood for so long but had no effect, Ye Ye could not help but shout anxiously.

"Don't panic! Don't panic!" Boss Xing said with a relaxed smile. Suddenly, all the resurrected corpses that fell on the ground stood up strangely. After that, they gathered together more strangely, and then slowly combined, and there were waves of vibrations from the ground, and suddenly, pieces of pale bones flew out from the ground.

They were the bones of dead animals or people who had been buried in this plain for many years.

Countless resurrected corpses and those skeletons kept combining, piling up higher and higher. And slowly combined into human form. They combined very quickly, and soon, a huge humanoid monster appeared on the plain.

Its body was made up entirely of resurrected corpses, and it was wearing armor made of skeletons.

"Quick, make a gesture of lifting the sky!" Boss Xing said anxiously. Hearing Boss Xing's words, everyone immediately made a gesture of lifting the sky, and the huge combined monster also slowly made a gesture of lifting the sky, surprisingly trying to use its body to resist the meteorite.

This move used the powerful blood of eleven people as the bottom line, and then it had to be used by eleven people at the same time. However, facing the huge meteorite, I don't know if it is feasible.

Chapter 42 Safe and sound

At this time, a strange scene appeared on this land full of holes and pits: in the sky, a huge meteorite seemed to be falling slowly but at lightning speed, and on the ground, a huge ugly humanoid monster, wearing white bone armor, made a gesture of lifting the sky, as if to use its body to resist the meteorite from outer space. Under the giant, there were eleven people, two of whom were lying on the ground with unknown life and death, and the other nine people made the same gesture of lifting the sky as the giant, but if you look closely, the ugly giant's hand was not upright and raised to the sky, but slightly bent.

"Master Ye, no, that guy has the blood of eleven of us, but only nine of us can control it, which is a little short." From his angle, Boss Xing saw that the hand of the giant composed of the resurrected corpse and other corpses was not upright, but slightly bent. He knew that if this continued, the arm would be broken the moment it touched the meteorite.

Ye Ye heard what Boss Xing said, and took a closer look. Sure enough, he thought about it, then picked up Qin Minglei and took out a Phoenix Thorn, and then forced him to lift up to the sky. After fixing it, he used the Phoenix Thorn to pierce his acupuncture points, making Qin Minglei solidify there. Then Ye Ye picked up Li Bin and repeated the same trick, making Li Bin also solidify there.

Instantly, the arm of the ugly combination giant raised a little again, this time, it was really raised straight, facing the meteorite.

"Hey, Boss Xing, even if we won't be crushed to death, we will be burned to death!" Before the meteorite landed, everyone felt a high temperature. On the ground, ants, crickets and other small insects all sensed the arrival of the disaster and moved their homes.

"Don't worry about this, get ready!" Boss Xing said to Ye Ye with a sidelong glance. After hearing this, Ye Ye no longer paid attention to the brothers of the Xing family. He looked at Qin Minglei and Li Bin, smiled confidently, and thought to himself: "Now that I have it, I will definitely survive, if I really can't resist it!" Thinking of this, he looked at the ugly combined giant.

Here it comes... The meteorite finally arrived late, with the power of destruction, breaking through the clouds and showing the whole picture to everyone. It was so huge that everyone in the Huangdao League, thousands of miles away, also saw its figure. Although it looked small from a distance, everyone knew the destructive power it brought!

And Ye Hen, with everyone in the Yemen, had already escaped for several miles in a row, which was also a safe position.

At this time, the eleven people who faced the meteorite directly were sweating profusely. When the meteorite broke through the atmosphere, it would burn with the air, and the temperature was extremely high. The tall giant was also roasted and smoke came out of his body.

"Now!" Boss Xing was extremely focused, saw the right moment, and then shouted at the top of his lungs. After that, he bit his tongue and spurted out a blood arrow. The blood arrow sprayed directly onto the stone slab and was directly absorbed. After Boss Xing spurted out the blood arrow, his face suddenly became like gold paper, and he looked extremely weak. What he spit out was actually his own blood.

After the stone slab absorbed the blood, it suddenly floated in the air in a very strange way, and then four ghosts suddenly appeared in the four corners of the sky. The four ghosts flashed and disappeared. After that, everyone saw that a layer of black protective film suddenly appeared on the body of the combined giant, wrapping it and the eleven people tightly.

As soon as this protective shield appeared, the combined giant, which was originally emitting green smoke during the test, no longer emitted green smoke, but looked more powerful. The originally extremely rough body of the combination became harmonious, and the black protective shield suddenly shrank to the outermost layer, looking like black skin. At this time, if you look from a distance, the combined giant suddenly becomes very humanoid, or it is a black-skinned giant!

"Here we come! Hold on! Haha! Brothers, we are destined to fight against the heaven! This is the battle of heaven!" Boss Xing suddenly said, and the brothers of the Xing family immediately showed fanaticism in their eyes after hearing it.

Silently, the meteorite fell and was actually held up by the combined giant, but the might of the huge meteorite fell so fast that the giant was also pressed down slowly. The land could not bear such a huge pressure.

The eleven people who made the gesture of holding up the sky had very painful expressions. The giant absorbed the blood of the eleven of them. They could control it, and they must bear it. At this time, even the unconscious Qin Minglei and Li Bin had very distorted expressions and endured great pain.

The giant kept sinking, and Boss Xing saw that there were flaws everywhere, and immediately shouted: "Brothers are united, and their strength can break gold." After shouting, the other six brothers of the Xing family suddenly vomited a mouthful of blood and sprayed it on the stone slab, and the light of the stone slab suddenly became more dazzling, and then, the ground they stepped on suddenly became very solid, like steel.

"Ah!" After doing all this, the Xing brothers suddenly became very weak, but they still insisted on lifting the sky and bearing the huge pressure. Ye Ye also resisted very painfully, but he could barely hold on.

After the ground became solid, the giant stopped sinking and his body slowly straightened up, but the remaining force brought by the meteorite was not easy to resist, and everyone resisted. In addition, the high temperature brought by the meteorite broke through the black protective skin attached to the outside of the giant, and instantly scorched the giant's arm.

The arms of the eleven people suddenly showed burn scars, which were slowly spreading and continued to worsen.

"Ah!" The Xing brothers kept howling in pain. But Ye Ye did not make any sound, because he strangely discovered the changes in his body: as soon as the burning pain and scars appeared on his body, a trace of coolness appeared in his heart, and then the wounds healed quickly and the pain disappeared.

Ye Ye looked at the other people around him. They were all covered with green smoke, but he was the only one who was fine. However, he could ignore the Xing brothers, but he was worried about Qin Minglei and Li Bin. Although they were unconscious, they were covered with green smoke, their expressions were distorted, and they cried bitterly. The two people in a deep coma were frozen by the Phoenix Thorn and could not move. Ye Ye was very worried.

Suddenly, just when Ye Ye was worried, a trace of coolness suddenly came out of his body and passed to Qin Minglei and Li

Bin. The pain of the two disappeared immediately. Ye Ye felt all this clearly and felt relieved immediately.

Time seemed to be frozen, and it was moving very slowly. The whole earth was covered with green smoke from the burning heat of the meteorite. The dead ants on the ground, crickets, and the birds falling from the sky were piled up. They were slowly evaporating the water in their bodies and turned into mummies.

I don't know how long it took, the sun had risen very high, and the power brought by the meteorite slowly decreased until it was only its own weight.

Seeing this, Boss Xing shouted, "Throw it!" After hearing this, the ten people made a unified and neat throwing motion. The giant howled and threw the meteorite in his hand. The meteorite was thrown very far, and then it landed on the ground with a bang, and a deep pit was smashed on the ground.

After all this was done, the brothers of the Xing family fell to the ground one after another, and then all laughed, thanking for surviving the disaster. With their laughter, the giant suddenly dispersed, disintegrating into resurrected corpses and skeletons, and then the black skin of the protective shield on its body suddenly disappeared and disappeared into the ground. Seeing this, Boss Xing raised his mouth slightly while no one was paying attention.

Ye Ye also sighed and smiled. He was about to pull his legs out of the deep ground, but found that his legs could not move no matter what, and were actually solidified in the ground by the land.

Boss Xing laughed when he saw this: "Haha, thank you, Master Ye, but I know how to repay a favor. How can I repay it? I thought about it for a long time, just send you to hell and be free!"

Chapter 43 Despair

When Boss Xing said that arrogantly and weakly, Ye Ye frowned suddenly, but soon healed, and then raised his mouth and said: "Oh? Hell? If I can, I really want to go down, but now is not the time. Don't forget that you are still weak. Forcing your own blood out will not heal so quickly!" Ye Ye was of course fearless, because he knew very well what the Xing brothers had just done. They forced their blood out, causing great damage to themselves. If they were not very strong, they would have fallen to the bottom at the moment of forcing their blood out, and would have fainted, or even died in serious cases!

Boss Xing was stunned when he heard this, then he said with a arrogant smile: "You are my biggest worry, and I have to avenge the blood feud! Yes, we forced you to bleed, but don't forget that you can't get out now, only I can untie you myself, otherwise you can only wait to die in the ground!"

Ye Ye shook his head helplessly, and said to Boss Xing who was lying on the ground in a tone of superiority: "Sometimes, don't be too absolute about some things, and don't even give yourself hope, because those hopes may turn into despair!"

There was a tone of command in Ye Ye's words, and Boss Xing frowned when he heard it, but after thinking about it, it was impossible for Ye Ye to escape from the ground that was integrated into the protective shield that could even protect against meteorites. Then he continued: "Good, you have courage, and heroes come out of youth! As expected, you are a hero, Sect Leader Ye, you are like a rising star in the sky, but there are too many rising stars that have been destroyed by me, Xing Xing, and I can't count them!" Boss Xing's original name was Xing Xing.

Ye Ye stopped talking and looked at Qin Minglei and Li Bin who were still holding up the sky. He knew that they were still frozen by the poison of the Phoenix Sting and had no sense of the outside world. He smiled with relief and turned to Boss Xing and said, "Boss Xing, do you know? There are some things that only dead people will not tell, such as..." Ye Ye said, and he stood up easily from the solid ground like steel, and then patted the dust and looked at Boss Xing jokingly. He touched his heart with his hand. He knew that it was a force coming from there that made him walk out and gave him a feeling of invincibility.

In fact, Ye Ye did not take such restrictions seriously at all. He could easily withstand the pressure of meteorites, so how could he not be able to walk out of this small restriction? But he suddenly felt like a cat playing with a mouse, so he said what he said just now. He wanted to give Boss Xing and others hope, and then let hope turn into despair.

However, Boss Xing didn't know all this. He stared at Ye Ye's mouth trembling and finally said, "You... How could you come out!" Boss Xing was finally scared at this time.

Ye Ye didn't rush to answer him. He was in an advantageous position at the moment. He slowly walked to Boss Xing, leaned down, looked at him and said, "I said, don't be too absolute about some things, don't have hope, otherwise hope will turn into despair, and it will feel worse than death." After that, he took out Ye Yang and slowly assembled it, and finally assembled it into a short blade.

Boss Xing looked at Ye Ye's actions, and after the fear in his heart slowly disappeared, he said, "Master Ye, are you so ungrateful? If it weren't for me just now, you would have died long ago! If it weren't for..." "Enough!" Boss Xing was interrupted by Ye Ye before he finished speaking: "You are afraid now? How about this, in order to make you more desperate, I will kill your brothers one by one?" After that, Ye Ye laughed a little crazy, which was completely different from the usual calm and kind Ye Ye.

After saying that, in the eyes of Boss Xing who was shocked and resentful, Ye Ye inserted the short blade fiercely into Xing Yu's heart, slightly prodded it, cut off the heart vein, and then pulled it out. Xing Yu only had time to scream in pain, and then his eyes were chaotic and he died!

Seeing Xing Yu die in pain without resistance, the originally weak Boss Xing suddenly stood up and rushed towards Ye Ye like crazy, wishing to eat him alive. However, he had no strength to compete with Ye Ye after forcing his heart blood out. He was kicked in the stomach by Ye Ye and fell to the ground again.

At this time, Ye Ye shook the blood on the short blade and said, "I've said it all, some things can only be kept secret by the dead!" After saying that, the short blade was immersed in Xing Tu's heart again, prodded it, pulled it out, and died.

Boss Xing was full of flaws and looked at Ye Ye with resentment. However, Ye Ye suddenly straightened his chest, and a momentum of controlling the world surged out of his body, and Boss Xing was terrified again.

"Alas, I said that if I want you to die, I will let you die knowingly. After all, I have known you for a long time... Forget it, let's not talk about this relationship. I'll let you know my identity. Only the dead will keep it secret!" Ye Ye's voice suddenly changed, and it turned out to be the voice of the Ghost King. And, while speaking, Ye Ye's body suddenly radiated bursts of five-colored cool light. These lights carried a chaotic power. It was the power of the Nuwa Stone.

"Who, who are you, who are you?" Boss Xing looked at the five-colored light in horror. He knew that it was the power of the Nuwa Stone, a power he was very familiar with, but what frightened him was that Ye Ye suddenly became a different person, and how could a person merge with the Nuwa Stone!

"Me? I am Ye Ye, the head of the Yemen!" The voice changed back to Ye Ye again, saying jokingly. "Okay, Ye Ye, I'll leave it to you. Kill him. You have too many secrets. Remember, be ruthless! I'm going back first!"

Ye Ye could actually communicate with the Ghost King living in his body? In fact, all this was due to the Nuwa Stone, which made him realize the power contained in his body. The Nuwa Stone was a divine stone produced at the beginning of the world. After Nuwa repaired the sky, she named it Nuwa Stone. How could the energy be small? After the nature transformed Ye Ye's body, Ye Ye had some changes.

However, from their tone, Ye Ye seemed to be unaware of the existence of the other person mentioned by the Ghost King.

Boss Xing felt the power of chaos, staring at the ground with lifeless eyes, looking extremely desperate, but he said in his mouth: "Brothers, you run away, run away if you can, quickly!" After saying that, Boss Xing jumped up suddenly, took advantage of Ye Ye's unpreparedness, immediately strengthened himself, and then hugged Ye Ye to buy time for his brothers.

"Quick!" Boss Xing hugged Ye Ye tightly, no matter how Ye Ye struggled or attacked, he couldn't break free. "Remember, as long as there is one still, we can't die!" After saying that, Boss Xing suddenly exploded, and a ball of flesh and blood covered the world. Mixed in the blood mist, three dark light balls took the opportunity to merge into one of the brothers of the Xing family. Seeing this, the brothers of the Xing family immediately ran away.

The flesh and blood scattered, and the other brothers of the Xing family had disappeared. Ye Ye waved his hand to dispel the bloody smell in front of him. There was no blood on his body.

"Forget it, I won't chase them. Next time!" After saying that, Ye Ye slowly walked to Qin Minglei and Li Bin. He touched the ground with his hand, and the black on the ground immediately dispersed. He pulled the two up, and then sat there, waiting for Ye Hen and others to rescue him. In fact, he could have carried the two and carried them back to Yemen, but I don't know what Ye Ye seemed to be deliberately hiding.

At this time, in the blind spot of Ye Ye's sight, a ball of light suddenly twisted, revealing a human figure, which was fleeting. Ye Ye only had time to look back, and then frowned in confusion. But he saw nothing.

Two days later, Ye Hen led the Yemen's men to this barren land scorched by meteorites and took Ye Ye and the other two away.

After they disappeared over the horizon, a person appeared in the place where the light was distorted. It turned out to be Xia Feng.

She looked at the direction where Ye Ye disappeared with a horrified look, but there was a trace of confusion in her horrified eyes.

Chapter 44 The Spirit of Meteorite

Xia Feng's heart was cold, like ice. With ice-like perseverance, she could hide beside Ye Ye for more than two days, which was beyond her ability, and she had to admire her.

After Ye Ye and others had left for a long time, Xia Feng woke up from her panic. She looked at the meteorite that was like a hill in the distance. She wanted to go over, but now she could vaguely feel the high temperature brought by the meteorite, and the idea was immediately dispelled. However, she always felt that since Ye Ye left, the meteorite actually emitted a call, constantly calling her to go, but now she had hidden for two days beyond her ability, her strength was greatly reduced, and she had no ability to find out the truth. She gritted her teeth and turned to leave.

However, when she left, the call from the meteorite was still lingering in her ears, and she could not dispel it until she walked a long way.

The war between the Zodiac Alliance and the Star Spirit ended just like that, but Gu Zihao, Ye Xincheng and Xia Wanjun, who were in a coma, didn't know all this. Their original intention was just to severely damage the Star Spirit, but they didn't expect that a coincidence that happened once in a thousand years would wipe out the entire Star Spirit, and even the seven brothers of the Xing family were killed or injured in the end.

On the Yemen side, Ye Ye led the Yemen people away from the battlefield. This battle also became a war without an end. The Zodiac Alliance was leaderless, and Feng Yi temporarily led the army to check the original camp of the Star Spirit. After finding that there was nothing on the ground except corpses and bones, he immediately ordered all the corpses to be buried and returned to the Zodiac Alliance base. The consumption of this army is not a small number, and those corpses are left on the ground like that. Over time, it will definitely become a plague.

Half a month later, on the Luping Plain where the decisive battle took place, there was no living thing on the empty plain, and the huge meteorite stood there alone. Suddenly, a group of people appeared from the east. They walked along, seemingly observing the illusion around them.

"Haha, judging from this environment, the war is really fierce." An old man with white hair and a youthful face in the group looked around and said with a smile on his face. It was Murong Di.

Hearing Murong Di say this, the people behind him agreed, expressed their own opinions, and finally flattered Murong Di. Murong Di and the few people closest to him twitched their lips, said nothing more, and continued to move forward.

"We're here, do you see it? It's really big!" When everyone arrived at the place where the stars fell at that time, they looked closely at the meteorite that had cooled down and exuded a metallic luster, and Murong Di laughed and said. Then they kept sighing around the meteorite, and after a long time, they said: "Okay, let's get started!" After that, evil appeared in his eyes.

As soon as Murong Di finished speaking, the people behind him put down their bags and took out tools, and then started digging at the meteorite.

Murong Di looked at the people working, smiled and said to someone beside him: "I didn't expect that such a big treasure would not be picked up by anyone! It's a bargain for me!"

"Master, do you think there is really a meteorite spirit in it?" the man asked carefully. Murong Di was in a good mood and sighed: "Meng Que, you have been with me in the Eight Days Pass for so long, don't you know me? How can I do something I am not sure of?"

Meng Que nodded and said nothing.

"Alliance leader, you'd better come out and take a look, you have encountered a problem!" While the two were talking, a person suddenly came in to report, but he didn't want to choose the wrong time. When Murong Di saw him come in, his face suddenly turned cold: "What did you hear?"

The man panicked, knowing that he had done something wrong, he immediately became anxious and knelt down: "Alliance leader, spare me, Alliance leader, spare me..." Before he finished speaking, his chest was strangely sunken, his eyes were also chaotic, and he died!

"Let's go out and have a look!" Murong Di was disturbed by someone, so he stopped smiling and walked out of the makeshift tent with a cold face. Meng Que followed him.

When a group of people outside the tent saw Murong Di coming out, several leaders immediately came out and surrounded him. One of them said, "Leader, there is a problem here, come and have a look!" As they said that, everyone made way for him.

Murong Di followed the road and found that a huge pit had been dug out of the huge meteorite. There is strength in numbers.

The leader walked five steps behind Murong Di and explained: "Alliance leader, this meteorite is very strange. Its outer layer is ordinary mineral soil."

Murong Di pondered for a moment and said: "Well, if I guessed correctly, then the outer layer should be left after being burned at high temperature. It is normal that it is not hard. Okay, continue."

You kept your head down and continued: "But after digging out the mineral soil layer, a very solid layer of soil with unknown texture appeared inside. The shovels and spades in our hands can't do anything." As he said, he lit a torch and walked into the excavated tunnel. The tunnel was not long. After walking to the bottom, a layer of silver material appeared inside.

Murong Di touched it with his hand, and the texture was cold. Then he closed his eyes. After a few breaths, Murong Di shook his head and said: "Use explosives. I don't want this thing, but it can be left. This material is extremely hard. Find a way to refine it into a weapon!" Murong Di just closed his eyes and rubbed it, and he sensed these things.

After saying that, Murong Di walked out of the pit and returned to the tent. Meng Que said, "Master, did you think that thing was the afterbirth of the meteorite?"

After hearing this, Murong Di nodded and said, "Yes, but I found that thing would block my spiritual sense to detect, and the meteorite is a spirit body that can only accept spiritual sense and communicate, and will not block it."

"Well, Master, you said that thing is very hard, it seems that it will take some time. Why don't you take a rest first?" Meng Que smiled and greeted Murong Di's back.

Murong Di suddenly laughed, grabbed Meng Que's hand and said, "Why don't you sleep with me?" Meng Que acted shy and agreed to Murong Di.

This Meng Que is a man, but he looks very handsome. He has low strength and has climbed to this step. In fact, it is Murong Di's strange hobby: he likes men! Although Murong Di is old, he is very energetic. But liking men is disrespectful.

Soon after, heavy breathing and groaning of men could be heard from the tent, but the people outside pretended not to hear them, as if they were used to it.

Chapter 45 Secret Request for Help

Half a month had passed since the war, and Ye Ye led a group of people back to Yemen. They had originally planned to be the yellow bird, but because of the appearance of the huge meteorite, the Xingling side was completely defeated, and Huangdao suddenly withdrew for unknown reasons, and Yemen also retreated safely.

"This time, it was lucky to escape!" said Li Bin, who woke up from a coma. Ye Ye smiled after hearing this, but did not speak. Among all the people, only Ye Ye knew what happened when the meteorite fell. Including the appearance of the ghost king... Only the few survivors of the Xing family and Ye Ye knew about this series of events.

Qin Minglei had been squatting in the corner without speaking. He looked at the heart area, where there was a black scar, not big, as if it had been pierced by a needle-like object. Qin Minglei had been thinking, he knew that it was the scar left after the phoenix thorn pierced, but he didn't know where it came from. He looked up, looked at the smiling Ye Ye and stood up and said: "Ye Zi, what's going on?"

Ye Zi? Qin Minglei hadn't called himself that for a long time. Ye Ye wondered, "Hmm? I stabbed him with a phoenix thorn."

"Why did you stab us? What happened? Ye Hen said that the power of the meteorite was not something that could be resisted by human power." Qin Minglei's eyes were red with excitement. He didn't know why he asked that. He had always had a question in his mind. He thought about everything that had happened in the past, from General Zixuan's house to the underground world, to the day when Uncle Chen and Ye Rui were rescued, and now, too many things had happened that he couldn't remember.

Ye Ye smiled and said, "It's nothing. The Xing brothers found a way to resist the meteorite, and then they got injured, and we escaped." Ye Ye said naturally and calmly.

"Really?" Li Bin also asked in confusion.

Ye Ye nodded and said, "Really, how could I lie to you?"

"But..." Li Bin was about to ask questions when he was interrupted by Ye Ye. "No buts, the important thing is that we are still alive now, right? Okay, I'll go to accompany Ye Rui." Ye Ye changed the topic and left.

Qin Minglei and Li Bin looked at Ye Ye's back as he left, and they were even more confused. Their understanding of Ye Ye became vague, and they even felt that they didn't know Ye Ye at all.

At night, in Li Ye Rui's room.

"Ye Rui, do you know that Brother Ye Ye is so tired? I really don't want to drag them down, but I can't be separated from them." Ye Ye looked at Ye Rui sleeping in his arms and said to himself. Then he sighed, put Ye Rui on the bed, walked to the window and continued: "Alas, maybe the disaster is really back!"

"Not maybe, but definitely, believe me, it's right. Haha!" Suddenly a voice sounded from Ye Ye's body. Ye Ye was not surprised. He knew that it was the Ghost King. Since the fusion with Nuwa Stone in the Eight Heavens Pass, he could sense the existence of the Ghost King and even communicate with him.

Ye Ye sighed and said, "But I really don't know if I can complete it. Besides, the world is peaceful now, how can such a problem arise?"

"The secret of heaven cannot be leaked. It will happen naturally when the time comes, just like the meteorite. Who can say for sure that it will come down at that time?" The ghost king said cynically.

After listening, Ye Ye clenched his fists, and his body radiated seven-color brilliance, but it disappeared in an instant, and then he said, "This power is really too great. I'm afraid I can't control it."

Suddenly, Ye Ye's body radiated black energy flames. The flames radiated from Ye Ye's body and left his body, fell to the ground, and finally condensed into a human form. However, the appearance of the human form was unclear.

"What do you think of my strength? I told you that the emperor and I can fight to a draw, right?" The flame condensed into the body of the ghost king.

Ye Ye hesitated and said, "At least among the people I have seen, there are only two people who are your opponents. One is Gu Zihao, who is definitely more powerful than that. The other is Murong Die who escaped from the Eight Heavens Pass. I can only describe him as a monster."

The Ghost King nodded and said, "Well, I can say that if you control the energy of the Nuwa Stone in your body, then the three of us will be killed by you in one blow." The Ghost King said helplessly.

Ye Ye said in astonishment, "Is it really that powerful?"

The Ghost King with a flaming body nodded and said, "Of course, and you also have..." Before he finished speaking, the flaming body of the Ghost King suddenly darkened, and then quickly returned to Ye Ye's body and disappeared.

"Ye Zi, what are you doing? Who are you talking to?" As soon as the Ghost King disappeared, the Ghost Queen broke in.

As soon as she came in, she looked in private. She must have sensed the Ghost King's energy.

"No, she's talking to Ye Rui. Didn't she just fall asleep? What's the matter?" Ye Ye said without any panic.

The Ghost Queen didn't ask any more questions. She continued to look for the familiar energy and said, "No, someone asked for Master Ye by name."

Ye Ye said, "I'll go check it out. Please take care of Ye Rui. She'll need to eat when she wakes up." Then he ran out of the room.

The Ghost Queen stayed in the room and looked around, but found nothing. She sighed and said, "King, are you really not going to pay attention to me? I just want to tell you that I have found my home." After that, she saw a strange black spot on the ground. She squatted down and looked at the black spot. It was burned by the flame body of the Ghost King just now.

"Olan Zi Ruixin, I am no longer a king. You can be happy and don't worry about me." The black mark burned suddenly showed a paragraph of text. Unexpectedly, the Ghost King had already sensed the arrival of the Ghost Queen and left such a hand.

The words turned into smoke and flew away. The Ghost Queen was stunned, then said to herself with relief: "King, thank you." After that, she sat on the bed, looked at Ye Rui and said: "Get up, girl, you saw everything just now, right?"

Just after the Ghost Queen finished speaking, Li Ye Rui suddenly opened her eyes, looked at the Ghost Queen with her watery eyes and said: "Aunt Zi Ruixin, hehe." Li Ye Rui had actually woken up.

"Are you going to keep it a secret?" The Ghost Queen asked. Li Ye Rui nodded and said: "Well, I know that Brother Ye Ye will not stay here for a long time. He has things to do. Just like your king."

"Dead girl, you are so talkative. Fortunately, I know how to change souls, otherwise you will be demented for the rest of your life. But you want me to keep this secret. Only the two of us know it. You still dare to tease me like this. Knowing that I have been combined with Huang Shang, you still say this. Do you want me to leak your secret?" The Ghost Queen said with a smile.

"I was wrong, hehe." Li Ye Rui said coquettishly. Then his hand scratched the Ghost Queen's waist, and then he started to scratch. The Ghost Queen immediately tightened her arms: "Good girl, are you looking for a fight?" After saying that, the two rolled together.

At this time, on Ye Ye's side. He slowly walked to the meeting room and saw that in addition to Ye Hen, there was another stranger in the meeting room.

"Are you the head of the Ye sect?" The man saw Ye Ye coming in and asked anxiously.

Ye Ye nodded in confusion.

The man immediately said when he found the right person: "My master asked me to ask for help!" After saying that, he handed over a letter.

Ask for help? Ye Ye was puzzled, then took the letter and read it. He immediately said: "Quick, notify them and discuss things immediately, big things!"

Chapter 46 Zixuan's Request for Help

The content of the letter was very simple: Ye Ye, Murong Di, is about to dominate the world! We are facing an unprecedented crisis, and I hope you can lead Yemen to come to rescue us."

Murong Di, Ye Ye didn't care about dominating the world, but saw the name Murong Di. A person who he felt was so powerful that he was terrifying.

After receiving the notification, everyone immediately came to where Ye Ye was.

"What's the matter?" Qin Minglei asked calmly, but seeing Ye Ye holding the letter with a serious expression, he did not ask any more questions, but took the letter and took a look, his expression froze immediately. Li Bin was curious and took a look, and the two of them froze at the same time, frowning.

Murong Die, the strong man who came out of the Eight Days Pass, dominated the world? A big question was placed in front of them, how did Murong Die dominate the world? The ancient Yin God of the Star Spirit was helpless and was broken, what did Murong Die rely on?

After everyone read the letter, Ye Ye said: "It seems that the matter is serious. Although we don't know what Murong Die did to make the army so worried, Zixuan has already sent out a request for help on behalf of the army. How can Yemen be immune? Besides, Murong Die, maybe you don't know, but Qin Minglei, Li Bin and the three of us know very well that his strength is not much inferior to Huang Shang. Moreover, he has many powerful subordinates around him, which is indeed a threat. Now, we can only go to General Zixuan and understand the whole thing, otherwise, Yemen will be finished. "Ye Ye clenched his fists and talked freely, expressing his opinion.

"Your strength is not much inferior to mine? Haha, I really want to see it. Ye Zi, take me with you?" Huang Shang is lonely when he is invincible. When he hears that there is someone with similar strength, he naturally wants to fight. But he didn't expect that the ghost queen grabbed his ear: "Where do you want to go? What will happen to us mother and daughter if you go?" Hearing your ghost queen say this, Huang Shang immediately flattered: "Madam, I won't go, I won't go. Hehehe!"

Everyone looked at Huang Shang's flattering look and laughed. Who is Huang Shang? Seeing him being defeated, how can he not be happy? Huang Shang's face suddenly blushed in embarrassment, but it soon disappeared: "What are you laughing at, you do your things, I will accompany my wife and guard Yemen by the way! No? "Everyone was happier knowing this, and they also eliminated the negative emotions brought by the news about Murong Die.

"Brother, you must be General Zixuan's confidant, right? Where is General Zixuan now?" After laughing, Ye Ye asked the messenger.

"Master Ye, I don't dare to be your confidant. I only ask you to save General Zixuan. The military department asked him to solve the problem of Murong Die in three months. If he can't solve it, he will be executed according to law. Now the general is on his way to Lu Ping." The man said, and his language was no longer firm and accompanied by his military temperament, and even pleaded.

"Lu Ping? Why go there? Not long ago, the war between the Zodiac Alliance and the Star Spirit began and ended there. Did Murong Die find the ancient Yin God Formation? Impossible, the main heart of the formation, the mysterious stone slab, has been taken away, it shouldn't be, what could it be?" Ye Ye heard the messenger mention Lu Ping, and immediately thought about it, but he didn't know: "So, do you know what they are doing there?"

The man shook his head and said, "I don't know. The general said it's a secret and you will understand it once you go there. Master Ye, let's set off quickly. You don't know that the general sent the most elite soldiers in the army to explore, but none of them came back! Then, we heard from the people that it was a dead zone. Some people saw a strange light there at night, but no one could get close to it. If you get close, you will die! This is definitely not an ordinary situation, otherwise the general would not ask you for help!"

"Strange light? Is it really the Yin God Formation?" Ye Ye thought with a serious face. Then he said, "Okay, let's set off immediately. This time we will enter in two batches. Qin Minglei and I will go first, and Li Bin, Yang Tianhai, and Yang Hengchao will lead the others to come later. Elder Ye, you stay to take care of the Night Sect. How about it?" Ye Ye said. Everyone agreed without saying anything.

No need to say more, Ye Ye and Qin Minglei, led by the messenger, walked down the night gate first, then got on the army car and quickly rushed to Lu Ping. However, Li Bin gathered people with the help of Ye Hen to provide backup.

This unit is very efficient. The three of them hardly stopped along the way, and they changed cars one after another. It took only two days to catch up with Zixuan.

"General, Master Ye is here." The messenger entered the army and led Ye Ye and the others to the command room.

Zixuan came out to greet him immediately after hearing it: "Ye Ye, you are finally here." After not seeing Zixuan for many years, Zixuan lost his sharpness and momentum at that time, and became more experienced, and even his eyes did not look as real as before. However, Ye Ye and the others also knew that in the officialdom, changes will happen sooner or later. If they don't change, they will only die or achieve nothing. For example, Yang Hengchao.

"Hello, General Zixuan! What happened? "Ye Ye didn't exchange extra polite words with Zixuan and went straight to the point.

Zixuan frowned, then sighed, stepped aside, invited the two into the command room, then called all the other people in the command room out, closed the command room curtain and said: "Big news!" Zixuan looked very anxious.

"What is it?" Ye Ye asked calmly, without the slightest surprise, which made Zixuan's eyes light up.

Zixuan sighed and said: "I'm afraid you two can't help me!" Zixuan actually thought that Ye Ye only asked them two to come and didn't help him with his heart.

How could Ye Ye not see Zixuan's thoughts: "Don't worry, our follow-up will be back soon. What happened? "Ye Ye was still worried that Murong Die had obtained the ancient Yin Shen Formation. If Murong Die really got it, then it would be over.

Zixuan frowned and looked at Ye Ye. Ye Ye looked at Zixuan calmly and firmly. After a long time, Zixuan moved his eyes away, sighed, squatted down, opened a safe, took out a stack of documents, threw them on the table and said: "Look for yourself!"

Ye Ye and the other man immediately picked it up and took a look. They both took a deep breath at the same time. This was more surprising than Murong Di's acquisition of the ancient Yin God Formation.

The information was full of the details of Murong Di and all the people who escaped from the Eight Heavens Pass. The army must have communicated with the Huangdao League, otherwise the information would not be so complete.

However, it was not the information that surprised people, but a row of bright red characters on the last page: Murong Di, opened the meteorite and obtained a rare treasure! However, he was greedy and would not leave for the time being. And, the rare treasure emitted light, and after the light slowly dissipated, it directly turned many people into ashes. No one could get close, and Murong Di was thinking of a way.

"Meteorite? Could it be... that meteorite!" Ye Ye was surprised.

Zixuan heard Ye Ye's surprise and said without any extra expression: "Yes, it is the huge meteorite you have seen. Murong Di opened the meteorite and took out something."

"Are you sure? "Although Qin Minglei fainted at the time, he only heard about the horror of the meteorite from Ye Ye, and combined with the information about the meteorite in his hand, he knew the seriousness of the situation.

Zixuan nodded, then took off his hat and said solemnly: "The soldier who spread the news is dead!" Zixuan looked sad, presumably, that person must have a close relationship with him.

Ye Ye ignored them, thinking quickly: "Meteorite, strange treasure, glow? What is it?" Ye Ye shook his head and sighed and said: "Qin Minglei, you immediately return to the original route and let them come faster!" Qin Minglei immediately received the order and left. Ye Ye looked at Qin Minglei's back and had some ideas in his mind, but he said: "General Zixuan, we can only make plans after the Yemen people come!"

Zixuan nodded without saying a word.

Chapter 47 Welcome

"General Zixuan, I'll go and rest first. I've been traveling overnight these days, so I should rest. I'll make a decision after everyone arrives." After saying that, Ye Ye looked at Zixuan indifferently.

Zixuan also looked at Ye Ye, but he couldn't see anything from his eyes, so he shouted, "Come on, take Master Ye to rest." As soon as he finished speaking, a man walked in immediately. Zixuan continued, "Master Ye may not be used to military life when he comes to the army. Take good care of Master Ye, okay?" The man nodded respectfully, then made a gesture of invitation and took Ye Ye out of the command room.

The man took Ye Ye to a tent. Ye Ye smiled, walked to the bed, sat down, and closed his eyes. Seeing this, the man walked out.

After the man walked out, Ye Ye pulled the corner of his mouth and deliberately threw an iron cup on the bedside table to the ground.

Crackling... As soon as the sound started, the man walked in immediately, but seeing that Ye Ye had closed his eyes for a long time to rest, he frowned slightly and walked out.

"Humph, as expected, he came to monitor my every move. But why did Zixuan monitor me? But..." After the man walked out, Ye Ye shook his head and muttered to himself, and then continued to close his eyes.

At this time, in the night gate.

Li Yerui suddenly got up and said sluggishly with sweat dripping, "No, don't, Brother Ye Ye, don't go." The sound attracted the attention of the ghost queen who was embroidering on the side.

"What's wrong? Li girl? Have a nightmare?" The ghost queen said worriedly.

After seeing the ghost, Li Yerui immediately held her hand tightly and said tremblingly: "It's so scary, Brother Ye Ye will die! I don't want it, and he doesn't want it either. That person is so powerful..." Li Yerui said randomly, and the ghost was confused and pinched Ye Rui's hand and said: "What's wrong? Don't be afraid, I'm here, talk slowly." Then he kept comforting her.

After a long time, Li Yerui calmed down, but he still said with horror in his eyes: "I dreamed of a person, so powerful, he held a glittering thing in his hand, and when that thing appeared, it burned all the people, the sky was full of smoke, and the ground was full of people burning and suffering. Brother Ye Ye was about to be killed by that person!" Ye Rui cried and told her dream.

The Ghost Queen sighed. She knew that Li Yerui loved Ye Ye, but Ye Ye treated her as a sister. She said, "Don't be afraid, don't be afraid. I told you it was a dream. It's a dream! Don't worry! Be good!" Although the Ghost Queen kept comforting her, Ye Rui kept crying, "Aunt Zi, please, go and save Brother Ye Ye, okay?"

The Ghost Queen looked at the pleading in Ye Rui's eyes and couldn't help thinking about how she felt when she was waiting for the Ghost King to return. But when she touched her belly again, she found that there was already Huang Shang's flesh and blood. If there was no child, the Ghost Queen would agree in one breath, so she said, "I'm pregnant, and it would be a burden if I go. How about this, I'll let Huang Shang go to help Ye Ye?

Don't worry, dear girl! Okay, I'll ask Huang Shang to save Ye Ye right now. If he doesn't go, I'll go with the son in my belly! Be good, wipe your tears and smile." After that, she stood up and walked out of the room.

However, Li Yerui was not completely relieved by the words of the Ghost Queen. Instead, he said to himself, "No, I have to save Brother Ye Ye by myself!" After that, he immediately put on his clothes, put on his shoes, and quietly walked out of the room.

"Hey, are you going or not?" At the Ghost Queen's place, she had already found Huang Shang.

Huang Shang pouted and said, "No, no, when I wanted to go before, you didn't want me to go, but now you want me to go. Besides, if I go, what will you and your mother do if something happens? Moreover, Ye Ye is not that simple, and the generals of Yemen have gone with him, so what are you worried about? No, no. I might as well enjoy my life in Yemen." Huang Shang resolutely refused to go.

The Ghost Queen looked at Huang Shang who was playing tricks, and said angrily, "Okay, you don't go! If you don't go, my mother and I will go together!" Then she touched her belly and said, "My child, it's a pity for you. You may die before you are born!" After that, she was about to step out. But Huang Shang grabbed him and said, "Nonsense! Okay, okay, I'll go, I'll go! Okay? You stay here in the night gate! Don't let anything happen! I'll leave immediately!" After saying that, he stood up and looked at the Ghost Queen. Thinking back to the time when Huang Shang was still the emperor, there were thousands of concubines in the harem. After a thousand years of loneliness, Huang Shang seemed to have settled down and kept his only happiness.

The Ghost Queen immediately wiped her tears and smiled, "Then let's go quickly, I'll pack your luggage for you! Then find someone to lead you, otherwise you, a road idiot, will get lost again and delay important things! Oh, by the way, I have to tell Ye Rui not to worry about that girl!" Women during pregnancy are moody and talk a lot. Huang Shang shook his head, looked at the ghost queen's back as she left, and smiled happily: "I'd rather win the beauty's smile than the kingdom."

"Ye Rui, girl, I tell you, Huang Shang agreed to help Ye Ye. You don't have to worry about that guy, right?" The ghost queen yelled before she even entered the door, and then pushed the door open.

However, when she saw the empty and cold bed, she immediately exclaimed: "Oh no, this damn girl should go save Ye Ye herself!" Then she immediately found Huang Shang, asked him to set off immediately, and search for Ye Rui's whereabouts along the way and bring him back to Yemen!

No one knew what happened in Yemen. Ye Ye was still sitting cross-legged with his eyes closed to rest. Qin Minglei rushed to Li Bin and others, and Huang Shang followed them. Ye Rui also chose a route to rush to Lu Ping.

Late at night, Ye Ye suddenly opened his eyes, and with the faint light outside, he twitched his lips: "Alas, it's time to act." After saying that, he pulled out the Night Sun, quickly combined it into a dagger, gently cut open one side of the tent, and gently turned out. Then he immediately lowered his body, stepped on his feet, dodged several searchlights, reached the edge of the wire mesh, cut a hole with the Night Sun, and turned out.

Ye Ye quickly did all this, then stood up and looked back at the troops, twitched his lips slightly, and went to the place where the meteorite fell according to his memory.

Ye Ye acted alone, very quickly, and Zixuan's camp was not far away from there. Ye Ye set out at midnight, and when it was close to Yinshi, he had already seen the place where Murong Di's camp was.

Then, Ye Ye continued to sneak. And successfully sneaked into the camp.

As soon as Ye Ye entered Murong Di's lair, he was shocked. It was still hot in the middle of the night. Countless workers kept coming in and out, pulling trailers, but there was only a small amount of silver-white stone on the trailers. Ye Ye looked at the location where the trailers came out and guessed that the stone must be a small part of the meteorite.

Ye Ye continued to walk, blending in with the crowd, not conspicuous.

However, Ye Ye found that there were fewer and fewer people around him. Suddenly, a hand gently patted Ye Ye's shoulder. Ye Ye turned around in surprise. A man with a clean face and a handsome appearance was Meng Que: "Welcome, Master Ye! My master invites you!"

Ye Ye didn't know when he had been discovered!

Chapter 48 The Battle of Babies

After being discovered, Ye Ye was surprised, then he instantly recovered, smiled and stretched out his hand: "Please lead the way."

Meng Que also smiled, stopped talking, and led the way in front.

Ye Ye observed Meng Que from behind and found that he was pinching his orchid fingers, frowning slightly, but he did not speak and continued to follow behind.

Meng Que led Ye Ye to a tent.

"It's you, you are not dead! But you came just in time, just in time for wedding wine!" Murong Di said happily when he saw Ye Ye coming in.

Ye Ye asked in confusion: "Wedding wine? Senior Murong Di, what is the wedding?"

"Oh, you, the master asked you to drink wedding wine, so you just drink it, why are there so many problems!" It was not Murong Di who answered Ye Ye, but Meng Que. Meng Que said, walked towards Murong Di, and snuggled into Murong Di's arms. Seeing this, Ye Ye frowned and thought: "They two..."

Murong Di smiled, said nothing, walked to the bed on the side, picked up a baby and said: "Come, Master Ye, look at my son!" Ye Ye walked over with doubts, and saw that Murong Di was holding a ruddy, jade-skinned baby in his arms. Although he was confused, he said: "Congratulations, it's a great joy to have a child in old age!"

Murong Di smiled and handed the baby to Meng Que. Meng Que took the baby to the side, picked up the bottle, and started feeding.

"Come on, come on, no matter what festivals we had before. Let's not talk about this happy day. Come on, come on, let's drink wedding wine together later!" Murong Di still said with a kind look.

However, Ye Ye knew that Murong Die had an ugly face under his kind face, a devil and a hungry wolf: "Since you are here, I will be disrespectful!"

"Okay! Meng Que, you stay here with the child. If you have anything, report to me immediately! In addition, no one is allowed to disturb you during this period." After saying that, he stretched out his hand and took Ye Ye out of the tent and turned to another tent. There were already drinks and only two seats. It seemed that Murong Die had already guessed that Ye Ye would come back here tonight.

After Murong Die sat down, he invited Ye Ye to sit down. Then he picked up the wine glass: "Come, drink!" After saying that, he drank it first as a respect. Ye Ye couldn't refuse and picked up the wine glass and drank it.

After three rounds of drinking, Ye Ye said, "Senior Murong Die, I wonder who you and Meng Que gave birth to that baby? Is it not true?"

After hearing this, Murong Die was stunned: "Haha, Master Ye, you are joking. How can men give birth to children? I picked up that child on the road. As you know, many people were displaced in the war between Xingling and Huangdao League a few days ago. I hit it off with this child and raised him. It can be regarded as finding a descendant for myself!"

Displaced? Humph, all the people have been evacuated since the beginning of this war. How could there be displacement?

Murong Die, your lie is too unreal! Fortunately, I witnessed it all! Otherwise, I was really deceived by you. Ye Ye thought about it and said, "Oh? Senior Murong Di, I hit it off with this child right away. I wonder if I can bear the pain of parting with him? You also know that you have no place to live now. It would be better for this child to wander around with you and come back to Yemen with me!" Ye Ye's words were tentative and mocking!

Murong Di was an old man, how could he not understand the meaning of Ye Ye's words? He ignored him and said, "No, I have already become the father and son of this child, which is a heaven-sacred bond. How can I give it to you? Yes, I am old now and have no place to live. I wonder if Master Ye can give up his love and give me Yemen as a place for cultivation?"

Ye Ye frowned slightly and thought, "Are you planning to take advantage of my Yemen?" Then he said, "Senior, Yemen is still in its growth stage. It is a small temple. How can it accommodate a great god like you? It is more appropriate for a small person like me to live there. Otherwise, give the child to me to raise first. When you find a place to live, I will definitely send him back in person!" When Ye Ye saw the child just now, he actually felt a familiar attraction. He guessed that the baby must be extraordinary, so he said this.

Murong Di sighed and said reluctantly: "Yes, I can't let the baby suffer. I have to find a place to settle down quickly!" He drank a sip of wine, raised the wine glass in front of him and said calmly: "Then Master Ye, tell me, is the Huangdao League better or the Xingling better, or is your Yemen more suitable for retirement?"

Ye Ye was stunned and couldn't help spitting saliva on Murong Di's face in his heart, thinking: "You are ambitious enough to seize other people's sects!" He sighed and said helplessly: "Alas, senior, this is your business. You want to come to my Yemen to retire, I don't object, but you seem to be the leader in your heart, right? How are you going to settle your disciples?"

Murong Di smiled disdainfully: "Ha, Master Ye, my disciples must follow me, I wonder if Master Ye can bear the pain and give up?"

Ye Ye frowned, exerted force on his hand, and unknowingly deformed the copper cup.

All this naturally fell into Murong Die's eyes, and he continued: "By the way, Master Ye, can you bring a gift when you come to celebrate my son this time? I remember that the gift I gave you last time when you were in the Eight Heavens Pass was very big!" After saying that, Murong Die acted distressed.

Ye Ye heard it, his face regained calmness and said: "Oh? Gift? Senior, I was lucky enough to survive last time, but I am lucky, I don't accept any gifts! Oh, wrong, the gift of enjoying death is really big!"

Murong Die put down the wine glass, pinched his nails and said: "What is the energy of Nuwa Stone? It can not only deform the wine glass in your hand, right?"

"Since you already know, why don't you come to get it back?" Ye Ye knew that the other party already knew that he and Nuwa Stone had merged into one, so he simply changed the topic.

Murong Di laughed and said, "Hahahaha, I am generous by nature, and I have never thought of taking back the things I have given away. But Master Ye, when you can't eat the gift, remember to remind me! I can't bear to give it up!" After that, he walked forward, filled Ye Ye's glass with wine, and then raised his glass. Ye Ye sighed and stood up, clinked glasses with Murong Di, and then drank the wine.

Ye Ye drank the wine, pursed his lips and said, "By the way, senior, I wonder what the baby is named?"

"Murong Tiansheng! My son is called Murong Tiansheng!" Murong Di said with a fiery look at Ye Ye. It seems that Ye Ye has been eaten to death.

"Tiansheng? Why is it named?" Ye Ye asked. "This child is given to me by God. I have a son in my old age, so I am called Tiansheng." Murong Di explained.

Ye Ye smiled: "Senior, are you really unwilling to give up your baby to me?"

"Of course not! This child is my life!" Murong Di said earnestly. After hearing this, Ye Ye sighed and said helplessly: "Okay! How about this! I just saw that baby and felt that we have a special affinity. Can I ask him to be my adopted son? I am also in my twenties and want to get married, but the burden of the Yemen is heavy and I don't have time or opportunity!" Ye Ye said something.

Murong Di suddenly laughed: "Haha, Master Ye, you really know the time! Okay, as long as you are willing!"

Ye Ye also laughed: "Okay, then take me to see our son first, I didn't see it clearly just now!" Murong Di threw the wine glass back and led the way with a smile. Ye Ye followed behind with a slight smile on his face.

Soon, they returned to the tent. After a long time, it was late at night and the baby had fallen asleep next to Meng Que. The two went in and woke up Meng Que. When Meng Que saw Murong Di coming in, he immediately looked anxious and wanted to say something, but was stopped by Murong Di. Then Murong Die picked up the baby, handed it to Ye Ye and said, "The guards here are very strict, don't worry, not even a fly can fly in here." Murong Die's words meant that Ye Ye should not act rashly, otherwise he would definitely fall here.

Ye Ye smiled, took the child, unwrapped the cloth wrapped around the child, and looked at him lovingly: "You know, my adopted son, who dares to snatch him?"

Murong Die smiled and walked aside, but still looked at Ye Ye vigilantly. How could he, a shrewd man, be at ease with Ye Ye? Even if Ye Ye had already released the intention of forming an alliance, or surrendering.

Ye Ye held the baby, and suddenly a familiar feeling rose from the bottom of his heart. The baby also opened his eyes and looked at Ye Ye with a smile. A voice suddenly sounded, it was the ghost king: "Ye Ye, take him away quickly, otherwise it will be a disaster!" Ye Ye nodded secretly. Then he caressed the baby and turned to Murong Di and said, "My dear, this baby is so cute! What a blessing!"

Murong Di did not speak, but laughed, but Meng Que on the side looked at Ye Ye anxiously, wanting to say something, but he knew Murong Di's temper. If he spoke at this moment, he would definitely die, so he just looked at Ye Ye and Murong Di anxiously, without saying anything.

"But, my dear, I still think this child is not suitable to wander around the world with you! I plan to take him back to Yemen!" Ye Ye suddenly raised his head and looked at Murong Di passionately.

Murong Di frowned and said, "What do you mean?"

"That's what I mean..." After Ye Ye finished speaking, black mist suddenly appeared all over his body, and a majestic force poured out. He was ready to forcibly snatch the baby away.

"Interesting!" Murong Di fought, not afraid of the pressure. However, Meng Que's strength was as strong as Murong Di's, and he was pressed to the ground by the pressure, and his urine and feces flowed out, and he said in horror: "Ye Ye will take the baby away!"

Murong Di suddenly became angry, turned to Meng Que on the ground, and then crushed his head with one foot and said: "Bitch, why didn't you say it earlier! You are looking for death!" After doing all this, he looked at Ye Ye coldly, emitting a pressure that belonged to him, and countered the pressure of the ghost king emitted by Ye Ye.

Chapter 49 The Battle of the Infant 2

As soon as Murong Die released the pressure, he said coldly: "This is not the power of the Nuwa Stone, who are you?" Murong Die had also stayed with the Nuwa Stone for some time, so he was naturally very familiar with the power of the Nuwa Stone.

Ye Ye also smiled coldly and touched the baby in his arms with his hand: "Who am I? I am Ye Ye. I will definitely take this child!"

After hearing this, Murong Die did not get angry but laughed: "Hahahaha, Master Ye, how about this? Give me your power, and I will give you this baby?" After saying this, the corners of his mouth rose evilly.

Ye Ye frowned, not knowing what tricks he was playing. Murong Die continued: "Don't be surprised or confused, I just want your power, it's very simple, just kill you!" After Murong Die finished speaking, he came towards Ye Ye with his hands in claws. Ye Ye quickly collected his mind, bent down, and dodged Murong Di's grab.

Since Ye Ye was holding a baby in his arms, his movements were restricted and he could not launch an attack. He could only dodge Murong Die's swift attacks. However, Ye Ye also saw a fatal point of Murong Die in these fights, that is, the baby in his arms. Murong Die would not hurt the baby, otherwise Murong Die's hand would have seriously injured Ye Ye, and he would not have dodged every time the baby blocked his claws. This baby must be extraordinary!

However, since Ye Ye had seen Murong Die's fatal point, he would naturally not miss this opportunity, and he could no longer dodge, but used the baby in his hand to force Murong Die back when Murong Die's hand grabbed him. Although doing so was shameful, at least Ye Ye did not have to worry about being injured by Murong Die.

Murong Die also saw Ye Ye's intention. After several unsuccessful attacks, he stopped and said, "Ye Ye, you'd better give me the baby honestly, otherwise don't force me!"

Ye Ye smiled and raised his eyebrows provocatively. Murong Di was furious. Then he suddenly put his hand down and put it behind his back: "You forced me to do it!" After saying that, a red claw emerged from his back and grabbed Ye Ye fiercely. Ye Ye smiled and quickly lifted the baby to force Murong Die to retreat. Who knew that the claw did not stop and went straight to the baby.

No, it was not going to the baby. The claw was very fast, and Ye Ye had already grabbed the baby before he could react, but Ye Ye was shocked. The claw actually went straight through the baby and rushed straight to Ye Ye. If Ye Ye continued to hold the baby, he would be killed by the claw!

In a flash, Ye Ye directly threw the baby up, and then he immediately rolled on the ground to avoid the fatal blow. Murong Di controlled the claw, and when Ye Ye threw the baby up, he caught the baby with his claw, took it back, and kept muttering: "Fortunately, I didn't wake him up!" There was little concern in his expression, and there was actually a little fear.

"Oh? You can actually control it like this! Awesome!" Ye Ye got up from the ground, but the voice changed, and the Ghost King controlled Ye Ye's body. "Leave it to you, I really don't have enough practical experience, I will learn from it on the side!" Ye Ye's voice came out of Ye Ye's mouth again.

Murong Di looked at Ye Ye in surprise: "You... Who are you! Who is it? " He said in surprise, and then he remembered whether his voice was too loud, and looked at the baby in his arms, and then a red mist formed an egg shape, wrapping the baby.

Just after doing all this, I turned around and found that Ye Ye had actually rushed up, and the Ye Yang in his hand formed a short knife. Murong Di was shocked and dodged quickly.

How could Ye Ye, who was controlled by the Ghost King, give up the pursuit. The Ghost King is very powerful, and his greatest hope is to find an opponent and have a good fight. Without any extra movements, 'Ye Ye' raised his knife and went up, slashing Murong Di who wanted to dodge.

"Ye Zi, look carefully, watch this move!" The Ghost King's voice sounded again. Murong Di knew that there must be a trick, and immediately became alert. But 'Ye Ye' just kept using the short knife to force back Murong Di, who was holding the baby and had limited mobility.

Suddenly, something strange happened. The ghost king shouted: "Watch it!" After shouting, he actually quickly 'broke' the Ye Yang in his hand into a pair of big scissors, and then cut towards Murong Di, and then merged the scissors into a dagger, stabbing Murong Di directly. Finally, he threw the dagger out, but a black line composed of a strand of energy was wrapped around it. After throwing it out, it was quickly pulled back. This series of actions tore Murong Di's defense apart.

"So that's it. As long as the Ye Yang is used properly, it can change continuously, making the opponent unable to react! And can't estimate the next move!" Ye Ye said thoughtfully.

However, all this is not over yet. After the dagger was pulled back, 'Ye Ye' actually gathered his strength under his feet, quickly flashed behind Murong Di, hugged Murong Di, and a thick black smoke of energy came out of his body. This is the unique energy of the Ghost King, which is highly corrosive.

"Be careful, don't hurt the baby." Ye Ye said worriedly. The Ghost King replied indifferently: "It's okay, I don't know the limit yet?" After that, the black mist immediately and quickly wrapped Murong Di, and the strong corrosive force kept corroding Murong Di.

When has Murong Di ever been hurt so much? If he hadn't been holding the baby in his arms and trying to protect him, how could he be so easily bound. Thinking of this, he became angry and immediately stretched out the red mist, constantly resisting the Ghost King's black mist.

A sound like glass breaking suddenly sounded. Murong Di was startled and found that the protective shield that had been protecting the baby had been corroded at some point, and the baby fell down, but Murong Di was wrapped in the Ghost King's black mist and could not move, so he had to resist with the red light.

"Oh no..." Murong Di had no way to catch the falling baby! Two words came out of his mouth lightly.

"Wow~~!..." A clear baby cry sounded. Along with the baby's cry came a powerful force!

'Ye Ye' retracted the black light and gave up the attack. Murong Di looked at the baby on the ground in amazement.

Chapter 50 The Battle of Babies 3

The crying of the baby on the ground was getting louder and louder, and more and more piercing. Outside the tent, the busy workers had to stop and look at the direction of the sound in surprise and confusion, and they could only cover their ears to reduce the piercing crying. However, the sound was everywhere.

The crying of the baby was getting louder and louder, and many people could no longer resist, and even bleeding from all seven orifices, which was terrifying.

As the parties involved, Ye Ye and Murong Di had to strengthen their defense and block their hearing to resist.

The baby kept crying, and suddenly, countless cold winds blew from all around. It made people feel cold. Moreover, there were terrifying faces in the wind.

Murong Di said inwardly, it's bad. He knew what was in those cold winds. Those things were evil spirits, coming from all directions for the crying baby on the ground. And Ye Ye sensed those powerful existences in the wind, but he didn't know why they suddenly gathered together.

In this world, there are many things that cannot be explained by science or at all. Those things are called ghosts by the people! And these ghosts are divided into many types, and the ghost clan of the ghost king is just one of them.

Ye Ye, who has read the Night Gate Sutra, naturally knows this and immediately becomes alert. Although he is not afraid of the current strength, it is always necessary to be on guard!

'Woo~' Suddenly, a series of wails came from all directions to the tent where Ye Ye and his friends were. With a 'squeak', the entire tent was suddenly torn apart, and the broken steps flew everywhere. And suddenly a group of black shadows appeared in the sky that could not be penetrated by the fire.

People are born with a fear mentality, especially when facing the unknown and death. Among the workers who were barely able to resist the piercing cry of the baby, someone suddenly shouted: "Ghosts!" The group of people suddenly became chaotic and ran away.

"Don't run! Stop!" There were also many people in the crowd who stopped the workers who ran away because of fear. Those people were the strong men who suddenly came out of the Eight Heavens Pass with Murong Di. However, facing the workers who were already in a state of chaos, they could not deter them. Although they had killed some of the workers who had escaped in anger, hoping to deter them, they did not expect that the workers would run away faster, and they all screamed loudly: "Ghost! Ghost!" Ordinary people are often afraid of these unknown things.

Soon, the workers had already fled like birds and beasts.

In the center, the baby on the ground was still crying, and the cry was piercing and penetrating. Ye Ye and Murong Di looked around vigilantly.

Murong Di looked around, then leaned down, picked up the baby, and stroked it: "Good baby, don't cry! I'll feed you milk." After that, he picked up a bottle next to the body of Meng Que and handed it to the baby's mouth, but the baby ignored it.

"You, clean them up for me! They disturbed my son!" Murong Di suddenly glared at Ye Ye and said. In his opinion, if Ye Ye had not fought with him for the baby, the workers would not have fled, and there would not have been any more trouble from the evil ghosts swarming in. After he finished speaking, the strong men who came out of the Eight Days Pass immediately began to attack the shadows, and the people and ghosts immediately fought in a melee.

Ye Ye ignored Murong Di's glare, looked at the people and ghosts fighting around him calmly and said: "Senior, I'm afraid this child's origin is not as simple as the child you picked up, right?" Ye Ye had guessed just now that this child must be extraordinary, otherwise the cry would not be so piercing, and the huge energy accompanying the cry was so terrifying that it even attracted evil ghosts from all directions to fight for it.

Murong Di suddenly laughed, pulled the cloth wrapped around the baby, and said to hide the baby's bloodshot face due to crying: "Haha, Ye Ye, I'll tell you honestly, this child was born from the meteorite, so he was named Tiansheng. Moreover, this meteorite stood in the wilderness, and I picked it up. Isn't this picking it up? Blame it on you for not knowing the treasure at the time!"

Ye Ye shrugged helplessly, waved the Ye Yang in his hand, cut a sneak attacking evil ghost in half, and said after it disappeared into the air: "So that's how it is, if you say so, then I'll take this child!" After that, Ye Yang slowly assembled, and a long sword appeared in Ye Ye's hand.

"Since I have told you the truth, then you must keep it secret for me, but I only believe that dead people will keep secrets!" Murong Di's face suddenly became majestic, and his body was red like the sun.

Ye Ye smiled disdainfully and said, "Really? Look, there are 'dead people' all around us. Did they keep it a secret for you?" After saying that, the black light on his body fluctuated up and down like a flame.

The two ignored the powerful evil ghosts around them. In their eyes, there was only each other. Murong Di wanted to kill Ye Ye, but Ye Ye just wanted to take the baby from Murong Di's arms. The ghost king just said that he wanted to take the baby away, otherwise there would be a disaster. Although Ye Ye didn't have time to know what the disaster was, since it was a disaster, he had to take it away.

Murong Di glared at Ye Ye, then put the baby on the ground, forced out some of the red light on his body, then circled the baby, bit his tongue, dipped his fingertips, and then drew a spell on the protective shield composed of the red light.

Murong Di is a Taoist master, how could this protective shield stump him. After doing all this, Murong Di looked at Ye Ye, pushed his own red light to the maximum, raised the corner of his mouth slightly, and his white hair moved without wind.

However, Ye Ye was surprised to find that he could not see Murong Di's actions clearly. He had to close his eyes, open his spiritual consciousness, and search for Murong Di.

"This way!" Ye Ye shouted, and blocked the Ye Yang long sword in his hand fiercely, blocking Murong Di's grab, but what surprised Ye Ye even more was that Murong Di's attack was several times more fierce than before, and when Murong Di touched Ye Yang, Ye Ye clearly felt that a trace of energy in his body was sucked away by Murong Di!

"Ghost power? How can there be ghost power in your body? Why don't you use the power of Nuwa Stone?" Murong Di retreated after one attack and said in surprise.

Ye Ye frowned after hearing this: 'He actually sucked away my energy and analyzed the type of energy. No, I must be less than him in contact, otherwise the energy will be sucked away sooner or later. 'Ye Ye thought, and then spread out the black light and wrapped the long sword, hoping to resist Murong Di's stealing energy.

But the result disappointed him. In the fight, Ye Ye not only failed to stop Murong Di's stealing, but also had a lot of his own energy stolen.

"Haha, Ye Ye, you can't compete with me. No matter how powerful you are, I have taken all the energy in your body! What about the person who just fought with me? Call him out. This energy is not yours, it's his. Tell him to play with me!" After absorbing a certain amount of energy, Murong Di not only analyzed the type of energy, but also the source of that ability.

"Let me do it, Ye Zi, you watch!" The ghost king naturally heard Murong Di's arrogance, said lightly, and then took over to control Ye Ye's body. After combining Ye Ye into a short blade, 'Ye Ye' went up.

The ghost king controlled Ye Ye's body, used the Ye Yang short blade, appeared and disappeared, like a ghost, and attacked Murong Di from all sides. And try to touch Murong Di's hands as little as possible. After fighting, the ghost king has realized that Murong Di can only steal energy through his hands. Despite this, a lot of energy has been stolen.

"Haha, Ye Ye, you should come back to control your broken body! If you let this ghost control you, your body will be empty and your soul will be broken. You will die! Haha! You can't hold on for too long! I'll play with you!" Murong Di blocked the short blade that Ye Ye attacked from behind, then jumped away and said.

"Really? Then try it! See who can hold on longer!" It was not Ye Ye who answered Murong Di, but the Ghost King. The Ghost King knew that his appearance would destroy Ye Ye's body, but Ye Ye had the Nuwa Stone in his body, which would constantly repair Ye Ye's broken soul, so the Ghost King was not afraid.

After saying that, he raised his knife and went up.

Around them, the evil ghosts were overwhelming, and there were even many strange beasts. They were spiritual beasts, and they were all attracted by the evil ghosts. Although they were weak, after being controlled by the evil ghosts, the two combined into one, which was not just one plus one. They seemed to have come for the baby, but they were controlled by the evil ghosts and kept fighting with Murong Di's men.

However, no one saw that the baby on the ground suddenly stopped crying, lying on the ground, looking around with his black eyes, and the corners of his mouth raised strangely.

Chapter 51 Weird Eyes

The baby on the ground suddenly climbed up tremblingly. At first, he only supported himself with his hands. Murong Di's protective shield prevented him from standing upright, but he just touched it with his fingers, and the solid protective shield shattered like glass. Then, the baby slowly climbed up. Logically, the baby could not stand up, but he did it. He slowly climbed up, and because his feet could not support his body weight, he kept trembling, and it took a long time to get used to it.

After the baby stood up, he looked at Ye Ye and Murong Di who were fighting each other, and his eyes actually showed greed. Then he slowly walked towards the two, but was blown away by the strong wind generated by the two when they fought. He was too fragile now. Everyone was fighting and didn't notice all this.

After trying several times, the baby returned in vain, and immediately limped back and forth anxiously not far from the two, with greed and anxiety in his eyes.

Ye Ye and Murong Di, who had no time to distract themselves, fought fiercely. The Ghost King directed Ye Ye's body, using the advantage of speed to fight guerrilla warfare with Murong Die, and tried to avoid Murong Die's strange hands that could absorb energy. Murong Die, however, was as steady as a mountain. He knew that his speed was not as fast as Ye Ye's, so he exerted his strength to sink, stood steadily, waited for Ye Ye's attack, and then stole a trace of energy in the gap of the attack.

"This is not a solution. Our energy has been constantly stolen. If it takes a long time, then our energy will slowly decrease. After Murong Die becomes stronger, he will definitely launch a counterattack." Ye Ye, who had been watching the battle, said. After hearing this, the Ghost King had to agree with Ye Ye's statement. He knew best that from the beginning to the present, he had not taken advantage of anything, but his energy was getting less and less. He also thought about getting away, but as soon as he stopped the offensive, Murong Die rushed up like a hungry tiger, and there was no way to get away.

Murong Die was going to exhaust them to death. Murong Di looked at Ye Ye's uncertain expression, and of course he knew what he was thinking. He didn't say anything, but just continued to defend himself. His red light was like the sun, and his hands emitted a light that was neither black nor purple, and a kind of devouring power was slightly emitted.

In fact, this is also the reason why Murong Di has the power to this day. The attack and defense of the skills he practiced are not outstanding. The weird thing is that in the skills he practiced, he can absorb energy, so as to steal the opponent's energy during contact and use it for himself. It is also simple to break this move, that is, to collect the energy of the whole body, and then attack with the body alone. However, how many people in this world can compete with Murong Di with full energy with their bodies?

In other words, Murong Di's move is invincible in the world today, and perhaps only a few people or non-humans can break it.

Although in terms of combat experience, the Ghost King has an absolute advantage, and Ye Ye's body has no resistance to the Ghost King, and has also been refined by the Nuwa Stone, the Ghost King is naturally handy to control. But facing such an invincible Murong Di, Ye Ye and the Ghost King had no way to deal with it.

During the interval between battles, Ye Ye looked at the sky. The sky was already full of fish belly, and it was almost dawn.

"It's almost dawn, we must leave the battle and go back, otherwise General Zixuan will definitely look for me everywhere. If he finds me here, then they are finished!" Ye Ye and the Ghost King communicated in their bodies.

The Ghost King said helplessly: "I want to, but there is no way. You don't want your body to be incomplete, right? As soon as I give up the attack, he will counterattack like a mad dog. There is no way to get away."

"Let me do it!" Ye Ye sighed and wanted to take back the command. The Ghost King was so smart. He used the short blade in his hand to wave away the Murong Di who was approaching and said: "No, I can't let you hurt yourself." Ye Ye actually wanted to take back the control of his body, and then endure the injury and leave the battle. How could the Ghost King watch Ye Ye get injured or even lose his life? So he held the command tightly and left without fighting. But Ye Ye was as stubborn as an ox. He would not go back on his decision and started fighting with Murong Di. The Ghost King had to attack or defend Murong Di while fighting for control with Ye Ye, so his offensive power weakened.

Murong Di could not hear the conversation between the two in his body, but he was happy because he thought that after such a long and fierce attack and he had stolen a lot of energy for his own use in the process, Ye Ye's energy must be very little, and he felt that the time had come to end. So, he used all the energy he had just absorbed, and then put aside Ye Ye's weak cut, and then formed tiger claws with his hands, causing gusts of wind to come towards Ye Ye's head.

The two people fighting for control of the body did not see all this, and when they realized it, they found it was too late. And Murong Di's mouth corners also rose, he was confident that his one-shot kill would be a sure kill.

'Dang'

A sound of metal and stone colliding suddenly sounded, and Ye Ye actually blocked the fatal blow that could not be blocked with Ye Yang in a flash. But it was also bounced away by the force, and then the strong wind left some blood marks on his face.

Murong Di was shocked and did not organize the next attack. Instead, he stood there in surprise and looked at Ye Ye who was hanging his head. He was very surprised in his heart: "Impossible, even if his strength has not decreased at all, it is impossible to block it. The body reaction is completely unable to keep up." Worried that Ye Ye, who seemed to be weakened, had a trick, Murong Di did not attack rashly.

Ye Ye, who was hanging his head, did not raise his head. He let his hands hang naturally and shook slowly with inertia.

Time seemed to freeze. Murong Di still looked at Ye Ye vigilantly. Although they were surrounded by shouts of killing and ghosts howling, he was not distracted at all. Only a few breaths of time passed, but Murong Di felt as if several hours had passed. Murong Die panicked, and was torn between his conscience and his desires: "Did he get killed by my blow?" Murong Die quickly rejected this idea: "No, it's impossible, he clearly blocked it just now!" "But why didn't he move? Isn't he afraid of my sneak attack?..." Murong Die hesitated. "Go up and take a look." Murong Die, who was naturally vigilant, finally decided to go forward and take a look at Ye Ye's situation.

One step... Murong Die took the first step, but Ye Ye still hung his head.

The second step... Murong Die was only about six or seven steps away from Ye Ye, and Ye Ye still didn't move after the second step.

Murong Die simply took the third step, and the fourth step. After taking two consecutive steps, Murong Die thought about the power that Ye Ye had just exploded, and couldn't help but stop and continue to observe Ye Ye's movements. Even the baby on the side stared at this side, his dark eyes kept turning, as if thinking. Ye Ye, who was hanging his head and his life or death was unknown, and Murong Di, who was vigilant against Ye Ye, did not notice this side.

The fifth step... Murong Di took the fifth step, but just as he took the step, a gust of wind suddenly blew up for no reason, blowing Ye Ye's long hair, and Murong Di's foot stopped in the air. Then, he froze like this, because he saw a scene he had never seen before!

Ye Ye slowly raised his head, his long hair swayed gently with the wind, his mouth slightly opened, and a little blood was slowly flowing out of his forehead, which was left when he just resisted Murong Di's fatal blow. The whole person looked extremely weird. But the weirdest thing was Ye Ye's eyes. His eyes were white and black! It exuded a fearful and uneasy atmosphere.

Murong Di was suddenly afraid. He hadn't felt that feeling for too long, so it burst out all of a sudden now, so violently. He froze in place, even forgetting to put down the foot he had raised, and just stood there strangely. And three steps away from him, it was Ye Ye who had become a stranger!

Chapter 52 Father and Heart

What happened to Ye Ye? Back to the moment when Murong Di launched a fatal attack. In Ye Ye's body, the Ghost King and Ye Ye were still fighting for control. When they realized that danger was coming, it was too late and they had to make a meaningless resistance.

However, at this moment, a strange thing happened suddenly. The Ghost King and Ye Ye forgot to fight for control, but made a resistance at the same time, but they were powerless. Suddenly, a huge force burst out from Ye Ye's body, and it forced the two to move and react several times, directly blocking the fatal attack. Not only that, but what was even more strange was that Murong Di's fatal attack actually became a catalyst, allowing the souls of the two to merge together at that moment. Indistinguishable from each other.

Ye Ye twisted his neck, making a "click" sound, then calmly looked at Murong Di in front of him and said, "It's almost dawn, I won't accompany you anymore, goodbye!" Ye Ye's voice was actually emphasized, and it sounded like two people were talking at the same time!

After saying that, Ye Ye ignored Murong Di who was still in a daze. He glanced at the baby and saw that the baby broke through the protective shield laid by Murong Di and looked at this side with surprise. He smiled and said nothing.

Ye Ye's words also woke Murong Di from his surprise, and he retracted his feet that were frozen in the air: "Master Ye, do you want to leave like this? If I let you leave like this, how can I explain to my men?" Murong Di is Murong Di, and he quickly calmed down.

Ye Ye turned his head and looked at Murong Di lightly, pointing to the baby standing not far away and looking at this side. The baby saw Ye Ye pointing at him, looked at Ye Ye in confusion, and the bloodthirsty greed in his eyes became more obvious.

Murong Die looked towards Ye Ye's direction with doubt. When he saw the power of the baby rising and looking at this side with doubt, he suddenly showed a look of fear. He remembered the horror that happened after the meteorite was blasted open that day, which he would never forget in his life!

That day, Murong Die ordered to use explosives to blast the meteorite to take out the treasure inside. The men under him quickly did as he said, and soon blasted a passage on the extremely hard meteorite. Murong Die was overjoyed and immediately led people in. In the meteorite, an embryo was actually bred! Murong Die tried his best to break the protective shield protecting the embryo and took out the embryo. The embryo immediately turned into a healthy and sleeping baby. It was the baby standing aside and watching them now. Murong Die naturally knew how precious the embryo bred by the power of heaven and earth was, and the embryo of the meteorite that flew in from the sky must have absorbed the power of the universe.

However, something terrifying happened. The moment the baby opened his eyes, a dark hole that was impenetrable to light suddenly appeared in the not-so-large space. As soon as the hole appeared, a huge suction force came, sucking in all the people who followed him in, and they were not sure whether they were dead or alive. However, it seemed that the black hole would not hurt the baby, and did not produce any suction force on the baby. Murong Die happened to be holding the baby, and was safe and sound. Murong Die walked out of the tunnel that was blown out in fear. He put the baby on the bed, and after letting Meng Que wrap him up, he observed the baby. When Murong Die and the baby looked at each other, Murong Die actually fell into an illusion. The illusion repeatedly replayed Murong Die's experience from childhood to adulthood, and Ye Ye's process of fusing the Nuwa Stone was also in it. Murong Die was surprised and happy. He knew the benefits of this doll. He could actually detect the past and the future! Therefore, Ye Ye was discovered as soon as he entered, and a series of things happened afterwards. Murong Die also thought that the horror had passed, and he had obtained this treasure, and forgot about the black hole.

Murong Die was sweating as he thought about all this. When he looked back at Ye Ye, Ye Ye had disappeared. He had quietly left while he was thinking. However, Murong Die did not care at this time. Instead, he looked at the baby with vigilance and worry, and thought in horror: Is the disaster not over? What on earth did I get?

The baby saw Murong Di staring at him, and the corners of his mouth curled up strangely, and slowly approached Murong Die. Murong Die did not show the baby, but kept an eye on the surroundings. He was worried that the terrifying black hole would appear around him again!

The baby walked in front of him, raised his head, and looked at Murong Di with dark eyes with a bloodthirsty light, and then uttered human words: "Submit to me, or die!" The childish voice, like his crying, was actually mixed with incomparable majesty.

Although Murong Di was afraid,. But how could he be so submissive after dominating things for so long? He looked at the extremely weak baby under him coldly and said, "Why? Who are you? What do you want to do?"

The baby smiled and said, "Hahaha, in fact, I should be grateful to you for letting me out, otherwise I would die in that meteorite. It is something that protects me and also something that takes my life. Maybe this is destiny! As for who I am, don't ask too much, it's not good for you." As he said that, the baby touched his chest and frowned, as if crying, and said, "I'm just looking for my heart and father!"

"Father and heart? What do you mean? Who is your father?" Murong Di continued to ask, he had too many doubts in his heart!

The baby suddenly frowned: "Don't ask anymore, help me find my heart and father, I promise you this world! Who is my father? If I knew who my father was, would I still need your help?" The baby said angrily.

Murong Di did not rush to speak, and thought in his heart: "Father and heart? You found it and promised me the world? You are so arrogant?" After thinking, he said: "Okay, I will take you to find your father, but I don't understand the heart!"

The baby continued to look at Murong Di, with surprise in his eyes, and then quickly resumed his anger and said: "Don't think of finding someone to replace my father. I can sense my father's energy! He is a powerful existence, and your energy is just an ant in front of him! Otherwise, you saw the black hole that day, right? It may just be that he waved his hand! Heart, I don't know where it was left! But I can sense that it appeared here."

Murong Di thought for a while and said: "In addition to the whole world you promised me, I still need your help, that is, the mirror images you let me see that day! You can't control it!"

The baby smiled, waved to Murong Di, and asked Murong Di to pick him up, and the two of them looked at each other. , Murong Di saw a scene again: Ye Ye, Ye Ye with black and white pupils, was holding his head in pain and rolling on the ground.

Chapter 53 Horrible Wail

When Murong Di saw Ye Ye like this, his mouth trembled and a trace of hidden regret flashed across his eyes. He thought: "It turns out that the boy is already at the end of his strength. Damn, I let him go!" Shaking his head, Murong Di said to the baby without thinking: "Okay, I accept your conditions! But don't try to make me surrender, otherwise we will all capsize together!"

The baby looked at Murong Di coldly and said: "Don't worry, I haven't thought about it, and it seems that you are not qualified! By the way, I want to borrow your blood, just two drops!"

"Blood?" Murong Di thought doubtfully, but still cut open his fingers and squeezed out two drops of red blood with a little golden color. The baby spread his hands, caught a drop with one hand, and said with a little surprise: "Not bad, the energy is very good!" After that, the blood on his left hand floated up, and when it floated to the position of his forehead, it suddenly rushed towards the forehead and disappeared. After doing all this, the baby seemed to be very comfortable, groaned and said: "Comfortable, although the energy is a little less, at least I am full! Put me down!"

Murong Di put him on the ground in response, and a surprising thing happened. The baby actually began to grow up, and it stopped until it was about four or five years old. The baby looked at his body that had grown a circle and said: "Take back what I said just now." After that, he stood with his hands behind his back, looking at the people around him who were still focused on fighting the evil spirits.

Murong Di didn't know whether to laugh or cry, and shook his head. He found that the baby actually looked like him 70%. After being surprised, he smiled warmly and thought to himself: "Maybe, I really picked up a son!" Murong Di couldn't help thinking that he was old, although he still had no descendants, because he had special hobbies and it was impossible for him to have descendants. However, Murong Di also cared a lot about his ability not being inherited by his descendants. Seeing that the baby had grown up so fast, Murong Di was surprised and sighed at the same time.

"Roar..." When Murong Die was thinking, he was suddenly awakened by a howl. The howl was mixed with all the negative emotions, which made people feel very depressed. Some people even stabbed their weapons at their hearts.

Murong Die had amazing concentration. He calmed down and looked at the source of the sound. It turned out to be the baby who had grown up. After he roared, he turned around and said to Murong Die: "People with low strength will naturally be eliminated!" After that, he ignored Murong Die and turned his head. A roar that was more intense than before came from him. Suddenly, even Murong Die felt a strong negative emotion constantly eroding his mind. Murong Die was startled, sat cross-legged, retracted his consciousness, and strictly guarded his heart to resist the erosion of negative emotions. The negative emotions that filled the world became more and more intense.

Among the others, only a few people with strong minds endured it. They all sat cross-legged and strictly guarded their minds.

However, this roar with negative emotions is harmful to humans, but it is beneficial to the evil ghosts. Those evil ghosts have accumulated a lot of negative emotions (commonly known as resentment) in their hearts since they died unjustly for people and things. This roar is like a strong medicine. Not only does it not harm them at all, but it even nourishes them! The strength is getting stronger and stronger. Many of their illusory bodies have become materialized! That is a sign of advanced strength, which means that these evolved evil ghosts have at least the strength of the ghost queen.

Those evolved ghosts have their own consciousness. Looking at the people around them who are still resisting negative emotions, they immediately show greedy eyes. Absorbing their souls, their strength can be doubled again! So, they are ready to attack.

"Hey!" Suddenly, a violent roar, like the power of the heavenly general above the nine heavens, immediately deterred the evil ghosts who were about to launch an attack to absorb souls. They looked back in confusion, and the one who made the violent roar was actually the child who had just made a "horrible wail" to make their strength greatly improved.

"Remember, you must submit to me in the future, or you will die!" The baby, who had grown into a child, said majestically. After that, he grabbed with his bare hands, and a small black hole appeared out of thin air.

The black hole emitted a burst of energy and a huge suction force, which frightened the ghosts. However, the black hole only sucked in one evolved evil ghost and stopped sucking.

"You will submit to me in the future, and you have already enjoyed the benefits. There will definitely be more and bigger benefits in the future." After that, the child glanced around and said, "Organize your people, lurk around me, and listen to my orders! Go!" After that, the black hole disappeared with a wave of his hand.

Those evil ghosts had self-awareness, so they naturally knew how powerful the child was. However, they had only been conscious for a short time, and the strong-willed consciousness in their hearts was still very strong. They immediately surrendered, bowed to the child, and then disappeared. However, some black light appeared from time to time around the child. They seemed to have been lurking around the child, and they would appear as long as the child gave an order.

After the child did all this, he looked at the sky and said sadly: "Father, where are you? The child without a heart needs you." After that, his eyes turned black and he fainted.

After falling to the ground, the child's body shrank immediately and turned into a baby again. After he fainted, the negative emotions that filled the world suddenly disappeared.

Murong Di sensed it and immediately opened his eyes and looked around vigilantly. But there was nothing. He lowered his head and saw the unconscious baby. He actually had a kind smile on his face, picked him up, and then cut his fingers, put them into the baby's mouth, and actually fed blood! The baby sensed it, and his throat began to move, constantly absorbing blood.

Looking at the unconscious baby in his arms who was constantly absorbing blood, Murong Di had some wonderful changes in his heart.

At this time, at Ye Ye's place. He was holding his head in pain, rolling on the ground, and was in great pain.

"Ye Ye, it's no good, one of us must give up! Otherwise, both of us will have nerve ruptures or even die!" The Ghost King said anxiously in Ye Ye's body.

It turned out that although Ye Ye and the Ghost King's souls wanted to merge, the energy carried by the fusion was not so easy to bear. It was not easy for Ye Ye to hold on until now and escape from Murong Di's range.

"No, no! Absolutely not! I... We must persist!" Ye Ye said, and after speaking, violent crying came from his mind, and he couldn't help but shout out in pain.

"Ye Zi, you are still young, remember to live well and help me take care of my people!" The Ghost King suddenly said with a vicissitudes of life.

Ye Ye naturally knew what the Ghost King wanted to do, and naturally didn't want to, so he was ready to forcibly stop the Ghost King's actions. But he found that his actions had been controlled by the Ghost King, which meant that the Ghost King chose to bear all the pain himself, forcibly interrupted the fusion of the two and controlled Ye Ye's body. Ye Ye wanted to stop all this, but found that he could not pull back any control. He could only be anxious.

"You will not die, because you... ah!" The Ghost King had just taken over the control of the body. The two of them could not bear the pain of the fusion. No matter how strong the Ghost King was, he could not bear it. The Ghost King had not finished speaking, but was interrupted painfully.

In just a moment, the Ghost King's spiritual sea exploded immediately. Ye Ye watched the Ghost King's soul dissipate, tears flowed from his eyes, but he still could not pull back control.

"Remember, I said, you will not die!" The Ghost King's voice suddenly sounded, he laughed, and then Ye Ye suddenly felt the surge of his own power and the strength of his soul. He knew that it was the Ghost King who gave up on him and let him survive, and it was the Ghost King who poured all his power into him.

The Ghost King is dead. Ye Ye also took back the control of his body, but he had not moved for a long time. At this time,

Ye Ye was very sad and didn't want to do anything. He just shed tears quietly. In the sky, a dark cloud suddenly turned into the appearance of the Ghost King, then made a howling movement, and finally disappeared gorgeously.

And the Ghost Queen, who was far away from Yemen, suddenly felt the death of the Ghost King. With tears in her eyes, she said, "King, is this your way?" After that, a black ghost-faced butterfly flew in, and the Ghost Queen caught it with her fingers, but the ghost-faced butterfly died in her hands. This is the situation after the death of their line of ghost clan strongmen, who turned into ghost-faced butterflies after death and died in the hands of the person they loved deeply!

After a long time, at Ye Ye's place.

"I can't cry, I still have a lot of things to do!" Ye Ye, who was crying, suddenly stood up, wiped his tears, looked at the sky and said. After that, he moved the stones on the ground, piled them into a tomb, and then used Ye Yang to cut a piece of wood into slices, and engraved it on it: Tomb of the Ghost King!

Chapter 54 Xia Feng

After Ye Ye built the Ghost King's tomb, he knelt down and then stood up to look at the sky without saying anything. To him, the Ghost King was both his master and his friend. They had controlled a body together and had deep feelings for each other. The Ghost King also died because of him.

After a long time, Ye Ye turned around and left without saying anything, heading towards the camp where Zixuan had set up camp. Although he knew that going back at this time would definitely arouse suspicion, after all, he still had blood on his head and his body was covered with mud from rolling on the ground when he was in pain just now. However, Ye Ye had no choice, because Qin Minglei and Li Bin, who were galloping today, would come with the people from the Night Gate.

"What? Ye Ye is missing? Hurry up, send someone to look for him immediately." Zixuan jumped up and said excitedly after hearing the news of Ye Ye's disappearance. Because of his excitement, the wound on his face from the left forehead to the right chin also turned red and swollen. He knew that if Ye Ye left... then he would lose his support, after all, according to his understanding, he could not deal with his opponent.

"Yes, General." The man who was arranged by Zixuan to monitor Ye Ye said respectfully immediately.

However, the curtain of the tent where they were was suddenly pulled open, and a voice said faintly from the door: "No need, I'm back." It was Ye Ye.

Zixuan looked at Ye Ye: the blood on his head had already solidified, and he was covered in mud. He immediately said in horror: "Where have you been? What's the matter?"

Ye Ye smiled and said: "I went to do something. General Zixuan, should you find me some clothes and let me take a bath? Do you want me to face my people in Yemen like this?" Ye Ye deliberately changed the subject and avoided answering. Ye Ye knew that Zixuan, who had been rolling in the officialdom for these years, was no longer the Zixuan that Ye Ye knew at the beginning. He had been poisoned by the officialdom.

Zixuan frowned. When did anyone dare to talk to him like this? However, because he had something to ask of Ye Ye, he couldn't say it clearly, so he said, "Well, if you don't want to say it, forget it. Go wash up and change into clean clothes. I will send someone to do all this."

Ye Ye nodded and turned away, not seeing the murderous intent in Zixuan's eyes when he turned around!

After washing up, Ye Ye came to Zixuan's tent again. At this time, Ye Ye was normal except for the slight swelling around the wound hidden under his hair.

"General, they should be here soon, right?" Ye Ye asked. Zixuan nodded and said, "Well, my spies have reported their whereabouts. It is estimated that they will soon enter the sphere of influence."

Ye Ye nodded, bowed slightly and said, "Then I will go out to greet them. They will be heroes in the future. The enemies we face..." Ye Ye's words hinted at the strength of the enemies they faced, and also hinted that Zixuan should go out with him to greet them as a welcome.

Although Zixuan was unwilling, when had he ever personally greeted anyone? Despite this, Zixuan still smiled and nodded, stood up and walked out with Ye Ye. He thought viciously in his heart: Humph, wait until you finish the matter, I will make you look good! Ye Ye, you owe me, you must pay it back! Thinking of this, Zixuan stared at Ye Ye's eyes, and the hidden murderous intent flashed across his eyes.

The two walked outside the camp, waiting for the arrival of the Night Gate team. After a long time, they heard a series of deafening engine sounds, and the Night Gate team arrived.

Seeing the car coming, Ye Ye and Zixuan immediately went forward. Ye Ye didn't have time to say hello, but Zixuan came to greet him, smiled and stretched out his hand to Li Bin who just got off the car and said: "Li Bin, haha, you boy, long time no see! All brothers of Yemen, everyone, hurry into the camp, good wine and good meat have been prepared for you, everyone enjoy it, but if you want women, we don't have them here! Haha." Zixuan's words were very appropriate, and he invisibly narrowed the distance between them.

Zixuan and Ye Ye are also old acquaintances, but Ye Ye and Qin Minglei have met, only Li Bin, Zixuan said so.

Li Bin saw that it was Zixuan, stretched out his hand and shook hands with Zixuan before saying: "General Zixuan, you are much older! Haha."

"Old? I'm still young! Come on, go in and have a rest, and then eat and drink to your heart's content!" Zixuan patted Li Bin on the back and sent Li Bin in.

However, Li Bin walked up to Ye Ye and whispered in his ear: "Ye Zi, there are guests!" Ye Ye looked at Li Bin in confusion. Li Bin smiled helplessly and pointed his finger. The crowd dispersed immediately. There was a woman in the crowd of Yemen! A woman with a hot body and stunning beauty.

Ye Ye walked up to the woman in surprise and said softly: "Xia Feng? Why did you follow them?"

"I just can't forget you, my Master Ye!" Although Xia Feng's voice was extremely charming, her face was cold. As she spoke, she leaned towards Ye Ye. Before Ye Ye could dodge, Xia Feng grabbed his hand. When she let go, it was a note.

Ye Ye clenched his fist cleverly, and then said: "So that's it! Haha, come on, go in and have a rest!" Ye Ye didn't know what Xia Feng wanted to do. Although he was confused, he sang the play with Xia Feng.

After hearing this, Xia Feng walked to Li Bin with a cold smile on her face, waiting to enter the military camp with Li Bin.

During this process, Zixuan kept staring at Xia Feng: There is such a beautiful woman in the world. Ye Ye is so lucky, but it's a pity that all of this belongs to me! Zixuan watched Xia Feng pass by, and a fragrant breeze made him feel relaxed and happy, but the murderous intention in his heart became heavier.

"General Zixuan, is it rare that you want us to go in by ourselves?" Li Bin's voice suddenly sounded. Waking up Zixuan from his deep thoughts, he smiled apologetically and quickly led the way into the military camp.

In the military camp, Zixuan prepared fine wine and food to entertain everyone in Yemen, and nothing happened during the process, except for Xia Feng. Ye Ye really couldn't understand what Xia Feng wanted to do. Ye Ye didn't have time to read the note, but put it in the treasure bag, but Xia Feng seemed to be arguing with him. During the meal, she kept leaning on Ye Ye, pouring wine and picking up dishes, which made the people in the army blow their noses and stare. After all, the army is full of men, hungry men, and Xia Feng is so hot and attractive, so it's natural.

Ye Ye was not fooled by Xia Feng's pretense. He knew that Xia Feng's eyes were still so cold under her flattery.

Time passed quickly. Everyone finished eating and was tired from traveling all night. Zixuan immediately ordered the servants to prepare empty tents for them. And Ye Ye also took advantage of the gap to read the note that Xia Feng secretly handed over: Meet under the headless tree two miles east at three quarters of midnight tonight.

Ye Ye was puzzled. How could this confidant of the leader of the Huangdao League come to the enemy alone, and so "intimate"! Before finishing reading the note, Ye Ye's hand trembled slightly, and a trace of black flame appeared, instantly burning the note to ashes, and it disappeared with a blow.

At night, Ye Ye used the same trick again, but Zixuan arranged another secret sentry. The vigilant Ye Ye cleverly avoided it and went to the small forest two miles away in the east.

Two miles is not far. Soon, Ye Ye arrived, and then looked for the headless tree mentioned in the note. Looking around, Ye Ye suddenly laughed, because he saw that a tree in the forest had its crown forcibly cut off. It must be Xia Feng's doing.

Ye Ye walked over and appeared from behind the tree.

"What's the matter? Tell me!" Ye Ye saw Xia Feng and immediately got to the point.

Xia Feng's voice returned to its coldness, looking at Ye Ye and said lightly: "Did you see the baby?"

Chapter 55 Kiss

"You saw the baby, didn't you?" Xia Feng said lightly, but Ye Ye was shocked. "How could she know the baby? Did she see it before? Impossible! Zixuan said that Murong Di got the glowing object from the meteorite a few days ago, and the glowing object was the baby." Ye Ye thought and said, "Baby? What baby?" Ye Ye planned to conceal it for the time being and make plans later.

"Don't pretend, you know the baby, tell me, where is he now?" Xia Feng still maintained that indifferent tone, but there was a hint of obscure understanding in her eyes.

Ye Ye smiled, looked at the tree whose crown was cut off by Xia Feng and said, "Baby? There are so many babies in this world, I can see them every day, which one are you talking about?" That hint of understanding fell into Ye Ye's eyes, and Ye Ye knew that Xia Feng must know something.

Ye Ye had just finished speaking when Xia Feng suddenly pulled out a dagger, rushed to Ye Ye, put the dagger against Ye Ye's neck and said, "Tell me, or you will die!"

Ye Ye felt the coldness on his neck and said, "I hate threats from others the most. I am timid and I remembered it, but you scared me so much that I forgot everything!"

"You..." Xia Feng knew that Ye Ye was teasing him, but although angry, he took back the dagger helplessly and continued, "Tell me! After all, someone has died for you." After saying that, Xia Feng actually showed a fearful expression.

Ye Ye was very surprised when he heard it, but he did not rush to speak. Ye Ye stared at the beautiful face close at hand, and Xia Feng also stared at him with a hint of fear in her eyes.

"What scares you?" Ye Ye asked lightly. Xia Feng gritted her teeth and said, "A few days ago, I had a dream! I dreamed..."

It turned out that Xia Feng had a strange dream. The dream was about the battle between Ye Ye and Murong Die. She also dreamed of the death of the Ghost King, and even dreamed of the baby intimidating the evil ghosts. This dream made Xia Feng feel a sense of terror, a sense of familiarity, and even a cry from the depths of her soul, which kept urging him to come.

After listening, Ye Ye shrugged his shoulders, sighed, and said with surprise in his eyes: "Do you know everything?"

Xia Feng nodded and said nothing. Ye Ye continued: "Yes, I have seen the baby, and I can feel that the baby must be extraordinary. Even the dead person told me that the baby will definitely cause a disaster. But what does all this have to do with you? Or what does it have to do with your Huangdao League?" Ye Ye said aggressively.

"My master didn't know that I came this time. I ran away secretly!" Xia Feng replied indifferently.

Ye Ye suddenly became serious and said, "In fact, I also have an inexplicable sense of familiarity with the baby, as if I knew him a long time ago!" After hearing this, Xia Feng looked at Ye Ye in surprise and did not speak for a long time. Ye Ye looked at him and told him everything about his visit to Murong Die last night.

After hearing this, Xia Feng trembled and took two steps back. It was not until he leaned against the tree that he said fearfully, "That was all true, it turned out that everything was true..." Xia Feng kept repeating this sentence, and Ye Ye asked in confusion, "What is it? What else do you know!"

Xia Feng shook her head and looked at Ye Ye with a complicated look in her eyes, unwilling to say it out. Ye Ye had no choice but to give up. Looking at Xia Feng who was afraid for some unknown reason, Ye Ye actually felt a kind of pity in his heart. He frowned and looked at her, and even wanted to reach out and hug her.

But no, Xia Feng suddenly recovered at that moment, looking at Ye Ye with cold eyes: "Master Ye, you'd better stay away from me in the future, otherwise you will lose your reputation!" After saying that, Xia Feng pulled out the dagger again and blocked it in front of him.

Ye Ye was very confused, not knowing why Xia Feng suddenly became like this again. He shook his head helplessly, shrugged his shoulders, and looked at Xia Feng without saying anything.

Suddenly, Ye Ye and Xia Feng frowned at the same time, and they said at the same time: "Someone is coming!" Sure enough, before they finished speaking, the bushes on the left of the two shook, as if someone was hiding in it.

"Come here!" Xia Feng suddenly said, and Ye Ye walked over in confusion.

Xia Feng put away the dagger, then suddenly hugged Ye Ye's neck, closed her eyes, and kissed Ye Ye's lips with her red lips. Ye Ye was startled and did not react, but his body was as if it was solidified by cement and could not move. Eyes

Feeling the coldness of Xia Feng's lips, and then thinking about the hidden person on the side, he suddenly understood in his heart, and then simply closed his eyes, hugged Xia Feng with his backhand, and touched Xia Feng's lips. After a few breaths, the person hidden in the bushes did not leave. And the two hugged each other like that.

As time went on, Ye Ye held the sexy body in his arms, and his mind became distracted unconsciously. After all, Ye Ye was still a novice to these things!

Slightly opening his eyes, watching the bushes still swaying slightly, Ye Ye's lips moved. He opened his lips gently, held Xia Feng's upper lip, and sucked gently. Ye Ye did all this, and clearly felt that Xia Feng's body suddenly tensed up, and her lips were tightly closed, no longer giving Ye Ye any chance to move.

"Boy, let me teach you something. When you kiss a girl in the future, remember to stick out your tongue! Haha!" Ye Ye suddenly remembered what the optimistic Qin Minglei said when Yin Lin, who was wearing a windbreaker, was still alive. Unconsciously, he followed suit. He slowly extended his tongue.

As soon as the tip of his tongue touched Xia Feng's gradually warming lips, Ye Ye suddenly became nervous. An inexplicable sense of comfort was transmitted from the tip of his tongue to his brain, and then he continued to lick Xia Feng's lips gently with his tongue. Feeling Ye Ye's actions, Xia Feng suddenly opened her eyes, looked at Ye Ye in disbelief, and struggled. Ye Ye also opened his eyes and looked at the bushes on one side. Xia Feng immediately reacted and stopped struggling, but also closed her lips to prevent Ye Ye from succeeding.

"Hey, don't squeeze me, don't squeeze me, why are you joining in the fun of my Ye Zi picking up girls." Li Bin's voice suddenly sounded. The two people who were hugging each other were startled and separated.

"I just listened to the general's words and came out to find Master Ye!" Another voice sounded.

"Come out, Li Bin!" Ye Ye said with a smile.

After that, two people walked out of the bushes, one was Li Bin, and the other was a soldier sent by Zixuan to monitor Ye Ye.

Li Bin walked towards Ye Ye with a smile, rubbing his hands and said, "Master Ye, I can't tell! Haha!" Ye Ye blushed when he heard it, but it was too late to tell, so he said, "What are you doing here?" After saying that, he suddenly felt a sense of humor in his heart, and hugged Xia Feng in his arms and whispered, "It's an exercise, so you have to act more realistically!" Xia Feng glared at Ye Ye helplessly, but did not resist. If the matter was spread, Xia Feng would definitely be killed by the army or captured and tortured.

"Master Ye, how can you go out so late at night? General Zixuan is worried about your safety and sent me to take Master Ye back to the camp!" The man said in a humble voice. After hearing this, Ye Ye was shocked, thinking that no one had discovered the route he took, and he couldn't help but doubt Zixuan: Since you invited me to help, why do you monitor me like this!

Thinking about it, Ye Ye said, "Oh, for a date! We must find a secluded place. In the army, there are only men, which is not romantic at all. Look, under this crownless tree, the moon is full and the wind is high. Isn't it nice to talk about love? Besides, this tree is the place where we are in love. But forget it, let's go. We are not interested in being disturbed by you! Go back!" After saying that, he let go of Xia Feng's hand and went towards the direction of the military camp.

Li Bin shrugged helplessly and followed him, and the man followed behind.

Xia Feng looked at the crownless tree, thinking about what Ye Ye had just said: "The crownless tree, the place of love..." Her face couldn't help but blush, a touch of happiness flashed across her eyes, but soon replaced by a touch of helplessness, she said to herself: "All this is true!"

"What are you mumbling to yourself? Let's go!" Ye Ye looked back at Xia Feng who was in a daze and shouted.

Xia Feng unexpectedly said obediently: "Oh!" and followed.

After they left, a shadow suddenly appeared behind the crownless tree. It turned out to be the evolved evil ghost. After Ye Ye and the others left, the evil ghost also went in the opposite direction.

"Really? She's here too? That's great! Haha! Father, I can find you now!" In Murong Di's tent, a fifteen or sixteen-year-old child looked 70% like Murong Di. It was the baby! And under him was the evil ghost that appeared under the crownless tree just now.

"Tian Sheng, when you find your father, I can also get this world! Haha!" Murong Di said happily on the left side of the child, but he looked a little weaker. It must be the sequelae of feeding the baby blood yesterday, and the blood must have been a lot, otherwise the baby would not have grown so much overnight, and he would not be so weak.

Chapter 56 Crisis Infiltrates

Tiansheng? The baby in the meteorite is called Tiansheng? That was the name Murong Die gave him.

Tiansheng twitched his lips and looked at Murong Die and said, "Let's find my heart first. It will be much easier to find my father with a heart. The world, I can't give you, but if you keep helping me like this, I think my father will definitely give you the whole world!"

Murong Die was immediately unhappy when he heard it. After all, Tiansheng changed his words, from 'I promise you the whole world' to 'My father promises you the whole world'. However, Murong Die did not show it, and his eyes looked at Tiansheng with that kind of tenderness: "Anything is fine! What are you going to do next! I plan to be a hands-off housekeeper, just waiting for my whole world!"

Tiansheng showed a naughty smile and said, "I plan to go out and play. After all, this world is still too strange to me!"

"I'll go with you, and I'll have someone to take care of me!" Murong Die has regarded Tiansheng as his own son and is worried about Tiansheng's comfort. After all, Tiansheng has his blood flowing in his body!

Tiansheng stood up, looked into the distance and said, "No need, you still have things to do, I can go alone, I won't go far, I must have something to do now. Are you worried about me going out alone?" After saying that, a black shadow flashed by Tiansheng's side. Murong Di felt the strong strength revealed by the black shadow. He was the strongest among the evolved evil ghosts, and was kept by Tiansheng as a personal guard. Murong Di smiled, and the stone in his heart was put down. He nodded and stopped talking.

"By the way, it's better to do it today than to wait for a day! I will leave today, and I will leave immediately! Haha, I can't wait to see..." Before he finished speaking, Tiansheng had already laughed happily. While laughing, he left the tent.

Murong Di looked at Tiansheng's back and didn't stop him. He smiled, so kindly.

And on Ye Ye's side. Ye Ye followed the soldier back to the camp. Zixuan did not ask where Ye Ye was going. He just smiled and said to Ye Ye: "Young man, if you want to talk about love, you should find a time and place. This is the army. If it gets out, how can I explain it to my subordinates? Be careful next time!"

Ye Ye nodded and said nothing, but he was confused: What exactly does Zixuan want to do? Why did he send someone to monitor me? Thinking of this, Ye Ye bowed and then went back to his tent that had been cut open to rest.

On the second day, Zixuan still did not tell Ye Ye what they were going to do, but asked them to check in the army, which was quite boring. However, Ye Ye took advantage of these gaps to sort out his thoughts.

Night fell, at the outpost of the army camp.

"Oh, the weather is getting colder, and I don't know when I can go back this time. I will miss going to the war zone. It's too boring here!" Soldier A said with a gun in his arms.

Another soldier, B, nodded and said, "Yes, I don't know when I can go back. I really miss my warm bed!"

"Bed? Your wife warmed your bed, right? Haha! How is her bed?" Soldier A said with an obscene smile.

"My wife, I'm not exaggerating. Anyway, she makes me feel like I'm in heaven! Haha!" The two soldiers talked about dirty jokes while standing guard.

Just as they were talking, a crisp voice suddenly sounded: "Excuse me, is there an army ahead?" The two soldiers turned around, raised their guns, and looked at the owner of the voice vigilantly.

"It turns out to be a boy! Little brother, what are you doing here? There is indeed an army ahead, not a place you can come to, go home quickly and hug your mother to drink milk! Haha!" Soldier A saw that it was a child of fifteen or sixteen years old and immediately relaxed his vigilance and joked. Soldier B also laughed.

The child was not angry, but said: "Thank you, my father said, be grateful, let me repay you!"

Hearing the word repay, the two soldiers' eyes lit up and looked at the child with a smile.

"Haha, a very good repayment!" After saying that, the child waved his hand, and a gust of cold wind blew, and the eyes of the two soldiers dimmed at the same time. "Father said that the best repayment is not to let you die in pain!" This child is Tiansheng.

"Okay, you can control their bodies, right? You control that one!" Tiansheng pointed at the dead soldier B with chaotic eyes and said. After saying that, a black shadow appeared from behind him and then merged into the body of soldier B. Soldier B suddenly came to life and knelt on one knee respectfully. His movements were not hindered at all, just like a living person, but the death in his eyes was very heavy.

Tiansheng looked at Soldier A, then took out a knife, cut Soldier A's finger, sucked two mouthfuls of blood, and then spit out two mouthfuls of saliva and said: "There is really little energy. The blood now is better, with a lot of energy. However, for fun, I will make do with it. This face looks good." As he spoke, Tiansheng's appearance and height kept changing, and finally he turned directly into the appearance of Soldier A.

On the side, the evil ghost who occupied Soldier B was not idle either. When Tiansheng transformed, he waved his hand, and a ghost-like giant wolf suddenly appeared from the darkness, and then ate Soldier A's body in a few bites, leaving no trace.

"Hey, you two, it's time to change guards, go back and have your spring dreams!" A voice suddenly sounded from not far away, startling Tiansheng and the evil ghost.

The evil spirit took over Soldier B's voice and his memory, so he said, "Okay, you bastards, when I go back and have a wife to warm the bed, you can go to your brothel! Be careful not to get sick!" After that, Tiansheng followed him to the military camp.

In the camp, Ye Ye still couldn't figure out Zixuan's motives, and he couldn't help but be alert. He also tried to see something from Zixuan's eyes and movements. After all, Zixuan has been rolling in the officialdom for these years, and his mind and scheming are very deep. Ye Ye naturally couldn't see it.

Ye Ye thought about it and walked to the camp. Shaking his head, Ye Ye looked at the hidden sentries who were always watching him around, shook his head, turned around and walked back.

But suddenly, Ye Ye felt a strong breath of death. Ye Ye was very familiar with death, after all, Ye Ye rolled among corpses. The death aura could be felt very clearly in this army of iron and blood. Ye Ye frowned and looked over to find the source of the death aura, but only saw two soldiers walking in from outside the camp. Ye Ye looked carefully, but could not see any clues, but could clearly feel that the death aura was indeed coming from one of the two soldiers.

The two soldiers also noticed that Ye Ye was looking at them, but they did not care, and then mixed with other soldiers, just like other soldiers. Moreover, the death aura disappeared immediately. Mixing with the soldiers who survived in the iron and blood at such a close distance, the death aura had been dispersed.

Ye Ye frowned, he knew that the crisis might have sneaked into the military camp. But when he looked for the two military camps again, he could no longer find them.

Chapter 57 Search

When Ye Ye saw that he couldn't find the two people, he frowned and rushed to Zixuan's tent. He said with a vigilant look: "Quick, notify everyone, there is a danger sneaking in."

Zixuan looked at Ye Ye's nervous look and knew that it must be true. He immediately sent someone to notify others to come. Qin Minglei and Li Bin were also called by Ye Ye.

The soldiers were very efficient and soon they rushed to the tent. They all looked at Ye Ye, waiting for Ye Ye to tell them the truth.

Ye Ye looked around and then told what he had seen in front of the camp gate.

"Impossible! Master Ye said that, you think our troops are not clean? We all came down from the battlefield, and no ghost can resist the evil spirit on our bodies. There is no way there is something unclean. I think you are worrying too much!" As soon as Ye Ye finished speaking, the major general with a gold plate and a star on his shoulder immediately refuted.

Ye Ye looked in the direction of the voice. The man was Zixuan's trusted general, Du Wei. Ye Ye stood up and stared at him closely and said, "General Du, do you think I am teasing you like this?"

Du Wei also stood up, looked at Ye Ye and said, "I don't know. There are so many more people in the army, there must be more trivial things, and there are women, which is not allowed in the army!" Du Wei's needle pointed at all the people in Yemen.

"General Du? Do you think it is me who let your masculinity leak out?" Du Wei had just finished speaking when a girl suddenly sounded from the door. It was Xia Feng.

Du Wei looked back at Xia Feng, hesitated for a moment, and did not speak again, but the disdain in his eyes became more and more intense. Xia Feng ignored him, walked straight to Ye Ye and sat down and stopped talking.

Ye Ye looked at Xia Feng, and then continued, "Everything I said is purely true, General Zixuan, the truth of the matter, you can judge it yourself!" After speaking, Ye Ye sat down and looked at Zixuan beside him.

Zixuan frowned and thought for a while, then stood up and said, "Since Master Ye is so sure, then everyone, you should immediately call everyone back and wait for inspection in the parade ground." Zixuan's words were full of irrefutable tone. Du Wei wanted to say something, but after looking at Zixuan's expression, he swallowed what he wanted to say.

After Zixuan finished speaking, his generals immediately withdrew and went to assemble their own troops.

"Then, Master Ye, since you suspect that there are unclean things in my army, then today you must give me and my men an explanation no matter what! Otherwise, my men will get angry, and I can't say anything." Zixuan said so, but he was ecstatic in his heart: "Ye Ye, there are unclean things in the army? This time I will definitely not let you leave this camp!" Zixuan didn't believe Ye Ye's words, but wanted to take advantage of this, and then after a search, if he couldn't find anything, he would instruct all his men to attack, and then it would be normal to cause any consequences, including getting rid of Ye Ye.

Ye Ye didn't know what Zixuan was thinking. After thinking for a while, he said affirmatively: "No problem, there will be, as long as those two haven't left the army!" After that, he clasped his fists and walked out of the tent. Qin Minglei, Li Bin and Xia Feng followed him.

After Ye Ye left, Zixuan revealed a sense of evil: "Ye Ye, that woman will be mine sooner or later! You owe me all this!" After that, Zixuan also walked out of the tent.

Not long after, in the military camp.

"Brothers, I called you here this time because someone said that there is a spy among you! I hope everyone will cooperate! Let us find the spy!" Dewey seemed to have a good reputation in the army. As soon as he finished speaking, the soldiers below immediately whispered to each other, but did not make a loud noise. Dewey continued: "Everyone, say what you have! I also want to hear everyone's opinions!" Dewey's move was extremely clever. He knew that these soldiers under his command would naturally not believe that there would be so-called spies among their brothers who had been through life and death with them. Saying this would only make them feel disgusted or even hate those who said that there were spies among them! He also cleverly pointed the finger at Ye Ye again.

"General, there can't be a spy among us! We believe in our brothers who have been through life and death together! If we can't find the spy, then please let the person who reported and framed us give us an explanation!" As soon as Dewey finished speaking, a soldier below immediately shouted, and his words aroused the support of all the people.

Dewey nodded with satisfaction, and then looked at Ye Ye. Ye Ye naturally knew what Dewey meant by doing this, without any fear. Ye Ye walked forward a few steps and said with a deep breath: "The person who reported and framed you is me, the head of the Yemen, Ye Ye!"

"Headmaster Ye, why did you frame us!?" The voice sounded dissatisfied again.

Ye Ye said with a serious look: "I didn't frame you. If I can't find the person I'm looking for among you later, then I will let you deal with it!" "Okay, then I hope that Headmaster Ye will keep his word! Brothers, we have been through life and death together, and we have seen all kinds of big waves. Let him check!" After that, the voice came out of the crowd. According to the official title, it seems that it is a regiment commander. As soon as the man came out, many supporters followed him out.

Ye Ye frowned and looked at the soldiers under him. He knew that if he really didn't find the two soldiers with death, then the anger of these iron-blooded warriors would definitely be directed at him. Although he was not afraid, it was also a big trouble. Thinking of this, Ye Ye looked at Dewey, the instigator, with a glaring look. But Dewey looked at Ye Ye with a playful look, as if saying, "Let you know how powerful you are!"

Ye Ye shook his head helplessly and walked down the more than one meter high stand. He wanted to check each soldier one by one. Qin Minglei, Li Bin and Xia Feng followed behind.

Ye Ye first walked to the head of the regiment who had just spoken, and then shook his head. No.

"It turned out to be a boy! Hey, boy, can you satisfy the delicate beauty behind you? Do you want us to help you?" The head of the regiment seemed to dislike Ye Ye very much.

Ye Ye ignored him and continued to walk forward. Seeing Ye Ye like this, the angry Qin Minglei and Li Bin didn't know what to say. They glared at the captain and continued to follow Ye Ye.

"Hey, beauty! Dump that boy and let the brothers love you. I promise they will be better than that boy! Haha!" Seeing that

Ye Ye and the others did not refute, the captain's words became more naked, but it seemed that the target was wrong. Xia Feng smiled at the captain, her face was charming but her eyes were still cold. She walked to the captain's side, gently stroked the muscles on the captain's chest and said, "Really?" Her movements seemed to be leaning on him, and the soldiers who saw it were booing. The captain also said very lustfully, "Of course, how about we try it tonight?" After that, he was about to reach out to hug Xia Feng.

Xia Feng turned around cleverly, avoiding the captain's bear hug, and said in a voice that only the two of them could hear, "See you tonight." After that, she followed Ye Ye's footsteps. The captain was left panting with a red face. "Captain, what did that girl tell you? Why are you so excited?" A soldier asked tentatively. "Fuck you, what's it got to do with you? Go to sleep tonight! I have things to do!" The soldiers knew what he was going to do and immediately started to make a fuss. The captains of other regiments could only be jealous.

Ye Ye also heard this. He looked at Xia Feng who was walking over, and then whispered: "Don't kill people easily!" Xia Feng listened, but rolled her eyes at him and said: "Yes, some people rely on women to show up!" After that, she didn't say anything else, and her face returned to indifference.

Ye Ye shrugged helplessly and continued to check.

Chapter 58: Imprisonment

At this time, at the end of all the soldiers, two soldiers quietly walked into the group of soldiers.

"What are you two doing! Hurry up and join the team. If you make any mistakes, you will be in trouble!" A man looked at the two and scolded them in a low voice.

"Hey, squad leader, I had a stomachache after lunch just now, so I went to set off cannons!" One of the two soldiers immediately said in a low voice. "Pay attention to me next time, soldiers, you must keep time!" The squad leader said earnestly. The two soldiers nodded their heads.

The two soldiers were the two soldiers controlled by the evil ghost and Tiansheng. At this time, the soldier controlled by the evil ghost no longer exuded any dead air, even if he got closer. But the soldier who turned into Tiansheng knew that his eyes were curved and laughed very playfully.

However, Ye Ye was persistent in checking each soldier one by one. Time passed slowly, and nine out of ten of the thousands of people in the entire army were checked, and it was the next morning. During this process, Ye Ye also suspected several soldiers, but after careful inspection, they were ruled out one by one.

"There are about a hundred more people! They must be here!" Ye Ye looked at the remaining soldiers and thought for sure.

However, Dewey's voice sounded: "Master Ye, there are more than a hundred people here, you haven't checked them out? I'm afraid you will find someone to fill the number!"

Ye Ye frowned and said: "Don't worry, I won't fill the number randomly!" After that, he continued to check.

Slowly, there are more than a hundred people, and there are still fifty... forty... thirty... twenty...!

"The last ten people, I want to see where you can escape! With such a close observation, the strong death aura can't be concealed from me!" Ye Ye thought in his heart, then walked to a soldier and shook his head. Not again!

At this time, Qin Minglei and Li Bin suddenly became anxious, not just them, but everyone in Yemen was anxious, and some people even quietly took out their weapons. If they didn't catch that person later, the soldiers in the army would attack their master, and they would definitely resist.

Ye Ye walked solemnly to the next soldier and shook his head again. There are still eight people.

"Master Ye, how can you bear not letting people sleep this night? The brothers all have dark circles under their eyes. If there is any war, how do you want us to resist the enemy?" A voice suddenly sounded jokingly.

Ye Ye looked in the direction of the voice. That person was the next soldier he was going to check, and the soldier controlled by the evil ghost. After hearing this, Ye Ye walked in front of him without saying a word, and then shook his head. Passed?

"Haha, no need to say more, it must be gone! Master Ye must not have rested well and had hallucinations!" Another voice also sounded, it was the soldier who was born.

Ye Ye walked in front of him and shook his head again. He was about to take a step, but suddenly he wondered: Why do the two of them have exactly the same breath? No.

Thinking of this, Ye Ye took two steps back, went to the soldier controlled by the evil ghost, and then to the soldier who was born, sensing back and forth. Ye Ye's action made all the soldiers' eyes jump constantly, thinking that he had discovered something. Dewey even stood up nervously.

After sensing back and forth several times, Ye Ye asked: "Why do you two have exactly the same aura?"

The soldier who was born said: "Report to Master Ye, he and I are inseparable. I have a strong body odor. It is normal for him to infect my aura!"

"Hahahaha! Xiao Wang, do you want your wife? Surprisingly, this kid is not as happy as your wife you said!" So the soldiers laughed when they heard it, but they did not deny it. After all, there are too many soldiers in the army who even sleep next to each other.

Xiao Wang, the soldier controlled by the evil spirit, bowed his head and said nothing.

But Ye Ye did not believe what he said, and continued to ask: "Then why don't you have his aura?"

The soldier who was born smiled and said: "I said, I have a strong body odor! Hehe!" Hearing him say this, all the soldiers laughed again.

Although Ye Ye was puzzled, there was indeed nothing unusual. If he continued to pester like this, then those soldiers would definitely say that he was just randomly finding people to fill the numbers. Shaking his head, Ye Ye continued to check, but everything was normal!

After a whole night, nothing was found, but Ye Ye was very sure that the two soldiers whose faces he did not see clearly were carrying death energy, but in the current situation, Ye Ye could not excuse himself. He frowned and walked up to the stands with a serious look, but kept thinking about where he was wrong.

"How is it? Master Ye, didn't you say that you can definitely find it? I remember someone said that if you can't find it, you can do whatever you want!" Du Wei saw Ye Ye coming up and said immediately.

Ye Ye looked up and said, "It's up to you!"

"Ye Ye, you are too ridiculous. I can't save you now." Zixuan looked at Ye Ye and said angrily, and then turned and left. Although he said so, Zixuan was very happy in his heart.

Ye Ye smiled and said, "General Du, I said I will do whatever you want. Don't you have the courage?"

Du Wei smiled and said, "Okay, you are a real man! Come on, tie him up!" Du Wei had just finished speaking when Qin Minglei and Li Bin rushed up at the same time and pushed Du Wei to the ground. All the disciples of Yemen also rushed out, with the intention of "if you dare to touch Master Ye, you will die together."

Ye Ye frowned and said loudly, "All disciples of Yemen, listen to my orders, don't make trouble, and remember to protect yourself. Qin Minglei, Li Bin, you two retreat!"

Qin Minglei and Li Bin were surprised when they heard it, and they stood there without moving. "Retreat!" Ye Ye suddenly roared violently, and Qin Minglei and Li Bin were startled and immediately let go of Du Wei. Then he walked down the stands.

When the two of them passed by Ye Ye, they heard Ye Ye whisper: "Remember, protect the Yemen disciples!" Qin Minglei and Li Bin nodded at the same time, then walked down and appeased the rioting Yemen disciples.

But Xia Feng shook her head and walked down. When she passed by Ye Ye, Ye Ye whispered: "Help, protect the Yemen disciples. Also... protect yourself!" Xia Feng was stunned, then smilcd coldly, walked down the stands, and walked into the Yemen disciples.

"Haha, girl, see you tonight! I didn't sleep all night, and I can stay up all night again tonight! Haha!" The captain also shouted.

Ye Ye ignored those people and said to Du Wei: "Come on!" After that, he stretched out his hands.

Du Wei laughed and said fiercely: "The head of the Yemen is not that good! I don't know what General Zixuan called you to do! Come on, tie him up and put him in jail." After that, he waved his hand, walked out two people, tied Ye Ye up. Then take him away.

In fact, Zixuan "invited" Ye Ye and the others to the army just to let Murong Di and his group deal with Ye Ye on his behalf, because he felt that Ye Ye owed him!

Chapter 59 Disaster in the Military Camp

Ye Ye was imprisoned. Yemen naturally refused to leave, and Li Bin also begged Zixuan to cede a small area to accommodate Yemen disciples. Zixuan hid himself and said regretfully: "You can stay in the east. I will find a way to release Ye Ye. Although I have the final say here, I don't want to appease the anger of the soldiers." Zixuan's move was perfect. On the one hand, Ye Ye was imprisoned, and on the other hand, Li Bin and Yemen were sold a big face.

After listening to Zixuan's words, Li Bin immediately nodded and said: "General Zixuan, thank you very much, please!" In fact, Li Bin was not worried about Ye Ye's comfort. He was just wondering why Ye Ye did this. He was worried that Ye Ye would be caught by the hidden Ye Ye who was looking for something in vain.

After Zixuan left, Li Bin and Qin Minglei also settled the Yemen disciples, and then patrolled and watched with Xia Feng. He believed Ye Ye's words that there must be a crisis hidden in this army.

At this time, in a remote corner.

"Not bad, right? Drinking blood feels good, right? This time, I let you drink this man's blood, so that we have the same breath, and it is mixed with Murong Di's blood, which buries the death aura." The soldier who turned into Tiansheng said.

The evil ghost nodded and said nothing, but his eyes revealed greed and bloodthirstiness. These evil ghosts were still illusory bodies before evolution, and could only absorb souls, so how could they taste the deliciousness of blood.

"Okay, okay, now the person who gave me a headache can no longer pose a threat to us for the time being. I don't think he can run out without any reason. Now he must be thinking about it. Haha, okay, you can eat as much as you want!" Tiansheng said evilly, and after that, a black shadow suddenly rushed out from the top of the soldier's head, and the soldier also fell to the ground limply. The death aura gradually spread.

Tiansheng was right. Ye Ye was really thinking about it at this moment. He clearly sensed the existence of the death aura. How could he be wrong when he was very familiar with the death aura? But why did everyone check it, but why couldn't they find it? He couldn't figure it out, he really couldn't figure it out.

When Ye Ye was extremely confused, suddenly the death energy came again. Ye Ye didn't act impulsively this time, but closed his eyes and tried his best to sense the death energy. The death energy was so majestic that Ye Ye could feel it very clearly. Ye Ye was anxious, his eyes suddenly swirled, and then he walked to the edge of the prison and shouted loudly: "Hey, is there anyone? Hey, are they all dead?"

"Why are you screaming? The brothers are studying how to deal with you. I heard that you are an old friend of General Zixuan? Then you hope that General Zixuan will forgive you!" A jailer suddenly said, and Ye Ye was immediately puzzled and asked: "Forgive me?"

The jailer smiled and said: "Oh, to tell you the truth, aren't you the head of Yiyemen? There are many people who have more backgrounds than you. I have even detained Wen Boqing. Who are you!!"

"Hey, brother, is the Wen Boqing you are talking about the old general Wen?" Ye Ye was shocked and asked in a flattering tone.

The jailer was also very satisfied with Ye Ye's tone. He straightened his chest, raised his head and said, "Of course, that old guy was too ignorant and had to disobey General Zixuan's wishes. As a result, he was locked up by General Zixuan and died here. I have been guarding him. He is a good person, but he is old and confused! Haha!" After hearing this, Ye Ye took two steps back. He couldn't help but think of the old General Wen who went out to greet him when he went home with Zixuan. He was killed by Zixuan. He was his father's old friend, so he was his uncle! Seeing Ye Ye in a daze, the jailer said loudly again: "So, you'd better be honest. Maybe General Zixuan is in a good mood and thinks you are still useful, then you can still live. Otherwise, no matter you are the king of heaven, the brothers will shoot you and your disciples." After that, he hit the prison door fiercely with the gun in his hand, then turned and left, muttering: "Wrong us? Wait for death!"

Ye Ye ignored the jailer's words, but kept combining what happened, from the secret call for help, the wrong call for help, the seriousness in his heart and the delay in action after arriving at the military camp, the sending of people to monitor him, the tracking, and even the inspection of the troops... A series of things kept breaking up in Ye Ye's mind, and then reorganized. Suddenly, Ye Ye's mind became clear: It turned out that all this was done by Zixuan. He first tricked himself here, and then originally hoped to watch Murong Di kill Ye Ye, but Ye Ye visited Murong Di not only did not die, but came back. Then he resorted to this desperate measure. However, there are two things that Ye Ye can't figure out: First, why did Zixuan do this? Second, who is that 'person' with a strong aura of death!

Ye Ye shook his head. Although everything was clear, he still didn't dare to gamble with all the people in Yemen. If he acted rashly now, it would be the people in Yemen who would suffer a catastrophe! This is also what Ye Ye didn't want to see.

However, Ye Ye suddenly laughed because he had smelled a faint smell of blood. "Hmph, I'll let you come and ask me out in person!" Ye Ye suddenly whispered, then sat down, closed his eyes, and stopped talking.

At this time, in the army, no one knew that the disaster had slowly come with the arrival of night.

"Howl~" A long howl suddenly sounded in the silent night.

"Hey, did you hear anything?" A soldier on guard suddenly asked in confusion, looking around vigilantly while asking. Another soldier said disdainfully: "Oh, spring is coming, and the wolves are going to be in heat! What are you worried about! You didn't seem to be afraid when you raped the paparazzi's wife that day, so what are you afraid of now?"

"I..." The worried soldier was frustrated and stopped talking. It was extremely boring to stand guard in the army. Seeing that he had picked up a topic, another soldier kept talking: "I remember that you seemed to be very powerful that day? Why are you soft now? Haha." The soldier ignored him and amused himself there.

"Haha, you..." Suddenly, the soldier who kept talking stopped talking before he finished speaking. The other soldier was also a little angry at what he said, and didn't turn around to care about him, but walked on his own. He didn't see that the man was like a plastic bag filled with water, and then pierced with countless small holes, but blood flowed out.

After the blood spurted out, it did not fall to the ground, but disappeared, as if countless mouths were sucking it constantly.

"Hey, let's go! Premature ejaculation?" The soldier walking in front suddenly felt something was wrong and turned back to shout at the man, but the man didn't move. It was late at night and the vision was not good, so he walked up to the man, pushed him and said, "Hey, let's go, go back!" But as soon as he pushed, the man actually fell straight towards him. He was shocked and shone the flashlight. He immediately threw the man away in fear, then raised the gun in his hand and aimed everywhere without a target: "Who... Who... Who, come out!" But no one paid attention to him. He looked at the soldier on the ground who had turned into a mummy again, thought about it, and then took out a flare from his clothes.

But as soon as he took it out, he felt a hint of coolness coming from his neck. He didn't care and continued to fiddle with the flare, hoping to attract reinforcements immediately, but the coolness slowly spread to the whole back, and with the coolness came the weakness. He pulled his hand back in confusion, but felt water marks. He put his hand in front of him in confusion, and when he saw it, he immediately shouted: "Ah~~" But before he finished shouting, a line of blood immediately spurted out of his mouth, and then his whole body slowly shrank and fell beside the soldier.

Although the shouting was not finished, it still came out, alarming several patrolling teams not far away. After hearing it, they immediately went to the source of the sound vigilantly.

In the darkness, dozens of black shadows flashed by.

Chapter 60: Life in Exchange for Brothers

"Haha, you all should taste the blood. Otherwise, when your father asks you what blood is, you won't know. Then you will lose face for my personal guards!" Tiansheng said with a smile, looking at the black shadow that flashed in the air.

As soon as he finished speaking, not far from him, there were a few muffled "bangs", and a few blood flowers suddenly burst in the sky. The strange thing was that the blood was actually drawn out in the air, and the broken meat was already shriveled when it fell to the ground. Obviously, the evil ghosts absorbed the blood.

"The smell of blood is getting stronger and stronger. I wonder how Qin Minglei and the others are doing." Ye Ye, who has superhuman perception, naturally felt the smell of blood and immediately worried about the people in Yemen. Thinking of this, he stood up and shouted, "Hey, is there anything going on outside now?" Ye Ye asked tentatively.

The jailer came over again, looked at Ye Ye drunkenly and said disdainfully, "Don't worry, nothing will happen to our troops!" After that, he picked up a bottle of wine and took a sip, then left Ye Ye's sight.

"Bang", like a glass bottle falling to the ground.

Ye Ye looked over in confusion, but it was just the bottle in the jailer's hand. He shook his head and was about to sit down, but suddenly felt something was wrong. He hurried to the side to see what happened, but his vision was completely blocked and he couldn't see.

While Ye Ye was looking around, the jailer slowly came over, buried his head, and padded, as if drunk, but Ye Ye frowned because he felt a strong breath of death. Without saying a word, Ye Ye took two steps back. He still couldn't figure out the other party's intention.

The jailer slowly came over, but when he walked to the door of the cell, he suddenly stopped moving and stopped in place. Ye Ye became confused, took out Ye Yang, and slowly approached vigilantly.

"Woo!" But as soon as Ye Ye walked to the edge, a black shadow rushed out from the jailer's head, grabbing Ye Ye with his teeth and claws. Ye Ye smiled calmly and said, "I didn't look for you, but you provoked me?" After that, he formed Ye Yang into a long sword, and then cut a small cut on his finger with a "squeak", smeared the blood on it, and then stabbed Ye Yang. Ye Ye was a virgin, and his blood had not been neutralized by the woman's yin energy. The yang energy was extremely strong, and he immediately caught the evil ghost off guard. The long sword passed through his mouth, and then the evil ghost turned into black smoke and disappeared. After the evil ghost dissipated, the jailer also suddenly exploded.

"Damn it, tell your men to be careful, don't provoke that kid!" Tiansheng sensed the dissipation of an evil ghost, and immediately said to the evil ghost who had been following him and had eaten his fill. The evil ghost screamed when he heard it, reminding other evil ghosts that Ye Ye should not provoke them.

After the blood mist dissipated, Ye Ye waved his hand to dispel the bloody smell, then shook his head, ready to sit down and rest, waiting for Zixuan to bring people to pick him up, but he suddenly saw the ground, then laughed and said to himself:

"Now you don't come to ask me, then wait until you can't find me!" Ye Ye said while looking at the bunch of keys on the ground, the keys left by the jailer after the explosion.

At this time, Zixuan didn't know that Ye Ye had walked out of the prison, but was busy and exhausted. He could only watch his brother who had been through life and death together being caught in the air by an invisible thing, and then the blood in his body was sucked away by an invisible force. Although he was terrified, he had often faced these extraordinary situations, so he still had a little calmness, commanding the remaining soldiers to shoot aimlessly with bullets soaked in chicken blood. However, the evil ghost is not a zombie, how can this entity's attack be effective?

It was not until Zixuan saw Dewey, who had been with him for many years and experienced all kinds of battles, being pulled into the sky and then torn into five pieces, and then having his blood sucked out, that the fearless general finally became afraid.

He kept retreating, repeating a name: "Ye Ye... Ye Ye..." At this time, Zixuan thought that Ye Ye was the only savior!

And those soldiers saw that their general had begun to retreat, and the enemy they faced was too terrifying and weird, so they had no intention of fighting. They either ran with Zixuan or took advantage of the gap to escape from the battle area, but they were torn to pieces and sucked blood by those evil ghosts.

However, when Zixuan arrived at the prison, he looked at the ground full of broken meat and the empty cell, and his face turned pale. He was at a loss and muttered: "It's over, everything is over, even he is dead! Shouldn't I be happy? Daddy, I have avenged you! It was Ye Ye who made you uneasy in the afterlife, I avenged you. But why am I not happy?" Zixuan was silent, and the soldiers behind him were also silent.

"I don't want to die! I just avenged my father, I don't want to die!" Zixuan was afraid at this time. It turned out that Zixuan thought that his father's corpse was caused by Ye Ye, and it was Ye Ye who disturbed his father's uneasy afterlife. He was a filial son, so he naturally hated Ye Ye. So, there was such a chapter. However, now he thinks that the revenge has been avenged, but he is going to die, he doesn't want to, he is afraid!

Zixuan's roar roared out the voices of those soldiers. Suddenly, a soldier shouted loudly: "Everyone, hurry to Yemen. They may have special abilities, and it may be safe there!" A stone caused a thousand waves. After a voice sounded, everyone seemed to see hope, and rushed out of the cell and headed towards the Yemen station. Zixuan also raised his head, thought about it with a complicated expression, and then went to the Yemen station.

Sure enough, they were right. The army stationed there was killing in the dark, bloody smell, minced meat, and dried corpses were all over the ground, while Yemen was quiet as usual, and all the disciples of Yemen were sitting on the ground eating.

The huge contrast made the soldiers see hope, and they immediately swarmed there. They could no longer withstand any more blows. On the way from the prison to here, they had experienced terror again.

"Stop, Yemen doesn't welcome you! This is the Yemen garrison. If you take another step forward, don't blame us for being rude!" Li Bin saw that all the soldiers had come here. He smiled and thought to himself, "Ye Ye is right! They are here! But the head of Yemen is not a prisoner, and Yemen is not a charity!" After Li Bin finished speaking, all the Yemen people stood up, holding guns that could be picked up anywhere on the ground.

Guns are useless against evil spirits, but they can make a hole in a person's body. The soldiers immediately stopped. One person stepped forward and said, "Brothers of Yemen, please protect us. Isn't that why the general asked you to come?"

Li Bin smiled, shrugged his shoulders and said, "Well, we are here to protect you. Return the head to us first!" This was also Ye Ye's trick, which made the soldiers collapse without knowing what was said.

After hearing what Li Bin said, the soldiers stopped talking immediately, and looked at Zixuan who was walking slowly from the back in embarrassment, but their eyes kept glancing around. And those evil ghosts disappeared suddenly and never appeared again.

"Let's watch the show first. I don't believe that guy has the kindness to accept the person who wronged him." Tiansheng said to himself standing on a high place.

Zixuan walked slowly to the front, with his head down, he didn't want people to see his tears. After a long time, after his tears dried up, he slowly raised his head, looked around at the remaining soldiers and said: "Brothers, I am sorry for you! It's me... it's me!" After that, he turned his tiger eyes and looked at Li Bin and said: "Li Bin, Ye Ye is dead! It can't be saved! But I am willing to exchange my life for another life. As long as you guarantee the safety of my brothers, I am willing to commit suicide in front of you!"

"General..." The soldiers wanted to stop him, but Zixuan refused: "Brothers, take care!"

Li Bin was embarrassed when he saw this situation, and then he looked into the tent behind him. Ye Ye said from inside: "Zixuan has finally recovered his tiger spirit! This is how a soldier should be, just follow him! Let him go with peace of mind! This is the respect for a real soldier, even though he was lost before!" Only a few people could hear Ye Ye's voice.

After listening, Li Bin smiled, and then said: "Okay, let you make up for your mistakes! Come over!" After Li Bin said, the disciples of Yemen made way for a way. But those soldiers refused to go in.

Zixuan looked at them with emotion, and then pretended to be angry and said: "Now that I am not dead yet, you don't obey my orders? I order you to go immediately! Otherwise, you will be shot!"

"I will not go even if I am shot! The general and I have been through life and death together, and death is just a request!" A voice suddenly retorted. Zixuan's tiger eyes were filled with tears after hearing this. He pulled out his gun, walked to the man, lowered his head with the gun and said: "Are you going?" "No!" The man firmly opposed.

"I'm sorry, good brother!" Zixuan said to the man in a low voice when he saw that his persuasion was useless. After that, he fired the gun in the man's surprised eyes, and his brains were splattered all over the floor. After doing all this, Zixuan gently put the man's body on the ground and roared: "Go immediately, or die!" After that, he fired three shots into the sky, step by step pressing his brothers.

The soldiers had no choice but to take off their hats, bowed heavily to Zixuan, and then walked into the crowd of Yemen. Of course, they knew why Zixuan did all this! So, they entered the night gate with tears in their eyes and looked at Zixuan respectfully.

Zixuan looked at them and smiled. Then Tiger Eyes returned the greetings one by one with tears in his eyes. After all the soldiers entered, he said, "Okay, watch, don't say that I, Zixuan, am a man who doesn't keep his word." After that, he put the gun to his throat, and the gun went off, and the man fell to the ground. For the sake of his brothers, a famous general restored his bloodiness that was obscured by dust in his last life, and exchanged his life for the lives of his brothers!

"Boring! Haha, are you really safe?" Tiansheng said boredly while watching this farce.

Chapter 61 Where the Heart Falls

Ye Ye looked at Zixuan after he exploded, and smiled faintly without saying anything. He was not a kind person, especially to those who dared to hurt him. However, Zixuan's words before his death also made him re-examine Zixuan, and he had to admire Zixuan's masculinity.

"Li Bin, what should we do next?" a soldier asked boldly.

Li Bin shrugged slightly, stepped aside and said, "I'm not sure, you should actually ask him!" After that, all the disciples of Yemen also made way. The soldiers looked in that direction, and when they saw Ye Ye sitting safely inside and then calmly holding up the tea, they were all shocked: he was not dead. This idea rose in their hearts.

Ye Ye smiled, then stood up, looked around and said, "Don't be surprised, those who are going to die should die." When the soldiers heard this, they naturally knew that Ye Ye was talking about Zixuan, but it was not easy to refute since they were living under someone else's roof, so one of them stepped forward and asked tentatively, "Master Ye, what should we do next?"

Ye Ye sighed, took two steps and said, "Alas... nothing to do, just wait! Maybe they will leave after they are full! Maybe they are already full at this moment!" Ye Ye said it easily, but the frightened soldiers did not think so, and immediately made a noise: "Wait? Do we have to wait for them to eat us all?"

"Of course not, they will only eat you! Now, hand over your weapons. Of course, you can also choose not to shout, but the result, I believe you have guessed it." Ye Ye said calmly. As he spoke, a faint pressure kept oppressing the already extremely fragile soldiers.

The soldiers had no choice but to take off all their weapons and throw them aside. Then they walked to the back of the crowd and did not talk to the Yemen disciples, forming an independent circle. Ye Ye did not care about them, but looked at the sky and said to himself: "It seems that the disaster has really come."

And Tiansheng, who was standing on a high place, watched all this quietly and said: "As expected of someone who has come into contact with my heart, this courage... However, if I want to find my heart, it seems that I can only ask you now." After saying that, he waved his hand, and the evil ghost beside him, who was already 70% human, immediately let out a low howl, and suddenly in the air around him, a group of black shadows became restless again.

"Finally can't help it? Come on! Hum..." Ye Ye felt the restless factor in the air around him and said lightly. After saying that, he immediately ordered all the disciples to prepare for defense.

"Woo~" With a whine, the battle between Yemen and the evil ghost broke out for the first time. The evil ghost was still a half-illusory body, but it had absorbed a lot of human blood just now. Now it was extremely excited and rushed towards the leading Yemen disciple with its fangs and claws.

Yemen disciples were people who had experienced many storms and had good mental qualities. The Yemen disciple was not panicked, but took two steps back and formed a defensive formation with the two people behind him. Then, when the evil ghost swooped down and was about to attack him, the three of them swung out the Yemen strange daggers in their hands at the same time. The daggers were smeared with corpse worm meat juice, which had a strong corrosive effect on any object.

"Ah~" The evil ghost was caught off guard and was cut by one of the daggers. Some black objects immediately fell from his body, and then turned into flying ash and disappeared.

"It works!" Li Bin and Qin Minglei cheered at the same time, while Ye Ye watched all this calmly and expressionlessly, and then suddenly shouted: "Be careful!"

Unfortunately, before he finished speaking, a deformed person suddenly appeared on the head of the Yemen disciple who was scratched by the evil ghost. That was his soul. They forgot or didn't know that the evil ghost was best at absorbing people's souls. The Yemen disciple fell down the moment his soul was sucked out of his body, and his vitality was instantly gone.

"Swish..." The evil ghost easily sucked out the soul of the Yemen disciple without much effort, and then took it into his body, shouting excitedly.

Li Bin became anxious when he saw this situation, and immediately said: "Everyone immediately form a defensive formation, retreat after one strike, don't fight lingeringly, and keep your mind while your soul is sucked away."

The disciples immediately formed groups of three or five, kept their minds, and carefully guarded. In front of them, a group of black shadows suddenly appeared out of thin air, all baring their teeth and claws and coming towards them.

"It's bad! No matter what happens, there will be losses!" Li Bin looked at so many evil ghosts and couldn't help but worry in his heart, but he still formed a double horn with Qin Minglei and stood at the front of the crowd.

And Ye Ye, however, watched all this calmly, as if there was nothing in front of him and he was not worried about anything happening. However, he had quietly drawn out Ye Yang and combined the short sword, ready to fight back against the evil ghosts who dared to offend them at any time.

Suddenly, Ye Ye, who had been expressionless, frowned: "Murong Di is coming!" Thinking of this, Ye Ye also became anxious. Originally, he could fully guarantee the safety of the Yemen disciples in the face of those evil ghosts, but now that Murong Di had arrived, if Murong Di mixed in with the evil ghosts and attacked together, then Yemen would be busy fighting with Murong Di, and Yemen disciples and even Qin Minglei and Li Bin would be in danger.

Ye Ye sensed the energy fluctuations of Murong Di, and then tried his best to look towards the place where the energy fluctuated. However, since the evil ghost blocked the sky and he couldn't see far away, he had to guard against Murong Di while protecting the disciples of Yemen.

Murong Di did come. But his target was not Ye Ye, but Tiansheng.

"What are you doing here? Didn't I tell you to wait for me there and take care of everything?" Tiansheng said to Murong Di behind him without turning his head.

Although Murong Di felt unhappy, he said softly: "Tiansheng, I'm not your housekeeper, and the news I brought this time is extremely important to you, otherwise I wouldn't come here in person."

Tiansheng raised his eyebrows, looked back at Murong Di and said: "Tell me, if you don't make me happy, then..." After that, the evil ghost beside him immediately roared threateningly.

Murong Di ignored the evil ghost directly. For Murong Di, the evil ghost in front of him was just a child who relied on the strong and picked up a gun. He said, "I finally understand that this heart is not that heart, Tiansheng, you are really a heart of stone!" After saying that, Murong Die put on a smile and looked at Tiansheng indifferently.

After Tiansheng heard this, his body suddenly trembled violently, and he looked at Murong Die with red eyes, and then his flesh twisted. In an instant, he recovered the appearance after absorbing Murong Die's blood and said, "What did you say!"

Murong Die laughed. All this was within his expectations. He continued to say indifferently: "This news is important enough, but it seems that you don't take it seriously!"

"I just ask you, what did you say!" Tiansheng suddenly became furious, stretched out his hand and grabbed Murong Die's neck. Murong Die was slightly startled and threw away Tiansheng's hand with both hands and said, "Isn't it just like that!"

Tiansheng panted quickly, then slowly calmed down and said, "Did you find it?"

Murong Di nodded, not angry because of Tiansheng's rash attack just now: "Yes, I found it!"

"Where is it?" Tiansheng continued to ask, with more hope in his eyes.

"You'll have to ask Master Ye about this!" Murong Di shrugged helplessly, pointing at Ye Ye who was alert not far away.

Tiansheng looked over and said, "Does he know?" He stared at Murong Di, who said nothing more. He smiled and looked at him, as if saying, "Whether you believe it or not, just ask and you'll know."

Tiansheng suddenly laughed and said coldly, "Okay, I'll go ask now!" After that, he slowly walked down the high ground. At the same time, the evil ghosts that had been attacking Yemen disciples all over the place also stopped.

Chapter 62 Unknown

Murong Di looked at Tiansheng's back indifferently and shook his head, his expression was like looking at his naughty child. With a smile, Murong Di followed Tiansheng.

While Ye Ye was wondering why all the evil spirits stopped attacking, he also sensed that Murong Di's energy was constantly approaching. Although the speed was very slow, it was constantly approaching.

Soon after, Ye Ye looked at the opposite side vigilantly, and his mouth moved slightly: "Here they come." Sure enough, as soon as Ye Ye finished speaking, three figures suddenly appeared in the thick fog that was originally caused by those evil spirits.

Ye Ye looked at them vigilantly. He didn't know that Tiansheng, who was still a baby at the time, was among the three. However, Tiansheng's strength was very weak now, and he only relied on the energy in Murong Di's blood to exist now. Ye Ye naturally filtered him out. However, the black hole that Tiansheng exploded was a terrifying thing. However, Ye Ye didn't know all this, and his attention was always focused on Murong Di.

The three people finally showed their faces in the thick fog. Ye Ye saw that Murong Di was among them. Ye Ye smiled and walked forward, looking at Murong Di and said, "Senior Mu, I haven't seen you for a few days. How come you are someone else's follower?"

Murong Di smiled and said, "I haven't seen you for a few days. How come Master Ye has become a shelter?" After that, Murong Di looked at the soldier hiding at the back of the crowd.

Ye Ye glanced at them lightly, and then said helplessly, "Yes, there is no way. We need to develop our Yemen!" Ye Ye shrugged lightly.

Murong Di was about to speak again, but was cleverly interrupted by Tiansheng. Tiansheng stepped forward again and said, "Master Ye? Excuse me, have you seen my heart?"

"Heart?" Ye Ye was puzzled. He didn't know that it was Tiansheng. But when Xia Feng heard the word "heart", her eyes immediately shrank into pinholes, and she took two steps back in fear. Her chest was constantly hurt by the violent panting, and she kept muttering: "Really... it's coming!"

Others did not see Xia Feng's abnormality. In the front, Ye Ye stared at Tiansheng. He really couldn't recognize that Tiansheng was the baby that he and Murong Di had been fighting for a few days ago. So he said: "Heart? What do you mean?"

Tiansheng raised his eyebrows, glanced at Murong Di, and saw Murong Di's calm expression, and then said: "Ye Ye, don't test my patience, tell me, where is the heart!"

Ye Ye smiled, so disdainful: "Do you believe me if I say I know? There are so many hearts here, just find one by yourself." After that, Ye Ye pointed to the bodies of soldiers whose souls were sucked away by evil spirits on the ground. He did not take Tiansheng seriously, because he clearly felt that the energy in Tiansheng's body was still so weak.

"You...Okay, it seems that I have to take action! I wonder if that gentleman is okay now?" Tiansheng suppressed his anger and said calmly.

Ye Ye frowned and said, "How could he know the Ghost King?" He still said calmly, "Take action? Come on! Which gentleman? I know many gentlemen. Isn't the one behind you the 'sir'?" Ye Ye deliberately said the gentleman's son very seriously, obviously targeting Murong Di, who has a strange hobby.

"You... Master Ye, watch your words and deeds!" Murong Di naturally heard what Ye Ye meant and said angrily. Then he said to Tiansheng, "Let me help you deal with him!"

Tiansheng refused and said, "No need, let me meet the head of Yemen!" After saying that, his body leaned down slightly, and he might burst out at any time. Murong Di knew Tiansheng's strength, and knew that Tiansheng had no tricks to save his life except the black hole at this moment, so he immediately wanted to stop Tiansheng, but Tiansheng wanted to, burst out. Murong Di was startled and hurriedly took a breath, ready to rush forward, but was blocked by the evil ghost.

"No need to help, he has his own plan!" The evil ghost's voice was as cold as hell, and it also woke Murong Di up, looking angrily at Tiansheng who was rushing up slowly. But Murong Di felt that although the evil ghost said so, he had already gathered strength and was ready to rush up at any time, and all the evil ghosts around him also emitted cold energy, ready to help at any time. Murong Di also calmed down, gathered energy, and looked at Tiansheng.

"You are overestimating yourself! Let me teach you how to respect your elders!" Ye Ye, who did not recognize Tiansheng, regarded Tiansheng as a newborn calf who had not been born deep in the world. He combined Ye Yang into a short blade and rushed forward.

Ye Ye's speed was much faster than that of Tiansheng, and he immediately came into contact with Tiansheng. Then Ye Ye stabbed the short blade first, quickly, accurately and ruthlessly, and the three-character formula was used so skillfully and impeccably.

Tiansheng's eyes shrank into pinholes. He didn't expect that Ye Ye would use all his strength against himself, who was much weaker than him. However, he couldn't be distracted at this moment. He absorbed Murong Di's blood energy and naturally gained some combat experience from Murong Di. He immediately leaned down, followed the momentum, rolled to the ground, rolled under Ye Ye's crotch, and narrowly avoided Ye Ye's stab. Then he immediately got up from the ground, made claws with both hands, and attacked Ye Ye's back.

Ye Ye smiled slightly, and suddenly kicked back with his right foot, a horse kick, to attack Tiansheng's grab.

With a muffled sound of "puff", Ye Ye's horse kick actually broke Tiansheng's grab and kicked him several meters away. He fell to the ground. However, Ye Ye also twisted his foot slightly, and there was a slight tingling in the sole of his foot. Tiansheng's attack also stabbed Ye Ye's fragile sole. A little blood stained the sole of his shoe slightly red.

"Asshole!" Seeing this, Murong Di, who regarded Tiansheng as his own son, could no longer hold back and released his condensed energy at once, rushing towards Ye Ye. Ye Ye was startled and quickly gathered his mind, preparing to resist Murong Di's full-strength attack in anger.

"Stop!" Suddenly, a voice sounded from behind Ye Ye. Murong Di was startled and the condensed energy also dispersed. He stopped and looked behind Ye Ye, and said with concern: "Are you okay?"

Tiansheng slowly got up from the ground, then patted the dust on his body, wiped the light golden blood from the corner of his mouth and said: "Don't worry, I'm fine!" After that, he slowly walked in the direction of Murong Di. Although Murong Di stopped attacking, he raised his energy and sent all his might to Ye Ye, as if saying: "If you dare to attack him, you will also be fatally hit!"

Ye Ye shrugged his shoulders lightly, neither resisting Murong Di's might nor launching an attack: "Go back! Remember to respect your elders!"

Tian Sheng had blood on his mouth. When he walked to Ye Ye, he stopped and said: "Okay, I remember. I will let you taste all this!" After that, he walked to Murong Di and said: "Let's talk about it all! Do more important things!"

Tian Sheng said, and left without looking back. Murong Di looked at Ye Ye fiercely and followed him. Then, the three disappeared in the thick fog. Finally, the overwhelming evil ghosts also disappeared.

Ye Ye felt Murong Di's energy going away, and only when he could no longer sense it did he let out a sigh of relief and turned to Li Bin and Qin Minglei and said, "Okay, let's go back to Yemen! Take the generals back, and then hand them over to Quanguo." After that, he kept thinking about who had just started the fight, and walked back to the crowd. He brushed past Xia Feng, and did not see Xia Feng's pale face because of fear.

When everyone in Yemen was packing up, at Tiansheng and Murong Di's place. Murong Di cut his finger again, poured the blood into a small bowl, and handed it to Tiansheng. Tiansheng took a sip and drank it. His complexion recovered a lot, and then he laughed and said, "It turns out that my heart is there, and they are there too..." After that, he laughed happily. Murong Di looked at him weakly and smiled softly.

At this time, on a long road. A girl with a sweaty face was squatting on the side of the road to rest. She casually took out a steamed bun and ate it, and said worriedly while eating, "Brother Ye Ye, where are you?" This girl was Li Yerui.

"I say, girl, I really can't persuade you. It seems that if I don't help you find your brother Ye Ye, you won't go back with me, right?" A voice suddenly sounded from behind him. Huang Shang picked up his clothes and slowly walked towards Ye Rui.

Chapter 63 Encounter

Ye Rui looked at Huang Shang who was walking slowly, smiled, and said with an apology but unable to hide the smile: "Uncle Huang Shang, I'm sorry!" After that, he gently covered his mouth, smiling.

Huang Shang sighed and shook his head helplessly. He had no way to deal with this girl Li Yerui. After all, in Yemen, only Li Yerui could contact Zi Ruixin. However, he thought that Li Yerui had not woken up from the coma. If it weren't for this incident, he might have been kept in the dark. Sighing, Huang Shang walked to Ye Rui, touched Li Yerui's head and said: "It's agreed that you must go back when you see your brother Ye Ye. This is not a place for girls to come. It's dangerous!" Maybe because he loves the house and the dog, Huang Shang also likes the smart and persistent Li Yerui very much. After saying that, he made a face.

Li Yerui frowned, pinched his nose and said: "Excuse me, did you wash your hands just now?"

"Uh..." Huang Shang groaned awkwardly, took his hand away, and then looked into the distance and said: "Girl, have you rested well? After resting, we are ready to set off again. Don't let Aunt Li wait too long! My baby is about to be born!" After Huang Shang finished speaking, a trace of happiness and anxiety escaped from his eyes.

Ye Rui naturally understood, nodded, and stood up: "Let's go, I guess we can see Brother Ye Ye in two days! If he is still safe." He said with worry.

Huang Shang looked at Ye Rui's worried look, shook his head and said softly: "Ye Ye, you can't let Ye Rui down!" A girl, who traveled thousands of miles to find him for a nightmare, how can such a girl be let down? Unfortunately, Ye Ye didn't know all this.

"I have a suggestion. I think we should change the route. How about it?" In the night gate team, Ye suddenly said to Qin Minglei, Li, and Xia Feng beside him. Xia Feng, the woman, has not spoken to Ye Ye since that incident, but she followed him strangely, which was puzzling.

After listening to Ye Ye's words, Li Bin pondered for a while, then nodded and said, "I agree. If the evil ghosts in front ambush again, we will be caught off guard. And changing the route may avoid all this." After that, Qin Minglei also nodded in support.

Ye Ye smiled. At this time, the three of them could make the decision. After all, except for the remnants, all of them were from the Yemen Sect. They only obeyed the orders of the Sect Master, not to mention the two hall masters. Ye Ye smiled, then stood up, and shouted loudly with a deep breath: "All Yemen disciples, listen to the order, immediately abandon the original route back to Yemen, go around from the northwest, and after resting and reorganizing, immediately form a team to go around." After Ye Ye finished speaking, the Yemen disciples did not react at all, and silently obeyed the order. Although those soldiers were a little dissatisfied, if they were not stupid, they would know that if there was an ambush ahead, it would endanger themselves, and they did not refute.

Ye Ye looked around, nodded, squatted down, fiddled with the bonfire on the ground, and glanced at the cold Xia Feng opposite, saying: "Hey, do you have to be so resentful?"

Xia Feng glanced coldly and ignored him. Ye Ye shook his head and said: "Heaven, earth, my wife must not be so cold in the future!" After that, he ignored Xia Feng and continued to fiddle with the bonfire. But when Ye Ye's words entered Xia Feng's ears, they seemed to have a different taste. She looked at Ye Ye with a slightly red face, sniffed slightly but did not speak. A strange feeling came from the two of them.

Li Bin quietly moved to Qin Minglei's side and said easily: "You are quiet, it's just that the young couple is having a quarrel! Let's retreat!" After that, Qin Minglei actually nodded and slowly moved.

"Okay, rest well, let's go!" But at this time, Ye Ye suddenly stood up and issued an order to march.

Li Bin and Qin Minglei also stood up, shook their heads and said, "The young couple had a quarrel and vented their anger on us. They have only rested for less than half an hour!" Although they complained, they had to obey Ye Ye's orders and followed the march. After a long time, on the way to change the route, Li Bin suddenly looked at Qin Minglei in surprise and found that a change had emerged in Qin Minglei.

Since Ye Ye and Xia Feng failed to communicate, Ye Ye seemed to change his calmness and became vigorous and resolute, which was unbearable for Qin Minglei, Li Bin and the people of Yemen.

On the other hand, Huang Shang and Ye Rui were walking slowly towards Ye Ye's original path, not knowing that Ye Ye had changed his route. And far ahead of them, three people were coming towards them quickly. These three people were

Tiansheng, Murong Di and the evil ghost. According to their itinerary, they would meet at noon the next day.

"It seems that I will finally meet him! Haha!" Tiansheng suddenly said softly. Murong Die was no longer surprised by Tiansheng's mumbling, perhaps he was used to Tiansheng's foresight. However, he did hope to know who the person he met would be, making Tiansheng so happy.

Traveling is lonely. Time passed quickly, and a day passed.

The next day, Huang Shang and Ye Rui traveled again, and Tiansheng and the others also traveled at the same time.

At noon, three people finally appeared in Huang Shang's field of vision. He shook his head and said softly: "Finally I met someone!" After that, he urged Ye Rui to speed up. He hoped to communicate with those people, perhaps to know Ye Ye's news, and also to make Ye Rui and the girl feel at ease.

Soon after, they met.

Huang Shang smiled, greeted and said: "Everyone, my niece and I have fled here. I wonder if it is safe ahead?" Huang Shang and Ye Rui have been traveling for several days, sleeping in the wind and rain, and their appearance is similar to that of the refugees.

Tiansheng smiled, his eyes showing some excitement, and said: "The front? It's not safe ahead. The army is fighting. We are hunters in the mountains. We escaped immediately after hearing about the war!"

Huang Shang heard it and confirmed that the front must be the place where Zixuan was stationed. Then he thanked him and said: "Thank you all, we will take a detour!" After that, he pulled Li Yerui, who looked hopeful, and prepared to move forward. He was also quite confused in his heart. Why did he feel a sense of death, but it was unpredictable.

But Tiansheng stretched out his hand to stop the two of them, and said with a smile: "You two, there is really a war ahead. You also know that it is really not peaceful recently." Huang Shang frowned slightly, he didn't want to entangle more. So he flashed by and continued to smile and said: "Thank you three, thank you for reminding us, we will take a detour! Besides, our roads are opposite, so I won't bother you three!" After that, he wanted to lower Tiansheng's hand.

"Do you have money?" Suddenly Tiansheng's voice sounded, and then he looked at Huang Shang, and his eyes revealed a strong greed. Huang Shang also looked at him. He didn't know what he wanted to do, but he relied on his own strength and was not afraid. He just looked at Tiansheng calmly without saying anything.

"Do you have money? I'm really sorry to tell you two that we have no money! If we go out like this, we will just starve to death!" Tiansheng's eyes were helpless and greedy, which were surprisingly vivid.

"Do you want to...rob?" Huang Shang said in a defensive posture. Tiansheng immediately pretended to be panicked and said, "You two, we are just for money. We are also very familiar with this place. If you don't mind, the three of us will take you there, and we men can temporarily protect you. However, we will only take you to the outer edge of the army stationed there, and this price..."

Huang Shang nodded and thought for a while, then said, "Okay, you will lead the way, and you can't do anything!" After Huang Shang finished speaking, Tiansheng looked at Murong Di beside him with surprise, but there was a touch of evil in his eyes. Then when he turned around, his eyes were full of surprise and he said to Huang Shang: "Okay, as long as the price is good, it's fine!"

Huang Shang nodded: "Let's go!" After that, he took Ye Rui and walked forward. Tiansheng also nodded, motioning the two to follow.

After walking for a day, they didn't communicate. Huang Shang just protected Ye Rui behind him, and let the three strangers who led the way for money in his mind. He didn't see Ye Rui's worried and frightened expression.

Night.

"Girl, what's your name?" Murong Die smiled and walked in front of Ye Rui, saying kindly. But Ye Rui shrank back and hid beside Huang Shang in fear. Murong Die smiled and said to Huang Shang: "You kid, you are really shy!"

"There's no way, it's hard to escape! It's hard for the child!" Huang Shang said with bitterness on his face. Murong Di smiled. He naturally didn't believe it, but he said, "Where are you from and where are you going?" Huang Shang avoided the question and said, "It's the past. I don't want to mention sad things. Sorry. Besides, maybe tomorrow you will take us to the gap in the army you mentioned, and we will separate and won't meet again!" After that, Huang Shang poked the campfire.

Murong Di also dressed very cleverly. According to the appearance of ordinary people after encountering such a thing, he stood up awkwardly and stopped communicating with Huang Shang. Huang Shang saw him leave, hugged Ye Rui beside him and comforted him softly, "Don't worry, your brother Ye Ye is fine!" However, Huang Shang did not see Ye Rui staring at Tiansheng's direction, with strong fear in his eyes, and his body trembling. Huang Shang felt Ye Rui's trembling, but thought she was cold, so he took off his coat and covered Ye Rui.

"It seems... that girl seems to know something! It's a bit troublesome!" Tiansheng stretched out his hand to warm the fire and said lightly. After saying that, the evil ghost beside him, whose breath was no longer dead, stood up, pulled up his pants, stepped into the darkness, and disappeared. But he looked like he had gone to the bathroom.

At night, the bonfire burned silently. In this climate, the night was especially cold, and Ye Rui had fallen asleep under Huang Shang's protection. Huang Shang also snored slightly. On the other side, Tiansheng, like ordinary people, huddled together to keep warm.

Suddenly, a gust of wind blew, blowing the bonfire slightly. Huang Shang frowned, but still pretended to sleep without opening his eyes. And the wind suddenly stopped. After a few breaths, the wind blew again. Suddenly, the wind became fierce, and the bonfire flashed out, leaving sparks flickering.

The night was dark, and you couldn't see your fingers. Silently, the wind caused by the rapid movement of a formation object blew. Perhaps it rolled up the dry grass on the ground, making a rustling sound. Then, there was a sound of breaking through the air and exploding, followed by a muffled sound, and then the sound of an object falling to the ground, and then the wind stopped. After the wind stopped, the bonfire with sparks suddenly ignited again.

Everything was the same as before. Huang Shang had been dozing for a long time, and Ye Rui had already fallen asleep. On Tiansheng's side, the three of them had been crowded together for a long time, and it was unknown whether they were asleep. On the ground, a trace of black powder slowly rose with the heat formed by the burning of the bonfire.

And suddenly, Tiansheng on one side opened his eyes. A sense of playfulness appeared in his eyes: "It seems that you are really strong! But you can't escape from my palm after all!" Tiansheng thought, and then closed his eyes again. And the human-shaped evil ghost beside him, his face kept changing strangely, but there was no energy overflowing. Obviously, he was seriously injured and was trying to suppress it at this moment.

At night, after such a commotion, it did not disturb the quiet of the night. The night passed quickly.

"Let's go... Hurry up and take us to the designated location, then we can disperse!" Early in the morning, Huang Shang got up, walked to Tiansheng and the other two, and woke them up, but there was a flash of teasing in his eyes.

Tiansheng rubbed his eyes, stood up and said: "Hey, okay! After taking you there, we can leave this dangerous place, and then you give us money, and then we have the capital to do business to make a living!" Tiansheng naively planned the future, and then walked to Murong Di while talking, but his eyes kept crossbowing Huang Shang, indicating that he would take action later!

"Hey? Why is that brother silent?" Huang Shang took out some steamed buns from his bag, and then heated them up and handed some to Tiansheng and the other two, and then asked tentatively. Before the man answered, Tiansheng rushed to answer: "He didn't sleep well last night. It's late at night, and he's afraid of some wild beasts, so he naturally needs someone to keep watch!" After that, he took the steamed buns and passed them to the two of them, and stopped talking. Huang Shang also smiled, turned around and walked to Ye Rui, handed the golden steamed bun to Ye Rui, and then ate it himself. However, his eyes occasionally glanced at Tiansheng and the other two.

After eating, the few people hurried on their way again. Not long after, they finally arrived at the gap where the army patrolled as Tiansheng said, a small forest. Of course, the army no longer exists, no matter what they say.

"We're here, this is it, this... money..." Tiansheng looked at Huang Shang and said lightly. Huang Shang smiled, took out a stack of banknotes from his clothes, and said earnestly: "Take it, remember to be a good person!" Huang Shang deliberately said the word "be a good person" very seriously, as if he knew who did it last night.

Tiansheng took the money, his eyes suddenly stopped being greedy, looked at Huang Shang lightly, and said: "One last request, lend me your blood!" Then he looked at Huang Shang. Huang Shang also looked at Tiansheng curiously and asked: "What's your name? Last night, you did it, right?"

Tiansheng smiled and did not deny it. Huang Shang continued, "Forget it, there are children here, I don't want to bother you, go away! Don't bother me anymore!" After that, he pulled Ye Rui to leave. But he found that Ye Rui's body was very stiff. He looked back in confusion, with a hint of surprise in his eyes. There was an overwhelming black shadow behind him, and then slowly formed an unformed human figure, which turned out to be countless evil ghosts.

As soon as those evil ghosts appeared, Ye Rui screamed in fear, but Huang Shang just looked at those evil ghosts indifferently, and then hugged Ye Rui in his arms, not letting Ye Rui look at those evil ghosts with majestic faces again.

"So that's what you did last night. Bully us uncle and nephew to escape?" Huang Shang said indifferently. With his strength, he didn't need to worry about these evil ghosts at all. However, in his words, the tone of the word "nephew" was emphasized. It must be said that Huang Shang was only worried about Ye Rui.

Tiansheng smiled and didn't deny it. He shrugged and said with a smile: "Escape? Haha..." Before he finished speaking, Tiansheng laughed like a lunatic. He laughed so crazily. After a long time, he continued: "Haha, Huang Shang is the emperor, the son of heaven, right?"

This shocking statement, Huang Shang looked at Tiansheng with cold eyes. There were only a few people who knew his identity, but why did the person in front of him know it so clearly? Huang Shang asked coldly in confusion: "Who are you?"

"The first two people were born by heaven, but you are the son, and I am just the birth." The clever answer, saying his name in the turn, can be regarded as Tiansheng's respect for Huang Shang.

"Tiansheng?" Huang Shang naturally heard the implication in the words and called out in confusion. Tiansheng smiled and nodded and said: "I said, Huang Shang, I will only use your blood for one use. If you don't give it to me, don't blame me for being rude." After Tiansheng finished speaking, the evil ghosts around him roared together, and the sound was about to shake the sky.

Huang Shang ignored the roaring evil spirits. He knew that those evil spirits were followers of the powerful. He looked at Ye Rui in his arms. Ye Rui's face was pale and frightening at this time. He kept saying, "They will kill... kill... kill." That was all. Huang Shang lowered his head and gently placed his hand on the back of Ye Rui's head. Under his skillful control, a force entered from the back of his head and compressed his blood vessels. Ye Rui rolled his eyes and fainted. After doing all this, Huang Shang smiled, raised his head and looked forward with bloodthirstiness: "Fight!" Obviously, Huang Shang was eager to fight!

Chapter 64 Let's Fight

Huang Shang didn't know why he couldn't suppress his anger. He had never been like this before. Even when he fought the Ghost Queen and the Ghost King, he didn't show such a love of war. But Huang Shang didn't bother to care at this moment. The overwhelming fighting spirit in his heart kept emanating, and his eyes were fixed on the evil ghosts, Murong Di and Tiansheng in front of him. He didn't rush to take action. Even though he was eroded by the fighting spirit, the pride in his heart told him to back up, because he knew very well that the opponent's strength was like paper in front of him.

Tiansheng looked at Huang Shang, curled his lips and said, "Nothing more, in that era, such strength could only be cannon fodder!" After that, the teasing in his eyes disappeared and turned into solemnity. Although he said that, Huang Shang is now invincible. Tiansheng waved his hand, and the evil ghosts swarmed up and covered the sky.

Huang Shang watched the evil ghosts rushing up, stepped back with his right foot, put his hands down vertically, and then the red and black flames emanated from his body, and a small strand of it wrapped up the unconscious Li Yerui on the ground. Huang Shang roared and rushed forward.

Even though those evil ghosts had evolved and had stronger strength than before, they were like paper under Huang Shang's arrogance. Huang Shang didn't need to do anything, just commanded the arrogance to burn the evil ghosts who dared to attack rashly into nothingness.

"Weak, too weak!" Huang Shang stopped and stood still and said. But those evil ghosts kept rushing forward as if they were not afraid of death. And Huang Shang didn't move either.

Suddenly, Huang Shang frowned slightly, and moved his body to one side to make way for a ball of golden light. The golden light passed by his side, and then disappeared again into the group of evil ghosts. Huang Shang smiled: "Finally, there is someone who can fight!" After saying that, he rushed to the place where the golden light disappeared, and the red and black arrogance burned the evil ghosts beside him into nothingness along the way.

"How come it's so fast..." The golden light was Murong Di. He wanted to hide again after failing to hit him, waiting for the next sneak attack. After all, he also felt Huang Shang's strength and did not dare to attack head-on. Just when he had just hidden in the group of evil spirits, he found that Huang Shang had already rushed up to chase his energy. He was shocked, but Murong Di was Murong Di after all. He made a choice quickly after being surprised.

Seeing that he could no longer dodge, he immediately raised his energy and concentrated it on his hands that turned into tiger claws. He saw the right opportunity and grabbed forward fiercely.

'Boom'. A sound of energy collision and explosion sounded, and a circle of energy spread out with the will of destruction. After the energy dissipated, it was found that Huang Shang was standing steadily in the position of Murong Di just now, and Murong Di had retreated several meters. A straight sliding mark under his feet was very conspicuous. Murong Di was actually knocked back several meters in such a blow. Huang Shang smiled and rushed up again.

Panting, Murong Di looked at Huang Shang in surprise, the fear on his face was so vivid. Seeing Huang Shang rushing up again, Murong Di did not choose to fight him again, but cleverly used his body to dodge, and then grabbed him from the outside and inside with both hands. Huang Shang also retracted his hand, blocked Murong Di's wrist, knocked down his claws, and then raised his knees to hit the wrist again. He actually wanted to break Murong Di's hands.

But Murong Di wrapped all his energy in his hands, then met Huang Shang's knee strike, and then followed that force and kicked out. But at this moment, Huang Shang rushed up strangely, grabbed Murong Di's long white hair, and then retreated and pressed, trying to press Murong Di to the ground. Murong Di immediately made a gesture of supporting the ground with both hands, and bounced up the moment he landed. Unexpectedly, Huang Shang was waiting for this moment.

Huang Shang grabbed Murong Di's hand with inertia after bouncing up, and then quickly flashed behind him and raised his foot to step down.

"Ah!" Murong Di was stepped on the ground, and his hands were dislocated by Huang Shang, and he screamed in pain. But Huang Shang did not stop like this, he raised his foot again and kicked down fiercely, the direction was Murong Di's head. He wanted to kill Murong Di.

At this life-and-death moment, Murong Di burst out with power beyond his ability. He first forced out his own arrogance completely, and then condensed the golden arrogance to form an illusory armor, especially thick on the head. Then he endured the severe pain from both hands, turned around suddenly, and kicked his feet in a rabbit-like shape, heading towards Huang Shang.

This was Murong Di's full-strength attack. Huang Shang did not stop the fatal kick because of this.

Murong Di kicked out with both feet, and Huang Shang's foot kicked into the gap between Murong Di's feet and stepped on his head, but Huang Shang was kicked out by Murong Di's full-strength attack and retreated two meters. After sliding back two meters, Huang Shang looked coldly at Murong Di, whose head was trampled on the ground, and smiled. Huang Shang, who was confident, had already thought that Murong Di was a corpse.

However, a strange thing happened. Murong Di stood up tremblingly. With his hands dislocated, he lost the power of his hands and slowly stood up with his legs and waist. At this time, the energy helmet on his head, which looked thick, also fell off piece by piece, revealing Murong Di's bleeding facial features. Huang Shang's attack had already injured him, but under the protection of the energy helmet, Murong Di did not die.

Surprise flashed across Huang Shang's face, but he did not attack again. He just looked at Murong Di jokingly.

Murong Di also looked at Huang Shang, but his eyes were swaying. He did not dare to look at him, nor did he dare to attack again, and even did not dare to use energy to repair his damaged body. He was afraid that once the energy was raised, Huang Shang would think that he was going to attack and rush up again to take his life.

Murong Di was scared. Murong Di was actually scared. Tiansheng looked at all this calmly. He looked at Murong Di's trembling body, shook his head and said, "Murong Di, come back!" After that, he walked to Murong Di and asked the evil ghost who had been by his side and had not participated in the battle to catch Murong Di and then brought him back to the camp.

"Sure enough." Tiansheng clasped his hands and said solemnly to Huang Shang. Huang Shang smiled lightly, retracted his arrogance and said, "You go!" Just now, a lot of fighting spirit had been vented. Huang Shang would not be controlled by fighting spirit for the time being.

Tiansheng shook his head and said firmly, "If I don't take your blood, even if I die today, I will die in humiliation!"

"Okay, you are a man! If you don't mind, come to my night gate, I will definitely treat you with courtesy as a distinguished guest!" Huang Shang didn't know Tiansheng's life experience and thought he was just a hot-blooded person.

"Thank you for the compliment! But I'm not interested in Yemen! I'm only interested in your blood. I just said I only want a drop of your blood, now I want all your blood!" Tiansheng said, his face became crazy. And he secretly raised his energy.

Huang Shang shook his head: "We are different! If you insist on doing this, I..." Huang Shang didn't finish his words, and was controlled by the surging fighting spirit again, and couldn't help but roaring to the sky. At this time, Huang Shang clearly felt that the man named Tiansheng in front of him could completely stimulate the fighting spirit dormant in his body.

However, although Huang Shang knew all this, he was already controlled by the fighting spirit. And this time the fighting spirit was stronger than before. Huang Shang immediately kept a trace of his mind, so as not to be eroded by the fighting spirit and become a madman who only knew how to fight. At the same time, the red and black flames ignited on him again!

Tiansheng looked at all this solemnly, and said to himself: "As long as I don't die!" After that, he rushed up first. The prelude to this battle with a huge disparity in strength was opened.

Chapter 65 Steal

Huang Shang looked at Tiansheng rushing up, with a hint of appreciation in his eyes. He didn't know Tiansheng well, but he actually took a fancy to Tiansheng. But at this moment, he was controlled by the will to fight, and had to fight!

"Ah" roared to the sky, and Huang Shang also rushed up. This time the collision was naturally no suspense. Tiansheng flew backwards under the collision and spit out a mouthful of light golden blood, but he quickly got up, but he looked listless and no longer had the same vigor!

But even though Huang Shang seriously injured Tiansheng, his brows frowned, and he raised his hands. The red and black aura on them dimmed a little. He was shocked: This kid can actually steal energy?

Just when Huang Shang was surprised, Tiansheng rushed up again, completely ignoring the injury he had just suffered. Huang Shang was confused, and did not attack, but defended. When Tiansheng's fists touched his arm, Huang Shang clearly felt that the strong aura on his arm dimmed a little. With this attack, Huang Shang was sure that Tiansheng could steal energy from the attack, and the energy he stole was not just a little bit, but a lot. Thinking of this, Huang Shang stopped fighting with him, dodged, and did not touch him.

"What are you dodging?" Tiansheng smiled, and his sluggish face regained some spirit, and his offensive became fiercer. After all, at this moment, he had temporarily paralyzed the enemy.

Huang Shang did not speak, and his fighting spirit became stronger. When had he ever been treated like this? The anger and the overwhelming fighting spirit became violent in Tiansheng's attack, and the only clear mind left in Huang Shang's heart also shook. Huang Shang, who was controlled by the fighting spirit, stopped dodging immediately, and met Tiansheng's fists with both hands, and forced Tiansheng back with both defense and attack. Then Huang Shang turned around again, and his elbow hit back, heading towards Tiansheng's chest. Tiansheng absorbed Murong Di's blood and obtained some energy from it, so his skills were naturally not bad, and he dodged the elbow that would surely break his sternum. However, Huang Shang's attack did not disappear like this. Instead, after the elbow strike dodged, the other hand followed with a reverse elbow strike.

Tiansheng's pupils shrank into pinholes, and then he crouched down dangerously. Huang Shang's elbow strike passed over his head with a tiger's wind, swept up some of his hair, and was immediately burned into nothingness by the flames. Tiansheng no longer cared about the flames above his head. He squatted and bounced his feet, and shot backwards. However, in this lightning moment, Huang Shang turned around strangely, and then grabbed Tiansheng who was about to fly back.

With a "boom", the flames rose, as if to burn Tiansheng. At this time, Huang Shang's other hand also launched, and the bowl-sized fist with red and black flames and the will to destroy everything smashed towards Tiansheng's head. If this strike hit, Tiansheng would have to die here even if he had eight lives.

However, Tiansheng looked at the flames, not only without fear, but also with a strong greed in his eyes. The corners of his mouth twitched and he smiled faintly.

Huang Shang had a clear mind and immediately felt something was wrong, but he could not withdraw his attack.

He simply increased his strength and was determined to take his name.

Just when his fist was about to reach Tiansheng, Tiansheng's body suddenly emitted a wave, which even distorted the air, and then a trace of attributeless energy was emitted, and a suction force was transmitted, and the energy on Huang Shang's body was also sucked over and then disappeared. People who have seen the wave will immediately know that the wave is the energy of the black hole summoned by Tiansheng.

Huang Shang was startled and wanted to retreat immediately. But he was surprised to find that he could not move, and the suction force actually sucked him firmly, and the energy in his body was also sucked out by the suction, and then passed to Tiansheng and disappeared.

He felt the energy in his body leaking out, but he could do nothing about it. Huang Shang roared angrily, and forced out all the energy in his body. The red and black aura turned black and wrapped around Huang Shang. Then Huang Shang sank his feet and bounced violently, finally getting rid of the terrifying suction.

The suction also brought a bit of bone-penetrating and soul-piercing coolness, which also woke Huang Shang from his fighting spirit. After Huang Shang retreated several meters, he looked at Tiansheng indifferently. At this moment, Huang Shang was wrapped in black flames, and his expression could not be seen clearly. Tiansheng still had that evil smile on his face, and the distorted fluctuations were slowly absorbed into his body.

"Haha, I'm really full. I haven't eaten such delicious food for a long time. But I still need your blood!" Tiansheng said, and took the fluctuations back into his body, and then smiled. Although he couldn't see Huang Shang's expression clearly, he could imagine his expression.

Hearing Tiansheng's words, Huang Shang's black flames trembled, but he didn't speak. Tiansheng continued to smile, his face no longer solemn, but said in a relaxed manner: "Arrogance? It is indeed arrogant, but..." As soon as he finished speaking, black flames appeared on his body and gradually enveloped him. Seeing the black flames burning on Tiansheng's body, the black flames on Huang Shang's body burned more violently, and he was obviously extremely angry.

"It's pretty good, but I can't operate it for the time being. But if I absorb your blood, then I can naturally control this power easily and freely!" Tiansheng waved his fist, with black flames on it, and said with satisfaction. After speaking, he put his hand down, then forced out the black flames, staring at Huang Shang: "But, fortunately there is a trial stone!" After speaking, he rushed towards Huang Shang.

Huang Shang was furious in his heart, and immediately went to meet Tiansheng. The same is arrogance, the same attack method, the same offensive, the two fought equally. As you come and go, arrogance is surging, and the wind is everywhere.

"Bold!" When Huang Shang and Tiansheng were fighting, Huang Shang suddenly saw evil spirits rushing towards Ye Rui who was protected.

The strength of one evil ghost was not enough to break the protective shield set up by Huang Shang, but what about hundreds or thousands? The protective shield was broken like an eggshell under the bombardment of the evil ghosts. Huang Shang saw this and immediately wanted to retreat to save Ye Rui, but was blocked by Tiansheng.

"Your opponent is me!" Tiansheng blocked the way and said jokingly. Huang Shang didn't say anything, but his anger became stronger. He looked at Ye Rui on the other side. At this time, Ye Rui had been caught by the evil ghost and flew into the sky.

Huang Shang looked at all this and sighed, and retracted his arrogance back into his body and said, "Let her go." Tiansheng smiled, so happy: "Okay, but give me a small cup of your blood!" After that, he took the jade cup handed over by an evil ghost.

Huang Shang glared at him, helplessly took the jade cup, then bit his finger and dripped a few drops of blood. Huang Shang, who had extremely strong recovery ability, bit another finger after the wound on that finger recovered, and continued to bleed until the jade cup was full.

Huang Shang's blood was red and black, with dark red blood beads flashing a faint glow in the red blood, mixed with some black blocks, which was extremely weird.

Tiansheng took the jade cup, greed in his eyes was clearly revealed. Then he waved his hand and asked the evil spirits to let go of Ye Rui who was caught. Then he strode away. Huang Shang rushed forward, picked up Ye Rui and looked coldly at the direction where Tiansheng left. Suddenly he remembered a book he had read a few days ago, which said: Tiansheng, born by heaven... "

Chapter 66 Successful Forced Seizure

This time, for Huang Shang, it was undoubtedly a failure. But for the proud son of heaven, when had he ever suffered such a failure? Although he was threatened, he had long been shocked by Tiansheng's strange ability - stealing the opponent's power in every contact and using it for himself, which was really abnormal. Moreover, Huang Shang didn't know whether that ability could be integrated with the energy absorbed from others. If it could, it would be unimaginable. Moreover, Huang Shang thought about the words written in the book, and his surprise became stronger.

Shaking his head, hugging Ye Rui, a feeling of resentment rose in his heart. Looking at Ye Rui, Huang Shang's eyes became firm, and an idea slowly took root.

At this time, on Ye Ye's side. Ye Ye didn't know what happened on Huang Shang's side, and still took everyone to take a detour back to Yemen, and sent some soldiers who wanted to go home back home along the way. It was not a big deal along the way.

As for Tiansheng, the winner of the battle just now, he was undoubtedly happy at this moment. At this moment, he was holding a jade cup in his hand, sitting cross-legged in the protective circle of the evil spirits, with Murong Di, who was seriously injured and recovering, beside him.

Tiansheng looked at the jade cup with his mouth raised, and the greed in his eyes was completely revealed: "Not bad, not bad, let's eat the main course!" After saying that, Tiansheng raised his hand and poured the red and black blood in the jade cup into his mouth, and then smacked his lips, which seemed to be delicious. But suddenly, he frowned in tears, and the black flame on his body appeared for no reason.

Each energy has its owner. No matter how powerful Tiansheng's skills are, it cannot change this fact determined by heaven. If you want to forcibly take energy for your own use, you will naturally suffer from energy backlash! However, Tiansheng's way of stealing energy during contact does not belong to this kind. He only steals energy, not forcibly depriving energy of ownership. Therefore, there will be no energy backlash, and it will dissipate in a very short time.

However, at this moment, Tiansheng wanted to forcibly extract the energy in Huang Shang's blood. Although there was not much blood, one was two, and two was four. . . . . . Until thousands and millions, this is a forced deprivation of energy ownership, which will naturally be backfired by energy, no wonder it is so painful.

In the pain, Tiansheng couldn't help but scream, but he clenched his fists tightly and endured it. He knew that as long as he could get through or suppress the backlash, he would have Huang Shang's thousand-year power for no reason.

The evil ghosts around were all sincere to Tiansheng. Seeing Tiansheng's pain, their hearts tightened. Some even wanted to help, but they were stopped by the strongest evil ghost who had been staying beside Tiansheng. He knew that Tiansheng must be standing on a springboard at this moment. Don't disturb him.

With the evil ghost blocking them, the evil ghosts were worried, but they didn't come forward again.

Suddenly, a wave of energy came from Tiansheng, but it disappeared after just a slight blow of the dust on the ground, and then a slight muffled sound came from his body. After that, everything returned to calm again. However, Tiansheng slowly opened his eyes. Judging from the curve of his mouth, he must have succeeded in forcibly taking away Huang Shang's energy.

At this moment, Tiansheng's eyes were as deep as Huang Shang's. This time, he just trembled slightly, and black flames appeared all over his body. This was the energy he had just stolen. At this time, Tiansheng had Huang Shang's original energy in his body, so he could easily control the energy and no longer let it dissipate due to time.

Feeling the energy in his body slowly multiplying and slowly filling up, Tiansheng excitedly roared to the sky, and the roar broke through the white clouds in the sky.

Ye Ye, who was on his way in the distance, suddenly looked at the direction they were coming from with doubts, and was shocked: "That's Huang Shang's energy. Did he go to find us? No, it shouldn't be. The ghost queen has a successor, and the ghost king should not be able to get away." Ye Ye quickly overturned the idea that Huang Shang came to find them, shook his head and continued on his way.

After the howl, Tiansheng slowly lowered his head, looked into the distance and said, "Let's go, let's go find my heart instead!" After saying that, he closed his eyes and saw the memory he stole when he came into contact with Ye Ye: seven people, several of them died, and then fled to the east with something, and beside them, a huge meteorite was quietly staying not far from them! The thing that was taken away was his heart. (I guess you have guessed what it is!)

Opening his eyes, Tiansheng raised his hand and pointed to the east. Then he looked at Murong Di, who stood up slowly beside him with a face as white as gold paper, shook his head, and let an evil ghost come forward to support him. Then the two ghosts went to the east.

Three days later, Ye Ye finally handed over the remaining soldiers to the military, and then took everyone from Yemen back to Yemen. Little did they know that those soldiers told everything that happened in Luping, and the military was very concerned about this matter and issued a shocking secret order!

"You're back?" As soon as he returned to Yemen, Huang Shang calmly greeted Ye Ye. He was traveling alone with the unconscious Ye Rui, so he was naturally very fast, faster than Ye Ye and his friends who returned to Yemen the day before.

Ye Ye was shocked. He had never seen Huang Shang greet them like this before, but he didn't ask much. He knew from Huang Shang's eyes that Huang Shang would definitely find a chance to tell everything, and he also knew the importance of the matter. However, he didn't ask much. After settling all the disciples of Yemen, he went to Huang Shang alone. And Huang Shang was already waiting for him.

"Huang Shang, are you okay? On the way back, I sensed..." Before Ye Ye finished speaking, Huang Shang interrupted him: "Yes, it was me!"

Ye Ye looked at Huang Shang in surprise. Huang Shang sighed and turned his back to Ye Ye, saying dejectedly: "I lost! Lost!" This was a shocking statement. Ye Ye naturally heard about the battle with the Ghost Queen from other people in Yemen and knew how powerful Huang Shang was, but at this time, Huang Shang admitted defeat! The god of war in Ye Men's heart admitted defeat! How could Ye Ye not be surprised.

In Ye Ye's surprised eyes, Huang Shang slowly told the story, but he didn't mention anything about Ye Rui, which was what he promised Ye Rui.

The more Ye Ye listened, the more surprised he was, and then he also told his own experience. After hearing this, Huang Shang turned his head and looked at Ye Ye in surprise: "You also contacted him, so did he steal your energy?"

Ye Ye shook his head and said: "No, but the moment he contacted me, I felt that someone was peeping in my head, I don't know what happened!" Huang Shang pondered for a while before saying: "He should have stolen your memory, even the ability can be directly stolen, stealing memory is no problem! But why did he steal your memory!?"

Ye Ye nodded and pondered, suddenly raised his head and said: "Heart, father... Did I contact his father?"

Huang Shang's face changed after hearing this and said: "It's very likely!"

Chapter 67 Birth of a Child

Ye Ye's face was slightly gloomy, and he kept sorting out some thoughts: born, heart, father... After a long time, Ye Ye slowly expressed his thoughts, and then told Huang Shang.

"This is just our guess, we can't believe it completely! Forget it, let's make plans for this matter later, go back and rest first! You are tired all the way back! I still have to go to Rui Xin, my son was born today!" Huang Shang shook his head and said excitedly. Ye Ye nodded with a slight smile, then bowed and walked out, but he didn't see the obscure look in Huang Shang's eyes that didn't know what it meant.

Everyone in Yemen didn't know what Ye Ye and the others were talking about, and they wouldn't tell it to others. Qin Minglei was staying in a room at this time, holding a child in his arms, that was his and Yinlin's child - Qin Feng. At this moment, Qin Minglei's eyes were actually more gentle and kind, as if holding the child would get the world.

With a creaky sound, a person pushed the door open and walked in. Qin Minglei turned his head back calmly, then immediately withdrew the kind expression on his face and looked coldly at the person who came in. "You are here indeed, how is the child?" The person who came in was Li Bin. When he came in, he also saw the kindness on Qin Minglei's face, and was startled and said.

Qin Minglei nodded: "Well, the child is fine. There are people in the night gate who take care of him. I am not a competent father!" After that, he put the child down, then stood up and continued: "What do you want from me?"

Li Bin looked at Qin Minglei holding the child gently, and felt happy for him. He smiled and replied: "The ghost queen is giving birth now. It is estimated that she will be born in the middle of the night. Shouldn't we go to celebrate?"

Qin Minglei frowned, but he was relieved after seeing Qin Feng: "Let's go! But we have to find the nanny first, so I can feel at ease." Li Bin listened, punched Qin Minglei and said: "I haven't had a drink with you for a long time. Let's drink happily!" After that, Qin Minglei let him hook his shoulder and walked out.

At this time, if they looked back, they would be shocked by what happened behind them, because behind them, Qin Feng, who was originally sleeping, suddenly emitted a faint halo, which was very strange in the dark blue, and there seemed to be something jumping in the halo!

"Oh my... Being a wet nurse is so annoying. In the middle of the night, everyone is going to a wedding, but I am here to take care of the baby!" The door was pushed open again, and a woman's voice came, and the halo and pulsation on Qin Feng's body suddenly disappeared. After the light disappeared, Qin Feng also suddenly cried. Seeing this, the woman muttered "Little ancestor, here it comes!" While running to the bed, she picked up Qin Feng and handed her huge breasts to Qin Feng for him to eat. Qin Feng stopped crying.

"Why haven't you heard the crying sound yet? I'm so anxious!" Huang Shang, who was once an emperor, was naturally familiar with the process of giving birth and had been anxiously waiting for the baby's cry at the door.

Ye Hen shook his head, covered his mouth, and then tried to hold back his smile and said: "Huang Shang, it's only been a short time, not so fast!"

"I don't know? You have to be so nosy?" Being hit on the point, Huang Shang at least pretended to be angry to ease the embarrassment.

At this time, many people were waiting outside the house of Ghost Queen Zi Ruixin. The Ghost Queen was a guest of the Night Clan. How could the people of the Night Clan not pay attention to the joy of having a child? So they waited there early. They also saw Huang Shang's embarrassment after the conversation between Huang Shang and Ye Hen, and they laughed out of joy.

"Oh, are you all here? What's going on? Why are you laughing so happily?" Li Bin and Qin Minglei heard the laughter of the crowd as soon as they arrived, and asked without knowing what was going on.

"Don't say it, no one is allowed to say it!" Huang Shang pretended to be angry again, and then looked in the direction of the house and whispered: "Why hasn't there been any sound yet? It's so anxious!" Huang Shang's move made the people around him laugh even more. Li Bin and Qin Minglei also learned about the incident from the people next to them, and Li Bin laughed. But Qin Minglei frowned, and a strong sadness gradually spread.

The careful Li Bin naturally noticed all this, and gently touched Qin Minglei with his shoulder and said, "It's okay, it's okay, just drink two more cups later!" Qin Minglei smiled and didn't say anything, but there was a touch of emotion in the sadness in his eyes. Li Bin looked at Qin Minglei without saying anything, shook his head, and stopped talking.

However, a bowl of wine suddenly appeared in front of Li Bin and Qin Minglei. The two looked at the wine glass and found that it was Ye Ye and Yang Hengchao. At this time, they each held two glasses of wine in their hands.

"What more can you say? How can you look at the time when you want to drink?" Yang Hengchao said lightly. The life and death together in these days have made the four people have a great affection. After Yang Hengchao finished speaking, Ye Ye also raised his head, handed the two bowls of wine in his hand to Li Bin and Qin Minglei, and then took the wine from Yang Hengchao's hand, and finally touched the bowls heavily: "Drink it!" After speaking, he raised his hand and opened his mouth, and the hot wine went down his throat into his stomach.

Li Bin and the other two did not drink until Ye Ye finished drinking. In Ye Ye's surprised eyes, the three of them actually pushed their glasses forward at the same time, indicating a toast, and the object was Ye Ye! Then they drank it all!

Ye Ye looked at the three of them, and an inexplicable feeling rose up, then shook his head and said: "Brothers are of one mind."

"Together we can break gold!" Qin Minglei and the other two echoed. Although the four of them are not brothers, they have been born and died, and they are no different from brothers or even better than brothers. Yang Tianhai, who was on the side, looked at the four of them, and his eyes suddenly shook, and a long-lost feeling was chaotic in his mind. That was the brotherhood of his tribe in his mind. Yang Tianhai also smiled, walked to Ye Ye and the others, and raised a jar of wine in his hand: "Drink it!" Ye Ye and the other four smiled at the same time, then raised the wine bowl, asked Yang Tianhai to pour the wine, and the five of them drank together, not caring at all what kind of illusion this was and who was next to them. When the disciples of the Night Sect around them saw the five of them drinking so passionately, they all suddenly became passionate and started drinking at the same time.

Huang Shang watched all this in a daze, but he couldn't say anything, because if he interfered, he would definitely leave a bad impression on the disciples of the Night Sect, and they would continue drinking under the pretext of celebrating! So, although Huang Shang was angry and irritable, he didn't stop them.

"Wow wow wow wow..." Suddenly, the crisp cry of a baby penetrated the noise of the drinking party and reached everyone's ears. The originally noisy drinking party also quieted down at this time.

Huang Shang was the most excited at this time. He jumped up and shouted, "It's born!" He ran into the house while shouting. Huang Shang had been lonely for thousands of years, and then he found the ghost queen in difficulty. Naturally, he was no longer as indifferent as when he was the king.

As soon as he ran to the door, a midwife ran out with a frightened face, her face pale. This situation also tightened everyone's heart.

Huang Shang retracted his smile, ran into the room faster, and then breathed a sigh of relief. In the room, the ghost king was weak after giving birth, and turned back to her original appearance, but her face was still beautiful, but her cheeks were dotted with sweat. But her body was a ghost's body.

The ghost queen was holding a tightly wrapped baby in her arms. When Huang Shang came in, she raised her head and looked at Huang Shang anxiously, and then under Huang Shang's puzzled eyes, she slowly pulled open a corner of the cloth wrapped around the baby in her arms.

Suddenly, a faint blue light emanated from the baby's body, painting the whole room with a strange blue. At the same time, in another room farther away, Qin Feng's body also emitted that light again, which was unexpectedly the same as the child just born by the ghost queen. Beside Qin Feng, the nanny was already sleeping soundly, and her originally huge breasts were now shriveled.

Chapter 68 Touched

Ye Ye looked at the blue light coming out of the door of the room and felt something was wrong. He immediately put down the wine glass in his hand and ran to the door to take a look. He was shocked and said, "What's going on?"

"I should ask this question!" Huang Shang's tone was not panic, but he even said with a little surprise: "My son is really gifted! This child is the most special one among my sons, although the others are all considered and died early." Huang Shang regarded this blue light as a sign of the strange phenomenon of his son after he was born.

However, Ye Ye kept frowning. He always felt that there was something ominous, but looking at Huang Shang's happy and excited look, Ye Ye did not say it out loud, but congratulated lightly, and then blocked the onlookers and pushed them out of the room: "Look, what are you looking at, haven't you seen a child born? The ghost queen is weak now, so you are not allowed to peek!" Ye Ye said in feigned anger and drove everyone out of the room. Then he continued to drink with them there. However, Ye Ye was no longer as bold as before. Although his face was calm and his hands kept feeding the wine to his mouth, his mind was clear. He kept thinking about where the familiar feeling came from.

He shook his head, shook off the dizziness brought by drinking and the boredom of thinking about things, and continued to drink with Qin Minglei and others.

"Wow wow wow wow..." The baby's cry came again, and everyone looked at the room again. Many of the Yemen disciples were married, and the experienced ones said: "The child is hungry, it's time to feed! Haha!" After that person finished speaking, the others laughed.

At this time, Huang Shang in the room suddenly broke out of the door and shouted loudly: "Quick, quick, please get me a wet nurse!" Huang Shang's anxious look made everyone laugh. After he finished speaking, a Yemen disciple immediately ran away.

Qin Minglei had also drunk a lot of wine at this time. He stood up and said, "The nanny is with Qin Feng! Don't wake Qin Feng up!" Hearing what Qin Minglei said, the errand disciple immediately changed direction and left.

Ye Ye took this opportunity to look inside the room. With his excellent eyesight, he saw that the ghost queen was weakly holding the baby, but the baby no longer emitted a blue light.

Seeing this scene, Ye Ye breathed a sigh of relief: Am I overthinking? But it is clearly a very familiar feeling! Ye Ye thought and became confused.

After this little farce, everyone returned to the wine party to drink again. Huang Shang looked at them happily persuading and drinking, and his heart was also happy, and he suppressed the boredom in his heart because of the defeat. After the year, he anxiously looked at the direction where the errand runner went: "Why haven't you come yet?" As he said, he walked around, and the people not far away laughed and shook their heads. Only some people who have been married and have children know this kind of mood. They no longer laughed, but continued to drink their own wine.

After a long time, the Yemen disciple who was running errands just now appeared in Huang Shang's sight. Seeing him appear, Huang Shang went over immediately, but he did not see the nanny but a baby in her arms. Huang Shang recognized it as Qin Feng from the Qin family, so he asked in confusion: "Where is the nanny? Why did you bring Qin Feng here!"

Who knew that the Yemen disciple said with a pale face: "Something happened, something happened, the nanny died!" It was a shocking statement. Someone died on such a happy day, which made people feel unlucky and angry.

"What happened?" Huang Shang said with a cold face after hearing this. Everyone suddenly lost the mood to drink, surrounded him, and looked at the Yemen disciple.

The Yemen disciple looked pale and continued, "I don't know what happened! Just now you asked me to pick up the nanny, and then Master Qin said the nanny was with him, so I went. As a result, I knocked on the door, but no one opened it. Then I pushed the door open and saw the nanny lying on the bed. I thought she was asleep, so I went to call her, but when I pushed her, she fell down. I was shocked and felt her breath, and she died. I was afraid that Qin Feng would be in danger, so I brought Qin Feng here."

Qin Minglei took Qin Feng and hugged him affectionately without saying anything. Ye Ye nodded and asked, "Do you know what kind of weapon did it?" Although there are many people in the world, they use different weapons. If you know what weapon did it, it will be much easier to know who did it.

The Night Clan disciple thought for a moment, then shook his head and said, "I don't know. I was in a hurry just now and didn't pay attention!"

"Don't think about it. Just go over and take a look and you'll know! Go find me a new nanny!" Huang Shang suddenly said, then turned his head and seemed to make some expression to the Ghost Queen. The Ghost Queen nodded, and Huang Shang closed the door and walked towards Qin Minglei's residence first. Ye Ye and his companions followed immediately.

"No wounds!" Ye Ye looked at the nanny's body and observed it carefully for a long time before saying angrily. "But you have to look at his chest!" Li Bin prompted. "Chest?" Ye Ye was puzzled, and then suddenly realized: "By the way, he was a nanny before, and the breasts of a nanny must be very big, but now they are shriveled, leaving only a layer of skin!" Ye Ye said, squatting down and grabbing the originally plump breasts on the nanny's body on the ground, but now the shriveled flesh, gently pinching, Ye Ye frowned, not only him, but everyone present frowned. What Ye Ye squeezed out was not milk, but blood, or blood mixed with milk.

"Everything was fine when Minglei and I went out just now. The nanny was called back to the room after we went out! Who could it be? He was so cruel that he actually sucked the blood from the heart veins!" Li Bin said embarrassedly.

"Wow!" Qin Feng in Qin Minglei's arms suddenly cried out. No one looked at him. Qin Minglei just patted him gently. No one saw that the moment Qin Feng opened his mouth, his scarlet tongue was like blood.

"Bury it first. It's unlucky to have these things happen on such a happy day!" Huang Shang said lightly. After that, he walked out of the room.

Ye Ye looked at Huang Shang and said, "Well, bury it first! Then comfort her family members. Minglei, you can sleep in another place these days!" After that, several people came forward and carried the body away. Then, several people also walked out of the room.

The new nanny was soon invited to the night gate again, and then she fed Huang Shang's son Huang Chen. Qin Feng was among them, and was forcibly "snatched" by the ghost queen with a sentence: A grown man can't take care of a child. Qin Minglei also agreed with this, and naturally knew how inconvenient it was for him to take care of the child alone.

After Huang Chen and Qin Feng were together, the two babies never showed any strange phenomena again. Moreover, Qin Feng, who was half a year older, seemed to be very good to Huang Chen. Qin Feng, who should have been young and incomplete in his thoughts, actually let the nanny's ** go in front of everyone's astonishment, and Huang Chen also consciously closed his eyes and rubbed over, drinking the ** that Qin Feng originally sucked.

This phenomenon, everyone thought that the two were destined to be together, and Huang Shang even pulled Qin Minglei to become relatives. But Ye Ye was uneasy from this abnormality.

Chapter 69 The restless atmosphere

Three days have passed since the birth of Huang Shang, the guest of Yemen, and Zi Ruixin. During this period, Yemen has been in a state of celebration. Only Ye Ye is alone. He is not unhappy, but feels that something will happen, but he can't figure it out. He can only look for it slowly while being anxious.

That night, Ye Ye was alone in Ye Rui's room. He comforted Ye Rui to sleep. He didn't know that Ye Rui had recovered. At this time, Huang Shang walked here, knocked on the door gently, saw Ye Ye turned around, and called him out.

Ye Ye closed the door and asked: "Are you not accompanying the ghost queen? It's so late, she should be asleep."

Huang Shang nodded, smiled meaningfully, then sighed and said firmly: "Master Ye, Zi Ruixin and Huang Chen will be left to you to take care of!"

Master Ye? When did Huang Shang call himself the master so solemnly? Ye Ye was startled, then looked at Huang Shang in confusion, and did not speak. He knew that Huang Shang must have his own ideas.

Huang Shang looked at Ye Ye, and then said: "The defeated ones must be taken back. Although, I know that maybe he is now stronger, maybe I am no longer defeated, but at least I have to redeem it. This is the dignity of a king!" Huang Shang is the emperor, and his pride has become stronger after thousands of years of baptism. Naturally, he can't stand the fact that he is defeated, and he is forced to do so.

"You don't care about the mother and son?" Ye Ye sighed and asked lightly. He could understand Huang Shang's thoughts. Huang Shang smiled, looked at Ye Ye and said: "I know you won't treat them badly, right?"

"When are you leaving!" Ye Ye knew that no matter how much he said, he couldn't organize Huang Shang, so he simply asked.

"Tonight." Huang Shang looked up at the bright moon in the sky and said. "So soon? Did you tell the ghost queen?" Ye Ye asked.

Huang Shang shook his head: "The land of gentleness, the tomb of heroes. Here is a letter. When she comes to find me, you can give it to her. Then tell her everything." After saying that, he took out a letter. Ye Ye reached out to take it and put it in his arms, then followed Huang Shang to look at the sky and said: "Have you found out the abnormality of Huang Chen?" Ye Ye naturally didn't believe that Huang Shang thought the blue light on Huang Chen was a divine sign.

"No, you be careful, I'm going." After saying that, Huang Shang no longer lingered, walked out of the next yard, then jumped onto the roof and disappeared into the darkness.

smiled. Then, his brows suddenly frowned, turned around, and looked behind him vigilantly. A black shadow suddenly jumped down from the roof and went straight to Ye Ye, but Ye Ye did not resist at all, but hugged it: "Yeyue, are you willing to come back?" The black shadow was Yeyue, the mysterious cat that had not been seen for a long time. The cat that swallowed the red blood snake bead!

Ye Ye said so, and then he meowed softly, and a white cat appeared from the roof, followed by three kittens. The white cat was Ye Yue's "inner cat" Ye Ling, and the ones behind him must be their children.

Ye Ye looked at Ye Yue's family, then sat on the ground, waiting for Ye Ling to slowly and gracefully jump down from the roof with the three kittens, and then wrapped them all in his arms, but because he couldn't wrap them, Ye Ye had to sleep on the ground, and then let them all play happily on his body, temporarily forgetting everything that was weighing on his mind.

At this time, in the room. Ye Rui also sat on the ground, gently patting his chest and muttering to himself: "It's okay, it's okay!" He hadn't fallen asleep until Huang Shang came, and she curiously followed to eavesdrop, and then saw Ye Ye suddenly turn around just now, thinking that Ye Ye had discovered her, fortunately it was only the cat.

"Yeyue, look at them, how gentle and elegant they are, and then look at you, you still look so dirty! Aren't you afraid that Ye Ling will dislike you?" Ye Ye said to Ye Yue while lying on the ground.

"Meow!" Ye Yue cried out in dissatisfaction, and then rubbed against Ye Ling as if to show goodwill, and Ye Ling did not hide and rubbed against him. Seeing this, Ye Ye smiled happily. Ye Ye had seen Ye Ling before, but he had never seen the remaining three kittens. After thinking for a while, he said, "Yeyue, let's call them Ye Ming, Ye Lin and Ye Teng!" After hearing this, Ye Ye and Ye Ling cried out at the same time, and their cries were full of joy.

Ye Ye looked at the family and suddenly envied them. As a man whose birth was unknown, he wished he had a family. As he thought about it, a woman with a devil figure and an angel face appeared in his mind. It turned out to be Xia Feng.

Ye Ye thought about it, smiled, shook his head, drove Ye Yue's family off him, pushed open Ye Rui's door, looked at Ye Rui still sleeping peacefully, and then left with Ye Yue's family at ease.

"No, I have to tell Aunt Zi all this. Huang Shang left, Aunt Zi and Huang Chen will definitely be sad to death! No, go now!" Not long after Ye Ye left, Ye Rui opened his eyes, talked to himself, and then got out of bed firmly, thinking about Zi Ruixin's residence. Then the night fell, and no one noticed her departure.

The next morning, Ye Ye's door was pushed open vigorously, waking up Ye Ye and Ye Yue's family who were sleeping.

Seeing the visitor, Ye Yue suddenly arched his back and stood up, as if he was facing a great enemy, and Ye Ling also protected the three kittens behind him and stared at the people who came vigilantly.

Ye Ye opened his eyes, looked at the door, then sat up and said, "Ghost Queen, what's the matter?"

Ghost Queen ignored Ye Ling's hostility, but walked to Ye Ye's bed and said angrily, "Where is Huang Shang?" When Ye Ye got closer, he saw that the Ghost Queen had not recovered from the rest of the past few days. She still had a little fatigue on her face.

Ye Ye put on his clothes, then got off the bed, touched Ye Yue's family, and said after settling them down, "Huang Shang is missing?"

Ghost Queen was furious and shouted loudly, "Ye Ye, don't pretend, tell me where Huang Shang went immediately? Ye... Ye, tell me quickly!" Ghost Queen was so angry that she almost let the cat out of the bag, but fortunately she took it back in time.

Ye Ye smiled faintly, "I guess you already know it, okay!" After that, Ye Ye took out the letter left by Huang Shang from under the pillow. When Ghost Queen saw the letter, she rushed to grab it and read it hastily.

"Rui Xin, I'm late for your letter. I'm sure you've noticed that your husband is feeling bored and uneasy when he goes out for a walk. Don't blame Ye Ye, I told him to do this, otherwise you can blame my selfishness and my extremely inflated self-esteem. I can't stand that, I really can't stand it. Rui Xin, don't worry, I will definitely come back, after all, Huang Chen needs me as a father, not the king!" Huang Shang had explained everything clearly in the letter, and also buried the foreshadowing that he would give up his former arrogance as long as this matter was resolved.

After reading it, the ghost queen dropped her hands, and two lines of tears flowed down her cheeks. Ye Ye sighed, and then slowly told the story. From meeting Tiansheng, to Huang Shang meeting Tiansheng, to Tiansheng's strange abilities, there was no concealment.

After a long time, Ye Ye finished speaking. After hearing this, the Ghost Queen trembled. She also understood the self-esteem of being a king, but he had really endured too much during this period, from the death of the Ghost King to the vision of the child. Huang Shang was supposed to bear it together, but now Huang Shang selfishly left. Although she is the Ghost Queen, she is still a woman.

Ye Ye shook his head, took out a handkerchief and handed it to the Ghost Queen, and then let her cry. For these things, Ye Ye has no idea.

After a long time, the Ghost Queen's crying suddenly stopped. Ye Ye looked over in confusion and found that the Ghost King's eyes were no longer sad, but like Huang Shang, they were determined.

"Master Ye, today, I, Zi Ruixin, took the initiative to resign and resigned from the position of guest official." The Ghost Queen said firmly. When Ye Ye heard it, he had guessed that the Ghost Queen must be looking for Huang Shang.

"Huang Chen..." Ye Ye was worried that no one would take care of Huang Chen, so he was ready to dissuade him.

Unexpectedly, the Ghost Queen interrupted and said, "Don't worry, I will take my son and Huang Shang's son with me to find him together!"

Ye Ye was shocked and said quickly, "No, absolutely not, Huang Chen was born not long ago and can't stand the strong wind and waves!"

"I am the Queen of the Ghost Clan, and I still have the strength to protect my child! Master Ye, don't persuade me anymore, I have made up my mind to leave, and I have nothing to do with Yemen from today. If I can find my husband by chance, I will definitely ask my husband for his help!" The Ghost Queen thought that all she did would bring disaster to Yemen, so she said this.

Ye Ye nodded and stopped talking. He knew that he couldn't stop the Ghost Queen. So he nodded: "Go!" In fact, Ye Ye just wanted to take a gamble. He bet that if the Ghost Queen could find Huang Shang, the gentle land, and the hero's tomb as soon as possible, Huang Shang might change his mind.

"Thank you, Master Ye!" After saying that, the Ghost Queen suddenly roared to the sky, and a thick layer of dark clouds suddenly came to cover the sun. On the ground, a dark mass of little ghosts came out from the ground. Their queen was calling.

After a few breaths, the entire Yemen Mountain was covered by the little ghost, and Huang Chen was also brought to the Ghost Queen's arms by the little ghost. At this time, the Ghost Queen left with tens of thousands of little ghosts. This is her capital, her capital for finding her husband!

Watching the Ghost Queen leave, Ye Ye sighed, and a feeling of deserted buildings rose up. Looking at the Yeyue family on the ground, he didn't feel lonely in his heart. He smiled, thought of Qin Minglei and others, and quickly stood up and walked out of the house.

Soon, he came to the door of Qin Minglei's residence.

But suddenly, an uneasy breath was transmitted across the entire Yemen Mountain!

Chapter 70 Qin Feng's Change

Ye Ye felt the restless breath, then looked around in confusion, and finally focused his attention on Qin Minglei's room. With a sense of surprise in his heart, Ye Ye ran into the room and saw a surprising scene.

Ye Ye pushed open the door, and the whole room was covered by a thick cloth by Qin Minglei. The moment he pushed the door open, a beam of faint blue light shone through the room. After the light dispersed, Qin Minglei was actually hanging in the air. His expression was not crying, but there was still surprise in his eyes. He looked along his eyes. It turned out to be Qin Feng. Qin Feng stood up at this time, holding his hands in the air, and a faint blue energy line connected his hands and Qin Minglei's neck.

Seeing this, Ye Ye was not too surprised, but took out the Phoenix Thorn. He didn't know what was happening now, and he didn't want to hurt Qin Minglei's child. However, just as he rushed up, Qin Feng stretched out his other hand, and then gently squeezed and lifted it, and Ye Ye was also lifted up.

Startled, Ye Ye immediately took the next step. He first forced out his own energy, then retracted his body, pulled out the Ye Yang on his leg, let the energy flame attach to it, and then tried hard to think about the energy beam emitted by Qin Feng's hand.

The energy emitted by Ye Ye was left for Ye Ye by the Ghost King after his death. Naturally, it was extremely fierce. After easily cutting the energy beam, Ye Ye landed gently, and then squatted down and bounced on the spot. The Ye Yang in his hand pointed directly at another beam that grabbed Qin Minglei. Who knew that at this moment, a head composed of energy appeared in front of Ye Ye, with a fierce roar, biting towards Ye Ye.

Ye Ye even felt the bloody smell in the mouth of the head. But at this moment, there was no time to hesitate. Ye Ye's momentum did not decrease, but his body was burning with the black and red flame that originally belonged to the Ghost King. As soon as the flame came into contact with the energy skull, the skull was vaporized. Ye Ye passed through the skull directly and cut off the energy line. Qin Minglei fell to the ground steadily, looking at Qin Feng with worried eyes.

"He is not Qin Feng!" Ye Ye shouted, and then rushed up again, seemingly without any spare strength. However, at this moment, Qin Feng suddenly showed a look of fear, and his eyes turned from dark blue to dark, but Ye Ye did not observe this carefully.

"He is Qin Feng, Ye Zi, stop!" Qin Minglei suddenly shouted excitedly, and the sound waves actually shook the whole room.

Ye Ye was startled and passed by Qin Feng dangerously. Qin Feng cried out when he saw this scene. Qin Minglei immediately stepped forward, picked him up, and kept comforting him. And Ye Ye, after retracting the flame, looked at Qin Feng coldly.

"What happened? Why is Qin Feng like this?" Ye Ye squatted down and inserted Ye Yang into his legs and asked casually. Qin Minglei frowned, then shook his head and said, "I don't know either. I was taking a nap just now, and suddenly this little guy brought me up. Maybe he was naughty! Ye Ye, don't worry too much. Maybe the offspring born by the Miao

Gu people and the corpse king are a little strange!" Qin Minglei's eyes showed joy and a hint of sadness.

Ye Ye shook his head and sighed helplessly. His intuition told him that things were not that simple. Huang Shang and the Ghost Queen left one after another. The Yemen was equivalent to having no masters to suppress the door. The nanny died inexplicably. Now that Qin Feng has suddenly changed... It seems that everything is so natural, but Ye feels that there must be a connection between them, because Ye Ye feels very clear about the strange phenomenon that appeared on the day when the Ghost Queen gave birth to a child, and the light emitted from Qin Feng and Huang Chen, who were born to the Ghost Queen, is all dark blue, and the attributes and even the frequency bands are the same!

Shaking his head, Ye Ye took out three phoenix thorns and handed them to Qin Minglei. Qin Minglei took it and naturally knew what it meant. Ye Ye wanted to take the initiative to control Qin Feng when he suddenly changed again.

Qin Minglei nodded, and Ye Ye frowned and walked out of Qin Minglei's room. After Ye Ye left, Qin Minglei immediately stepped forward, closed the door, and then suddenly leaned against the door, crying and covering his heart, and then beat his chest hard, making a "bang bang" sound. Qin Feng on the bed looked at Qin Minglei's painful appearance and suddenly sat up, with a smile on his lips.

This smile naturally fell into Qin Minglei's eyes, but at this moment Qin Minglei did not have the strength to care about Qin Feng. The phoenix thorn in his hand also fell to the ground. Qin Minglei bit his mouth tightly, then fell to the ground, and beat the ground hard, trying to restrain the pain caused by the love Gu in his heart.

Qin Minglei could have chosen to let the love Gu naturally leave his body when Yin Lin died, but he did not choose that. Instead, he chose to let it stay in his body as a reminder of Yin Lin. The love Gu was still alive and had not broken out because of the death of another love Gu, but now it suddenly broke out. Only Qin Minglei knew why all this happened, and that was Qin Feng, his son, who was sitting on the bed and laughing at his pain!

Qin Minglei could have asked Ye Ye for help, but Qin Feng was still his son, the son of him and Yin Lin. How could he do that? So, he could only endure the pain now.

"Hey, Minglei, are you okay? What was that sound just now?" Ye Ye's voice suddenly sounded from outside the door. Qin Minglei gritted his teeth and tried to speak in a tone that would reassure Ye Ye: "It's okay, Ye Zi, I'm fine. Qin Feng is already asleep. Just do your thing!"

"Take care of yourself. If there's anything, shout immediately. I'm sure Ye Men can hear it." Ye Ye, who was outside the door, said helplessly as he looked at the Ye Men disciples who had just heard Qin Minglei shouting, and then dispersed the Ye Men disciples, and left with his head buried in thought.

In the house, Qin Minglei cried even more bitterly when he heard the footsteps of the crowd disperse. He suddenly raised his head and opened his mouth, but did not make any sound. Qin Feng on the bed looked at Qin Minglei and smiled even more.

Qin Minglei buried his head and his face suddenly eased. During this period, since returning to Ye Men, after Qin Minglei saw Qin Feng, the love Gu in his heart would inexplicably break out intermittently, and he was in great pain. But Qin Minglei had been gritting his teeth to bear it. He didn't want his flesh and blood to be taken away and hurt. However, at this time, Qin Feng on the bed suddenly shook his head bleakly, a hint of teasing appeared on his face, and then he stretched out his hand and raised it upward. Qin Minglei on the ground was suddenly lifted up by a blue light. Qin Feng waved his hand downward, and Qin Minglei also followed the hand and fell to the ground. Qin Feng also continued this action, Qin Minglei kept going up and down, and then fell heavily to the ground. Then, a blue light went straight through the roof and rushed into the sky. And in a far place, the same blue light also rushed into the sky, corresponding to the blue light beam emitted by Qin Feng.

At this time, Ye Ye kept his head down, constantly sorting out his thoughts. He really didn't understand how these things were related. Now the only thing that can be confirmed is that Qin Feng and Huang Chen have the same energy, but why didn't Qin Feng attack before? Too many questions weighed on Ye Ye's heart.

Suddenly, Ye Ye frowned, looked back, and saw that the blue light rushed into the sky, and then looked into the distance, and a blue light in the distance was corresponding to it. Ye Ye was very familiar with these two energies. One of them was the energy that Qin Feng had just emitted, and the other one was very far away, but he could vaguely feel that it was exactly the same as Qin Feng's energy. Knowing the connection between the two, Ye Ye knew that the energy must be Huang Chen brought out by the ghost queen.

With surprise in his heart, Ye Ye felt that he ran into the house again. Not only him, but all the people in the Night Gate ran towards Qin Minglei's residence in surprise.

At this time, the light still did not dissipate, and even became more powerful. In the house, Qin Minglei looked at Qin Feng in surprise. Then he slowly trembled and climbed up. At this time, he finally believed that Qin Feng was no longer Qin Feng, or that this Qin Feng was not Qin Feng.

There was a touch of determination in his eyes, and then slowly became firm, and a murderous intent came out of Qin Minglei's eyes. Qin Minglei was not a person who didn't know the general situation. He would not harm the Night Gate or the world for his son. With pain in his heart, and hesitation mixed with the original strong killing intent, he sighed, then put down the strange dagger of Yemen, picked up the Phoenix Thorn on the ground, and his eyes were determined again. He leaned down slightly, and then shot out. The sharp part of the Phoenix Thorn in his hand emitted a little cold light.

At this time, Ye Ye also broke into the door again.

Chapter 71 Heart Appears

Ye Ye rushed into the house and was watching Qin Minglei holding a Phoenix thorn with a cold tip in his hand and stabbing Qin Feng, who was now glowing with a faint blue light. Even his facial features were now oozing blue light-like liquid. He looked up to the sky and opened his mouth, and a beam of light came out of his mouth, breaking through the clouds, which was extremely strange.

Seeing this, Ye Ye did not hesitate at all, and hurriedly forced out his aura, wrapped up the Night Sun in his hand, and then rushed towards Qin Feng. Ye Ye knew that Qin Minglei would be subdued if he rushed forward like this.

Sure enough, before Qin Minglei touched Qin Feng, beams of faint blue light were emitted from all parts of Qin Feng, and then tied up Qin Minglei like a dumpling when they touched him. Unable to move. At this time, Ye Ye also rushed over, and the Night Sun in his hand was wrapped in black and red aura, and gently cut towards the light that seemed to be real. Without the slightest sound, the light was cut off by the knife, and the light that entangled Qin Minglei also dissipated.

"Let me do it." Qin Minglei stood firm, rubbed his arm and said coldly. Ye Ye looked at Qin Minglei worriedly. At this time, Qin Minglei's eyes were red. Although he stared at the strange Qin Feng in front of him, his eyes were erratic, and he seemed to be hesitant. After two breaths, Qin Minglei suddenly retracted the Phoenix Thorn, then pulled out the Night Gate Strange

Dagger and walked towards Qin Feng. The tiger eyes were already full of tears.

Qin Minglei walked over, and Qin Feng did not summon those substantial lights again, but looked up at Qin Minglei. Except for the eyes that had returned to the dark, there seemed to be blue light flowing in his mouth, mouth, nose, and ears.

Qin Minglei looked at Qin Feng's eyes that seemed to be begging for real, and his heart softened, but he weighed it for a while, and then closed his eyes: "I'm sorry, Qin Feng, my child!" As he said, the dagger in his hand stabbed Qin Feng.

At this moment, Ye Ye's pupils suddenly shrank, and he hurriedly shouted: "Be careful." As he shouted, he rushed up, hugged Qin Minglei's waist in a flash, pressed him to the ground, and narrowly avoided the light shot from Qin Feng's mouth.

After falling to the ground, Ye Ye looked at the light, and the light actually penetrated the wall and went to an unknown destination. Looking at Qin Minglei, although Qin Minglei avoided the fatal light that was originally shot at the heart with the help of Ye Ye, he was still shot in the arm. At this time, the whole body could not move, and the position where he was shot was like being burned by a raging fire. The wound was also burned and solidified, and no blood flowed out.

Looking at Qin Feng, Qin Feng stopped the beam that broke through the sky, the blue light disappeared, and then fell softly to the ground. Seeing this, Qin Minglei hurriedly endured the pain again, hugged Qin Feng in his arms with one hand, and then gently stroked him. Ye Ye, who was standing on the side, saw this scene, but his vigilance was still there, and he was still staring at Qin Feng carefully.

"Ye Ye, don't worry. I won't let him leave my arms this time. If it happens again like before, I will solve it myself!" Qin Minglei said helplessly. Ye Ye frowned, and had to trust his brother who had been through life and death with him again, and then said, "I'm sorry..." After that, he turned around and prepared to summon the Yemen disciples who were watching just now. But when he turned around, he found that all the Yemen disciples were staring at the sky in a daze, with surprise on their faces.

Among these Yemen disciples, Li Bin was also mixed in. He had seen a lot of big things and woke up quickly, but he still said to Ye Ye with a trembling voice: "Ye Ye, you... come out and see!" After that, he looked at Qin Minglei on the ground, and the surprise on his face turned into worry. He immediately pushed away the Yemen disciples in front of him, walked towards Qin Minglei, and then took out the medicine and applied it on Qin Minglei's wound.

After seeing Li Bin enter, Ye Ye walked out of the room in confusion. He slowly raised his head and saw a scene that he would never forget.

If the huge meteorite last time was shocking, then this time was very shocking (hehe). At this time, there were two groups of faint blue light in the sky, slowly approaching. This was not the most amazing thing. The most amazing thing was that the two groups of light were shaped like half of a heart.

"Heart?" Ye Ye thought in his heart, and then he became more surprised. Could it be that the heart was born like this? The more Ye Ye thought about it, the more surprised he became. But there was nothing he could do, because that thing was in the sky and he couldn't reach it.

Ye Ye looked at the sky in amazement, and then he looked hard. In the place where the faint blue light was the most prosperous, there was something. From the shape, Ye Ye felt very familiar, as if he had seen it somewhere.

He thought about it, and then couldn't help but say: "The stone slab! It's the stone slab of Xingling! Is this his heart?"

At this time, at the foot of Yemen Mountain, on a small road, ten people wearing black cloaks were also looking at the sky, but there was not so much surprise in their eyes, and they even felt determined to get it.

"It seems that the other half is far away from here. It will take two or three days to attract it with the stone slab! I hope nothing goes wrong during these days!" One person said lightly, and then pulled down his cloak. It was Tiansheng. The others also pulled down their cloaks. It was Murong Di and the evil ghost, and the remaining seven people were actually the Xing brothers.

Didn't they die a few? Why are they standing here peacefully now?

Boss Xing looked at Tiansheng and said respectfully: "Young Master, I have a request!" Tiansheng said lightly: "Okay, just don't disrupt my plan to take my heart!"

When Boss Xing saw that Tiansheng knew his idea, he stopped talking and said directly: "Thank you, Young Master!" After that, the anger in his heart burned: "Ye Ye, I want you to pay with blood!"

Tiansheng and his companions did not speak again, but sat cross-legged on the ground, watching the changes in the sky.

After a long time, Tiansheng looked down at the sky and said with a tired head: "Rest first! Visit Yemen tomorrow morning!"

The changes in the sky were seen by almost the entire Shenzhou, and also attracted the attention of several forces.

In the Huangdao League, the Huangdao League, which was in the rest period, did not mobilize too arrogantly. Only Gu Zihao, Ye Xincheng and Xia Wanjun, Feng Yi and Sun Ye came, but this lineup was already the strongest team in the Huangdao League.

And in a valley somewhere, under a cave, there was actually a secret base.

"The sky has changed, we must get this thing! Otherwise, the world will be in chaos!" An old man with gray eyebrows and hair said majestically. If Yang Hengchao were here, he would be surprised, because this man is the person behind the military and even the entire conquest, known as Long Lao. It is said that he has lived for hundreds of years and has been living in seclusion. Unexpectedly, this change actually brought him out.

All the people under him are officials and immediately agreed. With the appearance of Long Lao, the army also began to spy on what happened after the change.

After a long time, everyone dispersed. Long Lao was alone in the secret room, and the corner of his mouth twitched slightly: "My second heart has appeared!" Who is Long Lao, and he actually knows the existence of this heart.

Chapter 72 Welcoming Guests from All Directions 1

The world was boiling at this moment. The strange phenomenon that could be seen by almost the entire Shenzhou attracted too many strange people. Ye Ye naturally knew all this. The thing was in the sky, and it was impossible to hide it. Moreover, how could such a huge and spectacular phenomenon be hidden? Moreover, this thing had only appeared for a short time. At this point, Ye Ye had already felt that several groups of powerful energy in the distance had approached Yemen again, and even two familiar energies were already within the range of Yemen.

"Looking at the two blue half-heart-shaped dark blue clouds in the sky that were slowly approaching each other, Ye Ye said to the Yemen disciples under him: "Immediately decorate the entire Yemen Mountain, how can the guests feel that my Yemen is not good at treating guests? "After saying that, Ye Ye laughed. After all, it was unnecessary to worry about the foreign object in the sky. Since this thing appeared in Yemen, let them fight for it. In this way, perhaps under the interference of many powerful people in the world, the natural person might not be able to get the heart of the sky. And Ye Ye's approach really ensured the safety of Yemen. After all, if he entertained everyone to seize the strange treasure as the host, those strange people would not be able to make trouble for Yemen.

Ye Ye thought, and then ordered people to open the gate of Yemen. Then the whole Yemen Mountain became busier than ever. They knew that if Yemen was not careful at this time, it would be in danger of extinction. Therefore, all the disciples of Yemen were very dedicated. Power.

Ye Ye's guess was correct. Since the strange phenomenon in the sky appeared, the strange people from all over the world are speeding up their pace to Yemen Mountain. They all want to get a share of it, or want to take that thing for themselves.

One day passed, and after the disciples of Yemen were busy all night, Yemen was finally set up. Waiting for the arrival of strange people from all over the world. Ye Ye also stood at the door.

After a long time, Yemen finally welcomed the first batch of guests.

The man was very familiar to Ye Ye and his friends, and even the entire Yemen. It was Shen Mo and his friends who lived in the city at the foot of the mountain.

"Master Ye, don't mind. We are not here to fight for the strange treasure. We just want to watch the fun, that's all! " How could Shen Mo not understand why Ye Ye did this? As soon as he reached the door, he clasped his fists and announced his purpose. Ye Ye looked carefully and saw Uncle Mu was actually there. Wasn't Uncle Mu dead? Could it be...

With many questions in his mind, Ye Ye smiled and clasped his fists and said, "Senior, please go in quickly, take a rest, and watch the fun. You may have to wait two or three days! I'll leave you for the next two days." "After Ye Ye finished speaking, he looked at the two half-heart shapes in the sky that were slowly approaching. He thought to himself: things seem to be getting more and more exciting.

Shen Mo didn't say much, and led a group of people into Yemen. Ye Ye looked at the shade of Shen Mo entering, and then nodded to Qin Minglei. Qin Minglei immediately followed him in, and then carried Qin Feng out for Shen Mo and his group to watch. Shen Mo and his group came here, indeed not to compete for any rare treasures, but just to watch the excitement and see the grandson who caused this scene. And Shen Mo also had a wide range of knowledge of the world's strange people, and was also invited to help receive guests, otherwise Yemen and others would not even recognize the people, wouldn't it be impolite?

After a long time, the second group of guests also arrived. Ye Ye didn't know these people. He quickly sent someone to invite Shen Mo out. After Shen Mo came out, he looked at the person who came, and immediately greeted him with a smile and said: "Brother Mu Ren, long time no see!"

When the man saw that the person who came was Shen Mo, he also clasped his fists and said: "Brother Shen, long time no see. I wonder if my brother is well? It's not a good feeling to live under someone else's roof when you have a home but don't live there. " His words were full of disdain.

Shen Mo smiled and ignored his mockery. He whispered something to a Yemen disciple beside him, and the Yemen disciple ran in. Soon, Butler Mu came out and shouted loudly: "Brother, what are you doing here? Go back! Don't peek at this thing. Even if you get it, the Mu family will not be at peace!" Butler Mu stopped Mu Ren.

Mu Ren just smiled and said: "It's better than living under someone else's roof as a butler. I think it's enough to be a dog or a human!" After saying that, Mu Ren turned his head and looked at Ye Ye and said: "I guess this is Master Ye? It's really a young hero. Are you going to treat guests like this? I came all the way here for the thing in the sky, not to stand at the door and talk to the dog."

Ye Ye raised his eyebrows and thought to himself: "This person is so conceited! I don't know how strong he is, but judging from the energy emanating from his body, it's not very good. "But he said without a trace on his face: "It's my fault for neglecting me, please come in!" After that, he waved his hand and asked someone to lead the way. Seeing this, Mu Ren followed the Yemen disciple who led the way. When he passed by Butler Mu, he gave Butler Mu a disdainful look.

Seeing this, Ye Ye walked to Butler Mu and said: "I'm sorry, Uncle Mu, this..."

"It's okay... It's okay! Ye Zi, it's okay, this is a family matter. "After that, he returned to normal. Seeing this, Ye Ye didn't know what to say, but looked at the sky, his face showing worry. Because he felt a familiar energy approaching. Moreover, those energies didn't seem to hide themselves and released energy wantonly.

Soon after, a group of people came to Yemen. One of them smiled, but his eyes showed hostility.

The people who came were Tiansheng's group. And the smiling person in the front was Boss Xing. When Ye Ye saw Boss Xing, his face was full of surprise: "Can't they die? "This is not the first time Ye Ye has seen such a situation. The last time was in the Huangdao League.

He put away the surprise on his face, pulled down Shen Mo who was about to go forward to greet the guests, and then clasped his fists and said: "Boss Xing, you are here early. It seems that this thing is still early!" After that, he pointed to the dark blue in the sky.

Boss Xing smiled, not hiding the hostility on his face and said: "Master Ye, you really know how to behave. The host is welcoming the guests, and the guests are really not easy to make trouble! But we are determined to get that thing!"

Ye Ye smiled, said nothing, made way, and then walked out of the way for a disciple of the Night Sect to greet him. Boss Xing just smiled, and retreated without giving face, and then in Ye Ye's puzzled eyes, he bowed respectfully to a man in a cloak who came with him and said: "Young Master, the gate of the Night Sect is already open, welcome young master in! "After saying that, he glanced at Ye Ye, with a cold murderous intent in his eyes.

The man twitched his mouth, pulled down the hat on his cloak, and then smiled at Ye Ye. Ye Ye was immediately shocked, wondering in his heart: "How could it be Tiansheng! What's going on?" Thinking of this, Ye Ye suppressed his doubts and said calmly: "Boy, go in!"

"Boy? Be careful when you speak!" The Xing brothers heard Ye Ye call Tiansheng like this, and they couldn't help but get angry. But they were stopped by Tiansheng: "Don't make trouble, the time is not right, and my plan has been disrupted!" Tiansheng's voice was only heard by the two of them. After hearing this, the Xing brothers suppressed their anger and followed Tiansheng awkwardly, ready to enter the night gate.

At this time, Ye Ye smiled and shouted loudly: "Welcome, Master Gu! "As soon as Ye Ye finished speaking, five people walked up the stairs, and they were Gu Zihao and his companions.

Gu Zihao was also surprised to hear Ye Ye say this, and then he walked forward, looked at Boss Xing following Tiansheng, thought about it in confusion, and then walked forward and said: "Haha, Master Ye, this is a great blessing from heaven for Yemen. Congratulations!" Gu Zihao meant that it was your bad luck that this thing fell into Yemen, and Yemen was waiting to suffer when you guys fought for it.

How could Ye Ye not understand the meaning of Gu Zihao's words, and ignored it, but said to Ye Xincheng: "Should I call you Elder Ye? Or Mr. Ye?"

Ye Xincheng was stunned, and when he was about to answer, Gu Zihao rushed to say: "Master Ye, have you seen my disciple? I wonder if Master Ye knows her whereabouts now?" He was referring to Xia Feng.

Ye Ye nodded, and then said: "Of course." Xia Feng had been hiding in Yemen, but no one could see her.

"Then I'm relieved! "After saying that, he turned to look at Boss Xing and said jokingly: "Boss Xing, oh, look at me, I accidentally took your place!"

Boss Xing did not answer, but Tiansheng said: "It doesn't matter. Master Gu, please go first, we are ready to go in. But suddenly I saw a dog on the ground (a kind of insect on the ground that can make bricks), I couldn't bear it, so I didn't step on it. Master Gu, please go first, I will wait for the dog to pass, then I will go in. "

Gu Zihao's eyes turned cold, looking at a strange face, the bold and careful Gu Zihao couldn't figure out the other party for the time being, but seeing that even the Xing brothers were inferior to him, he was shocked, and then perfunctorily said: "You are really kind." After that, he ignored them and prepared to go in.

"Gu Zihao, Ye Xincheng, Xia Wanjun! "But suddenly, a loud and sharp shout was heard. Gu Zihao and the other two looked over and saw that the source of the voice was Murong Di! Gu Zihao and the other two were startled, and then quickly wiped it off: "Who did I think it was? A fugitive." After saying that, he turned around and entered the night gate with disdain. But the three of them were thinking wildly in their hearts: Who is that young man, who made the Xing brothers and Murong Di willing to be inferior to him. They knew Murong Di's strength, so, that young man...

Tian Sheng smiled and said to Ye Ye: "Thank you, Master Ye, for your hospitality. I haven't eaten well these days!" After that, he led the Xing brothers and Murong Di into the night gate.

After they passed, Ye Ye looked at their backs and was no longer worried. Instead, he was surprised: This is fun! Tiansheng, you can't get this thing. Thinking of this, he clenched his fists, his left hand was red and black, and his right hand was colorful. The fierce energy was released wantonly.

Tiansheng and Gu Zihao and others who had just passed by naturally felt the two fierce energies, and looked back in surprise, but they only saw Ye Ye smiling calmly.

Chapter 73 Welcome guests from all sides 2

Ye Ye slowly turned his head and continued to greet people with a smile. However, no one came again. At noon, Ye Ye and others also took a rest. The greeters at the door were handed over to Shen Mo and Butler Mu. The two of them also knew a little about the heroes and strangers in the world.

But Ye Ye returned to the night gate. After dinner, Ye Ye, Qin Minglei, and Li Bin went to the temporary residence of Mu Ren and others.

Ye Ye pushed open the door and entered, but was looked at by several hostile eyes. Ye Ye ignored it directly, then walked into the room, looked at the food on the table that was not yet cold and said, "Are you guys afraid that I will poison you at night?" After that, he walked to the table, picked up the chopsticks, and picked up a dish. , after putting it into his mouth, he said vaguely: "Don't worry, I won't poison you!" After that, he turned around and left, closing the door. After walking out of the house, Ye Ye shook his head: "These people will definitely be the first losers in this fight!!" Thinking about this, Ye Ye continued to limp to the courtyard next door where the Tiansheng people lived.

Tiansheng and others did not enter the house, but stood or sat quietly in the yard, while Tiansheng looked at the two blue groups in the sky with unabashed greed. Except for the angry

Xing family brothers, Murong Spy and the others didn't seem to pay attention to Ye Ye's arrival.

"Excuse me, can you please entertain me at night?" Ye Ye asked lightly.

Hearing the sound, Tiansheng took his head back to look at the sky, looked at Ye Ye and said, "Yes, the food is delicious!" After that, he continued to look at the sky.

Ye Ye smiled, and then continued: "Little brother, don't look at it. It will take two more days to look at you again!" Ye Ye said. But Tiansheng didn't seem to want to talk to him, and continued to look at the sky. Seeing this, Ye Ye shook his head and walked out of the courtyard.

Not long after he walked out, he was about to go to Gu Zihao's place where the five of them were, but unexpectedly, he bumped into Ye Xincheng on the road.

"Mr. Ye, I don't know, how good is the reception at the night gate?" Ye Ye asked lightly. Ye Xincheng did not answer him in a hurry. Instead, he looked at the surrounding scenery and then smiled and said, "Everything seems so familiar. Of course the night gate reception is good, it feels like home."

After hearing this, Ye Ye tilted his head slightly: "That's good. I'm afraid that my night gate doesn't provide good hospitality. If you make trouble for the night gate, my little night gate can't afford it." No one in the night gate knew why Ye Xincheng He would go and join in the same deeds with Gu Zihao, so naturally he felt a little dissatisfied.

Ye Xincheng could naturally hear the dissatisfaction, but he didn't express anything, and smiled: "Master Ye, I won't disturb you anymore. I have to take a good stroll in the night gate." After that, he brushed against Ye Ye. And passed.

Seeing this, Ye Ye said to Ye Xincheng without looking back: "Mr. Ye, you can't wander around in the night gate. You should go back to your residence first!" After that, Ye Ye and the other three walked forward, leaving Ye Xin behind. Cheng stayed there alone and did not leave for a long time. Ye Xincheng himself also knew what his actions meant to Yemen. But he doesn't regret his choice. Thinking about it, he turned around, no longer lingering around, and left thinking about his residence.

"Ye Ye, is that too much? After all, he was once an elder of Yemen." Li Bin looked at Ye Ye and asked lightly. Ye Ye smiled, pointed to the sky and said: "If he can come back, it will be an elder, but this time it was that thing that brought him back." At this point, the three of them stopped talking and walked forward silently. .

"Hey, Master Ye. What brought you here?" Ye Ye did not enter the residence of Gu Zihao and his friends. He just passed by and Gu Zihao greeted them at the door.

Ye Ye smiled faintly: "Yemen treats you well, right?" Gu Zihao nodded and said: "Of course." After saying that, his face suddenly changed, and he whispered to Ye Ye: "Where is my apprentice? Where is he?"

Ye Ye smiled and said, "They are all over the night gate, look for them yourself!" No one knew why Xia Feng wanted to hide. After Ye Ye finished speaking, he clasped his fists: "I still have guests to greet, so I won't disturb you all!" Before he finished speaking, a disciple of Yiyemen hurriedly ran towards Ye Ye, and then he said something to Ye Ye, and Ye Ye's expression suddenly changed. Startled, his eyes flashed with excitement, and finally he turned around and ran away.

Arriving at the night gate, Shen Mo and Butler Mu were receiving a group of people. Among the crowd, there was an old man with white hair and a childlike face, who was extremely kind.

When the old man saw Ye Ye running out, he immediately trembled with excitement. The crutch in his hand kept hitting the ground, pointing at Ye Ye, and his mouth trembled, as if he had something to say.

Ye Ye looked at the old man suspiciously, looking up and down at him impolitely. He was still struggling to wake up from the words spoken by the Yemen disciple just now. That night disciple said to Ye Ye: "Master, there is a guest outside, claiming to be your grandfather!"

After a long time, the old man broke the silence and said, "Are you Ye Ye? You are indeed very similar to Feng'er!" After hearing this, Ye Ye took two deep breaths calmly and calmed down before saying, "Well. I'm Ye Night. Are you?"

The old man became excited again and wanted to say something to the people behind him, but he was too excited to say anything. After calming down, he continued: "Is your tail vertebrae more protruding than ordinary people? There are three more black moles on your chest, the middle one is larger and the other side is smaller?"

Ye Ye thought for a while and then nodded in surprise. Perhaps Qin Minglei and Li Bin didn't know these secrets. The old man became excited again: "That's it, I am your Ye Ye, Long Hengchen. My child, did you go out when you were dozens of years old? You did it because our Long family was attacked by enemies, Your father also died among them. Before he died, he sent someone to take you out of the Long family! Then something happened on the way, causing you to hit your head and lose your memory!" The old man said and sobbed. The people behind him also sighed.

Ye Ye looked at the old man named Long Hengchen in confusion and said calmly: "You said my surname is Long? Is it from the Long family?"

The old man nodded and said: "Yes, child, your full name is Long Ye! After the enemy attacked, I was a step late, so I had to eliminate the enemy and then send people everywhere to listen to your news. I finally found it today. Feng'er My soul is in heaven!" After saying this, tears burst down his face.

Ye Ye stood there in confusion. At this time, he was already doubtful. He was about to tell his strange dream and ask Long Hengchen what it meant. But at this time, Silence suddenly spoke.

"You all have come from afar, even if you want to recognize your relatives, why don't you come here at the gate of the Night Gate? If you don't mind, how about entering the Night Gate first, and then we can talk in detail later." Ye Ye's silent words made him feel his desire. Suppressing the thoughts spoken in the dream. He nodded and said, "Yes, everyone, go in first!"

When the old man saw this, he wiped away tears from his eyes and said, "Yes, go in first and see the career of the descendants of my Long family!" After that, he led a group of people into the gate. But when he met Yu Ye Ye, he pointed at the sky and said to himself: "With you, Feng'er can be resurrected!"

Ye Ye was the only one who heard this. After hearing this, Ye Ye was already doubtful. After hearing this, his pupils shrank and he slowly raised his head to look at the two blue masses in the sky.

Is this person Ye Ye's grandfather?

Chapter 74 Small Battle

The words of the old man Long Hengchen kept passing through Ye Ye's mind. "You are the descendant of my Long family, Long Feng's son, Long Ye!" "With you, Feng'er can be resurrected!" Ye Ye stood there, constantly recalling everything that Long Hengchen said.

How much he wished he had a father and a home, but today, why did Ye Ye feel uneasy and nervous? Ye Ye thought about it and looked at the sky, then said lightly: "Can it only be confirmed after my so-called father is resurrected as he said?" Ye Ye, who was calm and composed, looked very dull at this moment. But it is indeed understandable, just like when you were a child, your parents died, and then you wandered for decades, and then someone said that your parents were not dead, but you had no impression. Who wouldn't be nervous, who wouldn't be confused?

Li Bin and Qin Minglei saw Ye Ye in a daze, then walked towards Ye Ye, pushed Ye Ye with their shoulders, and after waking him up, they pulled Ye Ye to the door of the night. The two of them also knew what Ye Ye was thinking, and they also wanted to confirm whether Ye Ye's relatives were true.

The three pushed and shoved all the way, and finally came to the temporary residence of Long Hengchen and his group.

Long Hengchen and his group seemed to be extremely cautious, and there was someone guarding the gate of the courtyard.

"Young Master!" The two guards at the gate saw Ye Ye coming and immediately shouted respectfully. Ye Ye was startled and did not say anything. He looked at Qin Minglei and Li Bin anxiously. But what he was greeted with was the firm eyes of the two.

"Go and inform your master that Master Ye is here." Li Bin said lightly, and a gatekeeper ran in immediately. Soon, Long Hengchen came over with a cane, pointed at Ye Ye with trembling hands and said: "Child, are you finally here to recognize your relatives?"

Ye Ye hesitated and did not speak. Ye Ye, who was originally talkative and steady and calm, became so anxious.

Seeing that Ye Ye did not speak, Li Bin replied, "Mr. Long, our head of the Ye Sect came to see if there is anything that is not well taken care of in the Ye Sect!"

When Long Hengchen heard what Li Bin said, his eyes suddenly turned cold, and he turned his head away and ignored Li Bin. Seeing this, a strong man beside him said disdainfully, "Who are you? Why are you speaking for my descendants of the Long family? Let me tell you, this Ye Sect belongs to my Long family, and you are just a dog!" Li Bin raised his eyebrows and almost wanted to pull out the strange dagger of the Ye Sect to stab the man to death. But for the sake of the Ye Sect, Li Bin did not. He just said, "What about the dragon? There are snakes and insects hiding behind the dragon! Dogs are also nobler than them!" After that, he no longer paid attention to the angry eyes of the strong man just now, turned around lightly, and prepared to leave.

At this time, Qin Minglei suddenly shouted loudly, "Li Bin, be careful!" As soon as the voice fell, Li Bin turned back in surprise and found that the strong man had rushed in front of him at some point, and his fist as big as a bowl was heading towards Li Bin's head. If hit, Li Bin would have a concussion if not dead.

But Li Bin is the Undead King, how could he be defeated so easily. In a flash, Li Bin raised his right hand slightly, his fingers turned into knives, and after seeing the right moment, he skillfully chopped the strong man's wrist, knocked his fist diagonally, and passed through his side face. The strong man was startled, but soon calmed down, and then his other hand hit him again from bottom to top with a hook punch. Li Bin did not dodge, but pushed his hands down, pressed against the strong man's arm, and then flew backwards with the force.

After flying out, Li Bin twisted his body in mid-air, pulled out the strange dagger of Yemen, and then used the force of flying to suddenly bounce over, with a little cold light in his hand.

The strong man was also very extraordinary. In this flash, he also quickly pulled out the dagger on his leg. The dagger shone with cold light, and the back of the dagger was actually serrated.

At this time, Yang Hengchao had just finished his work. After hearing about Ye Ye's situation, Hu immediately followed. Seeing the dagger pulled out by the strong man, he exclaimed: "Military dagger?" Yang Hengchao had worked for the country before, so he naturally recognized these weapons, but Yang Hengchao had never seen those people. Confused, he walked over, and saw that Ye Ye and Qin Minglei did not stop him, so he asked lightly: "What's wrong?"

Qin Minglei did not answer him, but made a gesture of silence. Yang Hengchao looked at Qin Minglei lightly. He found that there was a trace of anger on his face, and he was confused, and then he looked at the two people fighting in the field without asking any more questions.

In the field, Li Bin and the strong man were still fighting, and no one stopped them. The sound of "click, click" was endless. Li Bin almost used all his strength at this time, and his clothes were cut by the strong man. There were even some cuts that could be seen that the wounds were slowly healing, and the whole person was in a mess.

Looking at the sturdy man again, his situation was not good at the moment. At this moment, the sturdy man who was originally wearing a white vest had several cuts on his white vest. Every time he moved, some blood flowed out of those cuts.

After all, mortals are mortals. How can they heal their wounds as quickly as the undead corpse king Li Bin? However, Li Bin was also more and more shocked as the battle went on. On the surface, he did have the advantage. But in the battle, Li Bin himself was very clear about the strength of the sturdy man's hands, and he had to admire the opponent's skills in using daggers. Several times, the sturdy man almost used the serrations on the back of the military dagger to hook the strange dagger of Yemen in Li Bin's hand. Moreover, what surprised Li Bin the most was that the more wounds the sturdy man had on his body, the heavier the strength in his hands!

After fighting for a long time, the cuts on Li Bin's body continued to increase, and the white vest on the sturdy man's body had been stained red with blood, and his eyes were also red, and he opened his mouth and let out a low roar.

At this time, Li Bin and the sturdy man were standing there, panting. Then the two rushed towards each other at the same time. This must be the last blow for the two.

When Li Bin was about to touch the sturdy man, he suddenly buried his body strangely, and slid over with inertia with a sweeping leg. The sturdy man jumped up vigorously, and Li Bin immediately squatted, grabbed the dagger with both hands, and stabbed upward fiercely. The sturdy man's performance was also very amazing. He actually turned a circle in the air, and after a little inertia, he also grabbed the dagger with both hands and stabbed at Li Bin.

A soft sound of "click" sounded. A scene appeared in front of everyone. The tips of the daggers in their hands actually touched each other, and then one up and one down, which was very strange. Finally, under the gaze of everyone, the light sound of "click" sounded again, and the two daggers actually cracked at the same time and turned into random. After the sturdy man landed from mid-air, he said nothing more and slowly walked to Long Hengchen. Li Bin also smiled and walked back to Ye Ye without saying anything.

At this time, Ye Ye finally woke up and looked at Long Hengchen with an apologetic look and said, "Long... Senior, I'm sorry to bother you! I hope my Yemen didn't treat you badly!" Ye Ye had been in a daze just now.

After that, Long Hengchen nodded and said, "It's okay, you young people can have a fight!" Ye Ye nodded and led the way out of the courtyard.

After walking out of the courtyard, Li Bin suddenly grinned, and a trace of black blood overflowed from the corner of his mouth. The last blow just now had injured him. However, in fact, Li Bin could have won. Because Li Bin's strongest posture is not like this, Ye Ye, Qin Minglei, Yang Hengchao and the other three knew it.

He supported Li Bin and slowly left the courtyard. In Long Hengchen's courtyard, the situation of the sturdy man was exactly the same as Li Bin.

"He's very strong, and I don't think he's using his full strength!" the sturdy man said to Long Hengchen calmly.

After hearing this, Long Hengchen smiled and said, "That's better..."

In a corner that they didn't notice, three people stayed on the roof and watched the farce. They were Tiansheng, Murong Di, and Boss Xing.

"Let's go, go back. It's too hard to wait, Xing Xin, I'll leave it to you later!" Tiansheng said calmly. Boss Xing's original name was Xing Xin. He nodded immediately after hearing this, and the three of them jumped off the roof and returned to their own residence. Boss Xing took out a dark blue bead in his hand. From the energy emitted, it was the same energy that attracted the two dark blue balls in the sky.

Chapter 75 Acceleration

Seeing Murong Di looking at the bead in his hand in confusion, Boss Xing smiled and said to him: "This bead is the main heart of the stone slab above. With its control and increased energy, the two halves of the heart will meet faster and then become the heart of the young master." Murong Di nodded thoughtfully.

Boss Xing smiled with satisfaction, and then suddenly exerted force with his hand. With a "click", the bead was crushed by him. "Be patient, only in this way will the stone slab feel the crisis, and then get angry and increase the energy absorption! And, in the end, after the two halves of the heart are combined, it will automatically fall to us!"

Boss Xing said so, the stone slab actually has self-awareness? Surprised, Murong Di continued to watch.

Boss Xing continued to exert force, and the bead was overwhelmed and kept making "clicking" sounds, and finally, it broke with a "snap". And those fragments did not fall to the ground when they broke, but flew towards the stone slab in the sky very quickly. After the beads were opened, there was a trace of something like a flame inside the beads.

Boss Xing smiled, put his nose close, and inhaled the flame before saying with a little discomfort: "This thing is the lifeline that can control it to put the heart back here!" After that, he turned to look at Tiansheng and nodded to indicate that the work was done.

Tiansheng smiled and nodded, then looked up into the sky.

After a long time, Boss Xing smiled and said: "It's finally started!" As soon as the voice fell, the sky suddenly changed. The two heart-shaped dark blue balls that were originally approaching slowly actually accelerated at this time, and the speed was increasing faster and faster, and the energy emitted by the stone slab in the center was getting more and more violent.

"Master... look at the sky!" A disciple of Yemen suddenly ran to Ye Ye's side and said in a hurry. Everyone looked up in confusion and saw this strange scene. Not only the Night Gate, but all the visitors sent people to check the movement of the thing in the sky at all times. Who would not know that such a drastic change had occurred at this time?

At this time, those who had not arrived at the Night Gate that day also felt the changes above their heads, exclaimed, and then accelerated their pace. They all wanted to arrive at the Night Gate when the two groups of dark blue merged together. Even if they could not get it, they would at least see the wonder.

At this time, the Night Gate became busy as more and more people came with faster pace. Fortunately, the Night Gate occupied the entire hill and was built quite grandly, otherwise it would not be able to accommodate so many people.

In his busyness, Ye Ye temporarily forgot about the family affairs that confused him, and concentrated on welcoming guests at the Night Gate. In his spare time, he would also look at the sky and the speed of the two dark blue flowers.

"It seems that we will meet tomorrow morning at the latest!" Ye Ye estimated a time in his mind, which was also the time estimated by most people. Ye Ye thought, looked at the lively Yemen, shook his head and whispered: "Who can imagine what tomorrow will be like with the laughter at this moment?"

Li Bin listened, patted his shoulder and comforted him: "If you have nothing to do, go and get familiar with Long Hengchen. If he is not your family, then at least he can be your family, right? You are missing a home now!"

After hearing this, Ye Ye looked up at Li Bin. Li Bin's family was also broken, his parents died early, and then he was in a corpse disaster and left his hometown. He also wanted a home, but he was thinking of Ye Ye. Ye Ye knew all this, but he didn't say much. He smiled, gave Li Bin a reassuring smile and said: "I know, I'll go see the guests, you take me here to welcome the guests!"

Li Bin nodded and let Ye Ye go. But he didn't know that Ye Ye thought of someone in his heart, Xia Feng, who went back to Yemen with him, but he was the only one who knew where that person was!

Ye Ye walked along the way, greeted the guests along the way, and slowly came to the backyard where there were few people. Then he quietly opened the door of the backyard and touched the back mountain. Finally, he found a wooden house in a hidden place in the dense forest of the back mountain.

Ye Ye smiled, walked over, and pushed the door open. The house was spotless, with two sitting cloths on the floor, and food was being cooked not far from the sitting cloths.

"Come out, it's me!" Ye Ye looked at the situation and sat on a sitting cloth, saying carelessly. Before the voice fell, a person appeared from the darkness, it was Xia Feng.

After Xia Feng appeared, she walked slowly, walked slowly to a sitting cloth opposite Ye Ye, sat down and said: "Why do you have time to come and see me? Why don't you go and do that thing?" While speaking, Xia Feng picked up the soup spoon and stirred the food on the fire, and a faint fragrance came to her face. This Xia Feng is not only extremely powerful, but also can cook well?

Ye Ye looked at Xia Feng stirring the food, smiled, and said with tenderness in his eyes: "Well, no rush, I guess we can meet tomorrow morning." Xia Feng raised her beautiful eyes and glanced at Ye Ye with doubts: "Why is it one day earlier?"

"I don't know, but nothing is absolute!" Ye Ye said lightly, and Ye Ye also stirred the food by himself.

After a long time, Xia Feng broke the silence: "You came to me today not just to tell me that the thing will meet one day earlier, right?"

Ye Ye smiled awkwardly, and then said: "Yes, I came for this. Don't you also want to win that thing? I don't understand, what's the difference between you winning it and your master winning it?"

Xia Feng stood up, picked up two bowls, filled two bowls of food, handed a bowl to Ye Ye, scooped up a spoon, blew it and said: "It's different, completely different. Or tell me why you came here!"

Ye Ye was not angry at Xia Feng's avoidance, but scooped up a mouthful of delicious food, and didn't Instead of blowing it cool, Ye Ye took it directly into his mouth, letting the hot food burn in his mouth. After swallowing the food, Ye Ye sighed and whispered, "Someone came to me and said it was my grandfather!"

Who knows, Xia Feng's hand suddenly trembled, and the bowl in his hand fell down, and he became very excited: "Grandfather? Ye Ye, I tell you, you can't have a grandfather, and you won't have a grandfather!"

Ye Ye looked at Xia Feng in confusion, not understanding why he was so excited, looking at the bowl in his hand and said lightly: "I don't know, but the evidence he produced really makes people believe it!"

"Humph." Xia Feng snorted coldly, Ye Ye felt that the temperature was a few degrees lower and then looked at Xia Feng. "Get out, get out, I said, you won't have a grandfather! You will know later!" Xia Feng's uncharacteristic behavior made Ye Ye very confused. Just as he was about to say something, he was interrupted by Xia Feng again. Helpless Ye Ye had to put down the bowl in his hand and said, "Thank you, it's delicious. It would be great if I could eat it for a lifetime!" After that, he left the wooden house without looking back, turned into the woods, and disappeared.

As soon as Ye Ye left, a figure appeared again in the darkness. Xia Feng looked over indifferently, ignored it, and quietly cleaned up the food that had just been spilled on the ground.

"Sister, do you like Brother Ye Ye?" The man said to Xia Feng in a crying voice. Xia Feng smiled bleakly: "Sister Ye Rui, don't think too much. You should go back quickly, otherwise he will find you. That would be bad." The person turned out to be Ye Rui. How could she find Xia Feng's temporary residence?

Ye Rui sighed and cried: "Sister, I heard what Brother Ye Ye said just now, I understand, I understand, Brother Ye Ye likes you!" Ye Rui actually loves Ye Ye deeply, but Ye Ye doesn't know it.

Xia Feng pulled Ye Rui into her arms, stroked his head and said, "What do you mean by like or not? Sister Ye Rui is so nice, who wouldn't like her?" "But..." "No buts, sister, I told you, maybe I will die tomorrow, and you will be the only one by his side!" Xia Feng suddenly became excited, pinched her right hand with hatred, and her nails dug into her flesh.

Ye Rui stopped talking and hugged Xia Feng tightly. Xia Feng also caressed his head, and after Ye Rui fell asleep, she said lightly, "Ye Rui, I'm sorry, I lied to you, and the one who will die is actually..." After Xia Feng came out of the Huangdao League secretly, she was deeply secretive. What secrets did she hide?

Perhaps, everything will be announced to the world. That night, the night gate had closed the door tightly and would not allow anyone to enter, and all the visitors were already resting their weapons and resting their spirits, preparing for tomorrow's capture.

In the sky, the two dark blue groups became more and more weird in the darkness.

Chapter 76: Fight

The sky gradually became brighter. That night, many people did not fall asleep. They were the ones who arranged to observe the blue sky for two days at night.

The sun rose, and the red light suppressed the dazzling blue color. As the sun rose, the two blue heart-shaped groups that had been traveling for several days were now close at hand, and they would merge together in a short time.

The sun slowly climbed higher. At this time, there was a commotion in the night gate.

"It's touched, it's touched!" Shouts came one after another. Those who were in no mood and pretended to sleep woke up from the exclamation immediately, and then rushed out of the house, staring at the two blue groups in the sky that were shining brightly at this time.

At this time, the two blue half-heart-shaped groups were already complete heart-shaped. Moreover, what was amazing was that the heart-shaped group looked like it was beating, like a living thing.

"It finally appeared. Xing Xin, wait for the right time and then take action to get my heart back. After that..." Tiansheng's eyes turned cold as he spoke. Suddenly, a group of black shadows flashed by his side. They were those evil ghosts.

Boss Xing looked at the sky enthusiastically, and a breath came out of his nose. A faint blue flame spurted out of his nose.

He stretched out his hand to catch it, and then smiled, determined to get the thing in the sky.

At the same time, it was not only Tiansheng and his men who were busy. Among the visitors, Gu Zihao and the other five had formed a formation. Gu Zihao was in the middle, and the other four were on all four sides of him, and then they raised their energy at the same time, and slowly a pair of giant hands formed above their heads. They actually wanted to use the giant hands to grab the heart that was about to complete the fusion.

Seeing a pair of giant hands appear out of thin air and point at the strange treasure in the sky, everyone was anxious and immediately used all their skills. Some people just took out their weapons and looked at those busy people with a covetous look. In their hearts, no matter who took the item in the sky, they would kill him, and then take the treasure from the army, and finally leave a good name and go home with the treasure. Some people, who came alone, formed teams at this moment. They were not very strong, but wanted to win by relying on numbers.

Look at Mu Ren again. Mu Ren and his party actually had their own secret treasures. At this moment, they actually took out strange tools one by one, and then kept assembling them, and soon they were assembled. The secret treasure turned out to be a crossbow, but what was shot out was an iron hand. Looking at the iron claw with a cold light, Mu Ren smiled and pressed the launch button. The iron hand immediately grabbed the air, but it was immediately retracted in mid-air. At this moment, the treasure was not fully integrated, and the smart Mu Ren did not want to be the target of public criticism. He just wanted to demonstrate.

Mu Ren's move touched the hearts of many people, but after the iron claw was retracted, they also breathed a sigh of relief.

At this moment, the calmest people were indeed the group of Long Hengchen and the people of Yemen who claimed to be Ye Ye's grandfather. Yemen was the master, so naturally they could not show too much purpose of competing for the treasure, otherwise, after this incident, Yemen would become the target of public criticism, so Ye Ye also said in the secret meeting that Yemen would remain a fisherman and let the clams and cranes fight. But Long Hengchen couldn't explain it clearly. Was his intention really just to find his relatives?

However, after a few breaths, Long Hengchen looked at the strange phenomenon in the sky, looked at Ye Ye, and then walked to Ye Ye with a cane and said, "Child, remember what I said? It can revive my son Feng'er." Pointing at the gradually forming heart shape in the sky.

Ye Ye looked at Long Hengchen solemnly and didn't speak. Long Hengchen continued, "Child, I know you doubt it, so let's join forces? Get that thing, revive Feng'er, and then talk about it, you will definitely believe me!"

Ye Ye hesitated, and he hesitated when he heard this. At this time, Xia Feng's words kept ringing in his heart, 'He won't be your grandfather, and you won't have a grandfather!' However, another voice lingered in his mind, 'Feng'er is resurrected, and you will definitely believe me later!' Unable to make a decision, Ye Ye looked back at Qin Minglei and others behind him. Qin Minglei and others were looking at Ye Ye firmly at this moment, with support in their eyes.

Seeing this situation, Ye Ye laughed immediately, and then said: "Well, no matter what, we will know the truth after resurrecting Long Feng, right?" In fact, Ye Ye's decision was not only supported by the people behind him, but he just didn't want Tiansheng to get that thing. Moreover, he felt that Long

Hengchen was strong, and the strength of the people around him was not bad, so it was really good to cooperate with him.

After that, Ye Ye stretched out his hand, and Long Hengchen smiled and said: "Okay, this is my descendant of the Long family!" After that, he stretched out his hand and shook it with Ye Ye.

Retracting his hand, Ye Ye looked at the sky. The two groups of dark blue had already parted with each other at this time, and the strong dark blue light even changed the brilliance of the sun. Everyone's eyes were focused on the sky, not only those in the Night Gate, but also many more people who were still unwilling to give up and wanted to come to the Night Gate.

Suddenly, the dark blue light slowly shrank, starting from the edge, and then slowly turned into a thin line and slowly disappeared from the place where the two dark blue balls touched. A blue heart appeared in the air.

This heart was surprisingly strange. Hanging in the air, it was beating like a living being, making a soul-stirring "thumping" sound, and at the center of it was the stone slab. After the heart was assembled, there were actually four black shadows next to it, which made the dark blue heart look even more strange.

Seeing the four black shadows, Gu Zihao immediately understood that this was the secret of the "Ancient Yin God Formation" arranged by Xing Ling. Gu Zihao was very familiar with the four shadows. After all, he defeated them, so Gu Zihao was very familiar with the four black shadows.

Others didn't recognize the four looming black shadows, but Gu Zihao knew them naturally. He gave the order to "go". The giant hand formed by the five of them immediately went towards the heart in the air. When Mu Ren saw Gu Zihao taking action, he immediately activated the strange crossbow, and the iron claws almost caught up with the giant hand's speed, grabbing the heart with both hands at the same time.

However, suddenly the heart emitted a faint light, and then flew rapidly towards the ground, and the direction was actually Tiansheng's direction. It was Boss Xing, who had a secret method to control the stone slab, and the stone slab seemed to be the main eye of the heart, so it could be controlled naturally.

Tiansheng suddenly smiled when he saw this: "This was arranged by me. Huang Shang left Yemen because of his defeated hatred, and the ghost queen followed him because of love. Qin Minglei's child and Huang Shang's child were born with extreme bodies, inheriting the energy of the heart, and the stone slab also belonged to me. It was not easy to trigger all this!" It turned out that everything was done by Tiansheng, and he had been directing all this.

Tiansheng was talking to himself, but the others didn't hear him. Instead, they looked at the place where the heart was flying to, and gathered their energy, ready to take it by force. Ye Ye and Long Hengchen, who were cooperating with him, also took action immediately.

In the air, the two claws grabbed nothing, and were immediately retracted by the owner, and then flew again towards the heart that fell in the direction of Tiansheng and the others.

Chapter 77 Fighting 2

"Opportunity." Ye Ye said secretly, and then suddenly forced out his anger, and rushed towards the rapidly falling heart at the fastest speed. Long Hengchen frowned, stood with his hands behind his back, and then angrily asked a tall and thin man beside him to help. After receiving the order, the tall and thin man was also very good, and his speed was even with Ye Ye.

Speaking of Ye Ye, he did see an opportunity. When he rushed up quickly, the two iron claws blocked the way, but all this seemed to be within Ye Ye's calculations. Ye Ye jumped up, and then twisted his body in the air forcibly, and then his feet actually tapped on the iron claws, refilling his own momentum that was about to end. Then, with the strength of the iron claws, Ye Ye went to the heart faster. But the tall and thin man sent by Long Hengchen did not have such ability. He just looked at Ye Ye in the air in surprise, and then continued to go to the heart quickly, as if nothing in the world would be missed.

However, how could Gu Zihao allow Ye Ye to get the heart so easily? He raised his hands and took off the mask. Then he shook his tail like a dragon. The giant hand in the sky also twisted around and flew towards the heart faster than Ye Ye.

The heart was already close at hand. The giant hand formed by Ye Ye and Gu Zihao flew towards the heart, but something changed suddenly. The heart suddenly stopped. Then Ye Ye and the giant hand passed by it at the same time. After the two flew over, the heart fell rapidly again.

Ye Ye looked down in surprise and saw Tiansheng's smug smile. Then he saw the spark on Xing Lao Da's hand. He could feel from a distance that the energy on the spark was the same as that of the heart. He immediately understood that it was Xing Lao Da who was controlling all this. He was anxious and roared loudly. He would not do it. Anger was mixed in the roar.

"Ye Ye!" Suddenly, a shout came from behind Ye Ye. Ye Ye was still in the air. He looked back and saw that it was Xia Feng. She was standing diagonally on the wall. Then, with a bang, the wall exploded. Then, Xia Feng flew towards Ye Ye quickly with the thrust generated by the explosion.

Ye Ye frowned and understood immediately. He stopped looking at Xia Feng and forced his body to shrink into the movement before ejection while retreating quickly. The two came into contact. Ye Ye's feet were bent and stepped on Xia Feng's shoulders. Ye Ye originally relied on the power of the iron claws shot out by Mu Ren's crossbow to fly so high and far, but although he didn't fly far, the force was already quite strong, while Xia Feng used the power of the explosion to eject. The two forces collided, and it was naturally difficult to bear, but she gritted her teeth and endured it. Then after Ye Ye ejected, she also lost her strength and slowly fell from the air. Fortunately, she was light and agile, and she squatted down and rolled gently when she landed, eliminating the force of falling.

Look at Ye Ye again, after borrowing the force again, Ye Ye went to the heart faster.

"Ah! Hurry!" Ye Ye suddenly shouted in the air, and then stretched out his hand to grab the heart. However, after all, Boss Xing could control the fall of the heart. Tiansheng suddenly shouted again: "Throw!" As soon as the voice fell, he was actually thrown straight into the sky by the strong Xing Yu. And Boss Xing also gritted his teeth at this time, and seemed to be very painful to control the heart. Surprisingly... the heart actually slowly floated upwards.

Ye Ye once again cursed Tiansheng and the others for being mean. He didn't know the truth and thought that Tiansheng and the others were cheating. Seeing Tiansheng flying straight up quickly and the heart also floating upwards, Ye Ye suddenly became anxious. He gritted his teeth and turned around, just in time to catch Tiansheng flying upwards.

"Come down!" Ye Ye shouted, and then used both hands to pull Tiansheng down. After doing all this, Ye Ye suddenly laughed and let Tiansheng go. Tiansheng looked at Ye Ye angrily, twisted his body in the air, and kicked Ye Ye sideways. Ye Ye smiled, then used his hand to resist the flying kick, and with the help of the force, the flying kick was not much, and he laughed even happier. Ye Ye, in the first place, would not let Tiansheng get the heart.

Tiansheng looked at Ye Ye angrily. He had already got the heart. His fingertips had just touched the heart. Feeling the breath connected to his blood, Tiansheng was very excited. But when he was about to grab the heart and merge it with it, Ye Ye did such a thing. How could he not be angry? Killing intent gradually emerged in his eyes. Then he shouted to the ground while falling: "Pull it down! You... waste, if it wasn't for my father's need... I would have killed you seven wastes!"

The ground had changed in the moment when Ye Ye and Tiansheng were fighting. The Xing Lao Da and the others who originally controlled the strange flame and thus the Youlan Heart were attacked by everyone at this moment, and they could not pull their hands out to control it. Tiansheng saw this situation, then turned around cleverly, squatted on the ground steadily, and then looked coldly at Ye Ye who fell not far away. The killing intent in his eyes became stronger, because after he fell, he saw clearly that the people who entangled Xing Lao Da and Murong Di were the people of Yemen!

When the killing intent accumulated to a certain level, Tiansheng couldn't help it, looked at the sky coldly, and then forced out the red and black flames, and rushed towards Ye Ye quickly.

Ye Ye looked at Tiansheng who was rushing towards him, but he frowned, and then forced out the same flames as Tiansheng, with his hands horizontally blocking in front of him. With a light "bang", the two identical flames collided with each other.

Ye Ye sank his legs, dodged Tiansheng's punch first, and then swept out the leg, forcing Tiansheng to jump up, but Tiansheng turned around at low altitude after jumping up, and forced Ye Ye to come directly with a high-pressure leg. Ye Ye couldn't dodge, and he pushed Tiansheng away with his hands, then smiled and said, "No more?" He pointed to the dark blue heart in the sky. At this time, the heart was actually clamped by Mu Ren's iron claws and Gu Zihao's giant hands, and slowly fell.

Tiansheng said inwardly, "Damn it!" Then he looked at Ye Ye fiercely and rushed back to his camp. Tiansheng returned to the battle, and the people of Yemen who were originally responsible for entanglement with the Xing brothers and Murong Die also withdrew.

Tiansheng used the same trick again, letting Xing Yu lift him up fiercely and then threw him into the sky. Then he first grabbed the chain of the iron claw and pulled it hard. The momentum plus his own strength did not break the iron chain. However, the root of the iron chain, the crossbow cart, suffered. It was pulled by Tiansheng and fell to the ground. It was considered that the iron claw could not be controlled temporarily. The iron claw that lost control also loosened its grip on the heart. Then Tiansheng forced out his anger and went straight to the giant hand composed of pure energy. The two energies collided with each other, and they were evenly matched, and they just confronted each other.

But, at this moment, people from other forces took action. After all, only after the heart fell down could they possibly snatch it. But they couldn't fly into the air and couldn't grab it directly, so they had to attack the people below. Gu Zihao and his companions were undoubtedly the first target.

Gu Zihao only had five people, and they formed a formation at this time, so he was proud to form the giant energy hand, but how could he have only one hand? While being attacked, he actually separated another hand to resist those who attacked.

Suddenly Tiansheng gave up the fight, and quickly descended, allowing the giant energy hand to grab the heart.

When Gu Zihao saw this, he frowned and thought in his heart: "What a cruel person, he actually wants us to be the first to come out!" It turned out that Tiansheng let Gu Zihao and his companions grab the heart not to give up, but to make everyone make Gu Zihao and his companions the target of public criticism.

Chapter 78 Fighting for Three

Gu Zihao is worthy of being the leader of the Huangdao League. Although Yibao Dang actually gave the order to give up, he operated the giant energy hand and released the heart. The heart lost its grip and slowly fell to the ground, while Gu Zihao's giant energy hand slowly fell with the heart, guarding against those who were ready to take it by force.

Tiansheng snorted coldly, as if he looked down on Gu Zihao's caution, and said coldly: "Get ready to grab it!" As soon as he spoke, the Xing brothers immediately changed into a fighting posture, and seven giants appeared, and Murong Di's face sank. It seemed that there was no change at all, but a heavy pressure emanated from him. Indeed, in terms of overall strength, Tiansheng's team is indeed the strongest.

Seeing this situation, Mu Ren and those who formed a temporary team were surprised at Tiansheng's strength. But they soon adjusted their mentality. In their hearts, they still thought that more people was an advantage.

Looking at those weak team members, Ye Ye sneered. Although a small number of those people were also powerful, they were still not as good as Murong Di. Seeing this, Ye Ye smiled, then looked at Long Hengchen beside him. The depression that had just been vented after the short battle rose again, so he said lightly: "Senior Long, it is not good for our Yemen to take action first! If after the incident, narrow-minded people attack Yemen, our Yemen can't bear it!"

"Hahahaha... kid, don't worry, as long as I'm still alive, or the Long family still exists, then no one dares!" Long Hengchen seemed very conceited, but his conceit was indeed based on facts. As soon as he finished speaking, the people around him immediately showed their momentum, which was a kind of iron and blood murderous aura that only existed after life and death on the battlefield. Unlike Ye Ye and his friends, Ye Ye and his friends had it naturally after experiencing life and death, while they had the murderous aura after killing countless enemies on the battlefield until they were numb. From this, it is enough to see that Long Hengchen must be a person from the military, or must have some connection with the army.

The heart kept falling down, and outside the walls of Yemen, people kept trying their best to enter Yemen from outside. Some people even entered directly from the walls several meters high and showed their strength without any scruples, which was quite eye-catching.

However, the more powerful people there were, the happier Ye Ye was, thinking that he would never get the heart! Then...

At this time, the whole Yemen was very quiet, so everyone was like a tight bowstring, ready to go. And the blue heart emitting a magnificent light in the sky also landed on the roof of Yemen at this moment, but it did not land again, but stopped there steadily.

Seeing the heart stop falling, everyone's pupils shrank, but no one was in a hurry to do it, thinking that no one wanted to be the first bird to stand out.

Time seemed to freeze, and the tense breath was transmitted crosswise in everyone's heart with ravines. Some people even had a lot of sweat dripping on their faces, and they were also panting. The wind suddenly stopped at this moment, as if it was isolated outside Yemen by the tense breath. The war was about to start.

"Go!" The heart was just controlled by Boss Xing to fall towards Tiansheng, and the place where it fell was closest to them. Tiansheng saw that his heart was in front of him, and after a long time, he could no longer hold his temper. Relying on the strongest combination, he gave a faint order.

Those who can come to Yemen to compete for the rare treasures are not ordinary people, no matter how strong they are. Naturally, their hearing is not bad. When Tiansheng whispered the order, everyone also moved their feet slightly, ready to rush up and snatch the rare treasures at any time.

After receiving the order, Boss Xing roared fiercely and rushed to a brother not far from him. The seven of them had a tacit understanding. Boss Xing did not say anything extra. The Xing brothers also understood and immediately made a gesture of support. Then, when Boss Xing stepped on his hand, he lifted his hand up violently. Boss Xing was lifted up and jumped onto the roof, and then went to the heart fiercely.

Seeing Boss Xing take action first, everyone immediately took action. Suddenly, the roof that Boss Xing was standing on suddenly sank, and then two people jumped out of the sunken cave. After the two jumped up, they ran towards the heart without hesitation. However, a pair of hands firmly grabbed their footsteps and threw them in the opposite direction. Then Boss Xing broke through the roof tiles again and jumped out.

"Got it!" Boss Xing suddenly showed a smug smile and grabbed the heart that was close at hand. However, suddenly a sharp sound of breaking through the air sounded, Boss Xing frowned and looked at the source of the sound, and his pupils shrank into needles, and then he retracted his hands that were grabbing the heart and blocked it in front of his chest.

What came with the sharp sound of breaking through the air was a crossbow, but the head was fist-shaped. The tail was connected to a chain, and Mu Ren was smiling smugly at the root of the chain. The crossbow turned out to be the iron claw just now?

Boss Xing was naturally blown away by the force. The heart was still there, and Mu Ren immediately shouted, "Quick, go!" As soon as he finished speaking, he rushed over and jumped onto the wall, heading towards the heart.

At this moment, the people who formed a team also started to act. They each formed their own group and headed towards the heart in their own way.

Chapter 79 Fighting for Four

The Night Gate suddenly became chaotic, fighting everywhere, just to prevent anyone who was not their own party from climbing onto the roof. The roof of the room where the heart was located was now destroyed and there was no place to stand.

Since Ye Ye stopped Tiansheng from taking the heart, he did not let the people of the Night Gate rush up to fight for it, but looked coldly at those people who were fighting for it. They could not form an effective attack at all, or they were blocked outside by the strong bodies of the Xing brothers. Even if some of the strong ones broke through the Xing brothers, they would be attacked by Murong Di and Gu Zihao. After all, it is easier to defend than to attack. However, the attraction of the strange treasure is indeed very great. Even if many people fell, many people still stepped on their fallen teammates and continued to rush forward.

"Kill!" Tiansheng had been watching all this coldly. He had been forced to be very irritable, and he could no longer bear it and reported the killing order. He also wanted to use his powerful strength to directly seize his heart, but he could clearly feel that Ye Ye's energy had locked on him. If he took action, he would be hit by Ye Ye's thunderbolt. Moreover, the energy giant hand formed by Gu Zihao's five people with a wonderful formation was constantly blocking those treasure snatchers who rushed in, but Tiansheng knew that as long as he took action, then the hand would also take action. At that time, Ye Ye and Gu Zihao would attack together. Tiansheng could not withstand the joint attack of the two even if his skills were strange. Tiansheng had no choice but to let his subordinates Murong Di and Xing brothers stop defending blindly, and attack those treasure snatchers who attacked rashly.

Seeing this, Gu Zihao immediately asked the other four to increase the control of the formation, and then the giant hand suddenly emitted a faint golden light and went towards those treasure snatchers. Gu Zihao naturally wanted to have a quiet treasure snatching environment. And Mu Ren immediately recalled the strong men of the Mu family, and then attacked the treasure snatchers together.

Ye Ye's face darkened, and he shouted in his heart, "Not good!" Then he shouted, "Those who don't want to die, retreat behind the Yemen disciples immediately." After Ye Ye shouted, those weak treasure hunters immediately went to the back of the Yemen disciples to grab treasures. Seeing all this, Ye Ye said, "Everyone, why do you have to kill so many people in the Yemen? If it gets out, it will damage the reputation of my Yemen!" Ye Ye's words seemed gentle, but everyone heard the murderous intent in his tone. What he meant was, "Whoever dares to kill privately will be hit by the Yemen! "

Yemen was the host, so everyone had to give face. Tiansheng snorted with disdain, and then called back Murong Di and the Xing brothers. Gu Zihao and Mu Ren also withdrew their offensive, but although the three of them successfully drove back the treasure hunters, they did not attack rashly. The situation at this time has changed dramatically. The temporary treasure hunters were scattered, but there were some who were quite strong. They did not want to lose the fight for the treasures, nor did they want to need the protection of Yemen like dogs.

They agreed verbally again, and then formed a team again, but this time the team was more than a little stronger than before. And all the people on Tiansheng's side have shown a strong fighting posture. Murong Di and the other five are still sitting on the ground to form a formation, forming a giant energy hand pointing at the heart. As for Mu Ren, although it seems that he has played all his cards, there may be something hidden under his confident smile. What.

On the other hand, the most mysterious person at this time is Long Hengchen. Among the people around him, except for two who exposed their powerful strength, the others did not leak their strength. If anyone said that Long Hengchen was an old man with no strength, then he would be a fool. Therefore, the mystery of Long Hengchen's team also weighed on everyone's mind.

As the host, Yemen seemed to be working with Long Hengchen at this time, but they didn't know what purpose they had. People who didn't know Ye Ye's purpose thought that Ye Ye must also have the heart to seize the treasure, but they didn't know that Ye Ye just didn't want Tiansheng to get it.

The sun gradually rose, and it was noon!

Several hours had passed, and everyone had not taken any action for a long time, and had been staring at each other for a long time. At this time, Long Hengchen suddenly stood up and shouted loudly: "Everyone, I am the oldest here, and I am only relying on my age once. There is no benefit in such a stalemate. Maybe no one will get it in the end! "After Long Hengchen finished speaking, everyone present nodded. Long Hengchen smiled and continued: "But you will not be willing to leave if you don't take this thing! How about we have a fair duel?"

"Duel? Old man, are you getting old and confused? Fair? Even if you win the duel, can you guarantee that other forces will not take the opportunity to destroy you?" The remaining powerful treasure hunters suddenly became noisy when they heard Long Hengchen's words, and obviously did not agree with his idea!

Long Hengchen stopped his subordinates who were about to get angry, and then said again: "Then what do you say to do?"

"I think, grab it! "The one who answered Long Hengchen was not the one who had just opposed, but Tiansheng. As soon as Tiansheng finished speaking, the strange blue flame appeared in the hands of Boss Xing again, and then Boss Xing roared, concentrating on controlling it, and the heart on the roof slowly went to Tiansheng again. It turned out that during this long period of time, Tiansheng took advantage of the gap between everyone's defenses to let Boss Xing concentrate again in the hope of controlling the heart. Moreover, the heart was closest to them, and if the control was successful, they would definitely get it.

However, Tiansheng must be too conceited. Seeing this situation, everyone was shocked, and then immediately went to Tiansheng in the hope of stopping or secretly taking away the treasure.

The giant hand controlled by Gu Zihao and the other five appeared again, and the huge palm opened wide, grabbing the heart. Tiansheng was shocked, his pupils shrank, and then he squatted down, then jumped up suddenly, jumped directly onto the roof, and then stepped on the pillars of the roof to ricochet towards the heart again.

"The sky and the earth are boundless, and the universe borrows the law. All things are wind, fast! "At this moment, Gu Zihao finally used the Taoist method and released it on the energy giant hand. The energy giant hand also burst out with an amazing speed and grabbed the heart faster than Tiansheng.

Ye Ye was shocked, but soon relieved because he saw Long Hengchen ordering his subordinates to take action. The man made a seal with his hand, and then the strong man who had fought with Li Bin immediately threw out a dagger quickly. The dagger was faster than Gu Zihao's energy giant hand and Tiansheng, and then it was nailed next to the heart on the roof. However, the man who had been holding the seal moved. The man only moved his hand He stretched forward, and then a burst of white smoke suddenly emerged from the position where he stood, and the smoke dissipated in a breath, and then there was only a dagger where the man stood just now, which was the dagger thrown by the strong man just now.

Ye Ye was shocked and smiled. When he looked at the position of the heart, the man actually appeared there and hugged the heart, and then the same hand seal was formed, and the white smoke reappeared and exchanged positions with the dagger again.

Long Hengchen laughed at this moment, walked towards the man, and said as he walked: "Substitute technique, his strength is within a thousand meters, any iron can be replaced! "As he spoke, Long Hengchen reached for the heart. Greed finally showed in his eyes, but it flashed by and no one saw it.

Everyone looked at this situation and immediately attacked Long Hengchen. Long Hengchen just waved his hand lightly, and the subordinates around him surrounded him and exuded a strong pressure. They were actually the most powerful team here. However, the temptation of the treasure was so great that everyone still rushed forward. Mu Ren and Gu Zihao also sent their claws to Long Hengchen. Only Tiansheng did not move. He could have taken the heart from Gu Zihao's giant energy hand by injuring himself, but it was taken away. He almost angrily used the black hole to kill everyone. But he quickly came to his senses. After all, if he summoned it, the black hole would also absorb his energy, and his only support would be gone, and the heart would also be sucked into the alien space. After calming down, Tiansheng looked coldly in the direction of Long Hengchen, and then suddenly smiled.

Suddenly, the change reappeared.

The man who was half-kneeling with the heart in his arms suddenly rolled up his back crying, and the heart was thrown high. A beautiful figure suddenly appeared at the place where the heart was thrown. It was Xia Feng.

Seeing Xia Feng appear, Gu Zihao shouted: "Good! Good apprentice!" Everyone heard his shout, but Ye Ye pulled the corner of his mouth with a smile. Xia Feng just glanced at Gu Zihao lightly, and then disappeared into the air! Gu Zihao and his group were left with dazed faces. But Ye Ye laughed and was very happy. Because the heart was not finally obtained by Tiansheng.

Chapter 80 Fighting 5

After Xia Feng disappeared again, Tiansheng did not panic too much, but retracted his arrogance, then raised his right hand and lightly snapped his fingers.

There was a crisp "pop" sound, and suddenly, the originally sunny afternoon turned dark. Everyone was shocked and confused to see that there were countless dark human-shaped shadows, which were the evil ghosts.

"Search for me. If you can't find anything, come to me with your souls!" Tiansheng shouted angrily. After yelling, those evil spirits began to dance in the sky, but they still attacked blindly! Even Ye Ye couldn't feel Xia Feng's direction. How could those evil spirits know? However, Tiansheng didn't want to rely on the evil ghost's super-human senses to find the hidden Xia Feng. What he wanted to do...

That's right, he could do whatever he wanted with overwhelming evil ghosts and wanton aerial attacks. Countless evil ghosts would definitely be able to attack Xia Feng. After attacking Xia Feng, Xia Feng didn't dare to show his body. If he didn't want to die with his hands, he could only use his heart to block the attack again. Blocking the attack would definitely reveal the collapse of energy. After discovering it, he could surround him. Of.

Ye Ye nodded and thought for a moment, and then figured out the tricks Tiansheng was playing. He said "despicable" to himself and then loudly ordered the disciples of the Night Gate:

"Disciples of the Night Gate, listen to the order. The evil ghost is here. There is no need for the disciples of the Night Gate to hide themselves." "Destroy the demons!" Ye Ye spoke angrily, and his voice spread widely, but Ye Ye's words were not only meant for the Yemen disciples, but also for Gu Zihao. The Huang Daomeng claims to be a well-known and upright family, but now there are so many evil spirits. If Gu Zihao doesn't take any action, then the Huang Daomeng will be disgraced.

"Master Ye, there is no need to panic. Our Zodiac Alliance will naturally take care of the matter of exterminating demons and defending the Way!" Gu Zihao was such a smart person that he naturally heard the meaning of Ye Ye's words and responded.

"That's the best!" Ye Ye replied simply, but instead of calling back the Yemen disciples who rushed up, his face suddenly darkened and he looked at Tiansheng coldly. He suddenly felt that something was about to happen. .

Among the disciples of the Night Gate, Qin Minglei, Li Bin, Yang Hengchao and Yang Tianhai were among them. They formed a simple formation with the strongest Yang Tianhai as the center, and kept stalking the evil spirits. Moreover, Tiansheng seemed to have given an order to those evil spirits, so that they could not fight back and could only continue to search blindly. The other people also temporarily stopped their actions because of the appearance of the evil ghost.

"Hmph!" Qin Minglei snorted coldly. With red eyes, he had already solved many evil ghosts. It was no problem for Qin Minglei to deal with one of those evil ghosts, but it became an absolute problem to deal with two or more. However, those evil ghosts were not. He refused to accept them, but forcefully allowed them to attack. On the side of the Zodiac League, Gu Zihao used his giant energy hand to crush the evil ghost in his palm, but Ye Ye knew that Gu Zihao did not use his full strength, or he was just playing for fun. Ye Ye smiled disdainfully, but Ye Ye didn't tell the truth. He didn't have the extra heart to pay attention to Gu Zihao. At this moment, he had been staring at Tiansheng closely. As long as he made any move, Ye Ye would immediately rush forward and launch the long-prepared thunder attack.

Gu Zihao continued to command the giant hand of energy, seemingly trying hard but actually killing the evil spirits nonchalantly. But suddenly, Gu Zihao was confused, and the strength to control the giant hand became stronger. Then he looked towards the giant hand.

A faint blue light actually emitted from the giant hand, and Xia Feng was suddenly caught in it. Gu Zihao was immediately surprised when he saw this, slightly increased his strength, and then quickly retracted his giant hand. However, the light suddenly exploded, and a huge force directly bounced away the grasp of the giant hand, just like the natural attack just now was offset and bounced away.

Then Xia Feng suddenly ejected from the ground, in the direction of Ye Ye. At this moment, Xia Feng's eyes were full of fear, and she was trembling to herself: "Oh no, it's really the same. Fortunately, I knocked that girl Ye Rui out!" But the heart in her arms was now blue. But the light never faded away, which meant that he would be discovered even if he hid, so Xia Feng had no choice but to run away.

Tiansheng suddenly moved at this moment. Not only him, but Murong spy, the Xing family brothers and all the evil ghosts also moved. Seven strong men on the ground were like tanks leading the way, and Murong spy released this pressure on Immediately following, Tiansheng showed his arrogance and jumped over the Xing family brothers. He was several times faster than Xia Feng and rushed towards Xia Feng.

Suddenly, there was a flash of red light, but Ye Ye stood in front of Tiansheng and said coldly: "Your opponent is me!"

Tiansheng didn't even look at him, but continued to shout loudly: "Boss Xing, it's yours!" As soon as he finished speaking, a giant shadow rushed towards Ye Ye, and Ye Ye had no time to avoid it, so he had to put his hand sideways. On the chest, he was knocked out at once, but a hand grabbed the clothes again, grabbed it back, and slammed it towards the ground.

Ye Ye's eyes narrowed. He didn't expect that Boss Xing's strength had improved so much. He was able to catch him back the moment he was knocked out, and he still endured the severe pain of being burned by the flames. . However, Ye Ye is Ye Ye after all. After absorbing a lifetime of energy from the Ghost King and a lot of combat experience, Ye Ye reacted immediately, and when he was about to be punched to the ground, Ye Ye condensed his arrogance into his hands, and then suddenly It was struck out, forming a counterattack force that shot up directly from the ground.

"Ye Ye, die!" As soon as Ye Ye broke free from the restraints of Boss Xing, he was immediately attacked by the other brothers of the Xing family. For the Xing family brothers, Ye Ye was the brother-killer who killed their brothers, that's why they attacked so violently.

"The seven brothers of the Xing family are a big trouble! What happened..." Ye Ye suddenly realized and then looked at Tiansheng. Tiansheng was still chasing Xia Feng, and the distance was already very close. Xia Feng holds the heart, which naturally affects its speed. Qin Minglei, Li Bin, Yang Hengchao and Yang Tianhai also rushed towards Tiansheng Hedge at this time. But judging from the speed, it's too late...

The corners of Tiansheng's mouth raised, and he casually pushed away the dagger Xia Feng threw back. Moreover, because of Xia Feng's throw back, Tiansheng was closer to Xia Feng. His hand had already been stretched out with high-temperature arrogance. If he caught Xia Feng, he would be seriously injured, and his heart would also be stolen by Tiansheng.

Ye Ye fended off another attack from Boss Xing, then stepped back a few meters and looked at the team of treasure hunters. At this moment, they were surrounded by countless evil ghosts. They couldn't escape from their origins and restrained Tiansheng. However, Gu Zihao's five people's energy The giant hand was also entangled by Murong Spy and the evil ghost who had been following Tiansheng, and could not restrain Tiansheng.

"What's wrong..." Ye Ye suddenly shrank. Tiansheng grabbed Xia Feng's hair and pulled it back violently. Xia Feng responded and flew backwards.

But suddenly, a strange-shaped Yemen dagger cut off Xia Feng's hair. A sudden voice sounded from the air: "Bullying a woman? Shame on you!"

Chapter 81 Fight for Six

After Xia Feng's hair was cut off by the dagger, Xia Feng immediately made a decisive move. While Tiansheng was in a daze, he stopped his retreat and ran to Qin Minglei and his men, temporarily safe.

Tiansheng, however, looked solemnly at the two figures flying towards him in the air. Startled, Tiansheng immediately retreated several meters and looked at the two people falling.

"Ah, it's the two guests! They're back, the guests are back!" It was Huang Shang and his wife who left Yemen. Huang Shang looked at Tiansheng, suppressed his fighting spirit, and then went to the dagger stuck in the floor, pulled it out, and then said, "How do you bully a woman?"

Tiansheng looked at Huang Shang and watched his movements seriously, then said calmly, "Who do you think he is? An old acquaintance. Bullying a woman? I'm just taking back my things!" Tiansheng's tone was very calm, but he was anxious in his heart: "Oh no, he's back. And the woman next to him is also very powerful." Thinking of this, he looked at Xia Feng, who was standing among the disciples of Yemen, holding her heart, with a touch of unwillingness and anger in her eyes.

"Don't say much, stand up!" After saying that, Huang Shang forced out his arrogance, and the monstrous fighting spirit surged again. Tiansheng shook his head solemnly, but withdrew his arrogance, and a layer of invisible and colorless fluctuations quietly covered him. Tiansheng had already used something to steal energy.

Huang Shang looked at the layer of fluctuations, raised his eyebrows, and then rushed up immediately, but he condensed all the arrogance on his palm and controlled it into a sphere. When Huang Shang was about to approach Tiansheng, he threw the ball of energy. Tiansheng was surprised: "You figured out a way to crack it so quickly?"

That's right, even if Tiansheng's technique was powerful, it couldn't absorb so much energy at once. And if you don't let your body touch Tiansheng, your energy won't be stolen.

After Huang Shang threw the energy ball, he didn't chase him, but let the energy ball repel Tiansheng. Then he looked at the direction where Tiansheng was knocked away, raised his left hand slightly, and grabbed it with his backhand. With a bang, the energy ball exploded.

"It's over!" Huang Shang said this lightly, and then went towards Ye Ye. The two of them joined forces, and no matter how powerful the seven brothers of the Xing family were, they were defeated very quickly.

After solving the problem, Ye Ye walked to Huang Shang and said, "You're back?"

Huang Shang nodded, and said a little embarrassedly, "Ye Zi, I'm sorry. I'm a guest..." Ye Ye didn't say anything else, but quickly returned to the disciples of Yemen, then took the heart from Xia Feng, and shouted loudly, "No need to fight anymore, the treasure has been obtained by Yemen!" The current Yemen is fearless. The return of Huang Shang and Gui Hou, the two guests, has brought Yemen the strongest strength that surpasses other sects.

Although everyone was unwilling to hear what Ye Ye said, they also saw Huang Shang defeat Tiansheng with one blow, so they didn't dare to attack rashly.

"That's my thing! Who dares to take it!" Suddenly, a cold roar sounded, and everyone was startled. They looked in the direction of the sound and were immediately surprised. That person turned out to be Tiansheng who was hit by Huang Shang's energy ball just now. At this time, his clothes had been blown into rags hanging on his body, his forehead was bleeding, and even his facial features were slowly oozing blood. He roared coldly: "That's mine... That's mine!" After saying that, he burst out at a faster speed than before and came towards Ye Ye.

Seeing Tiansheng's current appearance, everyone immediately scattered in chaos, each looking for a way to escape from Yemen. Because, behind him, a black hole slowly spread out. A strong suction suddenly burst out. Ye Ye and others looked at the black hole and were frightened. Then Ye Ye stopped the Yemen disciples who were about to flee and looked at Tiansheng coldly as he rushed towards them.

"That's mine... That's mine..." Tiansheng kept roaring, and the black hole behind him was getting bigger and bigger.

"'That's... me...'" But Tiansheng's roar suddenly stopped, and then he fainted. Ye Ye was right. Although the black hole was summoned by Tiansheng, it could not be used at will. Otherwise, Tiansheng would not have lost.

Huang Shang smiled, looked at Ye Ye and said, "Master Ye, let's finish it, otherwise there will be endless troubles!" Ye Ye nodded, then took out Ye Yang and slowly walked towards Tiansheng.

"Young Master! Young Master!" The Xing brothers were just subdued by Ye Ye and Huang Shang and could not move for the time being. Seeing Tiansheng faint, Ye Ye walked towards the unconscious Tiansheng with a weapon and suddenly became anxious and shouted loudly, "Ye Ye, you dog day, will you take advantage of others' misfortune?" Ye Ye paused and ignored him. "Ye Ye, please, don't! Don't! You can have anything you want, just don't kill my young master!" Seeing that he was too hard, Boss Xing actually begged. However, Ye Ye had ignored them for a long time and continued to move forward.

After a few breaths, Ye Ye walked to Tiansheng and raised his weapon. At this moment, everyone's eyes were focused on Ye Ye, and they didn't notice that someone in the crowd moved. The Xing brothers were all broken at this moment, shouting and begging.

Ye Ye smiled and was about to insert Ye Yang into Tiansheng, but Tiansheng, who had fainted from exhaustion, stood up tremblingly at this moment, and then did it very hard: "Do it!" Tiansheng said without fear. "I will, after all, it's too dangerous to keep you!" Ye Ye replied with a smile, with a victorious attitude. Tiansheng smiled self-deprecatingly: "Got it? Then do it, otherwise..." Before Tiansheng finished speaking, a triumphant laugh came from the direction of the Yemen disciples. Ye Ye looked puzzled and saw that the Yemen disciples fell one by one, and Qin Minglei, Li Bin, Yang Hengchao and Yang Tianhai were squatting on the ground at this moment, unable to stand up.

When Ye Ye saw the person who laughed, he was surprised: "It's you!" "Yes, it's me!" The person who laughed turned out to be Long Hengchen, who claimed to be Ye Ye's grandfather. In Long Hengchen's hand, he was holding the heart.

"Ye Ye, what is this?" Huang Shang and the ghost queen came later, and they didn't understand what happened during the period, so they asked. Ye Ye shook his head and frowned and said coldly: "Long Hengchen, unknown!"

"Damn it, he actually poisoned!" Suddenly, curses rang out from all directions, and everyone collapsed on the ground, looking at Long Hengchen with resentful eyes.

"So what if you poisoned? Oh? You three seem to be good, and you didn't fall down even after being hit by my "virtual dream". You are worthy of being my opponent! Hey, you, seem to be very powerful, come and play with me!" Long Hengchen did not hide the fact that he poisoned at all, but pointed at Huang Shang and said arrogantly.

Ye Ye looked at Long Hengchen with a puzzled look. "I like to see your puzzled look! I am not your grandfather, and the Long family also made it up to deceive you. It is your doubt that makes us have a cooperative relationship, that allows me to pretend to be a pig and eat a tiger, and that allows me to get this treasure without any effort!" Long Hengchen said, touching the slightly beating heart in his hand, and his originally kind face was covered with ugliness.

"Antidote!" Ye Ye was not angry because of Long Hengchen's deception, but said calmly. But Long Hengchen just shrugged his shoulders: "No, but the man behind you..." Long Hengchen said, making a look of "I won't give it to you even if you kill me".

Suddenly, Ye Ye frowned and turned around quickly, and found that Murong Di had come behind him without knowing when, and had taken Tiansheng to a safe place.

Chapter 82 Husband and wife go to battle together

Ye Ye watched Murong Di take Tiansheng aside and ignored him. Murong Di had saved Tiansheng by forcing himself to resist the poison, and the Xing brothers had been limp on the ground for a long time and could not escape from Yemen. After temporarily calming down, he turned his head and said to Long Hengchen: "What is your purpose?"

Long Hengchen raised the heart in his hand, indicating that it was his purpose, and did not speak. Ye Ye smiled and made a gesture of invitation, indicating that he could leave. Ye Ye just didn't want Tiansheng to get that thing. After all, Tiansheng...

Long Hengchen was stunned for a moment. He didn't know what Ye Ye was thinking. Then he smiled with a smile of "a man who knows the times is a hero" and turned around to leave.

"Wait!" Ye Ye suddenly shouted. Long Hengchen turned around and looked at Ye Ye in confusion. "Did you forget something?" Long Hengchen naturally knew what Ye Ye was talking about, but he continued to look at Ye Ye in confusion.

"Antidote!" Ye Ye said lightly. Long Hengchen pursed his lips and said reluctantly: "Since you have begged me, then I will give you the antidote!" After that, he threw out a jade bottle. Ye Ye caught it and gently opened the lid to smell it. The smell was very pungent.

"Haha, dreams naturally need stimulation to wake up!" Long Hengchen said, and then his subordinates handed over a gold bag with some words embroidered on it. He put the heart in it and could no longer feel any movement. Then he said "go" faintly and the group turned around and left.

However, the heart lost its energy fluctuations as soon as it was put into the gold bag. Huang Chen suddenly cried, not only Huang Chen, but also another baby crying in the distance, it was Qin Feng.

"Huang Shang..." The ghost queen called faintly, and then saw Huang Shang turned around and continued: "Same as before." Huang Shang nodded with a heavy face.

Ye Ye heard the couple talking to themselves there, so he asked them what was going on. Huang Shang thought for two breaths and then told what happened after they left.

It turned out that after Huang Shang left, the Ghost Queen used countless evil ghosts to search for Huang Shang's traces all over the world, and soon found him. She also learned from Huang Shang the reason for his departure, and then the couple's feelings deepened at this moment. Huang Chen was also very well-behaved. Although he had been running all the way, he had never cried. However, until the occurrence of the strange phenomenon, since the strange phenomenon, Huang Chen changed his well-behaved behavior. Every day, except for sleeping and eating, he kept crying. Then Huang Shang and the Ghost Queen followed the strange phenomenon to Yemen, and Huang Chen stopped crying the moment he stepped into Yemen Mountain. But just now, he cried again. And not only him, Qin Feng also cried.

Huang Shang and the Ghost Queen looked at each other. Then Huang Shang shouted loudly: "Hey, Long Hengchen? Please stay!"

Long Hengchen and his friends had just walked a short distance when they were stopped again. Long Hengchen looked back at Ye Ye in confusion: "Master Ye, what do you mean? Who is he?"

Ye Ye took two steps forward and replied: "Senior Long, this is our guest. We have no other intentions, but we hope that you can give Yemen or me a little compensation! I just remembered that you lied to me after all!"

"I thought it was something!" Long Hengchen said disdainfully, and then asked his men to hand over a briefcase, and then said: "Here is some money, just as spiritual compensation for Yemen! Also as a reward for your "knowing the times"!"

After hearing this, Ye Ye frowned, and a hint of anger was mixed in his words: "I'm not short of money!"

"Oh? What do you need?" Long Hengchen raised his eyebrows, looking impatient.

Ye Ye pointed at the gold bag in Long Hengchen's hand and said, "Leave it!" Long Hengchen looked over along the fingertips, then his face was full of anger, but after hearing the two bursts of babies crying one after another, he laughed, "I understand. You want me to give up the rare treasures and just these two babies? Humph, a fantasy!"

"These two babies must be the trigger for the heart! The heart needs too much energy to appear in the world. These two babies must have been born unusually, but when the heart was born, 90% of the energy was forcibly stolen, so they won't live long! What a pity, they will definitely be the pride of the world when they grow up, but if I leave within three days, they will definitely use up their own energy and die!" Gu Zihao on the side suddenly said lightly, his voice was very weak, but it reached everyone's ears.

After hearing what Gu Zihao said, Ye Ye frowned and looked at Long Hengchen again and said, "Senior Long, I will call you senior for now. If you leave your heart, I can ignore the deception."

"It's your honor to deceive you! I want to see how you, Yemen, who has not yet cured the poison, can keep me!" After saying that, he shouted away the subordinates who were ready to help. Then, a thick feeling of pressure that could crush people's hearts and lungs spread.

Feeling the terrifying pressure, Ye Ye, who was standing, and Huang Shang and his wife frowned at the same time. Everyone suddenly had a thought in their hearts: "Horrible!"

"Hahaha..." Long Hengchen suddenly laughed arrogantly.

Huang Shang stopped Ye Ye, and then the Ghost Queen handed Huang Chen in her arms to Ye Ye and said, "This is a matter between my husband and me. Besides, my husband and I have left Yemen and are no longer members of Yemen. There is no need to drag Yemen into this muddy water. Master Ye's intentions are appreciated by my husband and me!"

"But..." Ye Ye wanted to say something, but was interrupted by Huang Shang: "Ye Ye! Don't forget, you have more important things to do!" After that, he glanced at Tiansheng! After a moment of silence, Huang Shang continued: "Rui Xin, you go down too! This is not a place for women to come!"

"Have you forgotten what I said that day?" The Ghost Queen just said lightly, Huang Shang was obviously stunned, and then smiled: "Okay, let him see what it means that husband and wife are united and their strength can break metal!"

Ye Ye looked at Huang Shang and his wife, frowned and thought for a while, and then said: "Okay! Be careful, you can rest assured to leave Huang Chen to me for the time being!"

Huang Shang and his wife nodded, and then rushed towards Long Hengchen without saying a word. The couple went into battle at the same time. Huang Shang forced out his aura in front, and the ghost queen also forced out her ghost energy. He also held a strange-shaped dagger from Yemen in his hand. The blade was cold, and the ghost queen's ghost energy could not cover it!

And Long Hengchen just looked at the arrival of the two indifferently, and did not even make a defensive posture. He just tied the bag containing the heart to his waist and met the attack of Huang Shang and his wife. Huang Shang was in front, and a pair of fists wrapped in aura went towards Long Hengchen's cheek with the intention of destruction. The fist wind brought by the fist arrived before the fist, but the fist wind that could break the cloth actually slid clearly on Long Hengchen's cheek!

Huang Shang was shocked. He had always relied on the fist wind to hurt people before the fist arrived, but at this moment he clearly saw the fist wind sliding naturally from Long Hengchen's cheek to both sides! Despite this, Huang Shang still punched straight up!

However, Long Hengchen showed amazing fighting power at this moment. Under his kind appearance, he easily deflected Huang Shang's thundering attack. Moreover, the punch seemed to be very casual, but strangely it hit Huang Shang and pushed him back.

Then, he patted the hand of the ghost queen holding the dagger with the back of his hand, shook the dagger off, and took advantage of the situation to grab her arm and threw it towards Huang Shang who rushed up again!

"Weak! Too weak!" Long Hengchen said lightly, with a hint of disdain in his eyes.

Chapter 83 The First Corpse King in History

"Weak?" Huang Shang heard Long Hengchen's words, caught the Ghost Queen thrown over, and then asked angrily. Long Hengchen just shrugged his shoulders, with arrogance in his expression.

Huang Shang glanced at the Ghost Queen, and the Ghost Queen also gave Huang Shang a firm look. Smile. The couple rushed up again.

This time, Huang Shang did not rush directly as recklessly as before, but wrapped his whole body with aura, and then released it. His aura was black, like a demon god burning with black flames. The weapon was still a fist, but this time Huang Shang first shot out countless fist shadows out of thin air, confusing the opponent's eyes and ears. Then, at the moment of approaching, he retracted his fist and kicked out. What a clever attack.

However, Long Hengchen easily blocked it.

"Hmph!" Huang Shang snorted coldly, then increased the strength of his legs, but did not continue to attack, and suddenly dodged. Long Hengchen immediately shouted that it was not good. Sure enough, just as Huang Shang dodged, a black shadow came towards Long Hengchen with a whistling sound. Long Hengchen could no longer dodge, so he had to cross his hand in front of his chest in a defensive posture.

However, after the black shadow hit Long Hengchen's arm, his head was strangely bent. "Snap" hit Long Hengchen's face. This time, Long Hengchen was stunned.

The black shadow retreated after one strike, and then Huang Shang took the opportunity to dodge behind him and hit him fiercely. His fists were like two dragons, hitting Long Hengchen's back! However, Long Hengchen was still stunned in the same place. "Crack", the sound of broken bones made people's teeth ache. Long Hengchen himself was also knocked out by Huang Shang. His subordinates were also startled and ran over immediately.

After doing all this, looking back at the ghost queen, the ghost queen had already revealed her ghost-like tail and threw it behind her. Just now, the one who hit Long Hengchen was the tail.

"It's over!" Huang Shang said lightly, preparing to retract his arrogance. Hitting the spine and causing it to break, there is no doubt that he will die.

However, a weak voice came from Long Hengchen, who had been helped up by his subordinates: "Just now you deliberately let out your arrogance to block my vision, right? That tail whip is quite powerful. But why can't I move!"

"How can you mortals understand the power of the ghost clan?" The ghost queen smiled disdainfully. Long Hengchen nodded weakly and coughed twice to spit out some internal organs. Obviously, Huang Shang's attack was indeed fatal. After a few breaths, he continued: "I guess you are from the Nalan ghost clan! What? Your king divorced you? Follow this zombie!"

The ghost queen was obviously shocked after hearing this, but she didn't continue talking. There is no need to argue too much with a dying person.

"Do you really think I will die?" Long Hengchen said lightly, pursing his lips. Long Hengchen actually burst out with amazing momentum again. Huang Shang and his wife were shocked, and then immediately took a defensive posture.

"Hahahaha, you didn't kill me when I was weak just now! Then in order to repay the grace of not killing me, I will let you die!" After saying that, he stood up trembling, and then the subordinates around him slowly floated up.

Looking at everyone's surprised eyes, Long Hengchen clenched his fists, and the bodies of those powerful subordinates around him suddenly exploded, but the flesh and blood did not leak out, and they were still constantly compressed, and soon compressed into a blood-red bead the size of an egg!

"Human essence!" Ye Ye exclaimed in surprise. Human essence is the essence of human beings. It is a treasure like an egg that grows naturally in the body of those long-lived people, but I didn't expect that it was forcibly created now.

Long Hengchen smiled: "Let me show you what I really look like! I don't like this old man's look either!" After that, he opened his mouth wide and sucked all the human essences into his mouth! Then, red smoke immediately came out of his body.

Huang Shang and his wife were surprised and did not dare to attack rashly.

Ye Ye hugged Huang Chen in his arms and said lightly: "It's too late!" Human essence, the essence of human beings, contains the energy of a person's entire energy, and the predecessors of those human essences are those powerful people. Will Long Hengchen's strength be improved to such a level now?

Huang Shang and his wife suddenly felt bad and rushed up immediately, without any skills, it was a complete energy pouring collision. I hope to interrupt or even kill Long

Hengchen before he absorbs all the energy. However, it's too late after all. It's irreversible.

Their attacks were blocked by the red smoke, and the seemingly floating smoke actually blocked their attacks.

Huang Shang and his wife were startled, then frowned at the same time and quickly dodged backwards. A roar in the red fog reached the sky and the earth.

Everyone was startled, and all their eyes were focused on the red fog.

The red fog gradually dispersed, and a slender body gradually appeared, with fiery red hair fluttering in the wind.

"My own body is still more useful!" The man turned out to be Long Hengchen. He turned from an old man into a young man.

"Long Hengchen?!" Ye Ye shouted in surprise.

The man nodded, but said: "You are right, but now I hope you will call me Hanba!" After that, a red wave was transmitted from his body. Wherever the wave passed, the ground was scorched, and the plants on the ground dried up. Then, a hot breath was transmitted.

Hanba, the thousand-year-old corpse king. Or it can be said that he has been famous since ancient times, the corpse king Hanba! The disaster-bringing Hanba!

"Corpse king?" Huang Shang said lightly.

"Disappointed? That was me 6,500 years ago! Now, please call me the Corpse King Hanba! My people!" After saying that, he waved his hand and Huang Shang fell down with a painful expression.

Corpse King is the true king who is superior to all zombies. However, Huang Shang, who was at the level of Corpse King, fell to the ground with a wave of his hand. This terrifying strength is frightening!

"I said, you are too weak!" Hanba said lightly, shook his head and looked at Ye Ye and continued: "Humph, since you want to play, let them play with you!" After that, a wave of red bloodthirsty breath was transmitted again. In an instant, Qin Minglei, Li Bin, Ye Hen, and the corpses coming out of the imperial mausoleum all held their heads and rolled on the ground in pain, and a strange bloodthirstiness slowly appeared in their eyes. But Huang Shang still held his head in pain and kept struggling!

Corpse King Hanba actually controlled all the zombies!

Hanba came to the world, and disaster came! At this time, Tiansheng Youyou woke up, looking at Hanba's fiery energy that looked like flames and mist, and a strange smile appeared on the corner of his mouth.

However, Ye Ye looked at Hanba and those crazy people solemnly, and an unknown feeling rose from the bottom of his heart. Facing Hanba, the corpse king who had evolved after countless years, Ye Ye did not feel any fear at all.

Chapter 84: Extermination of the clan

Closing his eyes, Ye Ye stopped looking at the zombies with corpse poison in their bodies that went crazy because of the appearance of the corpse emperor Hanba. The Ghost Queen, holding Huang Shang tightly, then glared at Hanba, and rushed forward with a determined heart. The black shadow swung out, and the tail whip was swung out again.

Hanba didn't even look at the Ghost Queen, opened his mouth and stretched out his body in boredom, and raised his hand inadvertently, and grabbed the Ghost Queen's tail whip with one grab. The Ghost Queen was startled, but her years of combat experience made her sober quickly, and then she turned around, her hands turned into ghost claws, and grabbed Hanba's head with black ghost energy.

Hanba raised his eyebrows, and the corners of his mouth slightly pulled, and he blurted out two words coldly: "Looking for death!" Before he finished speaking, he spun around, and his hand was tightly holding the Ghost Queen's tail whip, and he turned around and swung it out. After the Ghost Queen was thrown out, she broke through several layers of walls before stopping, then she climbed up tremblingly, with a trace of scarlet blood flowing from the corner of her mouth. Then she looked at Huang Shang who was still holding his head in pain, and a trace of determination appeared in her eyes again. She roared to the sky, and black smoke came out of her body, wrapping him layer by layer, and her body kept growing. After a few breaths, the originally pretty Ghost Queen had turned back to her original appearance, with a tall body, black scales, sad barbs, sharp teeth, and a flash of determination in her bloodthirsty eyes.

"Ah!" The Ghost Queen roared again, and then the entire Yemen Mountain immediately responded to her one after another, and then a group of black ghosts immediately surrounded her from all directions. After doing all this, the Ghost Queen swung her tail and roared to the sky, then looked at Hanba coldly, and the battle was about to start.

The Ghost Queen, for her man, gave up her beauty and showed the most powerful fighting posture!

"Oh? Want to play? I don't have that much time!" Hanba looked at the Ghost Queen with disdain, then hung the gold bag containing the heart on his waist and said lightly. After saying that, a heavy breath covered the sky, and even the sun in the sky hid in the clouds. However, as soon as this momentum appeared, the little ghosts immediately fell to the ground in fear, and some of them even turned into a faint ghost mist and merged into the ghost mist of the Ghost Queen. The Ghost Queen had no choice but to push the ghost mist to the maximum to avoid the oppression of the momentum.

Looking at the people around her who lost their fighting power due to fear and died and turned into ghost mist to become her own power, the Ghost Queen was angry. Roaring again, the thick legs exerted force and flew towards Hanba at a high speed.

After the Ghost Queen turned into a ghost, the tail whip was still the most powerful weapon. After reaching the attack point, the Ghost Queen swung the tail whip, and the tail whip hit Hanba with the sound of breaking through the air. Hanba dared not catch the tail whip easily with his hands now, because the barbs and ghost mist mixed on it were also very destructive. Despite this, Hanba was the corpse king after thousands of years of evolution. If he dodged because of such an attack, wouldn't it be ridiculed as a corpse king?

So Hanba raised his hands violently, and a flame came out from his hands, but it did not leak out, but formed a fire shield.

With a "bang", the ghost queen's tail whip and the fire shield came into contact, but the gap in strength was irreparable. The ghost mist on the tail whip was burned away by the scorching breath on the fire shield at the moment of contact, and those hard barbs were also cut off by the hardness of the fire shield, and the fire shield also emitted a trace of flames, which went up along the tail whip, ignited and burned all the way.

"Ah!" The ghost queen roared in pain, retreated a few meters, and then immediately operated the ghost mist, wrapping it layer by layer before extinguishing the spreading flames. At this time, the ghost queen's people, the little ghosts, finally arrived.

First, there was a little ghost with purple skin. It rushed at a very fast speed, and then when it was about to approach, it immediately bent down and rolled down. There was a row of barbs on its back. The little ghost wanted to go to Hanba like a roller, but was still stopped by the fire shield, and then burned into nothingness, turning into a wisp of black ghost mist and melting towards the ghost queen. After this little ghost, there were still countless little ghosts. They all used strange tricks and kept attacking Hanba.

However, the gap in strength was like a chasm that could not be crossed at all. Whether it was the purple little ghost or the white ghost general, they were either blocked by the fire shield at the moment of contact, and then burned to death and turned into ghost mist. Or they went around Hanba, but after seeing Hanba's cold eyes, Hanba raised his hand and a wave of fire rushed out, burning the little ghosts into nothingness, turning into ghost mist and melting towards the ghost queen.

The screams of the ghosts continued to spread throughout Yemen Mountain. Ye Ye also opened his eyes, but watched it all calmly. The Ghost Queen, watching her people being slaughtered, became more and more angry. After feeling her people turning into ghost mist and melting into her body after death, which further strengthened her energy, the Ghost Queen suddenly screamed shrilly. She was ordering the suicide attacks of those ghosts! Only she understood why those ghosts did this. It was to use their meager energy to expand the energy of her queen after death, so that they might have the strength to fight!

The huge and terrifying body of the Ghost Queen suddenly trembled, and tears flowed from her bloodthirsty eyes. The tears did not fade away after falling from the huge inverted triangle cheeks, but formed drops of blue crystals. Ye Ye saw the crystals on the ground, and a trace of surprise appeared in his eyes, which were originally calm. He nodded and thought for a while, looking at the Yemen disciples who were crazy and painful because of Hanba's control, and the corners of his mouth pulled out a strange arc, and slowly walked towards Hanba.

At this time, the Queen of Ghosts saw that her roaring orders were useless, and she could only keep crying, and then looked at Hanba angrily, and worked harder to absorb the last legacy left by her people after their death. And those little ghosts, seeing their queen cheered up, roared at the same time, and rushed towards Hanba more violently. Hanba looked at the Queen of Ghosts with disdain. Although he was a little surprised at these little ghosts who died to strengthen his queen, the idea of being a superior in his heart made him arrogant and did not attack the Queen of Ghosts, but kept killing those little ghosts, and then watched the changes of the Queen of Ghosts.

However, the Queen of Ghosts did not change after absorbing the energy. In fact, the Ghost Queen did this deliberately. Originally, after absorbing so much energy, the ghost fog outside the body should become very strong, but it still did not change at this moment. The Ghost Queen kept the energy in her body, so that Hanba could not see it from the outside, and then gave him a fatal blow in the end. However, when the Ghost Queen did this, a trace of reluctance was revealed in her resolute eyes, and her eyes were looking at Huang Shang who was rolling in pain.

Huang Shang and the Ghost Queen have been together for so long, so he naturally knows the purpose and result of the Ghost Queen's doing this. That is, the Ghost Queen will pour out the stored energy without reservation to cause an explosion, but the Ghost Queen herself will also... This is self-destruction!

Huang Shang gritted his teeth in pain, and then looked at the Ghost Queen and shook his head hard. But the Ghost Queen kept crying, turned his head away and stopped looking at Huang Shang, and kept absorbing the legacy of her people after their death. And on the ground, a layer of the Ghost Queen's tears had gathered.

Although there are tens of thousands or even countless ghosts, there is still a number among the countless! Needless to say, Hanba is very strong. With just one defense, he can kill thousands of ghosts with a wave of his hand. At this speed, no matter how many ghosts there are, they can't stand his killing. After a long time, the endless ghosts that had climbed over the wall of the night gate also stopped their support.

"Gone? Humph! The weak are the weak! Let's end it all at once!" Hanba said lightly, then stretched his body lazily, and a circle of waves was emitted from his body. Wherever it went, the ghosts immediately turned into ghost mist and merged into the ghost queen. And Ye Ye walked towards Hanba with an expressionless face. The wave just passed through his body and did not cause any harm.

The Nalan ghost clan, except for the ghost queen who was temporarily alive, was completely destroyed!

Chapter 85 Battle

The Ghost Queen still had tears in her eyes. She looked helplessly at Huang Shang who was holding out his hand to stop her. She showed a touch of tenderness in her determination. Then she turned her head away with tears in her eyes. Her eyes became cold again and stared at Hanba: "The revenge of exterminating the clan. Today, I will leave you here to be buried with my Nalan Ghost Clan!" After the Ghost Queen finished speaking, she roared suddenly. The sound actually broke through the heavy clouds in the sky, and the sun came out from behind the clouds again. However, a stronger black ghost energy covered it again.

The sky suddenly became dark. This kind of darkness was not the night of the natural cycle, but the ghost energy accumulated by the Ghost Queen after absorbing countless little ghosts, which was formed by the ghost energy that covered the sky and the earth!

When Hanba saw the ghost energy that covered the sky and the sun, his face sank and his brows frowned. This was the first time that the Corpse King Hanba faced his opponent so solemnly. He shook his hands, and a layer of red crystals wrapped around his skin, and then suddenly a layer of flames ignited. The flames were not blazing, but they made people feel strange, because the flames looked very thick and made people feel very protective.

"Come on! I want to see how powerful the weak collective is!" Hanba said lightly, but while speaking, the flames burned more violently.

The ghost queen did not speak, and kept accumulating energy. The black ghost energy around the body became thicker and thicker. Finally, after a few breaths, the ghost energy condensed into a huge body on the head of the ghost queen. Huang Shang was shocked when he looked at the body, because the black shadow was 70% similar to the ghost king who fought in the cave!

"Come on!" The ghost queen said lightly, then shook her body and swung her tail back and forth, and the phantom on his body suddenly changed again. The phantom was originally in human form, but now it has become similar to the ghost queen, but the kingly aura revealed in it is not something the ghost queen can look down on!

"Just to disturb your ancestors like this?" Hanba was slightly startled, and then said calmly again. The Ghost Queen did not answer her, and made a posture of preparing for battle.

"There is no other way, let me kill your ancestors in my hands again!" Hanba said in a helpless tone. The words were shocking, and the Ghost Queen's body trembled when they entered her ears. She remembered a legend circulating among the ghosts: their ancestors disappeared for no reason countless years ago, and did not even turn into ghost butterflies to fly back to their loved ones.

The Ghost Queen thought about it and immediately concealed her surprise. The phantom behind her was not the ancestor, but the soul of the ancestor. In fact, it stands to reason that their ancestors did not come back, and even the ghost butterflies that their souls turned into did not come back, so how could there be the soul of the ancestors. Otherwise, this move was just a move created by the descendants of the ghosts to commemorate their ancestors, and then automatically inherited in the minds of every ghost at birth, but this move requires a lot of energy, and the ghosts are unwilling to use it unless they have no choice. But in the current situation, it is obvious that the entire Nalan Ghost Clan where the Ghost Queen belongs was destroyed by Hanba, and they also voluntarily entrusted their energy to their queen. Facing this life-and-death moment, the Ghost Queen had to use this trick that was imprinted in the minds of every ghost since birth.

After the Ghost Queen calmed down, her huge eyes were like thunder, and she glared at Hanba. Her legs sank slightly, and a horn with black lines suddenly appeared on her head. She lowered her head and aimed the horn at Hanba. The energy kept gathering at the tip of the horn, ready to rush towards Hanba. And Hanba also solemnly prepared a defensive posture.

But at this time, the Ghost King looked down in confusion. A person actually walked over slowly, then bent down, picked up the tears she had just left, and then continued to pick up the Ghost King's tears on the ground with a childlike smile.

That person was Ye Ye. Ye Ye didn't know why he was not afraid of the state of Hanba and Ghost Queen. He completely ignored them in his heart and picked up Ghost King's tears.

Hanba looked at Ye Ye with a smile in his eyes, then looked at Ghost Queen who didn't rush up, and smiled: "Facing the enemy, are you allowed to do this?" After that, Hanba flashed, and the red crystals on his body no longer wrapped around his body, but all flowed to his hands to form a red crystal sword!

Ghost Queen was startled and quickly whipped his tail towards Ye Ye, but it didn't hurt him, but rolled him up. Before he could throw Ye Ye out, Hanba's attack had arrived. Ghost Queen had no choice but to turn around and block Hanba's attack with her back. The red crystal sword actually cut through the strengthened scales of Ghost Queen. Not only that, the wound cut by the sword left flames, burning fiercely.

"Hiss!" The Ghost Queen took a breath of cold air in pain, and then prepared to throw Ye Ye out, but found that Ye Ye was no longer on her tail! Looking again, Ye Ye continued to pick up her tears on the ground as if possessed.

The Ghost Queen was startled, condensed the ghost energy on her tail, and then fiercely rushed towards Hanba who rushed up again. Hanba blocked the sword in front of him, but the tail whip was a soft weapon after all. After touching the red crystal sword, it still hit Hanba's cheek, and at this moment, Hanba arrogantly removed the red crystal covering his body, which means that this is the moment when his defense is the lowest.

A tail whip actually cracked Hanba's cheek. However, the Ghost Queen was not feeling well either. The red crystal sword was extremely sharp, and it also cut a deep cut in his tail whip, and then the wound was burning with flames. Although it was extinguished in time with ghost energy, the front part of the tail was already useless.

"Ah!" The Ghost Queen roared, on the one hand to protest, on the other hand to wake up the possessed Ye Ye.

However, Ye Ye was still picking up the tears condensed on the ground. The Ghost Queen had no choice but to passively defend, first withdrawing the energy from the black horn on the top of her head, then distributing it to her body, increasing the defense, and then protecting Ye Ye.

However, the fierce tail whip of the Ghost Queen just now made Hanba angry. "How many years have I not been injured for how many years, I thought I had forgotten the feeling of pain! Haha, cool... As a thank you, I will send you to hell!" Hanba suddenly went crazy, waving the red crystal sword in his hand wantonly, his tongue drooping at the corner of his mouth, his eyes red, his body twisted strangely, his legs bent and his hands bent. Then he suddenly disappeared. If it weren't for his symbolic red flame, no one would know where he went. At this moment, Hanba used his rapid attack on the Ghost Queen.

"Here it comes!" The Ghost Queen looked coldly at the red light rushing towards her, and then she groaned slightly, then crossed her hands across her chest, and when Hanba showed up, she grabbed Hanba with her claws. However, Hanba was in a state of madness at the moment, and was not afraid at all, and he staged a strange scene in the air.

Hanba, at the moment when the ghost claws of the Ghost Queen approached, forcibly twisted his body and flipped over the giant claws of the Ghost Queen. After breaking through the defense, the red crystal in Hanba's hand pointed directly at the right eye of the Ghost Queen.

The Ghost Queen was startled and immediately made a choice between life and death. She buried her head, and then tried to gather some energy to the sharp corners of her head, and then touched the red crystal in Hanba's hand!

The red hot energy and the black ghost energy of the extinction attribute collided with each other. The strange light shone brightly and then radiated.

"Huh." But Ye Ye seemed to have ignored the attack, sighed, opened the treasure bag on his waist and looked at the tears inside, smiled with satisfaction, and then looked at the Night Gate disciples who were controlled by Hanba but did not get Hanba's orders, including Qin Minglei, Li Bin and Ye Hen.

Everyone's eyes were focused on the battle between the Ghost Queen and Hanba, and no one noticed Ye Ye. Yang Tianhai suddenly looked at Ye Ye, and then shouted loudly: "Ye

Ye, what the hell are you doing?" After Yang Tianhai got familiar with Li Bin and the others, some dirty words came out of his mouth from time to time.

Ye Ye was stunned for a moment, then took out a tear and said: "Hold down the Night Gate disciples around you, there is a way to save them!" After that, he looked at Hanba who was fighting with the Ghost Queen with disdain, turned his head and went to the Night Gate camp. Ye Ye didn't know why he suddenly became like this at night, but ignored Hanba and continued his sonorous steps.

When the Ghost Queen saw Ye Ye had left the attack range, she no longer held back. After condensing the energy to the top corner of her head, she swung her head violently and blocked Hanba.

In fact, Hanba had the upper hand just now. However, Ye Ye looked at him with disdain the moment he walked away. He was immediately furious and more confused, and the strength of his hands was also lost, so he was blocked by the Ghost Queen.

"Save people? See how you guys saved so many people!" Hanba suddenly shouted loudly after being blocked. Obviously, his words were meant for Ye Ye and others. After saying that, he dodged the Ghost Queen's tail whip, and then a flame condensed in his hands, and then swung it violently. The flame was divided into many small flames in the air, and finally attached to the bodies of those zombie Yemen disciples. In fact, it was not that Yang Tianhai and his men wanted the Yemen disciples under them to be attached to the flames, but they had no choice. No matter how they dodged, the flames were like maggots attached to their bones, and they could not be driven away or avoided.

"It's over!" Ye Ye watched the flames merge into the bodies of the Yemen disciples, secretly said, and then sped up and ran towards the Yemen camp. The Yemen disciples who were attached to the flames suddenly became violent, randomly attacking the objects around them, even themselves! Among them were Qin Minglei, Li Bin, and Ye Hen. Huang Shang was also attached to a trace of flames, but he still gritted his teeth to hold back the bloodthirstiness and violence in his bones, and looked at the fighting ghost queen with tears in his eyes.

Chapter 86 Time Limit Expired

After Ye Ye left the battle area, the Ghost Queen also started to go crazy. She still gathered the ghost energy at the sharp corners and rushed over fiercely. Hanba was still in a frenzy. Seeing the Ghost Queen rushing up, he was not panicked but showed his superhuman fighting ability. He actually slowly retreated while using the red crystal sword in his hand to collide with the sharp corners of the Ghost King.

Suddenly, with a "click", the red crystal sword in Hanba's hand broke and turned into flying fragments. However, Hanba was still not anxious. Instead, he stopped dodging and laughed like crazy. When the Ghost Queen saw the red crystal sword shattered, she thought the opportunity to win had come. At this moment, the ghost energy condensed in the sharp corners on her head became more dense. She raised her head and stabbed Hanba. A simple stab changed the color of the sky and the earth.

However, the thunder strike suddenly stopped, and the Ghost Queen suddenly howled in pain. Moreover, countless small flames were burning all over her body, and they were still spreading. That was Hanba's flame. When did it attach to the Ghost Queen?

"Hanba's flame is extremely special. It was born at the beginning of the sky. Otherwise, how could droughts occur wherever he moved? And just now, the shattering of the red crystal sword was also arranged by Hanba. The red crystal was condensed from his destiny fire, comparable to a divine weapon, how could it be broken so easily. Then there is only one explanation, Hanba deliberately shattered the red crystal sword, the purpose is just to make it difficult for the Ghost Queen to be careless and then get hit... After all, it is condensed from flames, and it is naturally flames after breaking!" Tiansheng has been observing the battle between Hanba and the Ghost Queen since he woke up, and he has perfectly analyzed Hanba's attack.

The Ghost Queen, while howling in pain, used the ghost energy to extinguish the flames one by one, and then looked at Hanba coldly. And Hanba had returned to normal without knowing when. He said lightly: "It's nothing. I'm not interested! I'll finish you off!" After that, the red crystal on his body reappeared, and then condensed into a red crystal sword again, waving it towards the Ghost Queen.

On the other side, Ye Ye had already rushed back to the Night Gate camp, but those zombie Night Gate disciples went crazy. They not only attacked their fellow disciples around them at will, but also hurt themselves! And all this was done by Hanba. He just mixed his own order in the flames: "Destroy all life around you, including yourself!"

Seeing this, Ye Ye was shocked and hurriedly asked the Night Gate disciples headed by Yang Hengchao to try to hold down the crazy Night Gate disciples around them. Then he took out the Ghost King Tears that the Ghost Queen had just dropped and fed them into his mouth. After the Ghost King Tears entered their throats, the fanaticism and bloodthirstiness in the eyes of those Night Gate disciples suddenly eased a lot, and they also settled down. Then Ye Ye asked Yang Hengchao and Yang Tianhai to take good care of the disciples of Yemen, and then took the antidote for the virtual dream and the Ghost King's Tears, and went to Huang Shang. He first removed the weak toxicity of the virtual dream, and then fed him three Ghost

King's Tears. Suddenly, Huang Shang was no longer in pain, but he looked at the fighting Ghost Queen, and immediately endured the weakness and crossed his legs, hoping to replenish the energy lost during this period of weakness.

Ye Ye did not stop him. Ye Ye knew that Huang Shang must want to recover his strength as soon as possible and then go to help the Ghost Queen. After all, the couple is of the same mind.

After Huang Shang's breath stabilized, Ye Ye stopped disturbing him. Instead, he returned to the Yemen camp and gave the antidote to the Yemen disciples, asking them to detoxify the treasure-hunters one by one, but not to Tiansheng and the others. After all, Tiansheng looked at the Yemen disciples who passed by with the antidote, smiled, and was not angry. There was an inexplicable meaning in his eyes...

After everything was done, Ye Ye's attention finally returned to the battle between the Ghost Queen and Hanba.

At this time, Hanba finally showed its combat power. Although the Ghost Queen had absorbed the heritage energy of countless her people, she was still beaten back by the serious Hanba. After all, Hanba had lived for many years, and the accumulated combat experience was not comparable to them.

However, the Ghost Queen still held on. When she saw that Huang Shang was fine, she no longer held back. Although she was defeated and the wounds on her body gradually increased, her opponent Hanba was not doing well either. The originally vigorous flames were actually weakened at this moment.

The Ghost Queen also changed from simply attacking with horns to using horns, claws, and tail whips to barely resist the fierce attack of Hanba.

But suddenly, the Ghost Queen's eyes turned cold, and her pupils shrank into needles. Then the tail whip was pulled out fiercely. Hanba had already figured out the attack route of the

Ghost Queen and easily dodged the whip of the tail whip, but the Ghost Queen continued to chase, and her claws were like two black dragons, hitting Hanba's heart from top to bottom. Hanba was startled and blocked it with the red crystal sword, but he was also carried up by the force of the claws. However, he just fell into the trap of the Ghost Queen. What the Ghost Queen was waiting for was Hanba to jump up.

When the Ghost Queen saw Hanba jump up, she roared, and the sharp horns on her head suddenly burst into an extremely dazzling black light. This black color itself could not be dazzling, but on the sharp horns of the Ghost Queen, when the energy was particularly concentrated, the black light broke the routine and emitted an extremely dazzling light.

Hanba's face darkened, his eyes opened wide, his pupils shrunk into pinpoints. The faint words "I'm in trouble" burst out from Hanba's mouth. Before he finished speaking, the black light on the sharp corners of the Ghost Queen became thicker, and then with a sharp scream from the Ghost Queen, the black ghost energy on the sharp corners suddenly condensed into a black line, and went straight to Hanba in mid-air, who couldn't dodge. However, Hanba couldn't dodge at all because of the distance problem and the speed of the beam of light exceeded his limit!

With a "boom", the extremely condensed black light hit Hanba at high speed, making a violent explosion sound, and even vibrating the air, the air twisted, making it difficult to see what happened! One could only vaguely see the strong ghost body of the Ghost Queen standing proudly in place.

"Is it over?" This thought suddenly occurred to all the people watching the battle, but they still just stared at the battlefield, hoping to see the result.

But suddenly, a strong and dazzling red light suddenly appeared in the distorted air, just like the sun in the sky that was covered by black ghost energy. In the red light, there was a burning heat, a strong pressure and a destructive force.

The red light even covered the ghost energy that covered the sky in the sky, and the distortion of the air was also dispelled by the red light. Everyone looked at it carefully. In the center of the red light, there was a person standing in the air.

"Very good, it is really powerful. Let's finish it. I don't have much time. I will finish you. The group of people below are not his opponents!" Hanba said lightly, and then he slowly raised his hand, and the red light also slowly condensed to the top of his head with the rhythm of his hand. After the red light condensed, his appearance was also revealed. He was injured! A trace of red blood was flowing along his forehead, and then fell from his chin. It actually burned into a fierce flame when it landed, and it lasted for a long time.

The Ghost Queen was shocked when she saw Hanba gathering energy, and she wanted to move and hope to interrupt Hanba's gathering. However, just as she was about to move, Hanba suddenly screamed, and the scream actually formed a series of sound waves, and just like that, the Ghost Queen was bound in place!

The Ghost Queen struggled for several times but couldn't move again, so she made up her mind and gathered energy on the sharp corner on her head again, hoping that the same trick could match Hanba's move.

Everyone was shocked, including Ye Ye! No one thought that it would be like this in the end. Everyone knew that if the Ghost Queen didn't resist the fiery red energy on Hanba's head and fell to the ground, they would also be killed!

They wanted to escape, help, or even commit suicide, but they were intimidated by Hanba's roar just now, and they couldn't move like the Ghost Queen.

Huang Shang couldn't recover at ease at this moment, but looked at the two extremely condensed energy anxiously. In his eyes, there was not only panic, but also some relief. Maybe he thought that even if he died, he would die with the Ghost Queen.

Ye Ye shook his head. Maybe he was the only one who could move freely at this moment, but he didn't want to help. Instead, he looked at it indifferently. The two colorful lights in his hands were looming.

The energy of the Ghost Queen and Hanba was still condensed. Both lights would destroy the world.

However, there was a sudden change. Everyone knew that Hanba's energy had not been condensed. There was still a lot of energy outside, which had not condensed into a whole, but Hanba threw it out.

"Here it comes!" The Ghost Queen hummed in her heart, and then the ghost energy condensed on the sharp corners also burst out. The two energy collides together, and then the air twists violently, and the two bodies are blown out by the strong wind generated by the explosion at the same time. The huge body of the Ghost Queen regained its human form in the strong wind. Huang Shang had just rested and recovered some energy. When he saw the Ghost Queen being blown away, he immediately went to the direction where she fell. Then he caught the Ghost Queen. After the Ghost Queen fell into his arms, she looked at Huang Shang with gentle eyes, reached out and wiped Huang Shang's face, smiled with satisfaction, tilted her head, and fainted. Although the two clusters of energy were not fully condensed, after all, the energy contained in them was extremely terrifying, and injuries were inevitable. It was very lucky that he was not affected by the explosion and died.

And Hanba, who was blown to the other side, pulled the corner of his mouth and said to himself: "Energy, still not enough! But next time, I will definitely let you all die! All!" After that, he looked at Ye Ye and Tiansheng with a weird look, and then a ball of white smoke burst out from his body, wrapped him, and then landed steadily. After the smoke dissipated, Hanba had disappeared, and it was replaced by Long Hengchen!

He stood there, smiled, shook his head, touched the gold bag on his waist, and turned away. Ye Ye did not stop him again, and let him go, because Ye Ye was already deep in thought, and the last look he had just had with Hanba made him feel an inexplicable sense of familiarity.

On the other side, the Yemen disciple holding the antidote for the virtual dream was startled by Hanba's roar, and the antidote for the virtual dream fell to the ground, then rolled, and finally stopped in front of a person.

The man smiled, picked up the antidote, detoxified his nine companions one by one, and left Yemen quietly. And the direction they were going was surprisingly the location of the back mountain. That person was Tiansheng!

Chapter 87 Encounter

Long Hengchen left Yemen, taking the heart of the rare treasure with him. The treasure hunters in Yemen also left in fear and regret, and Yemen finally returned to peace. However, Yemen still has "guests" to entertain.

Gu Zihao and his companions were still poisoned by the dream, and they were now under house arrest by Ye Ye.

"Master Ye, may I ask why you force us to stay here?" Gu Zihao said with a smile while looking at Ye Ye. Ye Ye smiled, holding the antidote for the dream that Tiansheng and the others had not taken away, and put it on the table: "Master Gu, did I force you to stay?"

Gu Zihao and the others could only move reluctantly now. Gu Zihao stood up from the chair and looked at the antidote. There was no greed in his eyes, but he said lightly: "Oh? Then may I ask what Master Ye meant?"

Ye Ye shrugged his shoulders, and then said indifferently: "It doesn't mean anything, I just want you to stay in Yemen for a day! Now, you can do whatever you want, the antidote is there, please!" Gu Zihao looked at Ye Ye in confusion, Ye Ye smiled and left without saying a word.

Gu Zihao and the others were puzzled, but they still picked up the antidote, and then carefully tried the detoxification, and then left Yemen, and the disciples of Yemen did not stop them.

Ye Ye and the others stood in a hidden place and watched their backs going down the mountain and said lightly: "What will happen when they know that we have used them!" Qin Minglei and Li Bin laughed immediately.

Just yesterday, when those treasure hunters had just left, Ye Ye asked them to bring a message: Huangdao League Gu and several others were injured because of the treasure hunt, and Yemen let go of the past and let them stay to recover!

After Gu Zihao and others met Huangdao League, Gu Zihao was furious, but there was nothing he could do. Of course, this is a digression.

At this moment, what Ye Ye was most worried about was Tiansheng and others whose whereabouts were unknown. At that time, everyone's attention was focused on the battle between Hanba and Guihou, and they were frightened by Hanba's roar, and they were confused and didn't know the whereabouts of Tiansheng and others.

Ye Ye frowned and kept thinking about where Tiansheng and others had gone. Shaking his head, he walked alone. Unconsciously, he walked to a place where there were few people in Yemen. Sighing, Ye Ye looked around, then smiled and said to himself: "Why did you get here? You have been following me for a long time, come out!" As soon as he finished speaking, a person appeared out of thin air, it was Xia Feng.

Ye Ye turned around and looked at Xia Feng, with a look of concern and apology, and then said: "How is the injury?" Xia Feng did not dare to look at Ye Ye, lowered her eyes and said softly: "It's okay."

Ye Ye smiled, as if relieved: "That's good! You disappeared after arriving at the Yemen camp that day. Did you see where Tiansheng and others went?"

"Well... No! I didn't leave at that time. I hid aside and watched the battle. In the end, I was frightened by the roar of the drought demon and forgot everything around me!" Xia

Feng pondered for a moment and then said. Ye Ye frowned after hearing this. He already knew Tiansheng's life. Keeping Tiansheng would definitely cause a disaster!

"Walk with me!" Ye Ye said lightly, and then walked forward. Xia Feng was stunned for a moment, then followed his steps closely, and the two walked side by side. But the two of them were silent all the way. Until the two walked to the back door of Yemen.

"You..." Ye Ye and Xia Feng actually had something to say at the same time.

"You go first!" Xia Feng said lightly.

Ye Ye smiled awkwardly, then suddenly said seriously: "Take care of yourself!" After that, he turned around and left, and did not stay to listen to what Xia Feng wanted to say. Xia Feng was stunned, looking at Ye Ye's back and whispered: "Take care of yourself too!" After that, he disappeared like air, and the dry grass on the ground moved slightly.

In the dense forest on the back mountain, Ye Rui unexpectedly appeared in Xia Feng's temporary room again, and had already prepared the meal.

Suddenly, a sound of birds and beasts startled sounded in the woods. Li Ye Rui went out and said happily: "Sister Xia Feng should be back!" After that, he went back to the house and prepared the dishes.

Soon, the door of the wooden house was pushed open!

Ye Rui was still busy, and did not turn back and said lightly: "Sister Xia Feng, you are back! It's time to eat, otherwise it will get cold! After you eat, I have to go back or Brother Ye Ye will be worried!"

However, the sound of footsteps on the wooden board was wrong. Xia Feng was agile and would not make such heavy footsteps, nor would she be so messy. Ye Rui was puzzled, then turned around, and immediately covered his mouth and said in panic: "Who are you! Why are you here?" Ye Rui knew Tiansheng and Murong Di, but the wooden house was dim, and the people were backlit, so he could not see their faces clearly.

"Let's rest here today!" One person said lightly, and then looked at the panicked Li Yerui with a touch of evil in his eyes: "This time, Ye Ye will be in trouble! Little sister, the head of the Yemen, who is Ye Ye to you?"

Li Yerui was terrified and did not answer. The man squatted down and continued to ask: "Just now you said he was Brother Ye Ye, the head of Yemen, Ye Ye? Don't be afraid, we are his friends! He asked me to find you and take you back!" Hearing this, Li Yerui calmed down immediately. After all, Li Yerui has also experienced so many things. Looking at the blurred face of the man, he thought: "No. Brother Ye Ye can't know that I am here. Only Aunt Zi and Sister Xia Feng know. These people must be bad!" Li Yerui thought, and cold sweat remained. However, since he had calmed down, Li Yerui immediately replied: "How... How is it possible. If my brother is the head of Yemen, would I be here?" After that, Li Yerui returned to normal, and then took out a few more pairs of bowls and chopsticks, put them on the table and said: "You... You must be passers-by, eat and leave! I'll go make some more dishes for you! Oh, there are no more dishes, I'll go to the backyard to pick some!" Li Yerui is really smart. However, those people did not let Ye Rui go out, but stopped him and said: "Enough. No need to work hard! I haven't had a meal for several days." After that, a strong man imprisoned Li Ye Rui. Then he covered his mouth to prevent him from shouting. Then the man who just spoke sat down to eat, and the others did not move their chopsticks.

Li Ye Rui's eyes were filled with tears at this moment, and she kept thinking wildly in her heart: "Brother Ye Ye, save me!"

But how could Ye Ye save her at this moment. And Xia Feng, after returning to the back mountain, immediately ran towards the wooden house. Suddenly, she stopped, looked at the ground, and then grabbed a handful of soil: "Someone has been here! And more than one! I hope Ye Rui is not in the wooden house!" Xia Feng knew that the Yemen had been full of people recently. If anyone sneaked into the back mountain and entered the wooden house, Ye Rui would definitely be persecuted there. Thinking in her heart, Xia Feng quickened her pace.

Xia Feng ran at full speed at a very fast speed, and she did not walk on the ground, but bounced between branches and trunks, without having to go around trees on the ground, and she would not leave traces, and would not step on branches and dead leaves on the ground because of running.

Approaching the wooden house, Xia Feng first observed from a distance, looking at the messy footsteps at the door of the wooden house, she was suddenly shocked: "More than one person!" Thinking of this, she disappeared into the air, and then slowly approached the wooden house, and finally landed on the roof of the wooden house without a sound like a cat.

Looking from the gap on the roof of the wooden house, seeing Ye Rui being caught, her heart suddenly tightened, and then she looked at the people who broke into the wooden house. Ten people. Finally, looking at the most special person among those people who was sitting and eating, Xia Feng was immediately shocked, because that person was Tiansheng!

"Who!" Tiansheng suddenly shouted coldly. Xia Feng thought she had been discovered. When she was about to show her body, a voice came out lazily from the door of the wooden house: "How are you!"

Xia Feng saw that she was not discovered, so she calmed down and looked at the person who came. It would have been better if she hadn't looked. When she looked, Xia Feng couldn't help but retreat two steps on the roof in fear, and the roof also made a "creaking" sound!

Suddenly, everyone looked at the roof with cold eyes.

"It's bad," Xia Feng said lightly, and then she simply made up her mind that they were all injured, so she jumped off the roof and entered from the main door, shouting loudly: "What are you doing in my house!"

Chapter 88 Acting to Escape

Tiansheng saw that the person who came in was Xia Feng, and immediately remembered that day when he prevented him from taking the heart, and the resentment in his heart was also reflected on his face. He stood up gently and said with a smile: "It's you. I didn't expect to meet you here!"

Although Xia Feng was terrified, she still said calmly: "It's me, so what? This is the territory of the Night Gate. Moreover, this house is my house, please leave immediately and let my sister go!"

"Sister? You said she is a sister? Why do I feel that she and Master Ye have such an affair?" This was not said by Tiansheng, but by Murong Di. "You..." Xia Feng was speechless and suppressed the panic in her heart and said: "If you don't leave, I will send a signal immediately, and the people from the Night Gate will definitely arrive within half an incense stick." Xia Feng was alone, facing a large number of enemies, and he didn't dare to belittle himself and want to fight to the death. Besides, there was Long Hengchen sitting on one side, and he was the corpse emperor Hanba.

Tiansheng limped in front of him, smiled and said to the brothers of the Xing family: "She is still a beauty! Haha!" He turned around and said sternly: "Then call for help!" After that, red and black flames immediately appeared all over his body, and he grabbed Xia Feng with one hand.

Xia Feng did not expect the other party to attack like this, and was shocked, but she was also quite experienced in combat. She immediately calmed down, and a black dagger appeared in her hand with a tremor. However, she did not choose to fight Tiansheng head-on, but flashed and disappeared like air. When she appeared again, she was already behind Tiansheng, and the dagger was shining coldly.

"Humph" Tiansheng snorted coldly, and did not make any moves, but when Xia Feng's dagger was about to stab his back, a strong flame burst out from behind, Xia Feng was caught off guard, and she received all the flames, flying several meters away, punching through the wall of the wooden house and flying out.

One move, just one move, defeated the hidden killer Xia Feng.

Tiansheng stopped the Xing brothers who were about to rush out and said, "You won't die! But you can't move either!" After that, he returned to his seat, picked up the bowl and chopsticks and continued to eat. He said to Long Hengchen casually, "It's hard to imagine that you are the drought demon!"

Long Hengchen smiled and didn't answer him directly: "This food is good, who made it? You guys can't make it. It must be made by that little girl. I have a shortcoming, that is, I can't resist delicious food. This ordinary mountain food is also made so delicious. Sorry, I want this little girl!"

Tiansheng frowned. The other party actually ignored his existence, and he defeated Xia Feng in one blow and established his prestige first. However, Tiansheng immediately relaxed his brows after thinking about it. After all, the other party had the strength to ignore him. He took a dish and continued, "Who do you want? Just say it, please!"

Long Hengchen seemed to be waiting for Tiansheng to say this. He smiled and finally looked at Tiansheng and said, "Oh.

I'll take this girl first, and then I'll take the seven brothers around you. After all, the real body state requires a lot of energy!" Tiansheng frowned after hearing this. He certainly knew what Long Hengchen did when he turned into Hanba, which was to absorb all the blood, flesh and essence of his subordinates.

'This old guy actually paid attention to them. I wonder what his expression will be when he knows who his father is. ' Tiansheng thought to himself. Then he said, "This won't do. They are loyal to me, and I won't do anything unfavorable to my subordinates!"

Long Hengchen smiled and didn't say anything, but concentrated on eating. Tiansheng saw that the other party no longer paid attention to him, and knew that Long Hengchen had fallen into his trap, and then said to the Xing brothers, "You, go and bring her in!" With an order, the Xing brothers walked out of the house without any complaints.

Logically speaking, seven people should not be sent to capture a seriously injured person. However, this was Tiansheng's plan. He wanted Long Hengchen to see how powerful the seven brothers of the Xing family were.

Outside the wooden house, Xia Feng stood up slowly with a trembling body. There was blood flowing from the corners of her mouth. She was about to disappear like air again, but she saw the seven brothers of the Xing family come out, and her target should be her. She was shocked and immediately disappeared like air.

However, in this dense forest, the ground was full of dead trees and leaves, and Xia Feng did not dare to move easily. If she moved, she would be hit like thunder.

Boss Xing was so smart that he naturally expected this. He smiled, and then asked his brothers to surround the position where Xia Feng was just now, and then the seven brothers strengthened at the same time. Seven giants appeared in the forest.

"Since you can't see it, force it out!" Boss Xing said, and then the seven brothers of the Xing family moved and slowly walked towards the center. And the center of the seven people was Xia Feng who was hiding.

There is no way to the sky, and no door to the ground. Xia Feng was desperate, and she showed her body shape, with a dagger in her hand, and she wanted to fight to the death. However, Xia Feng looked in the direction of the wooden house, where Li Yerui was. As she thought, her hand loosened, the dagger fell to the ground, and then she closed her eyes.

"Be sensible!" said the elder Xing lightly, and then he carried Xia Feng back to the wooden house. ,

In the wooden house, Long Hengchen looked at the seven brothers of the Xing family coming in, and a hint of hidden greed suddenly appeared in his eyes, which flashed by but was caught by Tiansheng. With a smile, Tiansheng ignored Long Hengchen, but walked to Xia Feng and whispered: "I'm going to let you go now, you go and notify Ye Ye to come here immediately! Haha!"

Xia Feng's beautiful eyes suddenly opened, and she looked at Tiansheng in surprise. She didn't understand what Tiansheng wanted to do. Tiansheng looked at Xia Feng's surprised expression and suddenly said excitedly: "But she can't go with you, you have to leave me a hostage! Moreover, you must play a play with me, you must pretend to fight to the death, and then leave." Tiansheng said, twisting Xia Feng's chin with his hand. From Long Hengchen's perspective, Tiansheng seemed to be teasing Xia Feng. Long Hengchen shook his head disdainfully and continued to eat.

Hearing this, Xia Feng seemed to understand something, and Tiansheng seemed to want to express something. However, after all, he did not hear the conversation that just happened in the wooden house. Thinking of this, Xia Feng suddenly squatted down, and then kicked at the Boss Xing beside him, and a short blade appeared on his toes.

Boss Xing did not dodge, and went straight to meet him. A full-strength attack. However, Tiansheng cleverly stepped back two steps and patted his shoulder. Boss Xing understood, and the strength in his hand suddenly lightened a lot, but still broke the short blade on Xia Feng's toes, and then knocked him out. Tiansheng also blocked Long Hengchen's sight while retreating cleverly, so that he could not find out that Boss Xing was deliberately reducing his strength.

Feeling the other party's reduction of strength, Xia Feng immediately knew that this was a good opportunity, and immediately hid in the air, and then turned around at the moment of landing, and immediately launched out. Heading towards the night gate.

When the seven brothers of the Xing family saw Xia Feng escape from their hands, they immediately became angry, and an unmatched momentum emanated from their anger. Of course, this was arranged by Tiansheng.

Long Hengchen, who was on the side, looked at the seven brothers of the Xing family who were emitting momentum, and the greed in his eyes was revealed.

Tiansheng saw it from the corner of his eyes, smiled and thought: "Ye Ye, I hope you don't let me down! Otherwise..." Thinking of this, he returned to his seat, sighed and said to Long Hengchen: "You are so big, but you can't even deal with a woman. It's embarrassing!"

Long Hengchen smiled, then said: "Why don't you run away? Wait until someone from the night gate comes, you can't escape!"

Tiansheng also laughed and said: "With you here, why should we run away! The food is cold, that girl, come and reheat it and reheat a few more dishes, Mr. Long and I are not full yet!" After that, Murong Die let go of Li Yerui. Li Yerui was helpless, but knowing that Xia Feng had gone to ask for help and would arrive soon, he had to obey orders. At this moment, what he was most worried about was not that he would be trapped in injustice, but that he was worried about how she would face it when Ye Ye came and saw her. Ye Ye didn't know that she had woken up!

Chapter 89 Transaction

The dishes were soon heated up. Long Hengchen and Tiansheng picked up their chopsticks again and started eating. They chatted from time to time, and Long Hengchen would occasionally glance at the seven brothers of the Xing family who were already strong and standing outside the door (the house could not accommodate seven of them).

Tiansheng suddenly smiled, put down the bowl in his hand, and said with satisfaction: "Senior, this food is really good. The girl is yours!" Long Hengchen just smiled and looked at Ye Rui. Long Hengchen himself had a very kind face. He smiled and said to Ye Rui: "Girl, you will follow me in the future and cook for me. What's your name?"

Li Yerui rolled his eyes and said: "My name is Li Yerui." After that, he bowed and stood behind Long Hengchen. In Ye Rui's opinion, this old man was much better than those people, and maybe he could escape easily in the future.

Seeing the well-behaved Li Yerui, Long Hengchen nodded with satisfaction. He really had no other intentions, he just wanted to eat the food made by Li Yerui. After thinking for a while, he turned his head and said to Tiansheng: "Boy, do you think I don't know what you are playing? Tell me, what do you want to exchange!" Tiansheng pretended to be puzzled and asked: "Senior, I am stupid and don't know what you are talking about!" Long Hengchen smiled, sighed slowly, shook his head, and stood up: "Don't play dumb! You are very smart, otherwise how could you escape without the antidote for the dream!" Ye Ye's behavior of not allowing the disciples of Yemen to distribute the antidote to Tiansheng and others was also seen by Long Hengchen, who was fighting as a drought demon at the time. Tiansheng put away his smile, stood up solemnly and said: "This... insult, I will get it back one day!" Tiansheng regarded Ye Ye's behavior as an insult. After saying this angrily, he turned around and said to Long Hengchen respectfully: "Senior, that heart is very important to me! Can I..."

"No!" Tiansheng was interrupted by Long Hengchen before he finished speaking. Long Hengchen turned back and looked at Tiansheng coldly and said: "Absolutely not! If I have this heart, then I will get a second life. Life is more important than anything else!" After that, Long Hengchen stopped looking at Tiansheng and called Ye Rui, who was frightened, to leave.

Tiansheng looked at his departing back coldly and slowly opened his mouth: "What if I can let you own the state of Hanba forever?"

"Permanent possession!" The four words suddenly appeared in Long Hengchen's mind, and his steps stopped. He looked at Tiansheng with disbelief: "What did you say!" There was a sense of anger and unwillingness in his words. Even Long Hengchen himself did not notice that his hands began to tremble.

Hanba, evolved into the Corpse Queen, but could not maintain it. What a shame. Hanba naturally knew why. This was destined by God. God always wanted to maintain fairness in the world and would not allow such a heaven-defying thing to exist forever.

However, Tiansheng's light words surprised Hanba. Seeing that Tiansheng did not answer him, he became even more excited. He rushed forward, grabbed Tiansheng's collar and said, "Say it again!"

Tiansheng was lifted up by Long Hengchen, but he did not resist. Instead, he smiled and shrugged his shoulders and said lightly, "I said, if I let you have power forever, will you exchange it?"

"Nonsense, it's impossible!" Hanba also wanted to have power forever, but he had been trying for a long time since he became the Corpse King, but he returned in vain. How could he easily believe Tiansheng's empty words? Angry and humiliated, Long Hengchen threw Tiansheng out fiercely, smashed the wall of the wooden house, and then flew out. But he was caught by Xing Lao Da.

After Tiansheng was caught by Xing Lao Da, there was no hesitation or fear. He knew that Hanba had been hit. He smiled and patted the sawdust on his body. Although the force thrown out was terrifying, it was received by Boss Xing in full, and Tiansheng was not hurt. Smiling, Tiansheng walked back to the wooden house again, maintaining that victorious look and said: "Believe it or not!"

Long Hengchen was either afraid or shocked. He had never seen anyone who could be so confident that he could fight against Tian. After thinking for a while, Long Hengchen took off the gold bag tied around his waist and said: "Take it, but first tell me how to have power!"

Tiansheng smiled, called Boss Xing in, and then said: "Senior, untie the bag!" Long Hengchen was puzzled, untied the bag, and suddenly a dark blue light poured out. Boss Xing looked at the heart, and his breath sank immediately. An invisible force was transmitted to the heart. The heart also immediately emitted a more dazzling light, and it looked like Boss Xing was trying hard to make the heart more powerful.

Long Hengchen was shocked when he saw this situation. Tiansheng also took the opportunity to say: "You also saw that he can control the heart! In other words, he was originally a part of the heart, or the heart is a part of him!" Long Hengchen didn't know that it was just a little flame that was causing trouble.

"The heart is for you, and the seven of them are for me! How about it!" Long Hengchen thought that his choice was a sure win, after all, if. If the seven brothers of the Xing family were merged, then naturally the heart could be controlled. Then it was not impossible to get the heart back!

Tiansheng smiled. He knew what Long Hengchen was thinking, but pretended to be in pain. Instead, he turned around and asked, "Brothers of the Xing family, are you willing to exchange?" Tiansheng could arrange all this. The eldest brother Xing was also very smart. He knew that all this was done by their young master outside the house. He nodded and said, "For the young master, let alone exchanging with others, even if it means going through mountains of swords and seas of fire, I will not hesitate!" Tiansheng deliberately pretended to be reluctant and said, "Okay, okay! Then it's settled!" After that, he took the heart from Long Hengchen's hand, and then suppressed the surprise in his heart and pretended to be reluctant and said, "They will be yours in the future!" After that, he turned around and stopped looking at the seven brothers of the Xing family, looking extremely reluctant. Long Hengchen didn't care about Tiansheng: "So they are all mine!" After saying that, he threw the heart to Tiansheng, and then summoned Boss Xing out of the wooden house, and let the seven of them fight in a circle, and he stood in the middle, and then a force came out from him, and the seven brothers of the Xing family were sucked up, floating in the air, and then a red energy wrapped them up.

After absorbing it, it turned into a move of Hanba. The seven brothers of the Xing family naturally knew that Long Hengchen wanted to absorb their energy for his own use, and they would die, so they immediately struggled, but they couldn't break free, but slowed down Long Hengchen's speed.

Tiansheng looked at Long Hengchen, with a hint of evil in his eyes: "Alas, the heart is there, and my father... will soon appear!" After that, he turned to Murong Di and said: "Protect me no matter what. If it doesn't work, she must be a shield to ensure my successful absorption!" After that, he sat down cross-legged, then suddenly pulled open his clothes, clasped his hands to his left chest, and pulled them hard again. It was pulled open, and the place where the heart should have been placed was empty.

"Ah!" Ye Rui shouted when he saw such a bloody scene, and then Murong Di was also shocked, and then pulled Li Ye Rui to block in front of him, and looked at Tiansheng and Long Hengchen outside the house from time to time. The most bizarre scene appeared on both of them.

At this time, at Xia Feng's place, time had not passed long. Although Xia Feng was injured, he quickly arrived at Yemen, and then rushed straight to Ye Ye's residence, but Ye Ye was not there.

After all, Xia Feng's old injury had not healed, and a new one had recurred. In addition, she could no longer hide after running such a long distance with the injury, and her figure appeared in the Night Gate. Then she tilted and fell down.

"Someone, someone has fainted here." Suddenly, a Night Gate disciple happened to pass by there, and saw Xia Feng fainted, and shouted. The shouting attracted many people, including Ye Ye, who was upset and was about to visit Li Yerui's room.

"It's a beauty! Haha!" When Ye Ye walked to the crowd, he heard the Night Gate disciple say so, and then walked over with doubts in his heart. He pushed through the crowd and saw that it was Xia Feng. He was shocked, then walked forward, helped her up and said: "What's going on!"

Xia Feng opened her eyes weakly and said weakly: "The wooden house in the back mountain, born... Dragon lying horizontally... Save Ye Rui..." Before she finished speaking, her head tilted and she fainted.

"The wooden house in the back mountain? Tiansheng? Ye Rui?" Ye Ye thought about it, and suddenly got shocked. He immediately ordered the Yemen disciples around him: "Take her to the Ghost Queen, and then notify the people above the level of the hall master to wait for me in the meeting room immediately!" Ye Ye ran to Ye Rui's residence, pushed the door open, and found that the bed was empty.

"Ye Rui..." Ye Ye called out worriedly, and then went to the meeting room without any hesitation.

During the whole meeting, Ye Ye only said one sentence: "Tiansheng appeared in the back mountain and kidnapped Ye Rui. Long Hengchen is also there! Let's go immediately!"

Chapter 90: Fight Again

Ye Ye's words shocked the world, and everyone present stood up in panic, including Huang Shang. Huang Shang's strength has almost recovered, but the Ghost Queen has been in a coma, and a strong ghost aura surrounds her. No one knows his current situation.

Huang Shang heard Ye Ye say this, and immediately stood up and said solemnly: "Master Ye, let's go together!" Huang Shang no longer had the arrogance he had at the beginning, knowing that he was no match for those people, so he said to Ye Ye. Ye Ye shook his head: "No, Huang Shang, you are not a member of the Ye Sect now, and you can't be involved. Besides, you have someone to take care of!" Ye Ye refused mercilessly.

Huang Shang looked directly at Ye Ye and said, "Anyway, I will follow you!" After hearing this, Ye Ye smiled helplessly, sighed and said, "Okay, you are now the temporary foreign aid of Yemen, okay!" After that, he turned to the people of Yemen and said, "Yemen inner disciples, listen to my order, all the Corpse King-level disciples follow me, and the rest stay to guard Yemen!"

At Ye Ye's order, the most elite team in Yemen immediately stood up, Qin Minglei, Li Bin, Yang Hengchao, Yang Tianhai, Ye Hen, Huang Shang, Ye Ye. The seven formed the strongest combination of Yemen and rushed towards the back mountain.

At this time, in the wooden house in the back mountain.

Long Hengchen was still the same as before. Seven red suction forces sucked up the seven brothers of the Xing family at the same time, suspended in the air, and then constantly eroded the physical strength of the Xing brothers. After so long, the Xing brothers were all weakened, but they could still resist slightly.

"Hmph, in a little while, you will be my energy! If I can really have that ability forever, then I will take the heart back. If it can only last for a while, then I will still take the heart back!" Long Hengchen thought lightly, and then looked inside the house. The door of the wooden house was pressed tightly, and the only hole that could see inside was also blocked by Murong Di. Long Hengchen couldn't see the situation inside clearly, so he simply stopped guessing and increased his absorption ability.

Tiansheng, who was inside the wooden house, was in a stalemate at the moment. The heart in the left chest still had no reaction to being fused, but instead had a little rebound as if it was about to burst out of the left chest. Tiansheng also seemed to be in great pain, and then he moaned softly. The red and black flames ignited for no reason. After being wrapped in the red and black flames, Tiansheng seemed to be much more relaxed and began to fuse the heart.

With the red and black flames as a basis, the heart actually showed signs of fusion. A thick blood vessel actually grew on the top of the heart, and it was beating faintly. With every beat, a wave of energy would come out of the heart. However, soon, Tiansheng frowned again in pain... Although he claimed that the heart was his, it was still difficult to merge it.

On the other side, Ye Ye led Huang Shang and six others to the wooden house at a rapid gallop. The seven of them came all the way, without any concealment, with flying sand and rocks all the way, making a huge noise. Murong Di and Li Yerui, the only free people in the wooden house, were startled at the same time, showing two different expressions. Murong Di panicked, put Li Yerui, who looked happy, in front of him, and then stared at the source of the sound.

"Oh? Here it comes! Haha, just in time, let you see my peerless figure again!"; Long Hengchen looked at the huge movement of flying sand and rocks coming towards this side, pulled the corner of his mouth and increased the force of absorption. The Xing brothers could no longer resist, screamed, and then turned into flying ash in the red light. Then, seven gray-colored energies were sucked into the body by Long Hengchen.

"Hmm? Why is something wrong?!" After absorbing the energy, Long Hengchen immediately felt something wrong. He frowned, and a red light flashed. The surrounding trees and grass immediately dried up, and then spread rapidly, and Long Hengchen turned into the real body of Hanba. "Great! There is really no need to worry about recovering the fake body!" Did the seven brothers of the Xing family really stabilize him in the state of the corpse emperor Hanba forever?!

Feeling the changes in the surrounding trees and grass, Ye Ye and others shouted that it was not good, and then accelerated their pace. Then, at the moment of rushing out of the woods, the seven people dispersed at the same time and surrounded Hanba in the middle.

"You came so fast! Let's warm you up first, and then test whether this can really be a permanent corpse emperor!" Hanba said lightly, and then a red light flashed on his body, and layers of red crystals gathered on his body, and then rushed to his hands. In two breaths, a red crystal sword appeared in his hand. Then, Hanba made a simple straight stab, stabbing towards Huang Shang with a fierce burning flame.

The emperor felt the violent energy on the red crystal sword, and did not dare to take it rashly. With a shake of his hand, the Night Gate strange dagger appeared in his hand, but he did not meet the red crystal sword of Hanba. Instead, he suddenly fell down, used the Night Gate strange dagger as a point, spun it up, dodged the attack, and then exerted force with both hands, bounced up on the spot with his feet like a rabbit, and kicked Hanba. But Hanba suddenly flashed red, and a layer of red crystal appeared on his body again.

"Not bad! That kid didn't lie to me! No need to worry about insufficient energy anymore!" Hanba became excited. He really stabilized in the state of Corpse King Hanba, but he didn't think that he had become a natural...

Huang Shang knew the power of the red crystal, but the leg that kicked out could not be retracted, so he simply forced out the arrogance to hit Yu's legs and then wrapped the toes layer by layer, and continued to kick. However, the arrogance on Huang Shang's toes was shattered the moment it touched Hanba, and then Huang Shang was also bounced away, and then fell heavily to the ground.

All this happened in a flash. When Huang Shang was bounced out, the attacks of the other six people also arrived at the same time. Hanba's mouth twitched slightly, and then suddenly stood on tiptoe, holding the sword with both hands and spinning violently, and during the rotation, a stream of red flames was like a whirlpool, which immediately forced four of the six people away. The remaining ones were Ye Ye and the Punisher Yang Tianhai.

Ye Ye had already forced out the arrogance, and then fought against the waves of flames, while Yang Tianhai was even stronger, and actually used his body to resist. At this time, all the hair on his body had been vaporized, but he continued to resist as if nothing had happened. However, if you look closely at Yang Tianhai's skin, a layer of transparent film appeared there at some point. Although it could not control the temperature, it kept the flames out. At this time, Huang Shang also rushed up again. He had been a corpse king for thousands of years, and his strength was not weak. Moreover, thinking about the ghost queen who was unaware of the situation because of Hanba, the anger in his heart turned into strength. With a roar, he attacked Hanba. Although the strange-shaped dagger of Yemen in his hand was extremely hard, it was still a mortal object. It had turned into molten iron in the flames of Hanba in an instant. At this moment, he approached Hanba with his hands as weapons, and then roared fiercely, and his arrogance became extremely strong. With a grab of both hands, he actually grabbed the red crystal sword and forcibly stopped Hanba's rotation.

"Minglei, Li Bin, go save Ye Rui!" Ye Ye shouted, and Huang Shang, who didn't look back, grabbed the red crystal sword and immediately shouted that it was not good. With a strong arrogance on his body, he rushed in the direction of Huang Shang.

But before he arrived, the red crystal sword suddenly broke into countless fragments, and the fragments caught fire as soon as they touched objects, and it was difficult to extinguish. Huang Shang was holding the Red Crystal Sword, and was immediately hit by the flames all over his body. However, he did not panic, but used his Qi to resist and immediately retreated several meters, and then frantically used his Qi to extinguish the flames.

Ye Ye and the bald Yang Tianhai were also vigilantly guarding against the attack of Hanba, and then looked at Huang Shang worriedly. After a long time, the flames on Huang Shang's body went out. Looking at Huang Shang again, most of his body was burned, and what was even more shocking was that a large piece of flesh was burned on his face. Huang Shang's eyes were red at the moment, and with the burned face, he looked very scary. Qin Minglei and others on the other side were also stopped outside the house by Murong Die. He was holding Ye Rui in his arms.

The situation was suddenly in crisis

Chapter 91 The Power of Nuwa

When Murong Die saw that Qin Minglei and the others who rushed forward did not dare to move forward, he immediately laughed, then looked at Tiansheng who was emitting a faint blue light in the wooden house, and said calmly: "Come on, if you dare to take another step forward, I will definitely break her neck!" After that, he grabbed Li Yerui's neck with one hand, and then exerted a little force, and Li Yerui immediately groaned in pain.

Murong Die believed that it would not be a problem to defeat them, but if they were more than one person, and if he was dragged down, and one of them broke in, after all, it would interrupt Tiansheng's fusion with the heart at this moment.

Strangely enough, Murong Die didn't know when he really submitted to Tiansheng, and his mentality changed from temporary submission for hegemony to complete submission now. Murong Die said to himself: "Maybe, it's the aura of kingship in him!"

Qin Minglei and others saw Murong Die blocking the road and holding Li Yerui in his arms, so they stopped immediately and did not dare to attack rashly. They just stared at Murong Die closely, looking for a gap to attack.

Suddenly, Li Bin, the Undead King, whose body was covered with black lines, rushed towards the hole in the wall of the wooden house. Li Bin, who won by speed, wanted to break in with speed. However, Murong Die ignored Li Bin's sprint, and even shook his head slightly, stared with his eyes, and a mighty power was transmitted from his eyes. Suddenly, Li Bin was stunned.

Murong Die's attack actually intimidated Li Bin in the state of the Undead King. But it should be so, Murong Die is also extremely good at soul skills. As early as the Eight Days Pass, Ye Ye's soul was out of his body, but he was almost scared to death by Murong Die's stare. This shows how powerful Murong Di's soul is in spirit.

However, when Li Bin rushed up, Qin Minglei, Ye Hen, and Yang Hengchao also rushed up at the same time, but Murong Di did not make any move, but simply squeezed Li Yerui's neck tighter. Seeing Murong Di's behavior, Qin Minglei and the other four stopped their actions and looked at Murong Di coldly. They also kept looking for a gap to break through. They knew that there must be Tiansheng inside, but they didn't know why it didn't come out.

This side was temporarily deadlocked. Looking at the other side, Ye Ye, Yang Tianhai, and Huang Shang failed to besiege Hanba, but suffered a lot, which almost disfigured Huang Shang. However, such a blow did not stop the three from attacking. After failing to hit once, the three changed their formation.

Still led by Huang Shang, who was almost disfigured, the attack was launched. Huang Shang suddenly restrained himself at this moment, wrapped his arrogance around his body, obviously worried that Hanba would use the move just now again. The Ye Yang in Ye Ye's hand was an extraordinary thing. It could directly resist the blazing flames of Hanba, and then scratch some white marks on the red crystal on Hanba's body, and even directly cut off a small piece of red crystal. After the red crystal fell to the ground, it immediately turned into flames and burned for a long time.

And Yang Tianhai, at this time, was almost naked, with a bald head and no hair. However, her attack was so fierce. Yang Tianhai, who absorbed the memories of his tribe, the Punisher Clan, and all the war records, attacked like a surging river, continuously. Moreover, his attack was mixed with a spiritual attack, which kept eroding Hanba's spiritual sea. Although the red crystal had a strong defense, it still couldn't stop Yang Tianhai's spiritual attack. He also suffered a lot of losses.

"Brother, what are you doing..." Suddenly, this sentence appeared in Hanba's mind. Hanba, who was originally extremely defensive, also had a gap at this moment. It was Yang Tianhai's mental attack. The mental attacks kept accumulating, but only this sentence appeared in Hanba's mind. And Yang Tianhai knew that the direction of his mental attack was the area that Hanba was most afraid of. "Ye Ye, attack!" Seeing Hanba's brief mental trance, Yang Tianhai shouted immediately. Ye Ye and Huang Shang reacted immediately and turned defense into offense. The two groups of extremely strong arrogance went to Hanba from front and back. Hanba seemed to be still shocked by the words just now. When he reacted, Ye Ye and Huang Shang had already arrived in front of him, and it was too late to defend. Frowning, Hanba made a decision immediately.

With a "boom", a cloud of smoke formed by the explosion appeared from where Hanba was standing just now, and Ye Ye and Huang Shang also exchanged positions. But...their whole bodies were actually burning with flames at this moment, and then they fell down with a "puff". When the smoke dissipated, a trace of blood flowed from the corner of Hanba's mouth, and it seemed that he was seriously injured.

Smiling, looking at Ye Ye and Huang Shang who were burning with flames, Hanba thought about the life-and-death moment just now: just when Ye Ye and Huang Shang raised their arrogance to the peak and doubled him, he suddenly made a choice at this moment, and the red crystal sword in his hand suddenly shattered automatically, and the red crystals in the sky suddenly spread all around him. Not only that, the red crystals covering his whole body also suddenly shattered, and there were more red crystals in the air. Although Ye Ye and Huang Shang successfully hit him, they could not react to this variable and were all hit.

This Hanba actually exchanged his own serious injury for the destruction of the other two.

No, he didn't die. Suddenly, Huang Shang, who was not far in front of Hanba, suddenly moved. An extremely strong ghost energy suddenly covered him, and then instantly extinguished the flame. On Huang Shang's chest, an ordinary stone was emitting a strange black light, and death was coming out of it. Huang Shang still had a faint consciousness. He looked at the stone on his chest and suddenly remembered that when he caught the ghost queen flying down from the sky that day, the ghost queen handed him such a stone, and then the stone suddenly formed a rope strangely and was automatically worn around Huang Shang's neck. Huang Shang didn't think much about it, but he didn't expect that this stone was formed by the ghost queen compressing all the unreleased ghost energy before she fell into a coma. The ghost queen fainted not because she didn't release the ghost energy, but because she released too much. However, no one knew all this.

The ghost energy emitted by the stone slowly formed a cocoon, wrapping Huang Shang inside. The Ghost Queen didn't think that the thing that was originally used to protect Huang Shang at the moment of life and death, created...

Looking at Ye Ye again, the flames on his body were still burning, and Ye Ye didn't move at all.

Hanba laughed. Although he was startled by the black cocoon that wrapped Huang Shang, he looked at Ye Ye's unknown life and death and laughed immediately. In his heart, he had already won this battle. Shaking his head, a red light appeared again, and the red crystal sword and red crystal armor suddenly appeared on him. Then he looked at Yang Tianhai with disdain: "What can you do alone?" After that, the red crystal sword stabbed the cocoon formed by the ghost energy, but was forcibly blocked outside. Hanba laughed again. The attack just now did not break the black gas cocoon, and Hanba didn't mind. Then he said to Yang Tianhai again: "Kill you first, and then it won't be too late to absorb it! Punisher, the taste has probably not been tasted for a thousand years!" After that, the red crystal sword shook, and a flame wrapped around the sword, and the power was even stronger. Indeed, even the injured Hanba would not have a hard time dealing with Yang Tianhai.

But suddenly, Hanba frowned, turned around in confusion, and suddenly exclaimed: "The power of Nuwa!"

Chapter 92: Fighting on their own

Ye Ye, however, slowly climbed up at this moment, emitting seven-color light all over his body.

The fatal blow that had originally cost him serious injuries did not kill either of them. Hanba was startled, then turned his head and looked at Ye Ye. That was the energy that frightened him - the power of Nuwa.

Ye Ye was very clear-headed at this moment, and he knew that Hanba's fatal blow just now did not even cause him any harm. Because, when the red crystal broke apart and the flame attached to him, a layer of light seven-color energy suddenly attached to his skin, and the flame was burning on it. Ye Ye fell to the ground because he suddenly felt dizzy in his mind.

Standing up, Ye Ye shook his head, and then shook off the burning flame on his body. He looked at the black cocoon wrapped around Huang Shang in confusion and said, "Oh? What's going on?" After that, he looked at the seven-color light emanating from himself, smiled, and rushed directly to Hanba.

Hanba was startled, and the red crystals gathered and the sword appeared. But when he was about to attack, he found that Ye Ye was already in front of him. At this speed, Hanba had no choice but to block the red crystal sword in front of his chest and defend himself.

Ye Ye held Ye Yang and stabbed straight. After being blocked by the red crystal sword. Ye Ye shouted "Ah" and immediately added strength, and the red crystal sword broke into pieces, and then the red crystal fragments flew all over the sky, but when they attached to Ye Ye, they were blocked by the seven-color light and then slid away.

Hanba panicked when he saw this. His defensive moves were useless! But the situation at the moment did not allow him to panic, because Ye Ye's attack came again.

Everything happened too fast, and Yang Tianhai, who was watching the battle and waiting for an opportunity to intervene and help, was also shocked. His strength was not weak, but he knew that this battle was not a battle of the same level.

After Ye Ye shattered the red crystal sword, there was no obstacle under Ye Yang's blade, and he went straight to Hanba. However, Hanba was the first corpse king in history after all. At this time, he focused his mind, stared at Ye Ye's movements, and condensed red crystals at the same time, but this time he did not condense into red crystal armor, but only condensed a large amount of red crystals at the position where Ye Yang touched.

With a "click", the red crystal that had just condensed suddenly shattered again. The fragments flew all over the sky and blocked Ye Ye's sight. Suddenly, Hanba's eyes narrowed and saw an opportunity. He took advantage of the moment when Ye Ye's vision was blocked by the red crystal flame and kicked out. However, he did not want to hit Ye Ye, he expected Ye Ye to block it. And he used this block, and then bounced off Ye Ye's arm, temporarily leaving Ye Ye's attack range.

On the other side, Murong Di still threatened Ye Rui, and Qin Minglei and others did not dare to move forward rashly. In the wooden house, a burst of blue light suddenly appeared. Murong Die was shocked when he saw it: it was almost done. Thinking of it, he relaxed a lot. Qin Minglei's eyes suddenly shrank into needles. Seeing the right time, the strange-shaped dagger of Yemen in his hand flashed coldly. At this time, it was obviously too late for Murong Die to threaten Ye Rui, but he was also very strong, and he didn't care about Qin Minglei's attack. Instead, he looked at Qin Minglei indifferently, then grabbed the dagger in Qin Minglei's hand, twisted it, and the dagger slipped out of his hand.

However, Qin Minglei suddenly smiled. His whole body was red, and his eyes were bloodthirsty. He smiled horribly. Murong Die was shocked, and thought about it. He immediately took a defensive posture, and meanly let Ye Rui block him on the left.

Sure enough, after Qin Minglei's laughter, Li Bin, Yang Hengchao, and Ye Hen divided into three routes to encircle Murong Die. Each used his own skills. Murong Die sighed "not good" and immediately threw Ye Rui to the strongest Ye Hen on the left, making him stop attacking, and he also had an opening. However, Li Bin and Yang Hengchao came from the right and back, and there was also a temporarily restrained Qin Minglei in front of him.

Li Bin was extremely fast and arrived one step ahead of Yang Hengchao. The strange-shaped dagger of Yemen in his hand stabbed out quickly, and Murong Die blocked all of them. Then he waved his hand, and a golden light appeared, fanning Li Bin away. However, after Li Bin flew out, Yang Hengchao suddenly detoured from behind, then grabbed Li Bin's hand, and then used his running inertia to throw Li Bin to Murong Di again. And he rushed to Murong Die even faster, with a pair of strange fists in his hands, and the four barbs emitted purple cold light. It was poison, and it was the poison on the Phoenix Thorn.

After Li Bin was pulled back and thrown out again, he was not afraid, but had a serious look on his face. Then he stabbed Murong Die's heart with the strange dagger in his hand, but Murong Die blocked him again, and then grabbed Li Bin's wrist, and then a golden light flashed, piercing people's eyes.

'Ah!' was Li Bin's scream. After the golden light dissipated, looking at Li Bin again, he actually retreated several meters straight, and only stopped when he bumped into Yang Hengchao, and his arms were also hanging vertically on both sides. Li Bin was seriously injured in the golden light just now.

But Murong Die didn't have time to catch his breath, and a more fierce attack came in front of him. Murong Die frowned, and then the golden light reappeared, and he swung his fist, and the golden light suddenly gathered on his fist, and then his right fist with dazzling golden light hit the attacker-Qin Minglei.

With a scream, Qin Minglei was knocked away. After he stood up tremblingly, a trace of blood flowed from the corner of his mouth, and then he spurted out a mouthful of red and black blood with a sound of "puff", and there were some small pieces of objects in the blood. Qin Minglei, seriously injured.

Seeing that Murong Die had seriously injured Qin Minglei and Li Bin with only two hits, Yang Hengchao and Ye Hen were shocked, but they still rushed up. Because they knew that their partners would not be defeated so easily.

Yang Tianhai put Li Bin down and continued to attack from behind. And Ye Hen also put Ye Rui on the ground temporarily, and then forced out his not very strong arrogance and rushed up.

Murong Die shook his head. If it was the simultaneous attack of four people just now, he would still be quite afraid, but at this time there were only two people, he didn't need to take it to heart, even if Ye Hen had forced out his arrogance, even if he saw the purple light on Yang Hengchao's fist. This idea made Murong Die not defend with all his strength. Because in his heart, Ye Hen and Yang Hengchao were not his opponents at all.

But he overlooked one thing. Yang Hengchao arrived first, and his fists danced vigorously. Murong Die knew that he must be poisoned, so he did not take the attack directly, but cleverly hit Yang Hengchao's wrist to make him lose his strength. At this time, Ye Hen's attack also arrived.

Among the four people, Murong Die was most afraid of Ye Hen, and it was Ye Hen who forced out his arrogance. He ignored Ye Hen for the time being, but in a flash, he hit Yang Hengchao's wrist with both hands, making his hands lose their strength, and then he danced with both fists at the same time. Uppercut, hit Yang Hengchao straight up. After doing all this, Murong Die immediately turned around, and the golden light appeared, facing the arrogance of Ye Hen.

However, the defensive golden light arranged in a hurry could not match the red and black arrogance of Ye Hen that had been condensed for a long time. Suddenly, there was a sense of being suppressed. Murong Die did not panic, all this was within his calculations. He retreated lightly, and then the golden light suddenly became an illusory sword, and then pierced through Ye Hen's arrogance. Ye Hen was also startled, and then he attached his hands to the flames, and used the flames to control the sword.

However, Murong Di smiled, and then the sword body shone with golden light. The golden light actually had attack power, and Ye Hen was caught off guard and was hit immediately, but the golden light was radiating out, and the attack power was also much weaker. After Ye Hen endured it, the attack in his hand also decreased.

Murong Di smiled disdainfully, and when he was about to organize an attack, a black shadow suddenly jumped on his head, and then sat on his shoulders, and two pale thorns stabbed at his eyes.

That person was Li Bin, or Li Bin in a crazy state. Seeing this, Ye Hen also withdrew his attack. His attack was just a feint to cover Li Bin.

Murong Di grabbed the barbs growing from Li Bin's elbow with both hands and pulled them hard, trying to pull Li Bin off his shoulders, but Li Bin's legs were firmly fixed on it like the roots of an old tree. Seeing that he couldn't pull it off, Murong Di immediately grabbed the barbs tightly, and then a golden light emanated from his body. A sword appeared in front of him, and then slowly stabbed Li Bin. He could actually control the sword with his mind!

At this moment, Li Bin's hands were restrained, and he had no way to face the golden illusory sword. Murong Di smiled. If this sword stabbed someone, and then exploded in the body...

But suddenly a red light flashed from a distance. Qin Minglei stood up shakily, his eyes had turned into a red light, and then he immediately rushed up, and his figure left very quickly with a red line.

Murong Di didn't care, because he couldn't feel the energy in Qin Minglei. Continue to let the energy illusory sword attack Li Bin!

Suddenly, when Qin Minglei approached, an overwhelming energy emerged. Murong Di panicked, but he had no time to defend himself and froze in his place. This blow, he would die if he caught the barbs with both hands!

However, a ball of blue light came out of the wooden house, interrupting Qin Minglei, and a voice lazily said: "It feels good! Murong Di, you are really old!" As soon as the voice fell, a man opened the door of the wooden house and walked out. Ye Ye, who had just appeared and was fighting on the other side, Yang Tianhai and Hanba looked over at the same time, with surprise in their eyes.

Chapter 93 I want you to submit

Under the surprised eyes of the crowd, Tiansheng took a step slowly, walked to Murong Die and patted his shoulder, then smiled and said: "Don't worry, wait until I kill them all, and then I will give you what I promised you." After that, he turned his head to look at Ye Ye, frowned and said to himself in doubt: "The power of Nuwa is really a bit tricky, but..." As he said that, he ignored Qin Minglei and the others, but slowly walked towards Ye Ye.

Qin Minglei and Li Bin, who were in the frenzy stage, were interrupted by their attacks, and they were fearless in their madness. The anger in their hearts became more vigorous. The two roared in a low voice and launched an attack at the same time. Li Bin, with his hands put on his chest, two bones hidden behind them, suddenly raised his hands when approaching, and then jumped up suddenly, attacking Tiansheng from top to bottom. Qin Minglei's attack also arrived at the moment Li Bin jumped up. He was still the same. No energy fluctuations could be seen on the surface, but at the moment of punching, overwhelming energy and power were exerted at the same time.

Tiansheng didn't even turn his head back, and the corners of his mouth curled up. A dark blue energy flashed by. Before Ye Ye could say "be careful", Tiansheng waved his hand lightly, and a dark blue energy had already bound Qin Minglei and Li Bin.

Seeing this, Ye Ye frowned, and he knew what Tiansheng had done just now. Ye Ye knew that although the power of Nuwa was strong, it could not be as smooth and free as Tiansheng's command of the dark blue energy. Just now, it was Tiansheng who used extremely subtle control to let the energy bind Qin Minglei and Li Bin.

With a smile, Tiansheng ignored Qin Minglei and Li Bin behind him, but continued to walk in Ye Ye's direction.

Hanba was also very shocked at this moment. He asked himself that even though he had lived for thousands of years, he would not be as comfortable as Tiansheng in using energy. However, he smiled and said to Tiansheng calmly, "Boy, not bad. You can absorb the heart so completely." Hanba's tone did not reveal the embarrassment when he was attacked by Ye Ye just now.

Tiansheng looked at Hanba, shook his head and said, "Hanba, I think it is not easy for you to evolve to the Corpse King. How about you submit to me?" After hearing this, Hanba raised his eyebrows and his eyes became very cold: This guy is so arrogant just after getting the heart. However, after looking at the strength that Tiansheng seemed to deliberately show, he weighed it and said coldly: "I'm sorry, I'm used to freedom. Besides, do you think I will be subservient to others?"

Tiansheng ignored Hanba's cold words, but looked at Ye Ye calmly, and then said: "I don't know, if Hanba also becomes my person, then what do you have to rely on?"

Ye Ye raised his eyebrows, shrugged his shoulders helplessly and said: "It's okay, I can still give a life, but you can't give it, you still have to find your father!" Ye Ye deliberately said that the father and son are very serious. "Okay, okay, okay. It's really courageous. But it's no longer necessary. If I tell you that I can find my father at any time, what will you do?"

Ye Ye stopped talking, buried his head, and became very cold. He knew that if what Tiansheng said was true, then…

Thinking of it, Ye Ye's body suddenly showed a colorful light, and it became stronger and stronger.

If there is no point in talking, Ye Ye naturally doesn't want to entangle with Tiansheng. Prepare to launch an attack "Maybe Tiansheng has just completed the fusion of energy, maybe he is not as strong as he appears, and Hanba will not easily help Tiansheng." Ye Ye thought, constantly condensing the energy of the Nuwa stone in his body.

Tiansheng smiled, and ignored the increasingly strong Nuwa energy on Ye Ye's body, but calmly looked at the terrified Hanba and said: "I want you to submit to me!" After that, he slowly walked towards Hanba, but walked past Hanba, and then two black shadows flew towards Hanba. Hanba was in a state of tension, and a red light flashed, and caught the two black shadows in his hands. This defensive action was ridiculed by Tiansheng: "Haha, Hanba, if you don't want to eat it, just say it earlier, no need to burn it." Tiansheng's voice just fell, Hanba looked at the two black shadows in his hand, it was two people. It was Qin Minglei and Li Bin. Hanba was shocked, how did Tiansheng bring these two people here?

"Suck it!" Tiansheng said lightly, then looked at Ye Ye. The energy had reached saturation and would soon launch an attack, but Tiansheng still ignored it. Instead, he walked to the black ghost cocoon formed by Huang Shang, and then said: "Ye Ye, put away your energy, otherwise, the two people in Hanba's hands will definitely die! And he must die too!"

Ye Ye was shocked. When Tiansheng controlled the energy to throw the bound Qin Minglei and Li Bin into Hanba's hands, Ye Ye was shocked. But now hearing Tiansheng say so, he was even more shocked. The originally strong energy also swayed for a while, and then he looked up at Tiansheng.

Tiansheng smiled and said: "Qingyi, if you launched an attack just now, you could have killed the two of us! But now it's too late!" As soon as the voice fell, Tiansheng's hands suddenly burst into an extremely dazzling dark blue and grabbed the black cocoon.

The black cocoon that was hit by Hanba without any trace was actually inserted into it by Tiansheng's hands. Tiansheng couldn't let Ye Ye have such a partner. Tiansheng knew that Huang Shang was strong. If he succeeded in evolving, it would be very disadvantageous to him. So Tiansheng said what he said and did what he did just now, successfully attracted Ye Ye's attention, and then launched the attack that had been accumulating. He wanted to strangle the enemy in the cradle! Ye Ye was startled and launched the attack immediately without caring about anything. Although the power of Nuwa was shaken and dissipated a lot in Tiansheng's words, the offensive was still very fierce. Unexpectedly, Tiansheng not only did not panic, but continued to increase the energy in his hand, constantly grabbing into the black cocoon, destroying the black cocoon while saying: "Hanba, you are holding an important person in Ye Ye's heart in your hand. If I die, you will die too! So, start absorbing!" Hanba is so smart that he naturally knows that he is being used by Tiansheng, but Tiansheng is telling the truth. Without any hesitation, he threw Qin Minglei and the other two up, and a red light suddenly appeared on his body. A suction force pulled the two of them in the air, and a group of energy was sucked out of their bodies.

Ye Ye was startled and immediately turned around, grabbing Hanba with both hands with heavy energy. After all, Qin Minglei and the other two have no resistance now, and the black cocoon that wrapped Huang Shang is now emitting a strong black gas, resisting Tiansheng.

While grabbing Hanba, Ye Ye winked at Yang Tianhai, asking him to interfere with Tiansheng. Yang Tianhai understood and let out a low roar. A layer of transparent energy wrapped around his whole body. He rushed forward and swung his fists fiercely at Tiansheng who was fighting against the ghost energy emitted by the black cocoon.

Chapter 94 Evolution

Faced with Yang Tianhai's overwhelming attack, Tiansheng did not dare to take it with his body. However, he did not hesitate at all, turned his head, smiled, and then suddenly roared under Yang Tianhai's puzzled eyes. A roar, like the roar of a lion, makes people tremble. However, don't forget Yang Tianhai's fatal flaw-weak spiritual level.

Yang Tianhai just took the attack completely. A roar immediately hit his spiritual level. Not only did the attack on his hand stop, but it also caused a backlash. The layer of five-colored energy suddenly exploded. Although the explosion sound was very slight, it was an explosion of energy after all, and it was close to Tiansheng's skin. The energy that was originally protective now became a weapon. After a few explosions, Yang Tianhai opened his pupils wide and slowly fell down.

Tiansheng still ignored Yang Tianhai, but concentrated on outputting energy to fight against the heavy ghost energy. Ye Ye was shocked when he saw Yang Tianhai fall, but he did not stop his attack. The Ye Yang in his hand shone brightly under the power of Nuwa.

Hanba had to stop absorbing Ye Ye's attack, and then dragged Qin Minglei with the red crystal to block in front of him. Ye Ye frowned, and immediately forcibly withdrew the attack, then turned his body, passed Qin Minglei, and hit him with his elbow. Hanba easily blocked such an attack, and then when Ye Ye used the power of Nuwa, he immediately controlled Qin Minglei or Li Bin to block in front of him.

Hanba, the first corpse king in the world, is powerful, but he doesn't have to be so embarrassed. Ye Ye thought of it in his heart. After several rounds of fighting, Ye Ye clearly felt that Hanba's momentum and attack were not at the same level as that day when he seized the treasure. I don't know if Hanba deliberately hides or... However, this is a life-and-death moment, how can Hanba not go all out! Ye Ye thought about it, looked at Tiansheng on the side, who still couldn't break the ghost cocoon for the time being, and the ghost energy also had a tendency to overtake, so he was relieved for the time being, and then a small amount of Nuwa's power was under his control, quietly on his left hand, and then a Yeyang was constantly disassembled, and a short sword appeared in the hand of the tower.

Ye Ye did not attach Nuwa's power to Yeyang, but relied on his own strength to go towards Hanba fiercely. Hanba stretched out his hand, and a piece of red crystal appeared in his hand out of thin air, blocking Yeyang's attack. However, Ye Ye's attack did not end like this. At the moment when Hanba blocked the attack point, Ye Ye's left hand suddenly burst into dazzling colorful light, and then his hand formed a palm, and slapped Hanba's abdomen fiercely.

Hanba was startled and immediately formed a red crystal to protect himself. However, Ye Ye's seemingly fierce palm was just a light tap or even a touch on the red crystal part of his abdomen, and Ye Ye immediately withdrew. Worried that this was Ye Ye's trick, Hanba did not attack rashly, but blocked Qin Minglei and Li Bin in front of him.

And Ye Ye stopped attacking, but the corner of his mouth was pulled up. The palm strike just now was a test by Ye Ye. His guess was right. Something must have happened to Hanba. This red crystal did not have the hot temperature of that day!

Looking at Ye Ye's strange smile, Hanba was startled, but he was helpless because he felt something was wrong when he absorbed the seven brothers of the Xing family just now. Although, yes, he has obtained the permanent level of corpse king, but he can't play it at all, even the temporary manifestation of absorbing several of his subordinates on the day of the treasure. Hanba was also very helpless. As a corpse king, he actually hid so embarrassedly. Moreover, when Tiansheng ordered him just now, he was unwilling in his heart, but he had no choice, his life was in danger, and he had to ask Tiansheng about the strange thing that happened to him.

After a few breaths, Ye Ye suddenly put away his smile, and then a cold and stern look appeared on his face. He lifted up Ye Yang's hand, and a huge Nuwa force suddenly burst out, and the colorful light was beautiful and dangerous. Ye Ye, since he already knew what must have happened in Hanba's body at this moment, he couldn't use his full strength, so he wanted to defeat Hanba with one blow.

Without too much concentration, Ye Ye slowly took back Ye Yang, folded, and disassembled it. In an instant, a weapon shaped like Yemen's strange dagger appeared in Ye Ye's hand. After doing all this, Ye Ye rushed over. Hanba raised his eyebrows, looking at Ye Ye's figure rushing over, the word "damn" popped out from the red, but there was no hesitation, Qin Minglei and Li Bin were immediately dragged in front of him to protect themselves.

However, Ye Ye's attack did not stop at all. He grabbed Ye Yang's reverse grip and put it at his waist. Then, when he was about to approach Qin Minglei who was blocked in front, Ye Ye's right foot suddenly stepped out, then stepped on the ground, and his right hand swung out violently, but it was not an attack, but the huge inertia when swinging out drove the body to turn. When Ye Ye's front turned to the left, Ye Ye's left foot suddenly stepped out, but it was just a step, and then it was ejected. Ye Yang, who was originally holding his right hand reversely, was suddenly cut out. And the direction of the blade... was surprisingly Hanba's neck.

This series of actions startled Hanba, and also surprised Tiansheng who was standing beside him. And the ghost energy also took advantage of Tiansheng's distraction and suddenly increased again, instantly suppressing Tiansheng's dark blue energy completely, and then, with a bang, an explosion came from the contact point between Tiansheng and the ghost energy cocoon. The explosion brought a violent storm and swept all around.

On the other side, Ye Yang was about to break the red crystal that Hanba had hastily arranged and take his life. The explosion came with a violent storm. Hanba was immediately delighted, and then immediately followed the storm and was blown to other places, but Ye Ye stopped and looked at the location of the explosion coldly.

After a long time, the storm caused by the explosion dissipated, and then after a while, the dust blown by the storm subsided. At this time, everyone looked at the center of the explosion in surprise. At this moment, a person was squatting. A person with three barbs on his back, a black and red horn on his head with cold light, a tail drooping to one side, and a hammer-shaped tumor on the tail, it looks like he has been hit.

The man slowly raised his head, slowly stood up, and swung his tail twice. Then he looked at his hands in confusion, and roared violently, and the sound was almost the same as the roar of the ghost queen after she turned into a ghost. But the man spoke in human language: "What happened to me?" It was Huang Shang's voice. Huang Shang turned out to be like this.

Red skin, two fangs pulled down below the chin, red eyes full of bloodthirstiness, black ghost energy rising and falling from time to time on the body, black horns on the top of the head, barbs on the back, and a tail with a tumor... This is a complete fusion of zombies and ghosts! Except that the body is not as big as after the ghost.

"Huang Shang?" Ye Ye heard the voice and shouted in confusion. Huang Shang woke up from his doubts and looked at Ye Ye: "What's going on?" After saying that, he suddenly tensed up all over, then his body turned slightly, and his tail swung up with inertia, and then heard a "clang" sound, and a figure popped out from the tumor part of the tail.

"It's really good, suitable for the furnace top! Now that the furnace top and the carrier are both there, then..." The man was born, and after his tentative attack just now, he was hit by the tumor, and then slid on the ground for several meters before talking to himself.

Huang Shang's eyes immediately turned redder when he saw Tiansheng. The originally black ghost energy was gradually mixed with some arrogance, and it became more and more, and finally the ghost energy and arrogance were perfectly combined together. The ghost energy that was originally like fog was now like a real flame, and the whole person was like a demon bathed in black flames! A dangerous breath was transmitted.

Chapter 95 Confrontation

Tiansheng looked at Huang Shang after his evolution, frowning, and wondering what he was thinking. The most surprised person was Hanba. He had fought with the ghost queen after she turned into a ghost, and he knew how powerful she was. Now, Huang Shang not only had the aura of a ghost, but also the aura of a corpse king. The combination of the two made him feel nervous.

However, Huang Shang was not in a hurry to attack, but waved his hands randomly. He wanted to control the energy in a short time. After Ye Ye pulled Qin Minglei and Li Bin to a safe place, he slowly walked to Huang Shang and said, "What's going on?"

Huang Shang thought about it thoughtfully, then opened his palm, and there was a black crystal embedded there. Then Huang Shang said, "This is what Rui Xin gave me. Maybe she wanted to use this thing to protect me, but she didn't want to..." Ye Ye nodded, then laughed, and looked at Tiansheng jokingly. Tiansheng also looked at Ye Ye. Ignoring the provocation and teasing in his eyes, Tiansheng smiled, walked to Hanba, and then put his hand on Hanba's shoulder. Hanba wanted to break free immediately, but heard Tiansheng whispered: "If you want to control the energy in your body, don't move." After that, he pretended to say: "Okay, now it's fair, but I think the victory is still on my side." After that, a dark blue light appeared, and the dark blue was mixed with black and red arrogance. That was the arrogance of the corpse king! The energy that Tiansheng forcibly stole from Huang Shang's blood.

Ye Ye was shocked, looking at the two layers of energy of Huang Shang and Tiansheng, thought about it, and released the power of Nuwa. Then he looked directly at Tiansheng. Under pressure, the power of Nuwa also started to work at full capacity, and the colorful light even suppressed the brilliance of the sun in the sky.

After hearing what Tiansheng said, Hanba stopped moving, because he could clearly feel the energy transmitted from Tiansheng's hand. The energy was very strange and could control the energy that was sinking in his body. Suddenly, Hanba roared, and his body kept getting bigger. His clothes were torn apart until he was about three or four meters tall. At this time, Hanba's whole body was red crystal, and he even looked so crystal clear. His right hand turned into a red crystal sword, and there was a pair of red crystal fangs in his mouth, which looked sharper than Huang Shang's.

Suddenly, the temperature around him rose. The surrounding trees and grass dried up quickly. Hanba was in reality, and there was a great drought in the world! 'Ah' Hanba roared again, and then a fierce flame suddenly ignited on his body. He looked like a fire giant at this moment, even though he was a red crystal body. Under his feet, the land had even been burned and cracked.

Everyone present was suddenly surprised. This is the power of Hanba, the first corpse king in history! Tiansheng smiled, and stood on Hanba's shoulder and said, "Ye Ye, fight! The power of Nuwa is said to be able to mend the sky. Today I will see if it is as powerful as the legend says!" After that, Tiansheng disappeared from Hanba's shoulder, and when he appeared, he came to Ye Ye with an extremely dazzling blue flame. This is Tiansheng's true strength.

Ye Ye did not panic, and raised his left hand slightly, and then a shield composed of Nuwa's power appeared in front of him. As soon as the shield was formed, Tiansheng also came into contact with Ye Ye.

Tiansheng had no weapons in his hands, and a pair of fists smashed the shield. The shield was broken by the punch! Ye Ye was shocked. Although he arranged the shield in a hurry, he knew the energy in it. It was broken by such a blow, and he was very surprised. However, the situation did not allow him to be surprised, and Tiansheng's attack was still going on.

Without hesitation, Ye Yang in his right hand stabbed Tiansheng with colorful light, and then he lifted his right foot suddenly, and attacked Tiansheng from the bottom up with a knee. Tiansheng used his hand full of blue light to skillfully flick the sword and deflect the sword stab. At the same time, he supported himself with his other hand and resisted the knee strike. Moreover, he flew up with the force of the knee strike and bypassed Ye Ye's head. His hand immediately formed a palm and slapped Ye Ye's head. In a flash, Ye Ye made a prompt decision and dodged the palm strike with his head tilted, but his shoulder was hit hard. The whole person was also knocked to the ground by the force from above.

However, Ye Ye did not panic. At the moment he fell to the ground, his left hand skillfully touched the treasure bag on his waist, took out a phoenix thorn, and then skillfully broke the feather part, leaving only the sharp part of the feather handle, and then hid it between his fingers and clamped it tightly. When Tiansheng saw Ye Ye being knocked down, he immediately continued to slap from top to bottom, but this time he hit Ye Ye's heart.

Ye Ye pretended to be startled, and forcibly raised his energy, and used the hand holding the Phoenix Thorn to touch Tiansheng's palm strike. The energy that Ye Ye raised in a hurry was naturally not comparable to Tiansheng's abundant energy. The moment of contact, Nuwa's power was dispelled, and then Tiansheng continued to strike with a triumphant smile.

But suddenly, the dark blue energy on Tiansheng's palm retreated completely, and the speed of retreat was accelerating, retreating to the position of the arm in a short breath. Tiansheng was startled, and immediately pressed hard on Ye Ye's palm, and then bounced out of the battle circle. Looking at his hand again, a black wing handle was pierced into it.

The poison of the Phoenix Thorn itself is a temporary closure of a kind of energy in the body. Its toxicity itself depends on the quality of the material. But unfortunately, Ye Ye's treasure bag, because of his hasty arrival, only contained a Phoenix Thorn, which was made of Huang Shang's blood, the Corpse Demon Mother Stone and the peacock's wing handle when he was bored and before the Corpse Demon Mother Stone was damaged. The power, naturally, cannot be whispered.

Ye Ye smiled, slowly stood up, rubbed his arm that was numb from the palm strike, and said nothing. Tiansheng was very surprised, and immediately raised his energy to suppress the spread of the poison. However, Ye Ye dared to complete this plan with his death, so he naturally would not give Tiansheng time to suppress the poison. Ye Ye knew that the more powerful the poison was, the faster it would spread.

Without any words, Ye Ye's body was dazzling with colorful light, and the night sun in his hand had formed a short knife. And Ye Ye only used ordinary chopping movements, and Tiansheng also knew the principle of the spread of poison, while dodging Ye Ye's attack in a panic, he suppressed it with dark blue energy.

But suddenly. Tiansheng's eyes shrank into needles, and then when Ye Ye chopped down with a move, he stopped dodging, but instead used the hand pierced by the phoenix thorn to meet Ye Ye's attack.

With a sound of "hiss", a blue blood line rushed out of Tiansheng's arm. Ye Ye glanced at the blood on the ground. The blue blood was mixed with black blood. It was poisonous blood contaminated by the Phoenix Thorn!

Ye Ye dared to attack Tiansheng with his death, and Tiansheng dared to detoxify at the cost of breaking his arm. The battle between the two strong men was just the beginning.

Huang Shang and Hanba, who were standing by, were also using the energy in their bodies. Finally, they both opened their eyes at the same time, and two flames, one black and one red, suddenly became strong. Without any words, the two disappeared directly on the spot, and then the two flames collided in mid-air, sparking some sparks.

Chapter 96 Tiansheng's Identity

Compared to the pure power confrontation between Huang Shang and Hanba, the battle between Ye Ye and Tiansheng tended to be more skillful. Both sides were gifted and excellent in fighting. As they fought back and forth, the wounds on their bodies increased a lot.

But suddenly. Huang Shang looked at Ye Ye and the other two fighting not far from them, his eyes flickered, and he had an idea in his mind! Thinking of this, he would first force Hanba back, and then go in the direction of Tiansheng.

Sure enough, as he expected, Hanba immediately came forward to block him: "Your opponent is me!" Huang Shang smiled, ignored Hanba, swung his body, and the tail whip came with a sharp sound of breaking through the air, and Hanba did not resist. There was a sound of "bang" in the air, like a heavy hammer hitting a drum. However, before Huang Shang could retract the tail whip, Hanba had already firmly grasped Huang Shang's tail whip, and then swung his arm and threw Huang Shang out. Huang Shang was not panicked at all, but curled his lips inadvertently, then flew in the direction Hanba threw him, and immediately gathered the flames on his body with a smile on his face.

After Huang Shang was thrown out, he crashed into the dry forest, breaking countless dry trees like a bulldozer, stirring up dust all over the sky. Hanba, seeing this situation, immediately ran towards Ye Ye, but he frowned and stopped.

Hanba, a smart man, naturally saw the meaningless smile on Huang Shang's face just now. When he was wondering, a black shadow came towards Hanba. Hanba was startled, and the arm of the red crystal long sword blocked it, and the black shadow was immediately burned to ashes. Looking in the direction where the black shadow flew, Hanba immediately frowned.

That direction was exactly the direction Huang Shang flew out, and the black shadows were little ghosts with black flames all over their bodies. They were condensed by Huang Shang's energy! Moreover, countless little ghosts were coming towards him quickly. He was shocked and immediately waved his arm that had turned into a red crystal sword to block those little ghosts. However, there were too many little ghosts, and no matter how tightly the Hanba sword was waved, there would always be a ghost that slipped through the net.

The little ghost was burning with black flames all over his body. After breaking through Hanba's defense, he immediately stuck to Hanba's red crystal body. The black flames temporarily resisted the flames on Hanba's body, and the little ghost was not burned to death immediately. Hanba didn't know what trick Huang Shang was playing, so he immediately increased the flames on his body and instantly extinguished the black flames on the little ghost.

However, Hanba was suddenly startled. Because a violent explosion broke out from him. It was that little ghost, or rather, the little energy bomb ghost that Huang Shang kneaded with energy and then threw out!

All this was thanks to the crystal stone that the ghost queen gave to Huang Shang before she fell into a coma! That crystal stone was formed by the energy of all the ghosts of the Nalan ghost clan after they died, and it could naturally summon the souls of those little ghosts! Huang Shang himself knew that doing so would make those ghosts have no chance of resurrection, but in the face of the enemy, even his wife Nalan. Zi Ruixin and his people were so determined to sacrifice their lives, Huang Shang no longer thought about it and immediately used this trick. Those little ghosts were souls, and the black flames attached to them were just a mechanism. Huang Shang knew that it would not be of much use to summon those little ghosts, so he changed a method: he injected black flames into those little ghosts, and then when the black flames outside the body were dispelled, the black flames inside the body would explode! There were more than tens of millions of Nalan ghosts who died, and although Hanba was careful, he was still tricked. However, such an attack requires a long time to gather energy and summon souls, so Huang Shang made the move just now and successfully let Hanba throw him far away. After an explosion, Hanba's defensive attack also stopped, and then countless little ghosts immediately stuck to him. Suddenly, countless little ghosts stuck to Hanba's three or four-meter-tall body, and, Hanba's own flames dispersed those black flames. Explosion, a violent explosion appeared!

With a bang, a black mushroom cloud appeared where Hanba had just stood, and dust suddenly filled the sky. The storm stirred up a circle of waves, blowing away the surrounding trees that were already dry and had no grip. And Huang Shang, slowly facing the wind, walked out of the woods, and the black flames on his body became thicker.

The explosion shocked Ye Ye and Tiansheng, who were trembling together, and the two separated immediately. Then they looked at the explosion in shock. But, Tiansheng suddenly smiled. He had just injected energy into Hanba's body. With the energy induction, he knew that Hanba was not dead yet. However, before he could speak, a huge black shadow suddenly flew towards him. He was startled and dodged immediately. After dodging, he looked back and saw that the thing was actually a huge ghost! Although the ghost was wrapped in black flames, Tiansheng saw the ghost and summoned the ghost that day, and immediately distinguished that the ghost was equivalent to the blue ghost in the ghost clan.

Knowing the explosion just now, Tiansheng would naturally not take it hard. Instead, when the ghost rushed up, he grabbed it with both hands with a faint blue light, and then suddenly saw that the black flame on the ghost was gone. But there was no explosion. With a pinch of his hand, the ghost in the soul state immediately disappeared into nothingness and lost the opportunity to reincarnate.

"Hanba, you can't even do such a simple thing? Just suck it, this is a feast!" Tiansheng shook his hands and suddenly shouted. Then, an angry voice suddenly came from the center of the explosion: "You don't need to teach me! I know!" As soon as the voice fell, a red figure rushed towards Huang Shang with dazzling flames.

At this time, Hanba didn't seem to be injured at all, except that the red crystal sword in his hand was slightly smaller. Huang Shang was shocked and threw out a little ghost again, but Hanba's body was sucked, and a red line directly entangled the little ghost. In an instant, the little ghost dissipated, and then a black energy was transmitted to Hanba's body along the red line.

"It tastes good!" Hanba said, and then looked at Huang Shang coldly. Huang Shang shook his head, and a huge black flame appeared on his body, and rushed up. The two flames collided again and wrestled with each other.

But Ye Ye did not rush to attack. Instead, he looked at Tiansheng with a bored look and said, "I really don't know why you have lived for so many years! When you come back, you choose to look for your father who is missing and dying!"

Tiansheng heard the word "father" and his eyebrows were full of anger: "What do you know! My father can't be dead! You will see him if you can live to that time!"

Ye Ye shook his head and said lightly: "Tiansheng, is he really born by heaven? However, I really want to see Xingtian dancing with Ganqi! Tiansheng, born by Xingtian! What a Tiansheng!" Ye Ye said this neither humbly nor arrogantly, and his energy sank into Dantian, and everyone present heard it!

Tiansheng, born by Xingtian! Xingtian's descendant, Tiansheng! A baby who came out of a meteorite, a child who was looking for his heart and father.

"Father, I know you are not dead! But the shame of your defeat and the shame of being dismembered, I will make up for you one by one!" Tiansheng's eyebrows suddenly lost their anger and became very calm.

Tiansheng, there is a misunderstanding in his heart. He thought that his father Xingtian's defeat and dismemberment was a shame! He didn't expect that Xingtian's tenacious spirit of never giving up would be deeply imprinted in the hearts of future generations. The story of "Xingtian dancing with his halberd and halberd, his fierce will is always there" will be passed down through the ages.

Chapter 97 Tiansheng dances with Ganqi

"Since you already know, why pretend so hypocritically? I could have spared your life, but you knew my life story, so today, you have to die! I have to use you first to mourn my father!" Tiansheng said calmly without any anger, as if Ye Ye was already a corpse in his eyes!

Ye Ye said lightly without any surprise: "I don't know, if your father sees you now, will he cry or laugh!" After saying that, Tiansheng frowned, pondered for a long time, then turned his head to look at the collision between Hanba and Huang Shang, and then suddenly said: "It's none of your business, remember to say that I killed you when you go to hell!" Tiansheng's demeanor suddenly became very arrogant, then he stretched out his right hand, frowned again, and grabbed his hand. A small black hole appeared in front of his hand.

Ye Ye was startled, but he felt that the black hole did not have any suction force, and doubts made Ye Ye continue to watch. Suddenly, a stick-like object slowly emerged from the black hole. When the object appeared, Tiansheng smiled immediately, then grabbed it with his left hand, and exerted force, as if pulling the object out of the black hole.

However, the black hole seemed to tightly absorb the object, Tiansheng was helpless, and the dark blue energy burst out of his body. He roared "ah", and a huge object was pulled out by him, and then he immediately waved his hand to disperse the black hole, and gasped with a pale face.

Ye Ye then looked at the object pulled out by Tiansheng, how could it be a stick? It was clearly a huge axe and a huge shield.

"Ganqi...Xingtian dances Ganqi! Could it be the legendary Ganqi?" Ye Ye was shocked, and suddenly thought of Xingtian's weapon "Ganqi"!

Tiansheng was still pale, and then he suddenly raised his axe and shield. The size of the Ganqi was not a match for Tiansheng, but Tiansheng actually looked like he had no strength at all: "Die!" Tiansheng grabbed the Ganqi and the shield, exerted force on his feet, and immediately came to Ye Ye.

The axe arrived before the man. Ganqi was originally the weapon used by Xingtian. Xingtian's body was comparable to a giant, so this pair of weapons was naturally huge. Ye Ye was shocked, and saw the axe with runes coming with a sound of breaking through the air. He was shocked and did not dare to confront it head-on. He fell on the ground and rolled to avoid Tiansheng's huge axe. However, Tiansheng would not let Ye Ye go so easily.

After seeing Ye Ye dodge, Tiansheng's arm exerted force violently, and he actually stopped the huge axe horizontally, and then the huge axe face slammed towards the ground. This Ganqi and the axe of the giant axe were extremely special. At this moment, they were bent down instead of breaking. And Tiansheng's blood vessels burst. Obviously, although Tiansheng could control the Gan Qi like an arm, the change from the horizontal chop to the vertical slap that stopped the Qi Axe just now was quite strenuous for him.

However, since he had forcibly changed the chop to the slap, he was facing Ye Ye. At this moment, Ye Ye could no longer avoid the slap of the huge axe. Seeing the axe that was about to hit him and shatter him, Ye Ye made up his mind and simply opened up the power of Nuwa, then disassembled Ye Yang in his hand into a small shield and blocked it in front of him with both hands.

Just after doing all this, the huge axe arrived. With a sound of metal collision, the huge axe completely covered Ye Ye, and he could not see the situation below. And Tiansheng's attack was not over yet. Tiansheng suddenly roared again, and then pressed the Qi Axe down with force, and then a huge blue light appeared on his body, and began to slowly spread along the axe stick. Where the blue light passed, the runes on the Qi Axe lit up one after another, and then shone brightly. In an instant, a huge axe emitting a blue light appeared.

"Fire!" Tiansheng muttered, and then the Qi Axe ignited a blue flame, the flame on the axe face was the most intense, and the surrounding land was burned and cracked in an instant. 'Ice' Tiansheng muttered again, and the flame was immediately frozen, and snow-white crystals appeared around the Qi Axe, and the moisture in the air was frozen in an instant.

Ice and fire, how could Ye Ye, who was suppressed by the Qi Axe, feel good. Tiansheng thought, and then raised the Qi Axe. However, his brows suddenly frowned, because there was nothing under the negative side, and Ye Ye had disappeared. A hole appeared on the frozen and cracked land.

Tiansheng immediately became alert, how could such an opponent not make him alert. Tiansheng looked at the surrounding land and listened attentively, but the collision between Hanba and Huang Shang not far away hindered Tiansheng's hearing.

Suddenly, just as Hanba and Huang Shang collided again and made a loud noise, the land behind Tiansheng suddenly sank, and a pair of hands suddenly stretched out, grabbed

Tiansheng's feet and pulled him in. Tiansheng was startled and immediately raised the dark blue light.

The hole was too small, and the huge Ganqi could not enter, so it was stuck there. However, the sunken hole suddenly burst into an extremely dazzling colorful light, and Tiansheng flew out with a dark blue light. The huge pair of weapons in his hands fell to the ground. Then Ye Ye jumped out of the land dazzlingly, and the night sun in his hand formed a two-hooked iron claw. It must be that thing that broke the land. Looking at Ye Ye again, Ye Ye was pale at this moment, his clothes seemed to be burned by fire, and his hair was curled up.

Tiansheng, however, trembled and supported himself at this moment, with several deep scratches on his arms, and several strands of black scattered along the blood vessels at the wound. It was obviously scratched by the iron claw in Ye Ye's hand, and the black was the poison of the Phoenix Thorn.

In just a few breaths, Ye Ye and Tiansheng were under the ground, and they actually injured each other.

With a smile, Tiansheng covered the scratched place with his left hand and said: "When did the dignified head of the Ye Sect and the inheritor of the power of Nuwa become a dog? Haha..." Tiansheng laughed, and then secretly stimulated some blue energy in his left hand, and healed his wounds.

Ye Ye also smiled and said helplessly: "Didn't you become a dog?" After saying this, Ye Ye unconcealedly stimulated the seven-color power of Nuwa, and then the burn marks on his body slowly faded, and his hair regained its luster! (Is your hair dry? Try the new generation of Nuwa's power!) Then, Ye Yang in his hand immediately disassembled into a dagger and rushed towards Tiansheng.

Ye Ye knew that Tiansheng could not move at this moment, because Ye Ye would apply a layer of Phoenix Thorn poison on Ye

Yang whenever he had something to do. This Ye Yang is actually the most poisonous Phoenix Thorn! Ye Ye quickly approached Tiansheng, the Ye Yang in his hand emitting a cold light, but Tiansheng's eyes shrank into needles and he looked at Ye Ye coldly.

Chapter 98 Battle

Tiansheng looked at Ye Ye approaching slowly, and suddenly pretended to be afraid, and sat on the ground and slowly retreated. As he retreated, the blue light on his left hand, which was covering the wound on his right arm, was faintly visible, but it was cleverly blocked when Tiansheng moved.

Ye Ye looked at Tiansheng, shook his head, picked up Ye Yang, disassembled Ye Yang into a dagger, then sank his legs and exerted force, and suddenly shot out, piercing Tiansheng's heart.

But Tiansheng suddenly released his left hand when Ye Ye approached, and then his left hand immediately condensed into a real blue flame and waved it towards Ye Ye. Ye Ye frowned, and then used the dagger attached with the power of Nuwa to disperse it. However, he didn't expect that there was a black water behind the flame. Ye Ye was shocked, not knowing what it was, and didn't dare to attack again rashly, so he immediately withdrew.

But when he retreated like this, Tiansheng rushed up suddenly. Qi Fu danced vigorously and went towards Ye Ye who was retreating. Ye Ye stopped immediately. He knew that such a huge axe could not cause any substantial damage to him at such a close distance. Without hesitation, he raised the dagger again.

But he didn't think about it. Tiansheng threw the axe into the air while swinging it, and then raised the huge shield with both hands and smashed it towards Ye Ye. And Ye Ye had no time to withdraw. In a flash, Ye Ye suddenly turned around and left his back to Tiansheng, and then the power of Nuwa was superimposed on his back. He wanted to resist Tiansheng's shield attack with his back.

However, Tiansheng smiled disdainfully, and then immediately condensed a dark blue flame, which was attached to the dry shield in an instant. The dry shield attached with the dark blue flame, the inscription on it immediately glowed, and smashed towards Ye Ye with extremely strong force.

With a loud bang, Ye Ye was actually smashed away. Tiansheng also withdrew his offensive, stood in place, and looked coldly at Ye Ye who was knocked away. There was no rash attack.

But Ye Ye sat on the ground trembling. He was very surprised. Just now, he clearly felt that the huge shield touched the power of Nuwa on his back, and a severe dizziness was transmitted. He couldn't concentrate on gathering the power of Nuwa, so he was slapped out. Moreover, his ankle seemed to be firmly grasped by a hand, making him unable to dodge.

He unzipped his trouser legs and looked at them. There were two bruises on his ankles. He raised his head and looked at Tiansheng coldly. Tiansheng stuck the shield on the ground at this moment, Qi Fu held it on his shoulders and looked at Ye Ye and said to himself: "Who said that the shield can only be used for defense?" After that, he slowly walked towards Ye Ye, then stopped ten meters away and said: "Just now, that was just a secret that Gan Qi couldn't tell anyone. You have experienced four types. Next, I will let you experience them one by one!" Ye Ye was shocked after hearing this. He buried his head in thought, and after a breath, he asked: "Is the black water also the secret of Gan Qi?" Tiansheng was not surprised that Tiansheng, who could summon the black hole, could detoxify.

Tiansheng smiled: "Of course not, that was the poison you injected into my body just now!" Ye Ye frowned and breathed a sigh of relief. Fortunately, he did not attack rashly just now, otherwise he would be unable to move at this moment and be slaughtered by others! Thinking of this, he looked at the small wounds all over his body. Those were the wounds caused by the stones that popped out when Qi Axe hit the ground. If the poisonous blood containing the poison of the Phoenix Thorn was spilled just now, then the poisonous blood would enter along the wounds and slowly spread to the whole body. Then, Ye Ye is also worthy of being slaughtered by everyone.

Tiansheng suddenly put down Qi Axe, then sat cross-legged on the ground, and then closed his eyes. The dark blue flame outside his body was immediately retracted, but a heavy heartbeat came from his body, and every time the heartbeat beat, a dark blue wave came out of his body.

Ye Ye looked at Tiansheng and immediately closed his eyes to absorb the energy. The whole person immediately turned into a crystal statue.

At this moment, for the two of them, whoever can recover to the best before the other will hold the flag of victory!

Compared with Tiansheng and Ye Ye who have temporarily calmed down and recovered their energy. The battle between Huang Shang and Hanba is still fierce. The woods, plains, and grasslands have all become their battlefields. Whenever they change battlefields, all that is left is the messy, burnt and dry land.

Huang Shang and Hanba are definitely not feeling well at this moment. The flames outside their bodies have waned a lot, but the burning feeling is still intense. And every time they collide, red crystals or black scales will always burst out in the air. Despite this, they continue to collide, then separate, and then collide again...

The two separate again, and then breathe heavily. Look at the two again at this time. The scales on Huang Shang's body have almost fallen off, some places are flowing with bright red blood, and some places can even see burnt flesh. The tumor on the tail whip had already broken, leaving a long tail to swing back and forth. The body of Hanba, which was originally crystal clear, was now like the surface of the moon hit by a meteorite, with pits and bumps. The red crystal long sword in his hand could no longer be called a sword, but should be called a sawtooth.

Huang Shang suddenly roared fiercely and rushed forward again. The black flame on his body was forcibly huge, and the tail whip was swung out fiercely, but he did not want to use the tail whip to whip and produce a boring attack. It actually entangled Hanba, and then a little ghost immediately condensed in his hand. The tail whip pulled hard again and approached quickly. Hanba was startled and immediately raised a red flame to dissipate the little ghost.

However, Hanba's move, which was originally a defensive move, coincidentally became a catalyst. The energy of the two collided with each other, and the little ghost also lost Huang Shang's control in the energy. The little ghost was a bomb, but it suddenly exploded at this moment, and the explosion also caused the unstable energy when Hanba and Huang Shang collided, and the explosion became more violent. A fierce gale blew the two out.

The two immediately stood up trembling, and their already seriously injured bodies became more serious. However, the fighting spirit in their eyes was still strong. Huang Shang, to avenge his wife who was hurt by Hanba, while Hanba was for the dignity provoked by Huang Shang.

Roaring again, Hanba rushed up again. As he ran, the red crystals on his body kept falling into pieces, and the red flames on his body suddenly extinguished. The black flames on Huang Shang's body also extinguished, and his body was constantly flowing.

The two collided again. This time, it was a pure wrestling of strength. , There is no flame, no energy.

Teeth, fists, feet, heads, all became weapons for the two. They are like two bloodthirsty beasts, and they will die if they don't fight!

Chapter 99 The Destruction of Dignity

Qin Ming woke up tiredly, tremblingly supported his body, then frowned in pain, looked at Li Bin who was still sleeping beside him, and then temporarily felt relieved. But suddenly. A violent explosion woke him up from his peace of mind. Looking in the direction of the sound, he only saw a large number of trees being uprooted. Without hesitation, he immediately pressed on Li Bin, and then stuck to the ground. His scalp could clearly feel the huge trees flying over his head.

After a long time, the explosion subsided. He thought about it calmly, then stood up weakly, carried Li Bin on his back, and walked towards the direction of the explosion. He was already close to his limit, but at this moment he had to add Li Bin's body weight. His steps were slower than a snail. However, the sound of giants colliding kept stimulating him, and his memory was still stuck at the moment when Tiansheng appeared just now.

Ye Ye did not put Qin Minglei and Tiansheng far away. Qin Minglei quickly walked out of the messy forest with Li Bin on his back. Then, the scene in front of him suddenly shocked him. He let go of his hand, and Li Bin also fell to the ground. He saw that Ye Ye and Tiansheng's bodies were shining, sitting quietly on the ground; and a monster that looked like a ghost queen with black flames all over his body was fighting with Hanba. Around them, it was already a mess. I guess the explosion just now must have been caused by the two of them. And what surprised Qin Minglei the most was Hanba and the monster fighting with him. They were already covered with wounds at this moment. But after each collision, he still stood up, and then rushed forward, using his teeth, fists, and even the hard frontal bone of his head to collide. Every time they collided, a violent sound sounded, and every collision would have red crystals or black flesh and blood scattered. However, they were like dying beasts who knew no fatigue or pain, and fighting might have a glimmer of hope.

Qin Minglei was shocked. He was already very weak due to the energy being sucked away, but he actually took two steps back under the force and might of the collision. He looked ahead with his eyes wide open.

Suddenly, the black monster spoke in human language: "Hanba, today it's either you or I who will die." It was Huang Shang. Qin Minglei and Huang Shang stayed together for quite a while. He immediately recognized that the voice was Huang Shang's. He was shocked and looked at Huang Shang calmly again. However, Huang Shang's body slowly emitted extremely hot black flames, the temperature gradually increased, and the might gradually increased. Qin Minglei was already very weak and could no longer resist. His eyes rolled back and he fainted.

At this moment, Huang Shang had no intention of managing other things. He was concentrating the energy in his body on his own. The black flames became more and more vigorous and the temperature became higher and higher. Not only that, Hanba opposite him also began to condense the energy of his body. Red light ignited from his body, and Hong Jing's body became very transparent. In the center of his body, there was an extremely dazzling fire, which spread from his crystal-like body, and the whole person was as dazzling as the sun.

After fighting to such an extent, the two of them knew that extra collisions were useless, so they simply forced out their remaining vitality and turned it into flames on their bodies, preparing to launch the final attack.

After a long time, the two flames, one black and one red, suddenly stopped expanding. The surrounding air had been distorted, and the stubborn stones on the ground had even cracked. However, Ye Ye and Tiansheng were still normal, and the temperature and power were blocked outside the energy. The two continued to recover without knowing it.

The others had already fainted and were far away, so they didn't feel that strong, but despite this, their bodies had already shed dense sweat. Then it evaporated instantly and turned into salt crystals.

At this time, Huang Shang and Hanba moved at the same time. The two of them actually gathered all the flames into their hands in a similar way, then hugged the dangerous bomb tightly with both hands and rushed towards each other.

The whole world suddenly turned into a world of red and black. Then, the two colors, at the moment of contact, immediately turned into dazzling light. Instantly, the whole world was blind!

There was no explosion, no energy dissipation fluctuations, and even no sound. The only thing was the extremely dazzling light that made people unable to see clearly!

In the light, Ye Ye and Tiansheng frowned at the same time, but did not open their eyes. The energy outside their bodies suddenly condensed into an eggshell and wrapped themselves in it.

The light gradually dimmed, and then a gust of extremely violent wind blew out. After the light dimmed, you can even see the wind group in the center, which has even cut through the air, showing a shocking distortion! . Fortunately, the wind did not spread and disappeared in just one or two breaths. The whole world was quiet again. Only the light on Tiansheng and Ye Ye kept changing.

Look at the place where Huang Shang and Hanba collided with each other. There was a huge pit, and the surface of the pit was very smooth, as if it was cut quickly by a ritual vessel. However, Huang Shang and Hanba were nowhere to be found.

Suddenly, a hand stretched out from the soft soil at the bottom of the pit. It was an ordinary person's hand, with yellow skin and a few hairs. How could anyone survive the violent collision and the extremely terrifying gale?

Slowly, the hand was placed on the ground, and the muscles on the hand bulged slightly, as if the person was exerting force, and then a head slowly appeared. It was Huang Shang. It was Huang Shang who survived! After a long time, Huang Shang came out of the mud and fell to the ground. He looked around coldly, and when he was sure that Hanba's breath was gone, he closed his eyes with peace of mind and fainted.

Huang Shang was covered with wounds at this moment. Countless blood beads flowed out from the countless tiny wounds, and then replaced the blood that was just attached to the soil. The whole person instantly became a bloody man. And, in his palm, a black crystal suddenly fell from the place where his palm was embedded, and then broke into crystal powder.

The battle between Huang Shang and Hanba finally ended. Hanba's dignity as a corpse king was also destroyed.

But, is it really that easy? In the deep soil that no one knew, suddenly a small flame burned the surrounding soil into nothingness, and the flame slowly condensed into a human shape in that small space, and in the flame, seven strands of dark blue energy suddenly occupied the flame, and the condensation speed of the flame suddenly increased again, and then condensed into a human shape more quickly!

And, no one on the ground knew all this. Only Tiansheng's mouth corners slightly raised.

Chapter 100 The Passing of Life

With a smile, the blue light on Tiansheng's body slowly faded away. He stretched himself and looked at Ye Ye, who was still radiating the colorful power of Nuwa. He shook his head, picked up the Gan Qi on the ground, and the blue flame ignited.

Tiansheng recovered his strength one step earlier than Ye Ye! Qi Axe suddenly came towards Ye Ye with a sound of breaking through the air. Tiansheng didn't even use the blue flame to attach Gan Qi, but just waved the giant axe towards Ye Ye. But Ye Ye still closed his eyes and was still recovering. However, the Qi Axe was almost there. If it hit Ye Ye like this, without any defense, Ye Ye would die! Tiansheng's mouth suddenly showed a touch of cruelty, and his eyes looked at Ye Ye, who closed his eyes and had no perception of the outside world.

Qi Axe was about to hit Ye Ye. However, a figure suddenly rushed over and blocked the attack of the giant axe with his body. The black shadow was immediately smashed away by the giant axe, and two drops of blood dripped from the corners of his mouth and fell on Ye Ye's cheek. Ye Ye suddenly opened his eyes and touched the warm blood on his cheek. Confused, he looked at Tiansheng's vigorous blue flame and Ganqi shield axe, and suddenly turned around to look behind him. The black shadow who had just blocked his attack was lying on the ground, and his life or death was unknown. Ye Ye was immediately shocked and immediately ran to the black shadow, then picked him up and said, "Silly, why didn't you leave just now?" That person was Li Yerui, who was present and watched all the battles, and just now, she sacrificed herself to block Tiansheng's fatal blow to Ye Ye.

Li Yerui coughed twice, spat out some blood with internal organs, and said weakly: "Brother Ye Ye, I finally saved you! In fact... I have recovered a long time ago... It's just... I just want to see you every day... See you worry about me... and... Tell me your worries... My life belongs to Brother Ye Ye, otherwise... I would have destroyed myself long ago. I... also belong to Brother Ye Ye..." After saying that, Li Yerui's cheeks were strangely red.

Ye Ye nodded, holding Li Yerui's hand tightly, tears, one drop... two drops... dripped into the dry and cracked land, and then quickly spread and disappeared.

"Brother Ye Ye... Where are you? I... I... Why can't I see... you?" Li Yerui suddenly frowned weakly and stretched out his hand, touching randomly. Ye Ye knew that this was a sign of the disappearance of the six senses before death. He immediately grabbed Li Yerui's hand, put it on his cheek and said, "I'm here, don't be afraid, I'll always be here!"

Li Yerui felt Ye Ye and suddenly smiled. He touched Ye Ye's cheek and said, "Brother Ye Ye...you...why are you crying?" Ye Ye forced a smile and said, "No, how could it be!" Li Yerui smiled again, then spit out a mouthful of blood and said more weakly, "Brother Ye Ye...I like you...you...you...do you like me?"

Ye Ye was stunned and didn't answer. But Tiansheng on the side couldn't bear it anymore, and shouted loudly, "Are you close enough? Wait, I'll send you two downstairs to love each other."

Ye Ye ignored Tiansheng, but held Li Yerui's hand more tightly. Scenes of memories appeared in his mind, from the red clothes to the bloody night massacre to save Ye Rui, and then to Li Yerui's coma. Every time he came back, he would accompany her...do he really like her? Then what about the other her...Ye Ye's mind was confused, and he didn't know how to answer for a while.

"Okay, enough of the show. I still have things to do!" Tiansheng said lightly while looking at the pit after the battle between Huang Shang and Hanba. After that, the Qi Axe in his hand was immediately attached with dark blue flames, and then he came towards Ye Ye with the will of destruction. Before the axe arrived, the mysterious power of Gan Qi mentioned by Tiansheng arrived first. Suddenly, two black hands stretched out from the ground and tightly clamped Ye Ye's ankles, making him unable to move. Then the Qi Axe was lifted up by Tiansheng with the dark blue dazzling flames, and he also stood in the best attack position of the giant axe, and the Qi Axe slowly fell down.

"Ye Ye...Brother." Li Yerui suddenly called out weakly. Ye Ye woke up from his memory and confusion, and ignored the claws on his ankles and the naturally raised Qi Fu and said, "What's wrong?"

Li Yerui suddenly smiled very sweetly. Even though the bloody blood had already stained her cheeks, she said gently and weakly: "Brother Ye Ye...Don't answer! I don't want to know the answer in this life, so don't tell me, so that I will have a reason to find you in the next life. Remember that you must be happy and wait for me!" Li Yerui suddenly finished the whole sentence in one breath, and his body leaned forward excitedly, and then his hand tightly grasped Ye Ye's hand. In the end, he suddenly wilted, and his hands lost their grip and fell down. Ye Ye was startled and immediately hugged him tightly in his arms.

Ye Ye suddenly raised his head, his eyes filled with tears. For the second time, he clearly felt the departure of something—life! The first time was the death of Master Lao Wu, and this time it was because of the death of Li Yerui.

In extreme sadness, Ye Ye suddenly felt a fierce energy in his mind that opened a barrier, and countless memories came flooding in at this moment. His mouth opened slightly, his eyes suddenly became dull, but they shrank from time to time. Ye Ye was shocked by the memory, completely shocked.

And Tiansheng, with the Qi Axe held high, also chopped towards Ye Ye fiercely at this moment. The dark blue flame was fluctuating, and a layer of frost was faintly visible. But Ye Ye was still stunned in surprise.

Tiansheng looked at Ye Ye's appearance and smiled. The force on the Qi Axe suddenly became heavier, and the axe stick was even bent, which showed the force used by Tiansheng.

A "clang" sound, like the sound of a metal giant colliding, suddenly sounded when the Qi Axe touched Ye Ye. The colorful light and the dark blue flame kept colliding and disappeared. And on Ye Ye's chest, a fist-sized stone suddenly appeared.

Tiansheng was startled and immediately attached the dark blue flame more intensely. The dark blue flame on Qi Axe became more vigorous, carrying not only frost, but also thunder and strong winds...

However, Ye Ye was still immersed in that memory and still had no idea about the outside world. The stone on his chest suddenly became brighter, and the power of Nuwa that resisted Qi Axe became stronger and stronger. Tiansheng was also shocked at this moment, but he still looked at Ye Ye, who was stunned and dazed, calmly. With a determined heart, the dark blue flame on his body suddenly rose higher and fired at full power.

Ye Ye still didn't know that Tiansheng was firing at full power. And the stone became brighter, always able to stimulate the power of Nuwa that Tiansheng's energy wanted to counter, and resisted Tiansheng's attack.

After a long time, Tiansheng gave up the attack helplessly and retracted the dark blue flame. He looked at Ye Ye with anger, then gritted his teeth, sat down, and slowly recovered the energy he had just consumed. He didn't know what was wrong with Ye Ye, but Tiansheng recognized the shining stone on Ye Ye's chest. That thing was Nuwa Stone! Originally, he had recovered before Ye Ye and was able to kill Ye Ye completely, but he didn't expect an accident to happen in the middle. The woman named Li Yerui came out to block the attack. Although the obstructionist was dead, Tiansheng still couldn't let go of the cruelty in his heart. He gritted his teeth and said fiercely: "Sooner or later, you will all die!" After that, he looked coldly at Ye Ye who was stunned.

After a long time, Ye Ye's eyes slowly recovered. He shook his head gently, then looked at the Nuwa stone on his chest that was still shining, and gently covered it with his hand, and the light disappeared immediately. Then, he ignored Tiansheng who was sitting beside him, but picked up Li Yerui, walked to a safe place, gently put her on the ground, and then whispered: "Be good, wait until Brother Ye Ye finishes his work, I will take you home!" Ye Ye's voice was very gentle, just like the voice of Ye Ye when Li Yerui pretended to be unconscious. However, that was what Li Yerui could hear, now...

He sighed, shook his head, walked to a place more than ten meters away from Tiansheng and said lightly: "Do you want revenge? Come on!" After that, he stood with his hands behind his back, without any trace of energy use. Tiansheng stood up and looked at Ye Ye's actions in confusion. He felt uneasy. He didn't know whether he should attack. At this moment, Ye Ye had no defense at all. One strike... just one strike could kill him... But what if it was a trap?

Tiansheng was wavering in his heart. Ye Ye smiled: "What? Come on. Step over me, and you can start bloody revenge on the whole world. Xingtian's head, what I said... right?" With a shocking statement, Ye Ye actually said that Tiansheng was Xingtian's head, not Xingtian's son.

If it was really as Ye Ye said, then Tiansheng's resentment could be easily explained. Xingtian fought with the emperor, his head was cut off, and he was buried in Changyang Mountain. He did not experience the next battle with the rest of his body. Misunderstandings are inevitable.

Tiansheng's body trembled violently after hearing Ye Ye's words, and then he laughed like crazy: "Hahaha, why are your IQs so low? I said, I am the son of Xing Tian!" Ye Ye shook his head and ignored Tiansheng's madness and continued to say lightly: "If you were the son of Xing Tian, then you wouldn't hate the world so much! Jingwei carried a small piece of wood to fill the sea. Xing Tian danced with Ganqi, and his fierce ambition was always there. Since there is no similarity between the same things, there is no regret for disappearing. It is just in the heart of the past, how can the good time be expected. This is the spirit of Xing Tian who continued to fight despite his failure, which was recognized and praised by later generations. You, although you can use Ganqi, you can't bring out the full power of Ganqi. Ganqi, an axe and a shield, symbolizes: 'Never compromise!'" Ye Ye said lightly, the syllables were slowly raised, and in the end he became very excited.

But Tiansheng took Ganqi and watched it. He knew very well that he really couldn't fully control Ganqi. After a moment of hesitation, Tiansheng's face became crazy and he said, "Nonsense. I, Tiansheng, am Xingtian's son and descendant! Ganqi, I can also fully exert my power!" After that, he waved the Qi axe and came towards Tiansheng again. He really didn't know that Ye Ye seemed to have become a different person in an instant. Even when facing the tremendous power he exerted, he was very calm. He began to be afraid in his heart, but he did not retract the power in his hand at all, and chopped towards Ye Ye without regret.

Chapter 101 Black Hole

Ye Ye looked at Tiansheng who was rushing towards him furiously and frantically. He shook his head, a trace of pity appeared in his eyes, he sighed helplessly, then shook his hand slightly, Ye Yang switched to his left hand, and then kept combining his hands, finally, Ye Yang combined into a long sword, gently holding it in his hand, when Tiansheng's axe chopped down, he suddenly took two steps forward, then raised his right hand holding the sword very calmly, unexpectedly so calmly resisted Tiansheng's mighty vertical slash.

Tiansheng was startled, his eyes slightly glanced at the position where Ye Ye was standing just now, the pair of claws that had clamped Ye Ye's ankles were now limp on the ground, and then slowly dissipated. With surprise, he thought in his heart: So quickly, he found a way to crack it?

Seeing Tiansheng's surprised look, Ye Ye smiled, and after blocking the Qi Axe with force, he said lightly: "Sure enough, you can only use the function of the inscription on the axe, not the entire Qi Axe!" Tiansheng raised his eyebrows, was stunned for a moment, and then immediately changed to disdain: "So what? I have only gained my own power for a short time, so naturally I can't use it all. I will definitely be able to use it all in time."

Ye Ye didn't seem to listen to Tiansheng's words, but suddenly changed the subject: "By the way. That heart must be the heart of Xingtian, right? I really don't understand why the heart is divided into two halves and appears in two babies?"

"Hahahaha, father's wisdom, how can you mortals understand it?" After saying that, Tiansheng swung the axe and forced Ye Ye back. It seems that he is still quite afraid of Ye Ye now. Ye Ye smiled and said nothing, stepped back a few meters and stared at Tiansheng. Tiansheng smiled: "Haha, since you already understand, I will tell you, so that you don't have doubts when you die, and you will be a ghost!" Ye Ye shrugged his shoulders and said nothing.

"In fact, the heart was not placed in the two babies by anyone. Rather, it was already there in the heavens. I was just able to sense it, or I became a catalyst. You must know their parents, right? A ghost, a corpse king; then a half corpse king and a love Gu. With such a combination, the probability of producing a child is definitely higher, and when they were born, they all had strange visions, a faint blue light! That was not because they were gifted, but to remind Xingtian's descendants that the heart appeared!" After saying this, Ye Ye immediately nodded and pondered.

Indeed, when Huang Chen was born, the faint blue vision did appear; but no one could see Qin Feng, so there must be something strange about it. However, since Tiansheng said so, Ye Ye immediately understood, and then said lightly: "So that's it, but why don't you look for Xing Tian's body, but look for Xing Tian's heart instead?"

After hearing this, Tiansheng suddenly waved the Qi Axe, exuding a fierce momentum, and a meaningful smile hung on his face: "Hmph, this... you don't need to know! You just need to know that you are dying!" After that, the Qi Axe ignited the dark blue flame again, and Tiansheng also sank his feet, exerted force violently, and shot towards Ye Ye at a high speed.

Ye Ye frowned and dodged immediately, and did not fight with the Qi Axe head-on, but attacked in the gap when the Qi Axe was dancing, either swinging the axe stick to block the attack, or cutting along the axe stick, forcing Tiansheng to retreat or defend with a shield.

For a while, Ye Ye still fought very calmly, but Tiansheng became more and more shocked, because he felt that all his attacks were either dodged or counterattacked, and after such a long battle, the energy consumption was also very huge. Gradually, Tiansheng stopped his aggressive attacks and used shield and axe together, using shield strikes for close range and Qi axe for far range, so that Ye Ye could not get close. It also saved a lot of energy.

However, Ye Ye suddenly withdrew from the battle circle at this moment, looked at Tiansheng coldly, and his gentle smile turned into a cold and fierce killing intent: "Don't waste your energy, I'll give you two ways. One, go back to where you came from. Two, die!"

Ye Ye's cold and fierce killing intent made Tiansheng feel cold all over. He really didn't know why, just for a moment, Ye Ye became so powerful. However, he still refused to admit defeat, and the energy in his body burst out, and the whole person became a blue streamline, hitting Ye Ye.

Who knew that Ye Ye actually put Ye Yang away, and then stretched out his right hand, and layers of Nuwa's power slowly condensed. Tiansheng was in the stream of light, and his speed was extremely fast. Looking at Ye Ye's movements, Tiansheng couldn't help but laugh, because he still used the same trick this time, using Qi axe attack as bait, and then a thunderous shield strike!

However, Tiansheng miscalculated! When the Qi Axe in his right hand chopped out and touched the power of Nuwa, a suction force suddenly came from the power of Nuwa, sucking him towards Ye Ye. Tiansheng was not surprised but happy to see this, and the dry shield inscription on his left hand lit up. But suddenly, a repulsive force stopped his movement.

Surprise hung on his face in an instant. Ye Ye smiled at this time, and his eyes suddenly turned red, bloodthirsty and fanaticism revealed in his eyes. Tiansheng was sweating all over his back, terrified in his heart, and forgot to defend himself. Suddenly, the bloodthirstiness and fanaticism in Ye Ye's eyes disappeared, and then a Yeyang long sword in his hand stabbed out, aiming at Tiansheng's heart.

"It's over." Tiansheng suddenly had this thought in his mind. Unexpectedly, when the long sword in Ye Ye's hand was about to stab Tiansheng's heart, which he had no time to defend, he suddenly turned his head and hit the heart area hard with the hilt of the sword, and the force also knocked Tiansheng out.

"I won't kill you because Xing Tian is worthy of respect!" Ye Ye said, turned around and stood with his sword on his back, no longer paying attention to Tiansheng who looked terrified.

One strike, just one strike, and Tiansheng was defeated. What happened to Ye Ye?

Ye Ye's words entered Tiansheng's ears, and Tiansheng, who was narrow-minded, naturally understood it as an insult. He collapsed on the ground in fear, and suddenly his fear flashed away, and then slowly turned into madness again.

Holding his head, bending over, Gan Qi fell to the ground casually, his eyes began to turn red, and then he roared fiercely: "Die, die, you all have to die!" After that, he suddenly ignited a dark blue flame on his body again, and when the dark blue flame reached its peak, it suddenly turned black, and then a dangerous breath came from the sky.

"Hahahaha... Die, die, you all have to die! Who said that my father would blame me? My father will also take revenge on the whole world." Tiansheng was still complaining at this point, and the resentment accumulated to a certain extent. Tiansheng ignored his own life and used the life-saving skill: black hole.

As soon as the black hole appeared a little, the sky was suddenly filled with evil spirits, and the leader was the human-shaped evil spirit that had been following Tiansheng!

"What are they going to do?" Ye Ye suddenly became alert, and the power of Nuwa poured out again. He felt the danger coming.

Chapter 102 Resentment

The sense of danger gradually became stronger. Tiansheng's expression became more and more crazy, and even his body had turned into a ball of dark blue flames, and it was impossible to see clearly what was going on inside. At the same time, under the deep soil of the pit where Huang Shang and Hanba fought, seven rays of light appeared, reflecting the dark blue flames of Tiansheng.

Then, suddenly, the seven rays of light broke through the soil and flew towards the black hole. The seven rays of light were so bright that Ye Ye could not see clearly what they were, but Tiansheng suddenly said crazily: "World, destroy it!" After that, he was slowly sucked up by the suction from the black hole.

Tiansheng was sucked in. Ye Ye looked at the black hole in the air nervously. Suddenly, the suction disappeared and everything became calm. Ye Ye knew that this must be a sign before the storm. Because the black hole was spreading slowly.

"Could it be that the world will be destroyed as he said?" Ye Ye looked at the slowly spreading black hole in the sky, with a worry in his eyes. It must be that it was not something he could solve. After thinking for a while, he shook his head, opened the treasure bag, and then took out a bamboo tube, pulled open the tail, and a sharp scream suddenly sounded, and then a ball of fire flew into the sky and exploded violently. That was the signal fireworks of Yemen.

Soon after, all the inner disciples of Yemen arrived here, and then Ye Ye ordered them to take the unconscious people back to Yemen, but he stayed in the dilapidated wooden house. He still had one thing to do...

He asked the disciples of Yemen to take Huang Shang and even Murong Di back to Yemen, but only left the dead Li Yerui!

After watching all the Yemen disciples leave, he gently picked up Li Yerui, then walked to the wooden house, gently put her down, and said, "Sister Yerui, I'm sorry. I'm telling you my answer now, and my answer is: you will always be my sister! I love my sister the most!" After that, he put Yeyang away, then knelt down and pressed the ground with his hands. He actually wanted to make a grave for Li Yerui with his hands!

At this time, Ye Ye didn't see that behind him, a black-clad figure leaned against a giant tree, tears kept falling. It was Xia Feng. In fact, she had already woken up when the black hole just appeared, and then immediately hid here. Seeing Ye Ye like this, she actually felt a kind of pain of exhaustion.

After a long time, Xia Feng wiped her tears, then slowly walked to Ye Ye and said, "Let's do it together!" After that, she wanted to squat down and dig the soil, but Ye Ye stopped her and said, "No need. Let me do it myself." Xia Feng was stunned, then smiled gently, turned around and walked into the wooden house. When she came out, she held a beautiful mirror box, a basin of water, and a handkerchief in her hand. Then she walked to Xia Feng, squatted down, wet the handkerchief, and slowly and gently wiped the blood on Li Yerui's face. After wiping, she looked at Ye Ye, and a trace of sadness appeared in her eyes, which disappeared immediately. Her eyes became firm, and she gently touched Li Yerui's face, and finally opened the mirror box. It was actually filled with women's cosmetics.

Ye Ye looked back at Xia Feng, and the sadness in his eyes became more intense. He turned his head and continued to dig with his hands. Both hands were already bloody, and even every handful of soil he grabbed was accompanied by a little blood. However, Ye Ye seemed to be unaware of the pain, and kept digging with a cold face.

After a long time, Ye Ye finally dug a hole that could hold Li Yerui. Just as he was about to pick up Li Yerui, he heard Xia Feng say coldly: "Do you want to bury sister Yerui like this?" Ye Ye looked at Xia Feng in doubt. Xia Feng stood up again, walked into the wooden house, took out a black but gorgeous dress, which must be her clothes, and said lightly: "Should I avoid it?"

Ye Ye immediately understood, then turned and walked to the pool, gently washed the wound on his hand, and did not look back at Xia Feng changing clothes for Li Yerui. After washing, he looked at the black hole that was spreading in the sky. I don't know when a circle of evil spirits surrounded the black hole. But they were very quiet, just surrounding the black hole. Ye Ye lowered his head and slowly walked towards Li Yerui.

Xia Feng had finished putting on the clothes. Ye Ye gently picked up Li Yerui and gently put him into the hole. A handful of soil gently covered it, and soon, Li Yerui's beautiful face was covered.

Li Yerui, dead. He saved Ye Ye's life at a critical moment, and died.

Ye Ye and Xia Feng covered the soil at the same time, and soon Li Yerui was completely covered. Ye Ye finally walked to a dead tree, folded Ye Yang into a sword, cut the dead tree into a square, and then carved a few words: Tomb of beloved sister Li Yerui.

In the end, Ye Ye could not admit Li Yerui's love.

After doing all this, Ye Ye said lightly: "Let's go." "Where to?" Xia Feng asked. "Wait." After saying that, he looked at the black hole in the sky surrounded by a group of evil spirits, then sighed and walked towards the direction of Yemen.

Ye Ye and Xia Feng did not notice that the evil spirits surrounded by the black hole were actually sucked into the black hole little by little. In the black hole, a trace of evil and bloodthirsty red light slowly appeared. But it flashed by. Even though the black hole had attracted worldwide attention, no one noticed the flash of red light.

Three days later, the black hole suddenly stopped expanding. And all the evil spirits around it suddenly disappeared!

And Ye Ye had temporarily disbanded the Yemen. After all, the black hole was closest to the Yemen, and no one knew what would happen, and now only he and Xia Feng could fight. So, he dispersed all the ordinary disciples of the Yemen, leaving only the inner disciples of the Yemen. The others, however, watched the fire from the other side of the river.

Two days later, a breeze suddenly blew for no reason. The wind was so strange that it actually floated upwards. Ye Ye was startled and immediately looked up. The black hole was actually slowly emitting a suction force. He was startled and on guard at all times. However, the wind disappeared again overnight, and then replaced by a wind blowing from top to bottom, and the wind force was gradually increasing.

One night later, Ye Ye looked up again and found that the black hole had covered the entire range of Yemen Mountain without him noticing.

At noon, the sun still hadn't appeared. The sky was gloomy.

Ye Ye looked up, and a resentment suddenly came out from the black hole. Everyone immediately felt a resentment that made their hearts tremble.

Ye Ye frowned and said lightly: "It's coming! What will it be?" Beside him, Xia Feng had a cold face, but there was a trace of fear in her eyes that was difficult to conceal. She looked at Ye Ye worriedly, and said in a voice that only she could hear: "Don't be him, don't be him!"

Chapter 103: Xing Tian Reappears

Ye Ye did not notice Xia Feng's frightened expression, but looked at the black hole in the sky with a serious face. However, after a long time, there was still no response, only the huge resentment kept spreading. Anger, unwillingness, complaints... and other negative emotions constantly affected everyone in Yemen. Moreover, Qin Minglei and Li Bin were also awakened by the resentment, and then they came to Ye Ye's position with injuries and supported each other.

Ye Ye saw Qin Minglei coming, lowered his head, looked at Qin Minglei and said: "Minglei, you should know Qin Feng's situation. Now he has been sent down the mountain. If you want to go, I will never stop you!" Qin Minglei shook his head lightly, and his weak expression immediately changed to determination: "No, if I run away, I must not be worthy of being the father of the child." Ye Ye was stunned and stopped talking. He looked at Li Bin again, but found that two words were written on Li Bin's face as white as gold paper: firm!

Nodding, continued to look up at the black hole in the sky, and stopped talking. Huang Shang had already woken up, but he did not leave the room. He just squatted on the ground and gently stroked the Ghost Queen who seemed to be sleeping. He was holding two babies in his arms, Qin Feng and Huang Chen. He said lightly: "Rui Xin. Qin Feng is also destined to be with our Huang Chen. Why don't we save them together? Anyway, there is nothing for us to do now." After saying that, Huang

Shang glanced at the black hole in the sky with a trace of sadness in his eyes.

He actually found Qin Feng back.

"Haha, okay. We should have a good rest! I promised you that we would be ordinary people. Let's start!" After saying that, he lay down next to the Ghost Queen and put the two babies between them. Finally, he smiled, squeezed the Ghost Queen's hand tightly and said: "Rui Xin, let's start!" As soon as he finished speaking, black flames suddenly ignited on his body, but the black flames did not have any temperature at all, and the black flames condensed into two lines in the air, connected to Qin Feng and Huang Chen, and then the two babies suddenly ignited black flames. Not only that, the ghost queen, whose life and death were unknown, also had ghost energy coming out of her body for no reason, and then wrapped around Huang Shang's black flame, and kept infusing it into Huang Chen and Qin Feng's bodies.

The whole room was suddenly filled with dark air and emitted a dazzling light. However, no one noticed the strange phenomenon in the room at this moment. Because a hand suddenly stretched out from the black hole in the sky.

A hand, a thick hand, with a golden ring on the wrist, and the weapon held in that hand, Ye Ye was very familiar with. In that hand, it was a huge axe, or it was the Qi axe in the Gan Qi!

"Ah" a roar, like pain, like struggle, came from the black hole. Everyone was shocked, and some people even collapsed to the ground. Just a roar was so powerful. After the roar, a burst of red light suddenly appeared. The red light was like a human eye, but at this moment it exuded bloodthirstiness and oppression, making people dare not look directly at it.

The red light disappeared, and a body appeared in the black hole, a body without a head! The breasts are eyes, with a faint red glow, and the navel is a mouth, looking at the world indifferently.

But suddenly, a painful roar came from the navel, a blue glow flashed, and then stopped on the headless body. Ye Ye was shocked when he saw it, but soon he said to himself in relief: "This is easy to solve, but the black hole..." Ye Ye was not afraid! Moreover, he knew that the blue thing was the head of Tiansheng, Xingtian.

Ye Ye was not afraid, but Xia Feng behind him was already covered in cold sweat and couldn't even move. She knew that as long as she moved, she would definitely go soft: "How could this be... It's really him, it's really him... God of War, Xingtian!"

Qin Minglei and Li Bin behaved very naturally, standing behind Ye Ye, looking down at the strange phenomenon in the black hole above their heads, with a touch of determination in their eyes!

When the dark blue stopped at the head, the body suddenly stopped struggling, and then the dark blue in between flashed violently, and the light fell. A head appeared on the headless body, with braids all over his head, eyes like tigers and dragons, a firm and disdainful smile at the corner of his mouth, and then he looked at Ye Ye coldly. Then, he looked away and struggled violently.

Suddenly, the whole black hole became restless. A strange suction force suddenly came out, as if it wanted to suck Xing Tian in again. Moreover, bursts of black lightning appeared around the black hole, and Xing Tian's body stopped struggling. Suddenly, all the movements were quiet again.

The corner of his mouth twitched, and then Xing Tian suddenly stretched out another hand from the black hole, holding a dry shield in that hand. Suddenly, he actually threw the dry shield down violently, and the people below immediately dodged, and the huge shield was embedded in the mountain.

After doing all this, Xing Tian smiled, then held the axe in both hands and chopped fiercely at the black hole. Ye Ye took a look and shouted in surprise: "Hurry up and find a safe place, and try to grab the object... He...

Before he finished speaking, a huge suction force suddenly came from the black hole. Suddenly, trees... house tiles... even smaller stones were sucked up. Ye Ye's body was covered with colorful light, standing firmly in place, looking coldly at the sky.

The black hole was actually split open by a crack, and suddenly, the black hole became more hideous. The huge black hole itself was like an arm growing out, spreading thousands of miles in the sky. Xing Tian's split actually split the sky.

The whole world suddenly became chaotic. The sea began to rise violently, and the land was shaking restlessly from time to time. Moreover, a meteorite would fly out from the cracked sky from time to time, and then hit the ground with a long tail!

The sky is cracked!

Suddenly, a voice sounded from Ye Ye's left, where Xing Tian dropped his shield: "Ye Ye, die!" Ye Ye turned back in surprise, because the voice he heard was actually... Tiansheng!

Tiansheng, or Xingtian at this time. Naked, he had become the height of an ordinary person, holding the Ganqi firmly in his hand. Ye Ye looked at his body in confusion. The breasts that were originally like eyes were now just squeezed, and the navel was just closed. Suddenly, a bad premonition arose from the bottom of Ye Ye's heart.

Tiansheng smiled, then suddenly stopped laughing, and said with a grim face: "Resentment!"

'Resentment?' Ye Ye suddenly frowned, nodded in thought, and suddenly looked at Tiansheng as if he had realized something. Tiansheng also smiled, and then a black mist emerged from his huge body. Everyone clearly felt that the mist was filled with all the hatred and murderous intent...

"No wonder, all the evil spirits in the world were sucked in. No wonder the resentment is so great that it can corrode Xingtian! "Ye Ye thought. It turned out that Tiansheng did not summon Xingtian, but used the resentment of countless evil spirits to corrode Xingtian, and then let his body be used for his own purposes.

"Die!" Tiansheng suddenly shouted loudly, and before he finished speaking, Qi Axe had already swung out, and under the sharp axe wind, countless giant hands suddenly stretched out from the ground, clamping everyone tightly, and then cold wind, fire, thunder and lightning... suddenly broke out!

This power... is indeed not comparable to the power exerted by Tiansheng's hands that day!

Chapter 104 Environment or Dream

Ye Ye looked at the colorful sky and was startled. Then he looked at the Yemen disciples around him and saw that they were all in a safe place. He no longer had any concerns. The colorful light on his body suddenly condensed into a real flame. This was the first time that Ye Ye faced the enemy so solemnly. When he faced Tiansheng, he did not condense the colorful power of Nuwa into flames. And this flame was the aura of the ghost king that he inherited. When Ye Ye saw Tiansheng and Huang Shang combine their own energy and aura, he knew in his heart that he would definitely be able to do it. But he did not use it, but kept it as a trump card now.

However, is Ye Ye still Ye Ye at this moment?

Ye Ye looked at the mighty axe, slightly turned sideways and bounced, flew out diagonally, avoided the axe, and the colorful flames on his body also blocked those energy attacks outside.

Looking at Xing Tian, whose body was controlled by Tiansheng, Ye Ye shook his head and suddenly remembered the illusion he had after Li Yerui died that day, or...his memories!

Ye Ye had seen these illusions before, and had seen them several times, but not as strong as this time. He saw the people around him clearly, and even heard what they said.

Those people surrounded him and said respectfully: "King, are you tired? Why don't you come back?" Others said with hatred: "Why? Why did you create us?" Their words were full of resentment.

He waved his hand gently, and those people immediately dispersed, and he saw a peerless scene. This scene was far more spectacular than what he saw when the meteorite fell to the world, the black hole summoned by nature, and the heart fusion!

Ye Ye saw: meteorites all over the sky hit the ground everywhere, volcanoes sprayed wantonly, giant monsters and tall giants kept running towards him. And beside him, a gentle hand suddenly held him, and turned back lightly, that person...that person was exactly the same as Xia Feng!

And those people respectfully called her - mother!

But suddenly, a huge suction force suddenly came from the sky, and countless giant beasts and humans were sucked up. They looked up in horror, and the sky suddenly cracked, and the crack kept getting bigger. Then a red and a blue figure suddenly appeared beside him, kneeling on the ground and said: "Wang, mother. I'm sorry, we..."

Before Ye Ye could get angry, a woman who looked exactly like Xia Feng took two steps forward and said gently: "It's okay. You, run away!" While speaking, she used more force and then tightly grasped Ye Ye's hand.

The group of people showed fear in their eyes, and then showed reluctance and determination. In the end, they all left every three steps under the woman's drive.........

After the people left, the woman suddenly let go of Ye Ye's hand, and then her eyes showed a trace of sadness and reluctance, holding a colorful stone in her hand, which was the Nuwa Stone. Then, she chanted a spell that Ye Ye couldn't understand. In an instant, the Nuwa Stone became very huge, and then the woman's figure flashed, and the colorful light forced Ye Ye away. Then the woman turned into a human body with a snake tail, and slowly carried the Nuwa Stone that was still growing bigger and flew towards the sky.

And Ye Ye wanted to move, wanted to stop it. But he found that he couldn't move, and the colorful light trapped him there. Helpless Ye Ye screamed hoarsely: "Wa... Come back! Don't!" Tears flowed from the corners of his eyes while shouting. The color of the tears was also very strange. Although it was colorless, it was like a crystal, and thousands of colors kept changing.

After a long time, the sky suddenly burst into colorful light. Then a burst of light flashed by, and the whole ground suddenly shook, and then the dazzling light pierced people and couldn't open their eyes. After the light dissipated, the cracks in the sky were stitched up, and the woman disappeared.

Heartache, the heart is like a torn pain transmitted to the heart. Ye Ye also gained the ability to move, but he stood in the same place, tears kept flowing, and the whole person kept getting bigger. In the end, he turned into a huge mountain, and the tears from his eyes turned into two waterfalls that flowed down the cliff.

I don't know if it was in a dream or an illusion, time passed quickly.

Thousands of years passed, and tens of thousands of years passed. The two waterfalls stopped flowing. Ye Ye had been turned into a mountain and stayed there. Slowly, the mountain was weathering, and the crust moved slowly. The mountain slowly became smaller, from a mountain that reached the sky, to an ordinary mountain, then a small hill, and finally a mound of earth... I don't know how many years later, the hill disappeared. Ye Ye also turned into a human form, and then walked in this world. He forgot everything and walked in a daze, until one day, a man took him home and named him Ye Ye. Then, he also knew the man's name—Wu Daoming!

And now, Ye Ye finally knew his original name—Fuxi! The person who looks exactly like Xia Feng is called Nuwa!

He shook his head and turned his attention to Xing Tian again. The huge Qi Axe was still in front of him, but it was blocked by the colorful Nuwa power. Sadness suddenly appeared between his eyebrows and his heart ached. He looked at Xia Feng not far away. Her face and temperament were exactly the same as the Nuwa in his memory. An unknown feeling suddenly rose in his heart, and then he closed his eyes silently. The Nuwa power on his body also withdrew. Qi Axe lost the energy to resist and suddenly chopped down.

Seeing this, Xia Feng on the side suddenly burst into tears and shouted loudly: "Xi! Don't!"

As soon as the voice fell, the Qi Axe chopped down. Tiansheng pulled the corner of his mouth, and a touch of fanaticism appeared in his eyes, but he didn't feel any feeling of hitting an object, and his heart was immediately shocked.

"You... As expected, you have remembered me!" A gentle voice suddenly appeared behind Xia Feng. Xia Feng looked back with joy, and immediately said with surprise: "Xi, I'm sorry...I'm sorry!"

Ye Ye stretched out two fingers, then blocked Xia Feng's mouth, looked at Tiansheng who controlled Xing Tian's body and said: "It seems that your original actions and my indifference to the world have caused many problems. No need to apologize, I will solve the current problems first!" After that, he pulled Xia Feng behind him, and the colorful Nuwa power on his body suddenly weakened and turned colorless. If it weren't for the energy fluctuations that distorted the air around him, he wouldn't even see the energy on Ye Ye's body.

"The power of chaos!" Tiansheng was suddenly afraid, but his eyes immediately became very cunning and said: "If you have the ability to kill me, you will definitely not be able to make up for the things of Tiansheng. Nuwa...is no longer there. Even if she is, you can't make up for it with the little Nuwa stone in your body!"

Ye Ye frowned and shouted: 'Asshole! "After saying that, his figure flashed, rushed up, and then suddenly disappeared in the air, leaving only a belt of air that distorted the air.

When he appeared, he was already in front of Tiansheng. Tiansheng only had time to slightly lift the dry shield, and was stabbed by the night sun in Ye Ye's hand. And the force also knocked Tiansheng out.

One blow, just one blow. Tiansheng, who was the body of Xingtian, was seriously injured and knocked away! But it's true, if Ye Ye, as the human king Fuxi, can't do this, then he doesn't deserve to be Fuxi!

Chapter 105 Sealed Energy

Tiansheng suddenly stood up trembling at this moment, and then said with a crazy look: "Haha, it's just like that." Ye Ye looked in the direction of the voice, and a trace of fear appeared on his face, but he immediately dispelled it, and then the energy on his body reappeared. He looked coldly at the body of Xing Tian controlled by Tiansheng.

However, Tiansheng suddenly spit out a mouthful of blood, but his face did not show a trace of weakness, but he was more energetic: "Xing Tian, why can you fight with the emperor for so long, and you can fight without cutting off your head? Why? Haha, tell me, why!" After saying that, Qi Fu grabbed it fiercely and danced it vigorously. Ye Ye frowned and was about to rush forward, but he saw Tiansheng continue to say: "That's it..." After saying that, he suddenly disappeared, and when he appeared, Qi Fu's huge axe face was already in front of Ye Ye.

Ye Ye's face sank, but he was not surprised. Instead, the colorless energy on his body surged, and then he slightly turned his body before the axe face hit him again, avoiding the chop. With the short sword in his hand, Ye Yangcheng raised it up suddenly, firmly pressing against the axe and stick of Qi Axe, and then moved along the axe and stick, heading straight towards Tiansheng's hand holding Qi Axe.

Tiansheng was startled, and when Ye Ye approached, he suddenly let go of Qi Axe, and smashed Ye Ye with the dry shield of his other hand. Ye Ye had no choice but to retreat immediately. Tiansheng saw Ye Ye retreating, stretched out one foot, tiptoed Qi Axe, and grabbed Qi Axe again, and slashed at Ye Ye again.

At such a close distance, Ye Ye didn't need to worry about the huge Qi Axe causing any damage. He didn't dodge, but went forward. However, he cautiously separated a trace of energy for defense.

Tiansheng saw this, and the corner of his mouth twitched. There was only a sound of metal collision, and the Qi Axe shrank without knowing when. Fortunately, Ye Ye separated that trace of defensive energy in a flash to block the axe attack. Then he immediately stepped aside, because Tiansheng was close, and then the dry shield in his hand smashed over with dazzling blue flames.

After Ye Ye dodged, before he could catch his breath, the Qi Axe in Tiansheng's hand turned huge again, and then chopped fiercely. Ye Ye was shocked, but he couldn't dodge it. At least he raised Ye Yang, and then supported the energy to protect the vitals. He wanted to use the fierce slash to retreat.

However, Ye Ye miscalculated this time. Because, at the moment when he was in the Qi Axe, countless hands stretched out from the huge axe face, and then tightly wrapped Ye Ye up. Those hands were black, and they would be vaporized by the colorless energy the moment they touched Ye Ye, but the huge number actually restrained Ye Ye and made him unable to move temporarily.

Tiansheng smiled. Then he grabbed the axe stick of Qi Axe tightly with his hand, and the Qi Axe suddenly became smaller, while Tiansheng grabbed the smaller Qi Axe and was pulled over. The inscription on the dry shield in his other hand lit up and bloomed an extremely dazzling blue light.

Ye Ye was helpless. He felt as if he had fallen into the desert quicksand. No matter how powerful he was, he could not get rid of the comfort of those strange hands. Although those strange hands would disappear and vaporize the moment they touched him, he could do nothing about the huge number. What's more, Tiansheng was holding the dry shield and was approaching.

"Die!" Tiansheng roared fiercely and smashed the shield in his hand towards Ye Ye. In an instant, the dry shield emitted a dazzling light that blocked everyone's vision. Only a sound of hitting an object came from the light.

"Xi..." Xia Feng could not see the situation in the light and called out worriedly.

After the light dissipated, Tiansheng was the only one who stood proudly with an axe in the place where Ye Ye had just stood. Ye Ye had disappeared.

"Dead?" Tiansheng did clearly feel that he had hit the object just now, but at this moment Ye Ye disappeared. He immediately became cautious and held the dry shield in his hand to be on guard at all times.

Suddenly, the ground sank. Tiansheng was startled, and before he could react, he fell in. Then a wave of waves emanated from the pit, distorting the air. After that, Ye Ye jumped out from inside, and then kept gathering energy, preparing to give Tiansheng a fatal blow.

Just now, the moment the dry shield touched Ye Ye. Ye Ye actually made an amazing move. He actually drove the energy to rotate, and then took advantage of the blue light to cover the field of vision, and rotated into the ground. Rotating into the soil, the ground could not be seen, because Ye Ye had been under Tiansheng's feet, but Tiansheng did not pay attention to his feet, so there was the scene just now. And the sound of Tiansheng hitting the object just now was just a stone.

A huge axe suddenly appeared, broke the ground, and chopped towards Ye Ye. But Ye Ye frowned, and then released the energy that had been gathered for a long time. The energy not only blocked the huge axe face, but also immediately attached to the axe face, immediately dispelling the blue flame attached to it, and went to the ground.

Suddenly, a scream came from the ground, and a man jumped out of the ground, covered with wounds and bleeding from the corners of his mouth. The blue flame on his body slowly dissipated.

"Surrender! Your energy is being devoured by my energy, seal..." Ye Ye didn't finish his words, but Tiansheng said angrily: "No, it's impossible to surrender. If I die, I will also drag this world to be buried with me!" After that, he jumped up suddenly, and then the axe in his hand suddenly grew longer and chopped towards the black hole in the sky. He actually gathered the last energy a second before the seal

Ye Ye was startled, and then jumped up. He wanted to stop Tiansheng, he knew what Tiansheng wanted to do. Tiansheng wanted to split his black hole, and then, the energy in the black hole would... Ye Ye didn't dare to think about it, and the energy on his body suddenly surged.

However, it was too late after all. Ye Ye didn't catch up with the speed at which the axe in Tiansheng's hand grew, and he chopped towards the black hole one step earlier than Ye Ye.

Instantly, the suction came out suddenly. Tiansheng was sucked up. Ye Ye's attack missed, and then Ye Ye immediately gathered energy to resist the huge suction force, slowly landing on the ground, but saw that many of the Yemen disciples around him were sucked up.

He grabbed Xia Feng who was slowly sucked up beside him, his face sank, and he looked at the black hole blankly.

"No, don't! Don't!" Ye Ye suddenly muttered to himself.

Suddenly, the expansion speed of the black hole increased sharply, and shining meteorites with long tails appeared from the black hole, and then fell to the ground, hitting a huge meteorite crater! Even some meteorites fell into the city and houses. The screams shook the world and Ye Ye's heart!

Chapter 106 How can we be missing

With a sound of 'meow', a black shadow suddenly jumped in front of Ye Ye. Ye Ye frowned, then picked up Ye Yue without saying anything. Xia Feng said at this moment: "Have you recovered your memory?"

Ye Ye nodded, looked at the gradually spreading black hole and said worriedly: "I don't know, maybe. But, am I still the same person as before?" After that, he shook his head and touched Ye Yue in his arms. Xia Feng returned to his indifferent look and stopped talking, but said in his heart: "Xi, if possible, I…"

"No! Absolutely not!" Ye Ye suddenly said, Xia Feng was startled and immediately asked 'What's wrong?'

"I can't let that ending continue! This time, let me do it!" After that, the colorless energy suddenly burst out, and then gradually transformed into colorful flames. Xia Feng shook her head, grabbed Ye Ye's hand tightly and said: "It's useless, as Tiansheng said, we have too few Nuwa stones!"

Ye Ye was stunned, his face sank and he regained his composure. Shaking his head, "Is it really the only way to destroy the people of the world?" Ye Ye is Fuxi, the king of men Fuxi. How can he not consider the people of the world?

Xia Feng is the reincarnation of Nuwa, and has the memory of Nuwa. She is also very helpless. The sky leaked again, but she can't do anything! Insufficient Nuwa stones, this is a serious problem! Originally, Nuwa piled up huge stones on the top of Tiantai Mountain as a furnace, took five-colored soil as material, and borrowed the sun god fire. It took nine days and nine nights to refine 36,501 five-colored giant stones. Then it took another nine days and nine nights to repair the sky with 36,500 colorful stones. The remaining piece was left on the top of the mountain in Tanggu, Tiantai Mountain. It took 36,500 pieces to repair the sky, but now there is only one piece! How can it be enough!

However, Yeyue in Ye Ye's arms suddenly scratched the back of Ye Ye's hand, then "meowed", jumped out of Ye Ye's arms, and went to the back mountain. After walking two steps, he would look back at Ye Ye. Ye Ye was puzzled, and suddenly remembered the situation when Yeyue took him to find the Yemen Sutra. He immediately followed and said, "I don't know what this cat spirit has found!" Yeyue was originally a cat spirit, a pet of Fuxi. After Fuxi turned into a mountain, it waited for countless years. In exchange for life, it used its own power as an exchange!

Xia Feng was startled and immediately followed Ye Ye. Yeyue and Xia Feng ran towards the back mountain with Ye Ye. After a long time, they stopped, and then Yeyue gently called "meow", and three cats suddenly turned out from the bushes. They were Yeyue's belongings.

"Yeyue, why did you bring me here?" Ye Ye asked in confusion. Yeyue couldn't speak, so he had to shout, and then turned into the bushes, and his wife and children followed him immediately. Ye Ye was shocked and followed him in immediately, but he found that there was a hole in the bushes. The entrance was very narrow and only allowed one person to crawl through.

The corridor of the cave was also very long. Ye Ye and Xia Feng crawled for a long time in the dark. If it weren't for Yeyue or Yeyue's wife leading the way, they would have lost their way long ago. After a long time, several people finally got out of the corridor and stood in a hall.

But it was dark and nothing could be seen clearly. Ye Ye thought about it and prepared to raise the flame of Nuwa to illuminate the darkness. But he heard Yeyue's excited cry, and Ye Ye stopped condensing in surprise. Shaking his head, he had to take out the fire, and then illuminated the faint range. Looking around, there was a huge stone there! Five-colored stone!

"Nuwa Stone!" Ye Ye and Xia Feng exclaimed at the same time. The number of Nuwa stones is absolutely limited. If you use a little, you will have less. Moreover, when Nuwa repaired the sky, she refined 36,500 pieces! The Nuwa stones that should have been extinct actually reappeared, and they were no smaller than the one that Nuwa refined! Ye Ye smiled, and Xia Feng also smiled! The common people are saved.

However, another problem was placed in front of them again. At this moment, Nuwa did not have the power of the past. Now Xia Feng only had Nuwa's memory, but did not obtain the power passed down.

Who will repair the sky, who will refine it?

Ye Ye silently extinguished the fire, and then said softly: "There is no way! A good cook cannot cook without rice. We haven't seen each other for thousands of years, right? Let's enjoy this last time! I am willing to see you at the end!" Ye Ye suddenly said, and Xia Feng's body trembled immediately after hearing it in the dark. Suddenly, she felt Ye Ye hugging her tightly. She was startled and tears flowed down.

She herself didn't know where her so-called Nuwa memories came from. It seemed that she slowly woke up after she saw Ye Ye for the first time! However, that memory made Xia Feng very entangled, and she seemed to be dominated by that memory and did everything after that!

Seeing that Xia Feng didn't speak, Ye Ye said again: "Remember? We were originally brothers and sisters, and it was a forbidden love. However, we broke through all the obstacles, but in the end we didn't get together! I thought I would never see you again. No matter how powerful a person is, he can't fight against the sky. Unexpectedly, after so many years, I saw you again!" Xia Feng was in Ye Ye's arms, and she couldn't stop crying. She shook her head and didn't speak.

Ye Ye's voice suddenly became very gentle: "Wa. Remember you chose the common people? It's a good choice! But now I have to make the same choice, I'm sorry!" After Xia Feng heard it, her body immediately tensed up, and then she struggled, but was hit on the back of the head by Ye Ye and fainted.

"I'm sorry! If God wants, we will meet again in tens of millions of years!" Ye Ye, or Ye Ye as Fuxi, is willing to do it? No, of course he is reluctant! However, the current situation does not allow him to do it!

On the ground, the speed of the black hole's expansion keeps getting faster and faster, and meteorites, earthquakes, and tsunamis suddenly rage. The whole world is in chaos, or it is heading towards destruction! That is the natural will that distorted the will of Xingtian!

Underground, Ye Ye gently put the unconscious Xia Feng aside, his face was as gentle as when he buried Li Yerui, smiling calmly, his face was not sad at all! After doing all this, Ye Ye suddenly walked towards the huge five-colored stone, the flame of Nuwa on his body ignited, and then the whole person also stuck to the five-colored stone. He wanted to use himself as a furnace to refine the five-colored stone!

However, Ye Ye is Fuxi, the king of men Fuxi. However, at this moment, he did not have or recover much power. The five-colored stone was burned by him and turned red, but there was no sign of being refined. Ye Ye was anxious, so he took out Ye Yang and cut his left wrist. The blood flowed out desperately, and then flowed on the colorful stone. The colorful stone that was touched by the blood immediately softened and showed signs of melting! However, compared with the hugeness of the colorful stone and the softened part, it was really just the tip of the iceberg.

Ye Ye was helpless, his face sank again, and Ye Yang changed hands, and then cut his right wrist and ankle. He immediately stood on the top of the huge colorful stone and let the blood invade. However, how could one person's blood cover a huge stone of about ten feet! Moreover, the long-term blood loss made Ye Ye dizzy and dizzy. He could no longer stand and slid down from the stone! Then he stood up weakly again.

But suddenly, five dazzling lights suddenly lit up behind him. These five people turned out to be Qin Minglei, Li Bin, Yang Hengchao, Yang Tianhai, and Ye Hen! None of them had followed Ye Ye here, and then groped in in the dark!

"Ye Ye, how can we be missing out! Don't think you can be a hero alone! No matter who you are, you are just the head of our Yemen! Ye Ye!" Li Bin stepped forward to support Ye Ye, and then said.

Ye Ye smiled weakly. Although he didn't think the five of them could help, he was very moved. After standing firm, he looked at the five of them and said, "Okay, let's become a new generation of heroes together!" After that, Ye Ye turned around again, forced out the flame of Nuwa, and with Ye Yang in hand, he was ready to bleed again, but was stopped by Li Bin: "Ye Ye, no matter how powerful you are, how much blood can one person have compared to the blood of five people?"

After Li Bin said that, the other four people pulled their mouth corners at the same time, and then smiled strangely at the same time! The five people actually made a move at the same time. They jumped onto the huge five-colored stone at the same time, and then cut their arteries in both hands, and bled on the five-colored stone. Their blood would not soften the five-colored stone directly like Ye Ye's blood. However, they are not ordinary people after all, and the energy in their blood is naturally huge, not to mention the blood of five people at the same time!

"Ye Zi, stop being dazed! Refine it!" Qin Minglei suddenly shouted, and his clothes immediately broke and scattered, and then he began to bleed. He actually used his Qi to break through the blood vessels in his body, letting all the blood flow out. The pores, facial features, and any place that could flow out were bleeding like a faucet. Seeing this, the other four people also smiled, without any complaints, and immediately forced their blood vessels to break like Qin Minglei, letting the blood soak the huge five-colored stone!

Ye Ye was shocked, but this was not the time to be surprised. He smiled calmly, and then immediately drove the flame of Nuwa to burn the five-colored stone. At first, Ye Ye did not dare to burn with all his strength, for he was afraid of accidentally burning the five people above to death. However, the five people heard at the same time: "Damn, Ye Ye didn't eat? We have no clothes and we are cold!" Ye Ye gritted his teeth and immediately drove the Nuwa flame with all his strength. The five people on the five-colored stone were naturally burned by the Nuwa flame, but the five people actually put their hands on each other's shoulders at the same time and laughed. In the laughter, the five people were burned to ashes in the Nuwa flame and then vaporized!

At this time, on the ground, the black hole expanded more and more. The suction force and meteorites kept torturing the people below. Human lives were taken away at will like stones at this moment! As the center, Yemen Mountain was now bare, and even the mountain was slowly being pulled into dust by the suction force, slowly reducing its altitude! However, there was a place that was giving off a strange scene.

There, the black ghost energy actually resisted the suction of the black hole. Let the surrounding mountains lower, and the room wrapped in black ghost energy was no problem at all! And the last person in Yemen was there. Their eyes were all focused on the bed. There, Huang Shang and the Ghost Queen had fallen into a deep sleep, and the two babies were suspended in the air above the disaster, with thick, strong ghost energy constantly emanating from them, and then resisting the suction.

But suddenly, a meteorite appeared from the black hole with a long tail, heading towards Yemen Mountain. If the meteorite hit, it would be a complete destruction!

Chapter 107 Ending

Before the meteorite fell, the people on the ground had already felt the power and temperature of the meteorite, and the strong wind formed by the meteorite's rapid impact blew his hair up. The remaining disciples of Yemen, who were already scarred, looked at the huge meteorite in the sky with even more despair in their eyes.

But suddenly, two groups of black light broke through the roof from their side and shot towards the meteorite. Then they hit the meteorite violently, and suddenly there was a violent explosion. The two beams of light actually smashed the meteorite into pieces, and the meteorite fragments with flames fell all over the sky. Although many fragments hit the house where the Yemen disciples were, they were stopped by the strong black ghost energy and did not cause any casualties.

The remaining disciples of Yemen, who escaped death again, looked up. The two beams of light had disappeared at this moment, and two small bodies were floating in the air and slowly falling, and finally suspended outside the eerie ghost energy. At this time, the ghost energy suddenly disappeared. But they didn't feel any suction at all. Everyone was shocked and looked at the two people. They were very familiar with the two people. They were Huang Chen, the son of the two guests Huang Shang and the ghost queen Nalan Ziruixin, and Qin Feng, the son of Qin Minglei!

The two babies were floating in the air with their eyes closed and serious faces, and the eerie ghost energy kept surging outside their bodies. The originally cute two people now looked as majestic as the sons of the devil.

When everyone looked at Qin Feng and Huang Chen, Huang Shang and the ghost queen who were originally lying on the bed slowly turned into two black butterflies and flew away quietly. They were not sucked away by the suction force from the black hole at all, and slowly flew away. Their destination was the tomb of the ghost clan!

Huang Shang and the ghost queen used their last vitality to create the current Qin Feng and Huang Chen, and their lives have been extraordinary since then. However, perhaps no one will have a future.

With the support of Qin Feng and Huang Chen's energy, everyone in Yemen is temporarily safe. However, watching the black hole in the sky that kept expanding and spinning out meteorites, everyone became more and more desperate.

Suddenly, the entire ground began to shake violently and could not stand at all. Then a huge crack started at the foot of Yemen Mountain and extended in all directions. The ground could no longer withstand the huge suction of the black hole and cracked, breaking into pieces.

A huge crack slowly moved towards the remaining disciples of Yemen, and actually split Yemen Mountain in half. The Yemen disciples looked at the huge deep pit, kneeling on the ground, but their eyes suddenly became clear. I don't know who suddenly shouted: "Damn it! We have been dead for a thousand years, and we are still afraid of death?" Although the man's voice was trembling, it became extremely encouraging at this moment, and the remaining Yemen disciples were zombies from the imperial mausoleum. After being encouraged by those words, they were no longer afraid, but watched the crack spread rapidly towards them!

It's not just this crack that's spreading, countless cracks are spreading everywhere from the foot of Yemen Mountain. If this continues, the whole world will be completely destroyed!

Hundred meters... Fifty meters... Thirty meters... Twenty meters... The crack spread very quickly, and in a blink of an eye it reached the front, and all the disciples of Yemen closed their eyes, waiting for the final destruction of their fate! But Huang Chen and Qin Feng were still floating in the air with their eyes closed, and their ghostly spirit was still strong!

Ten meters... Just when the crack was ten meters away from the disciples of Yemen, suddenly, a violent roar came from the ground, and then a person with colorful flames all over his body, even the whole person was colorful, jumped out of the ground. After he jumped out of the ground, he landed on his feet, and then a shining colorful light was thrown into the crack by him. Suddenly, the crack emitted a dazzling light, and then stopped spreading, and slowly sewed up.

It was Ye Ye! He actually refined the huge colorful stone at the last moment, forming a real Nuwa stone. He slowly walked towards the Yemen disciples, then put down Xia Feng in his arms, gently touched Xia Feng's beautiful cheek, and smiled happily. Then he looked at Qin Feng and Huang Chen who were suspended in the air in surprise. In front of him, Qin Minglei suddenly walked towards Huang Chen with a cigarette in his mouth, but his eyes were gentle. Ye Ye smiled, took out two smaller Nuwa stones and put them into the ghostly aura of Qin Feng and Huang Chen, and then watched the ghostly aura slowly merge with the Nuwa stone and said: "Child, remember. The Nuwa stone here contains the spirit and blood of your parents!"

After that, his feet suddenly sank and rushed towards the black hole in the sky.

It turned out that at the last moment. Qin Minglei, Li Bin, Yang Tianhai, Yang Hengchao, and Ye Hen used their lives as the price to help Ye Ye soften the colorful stone. Sad and furious, Ye Ye naturally knew that he could not waste their lives, and finished refining the Nuwa stone at the last moment, but the price he paid was not small. Of all the Nuwa stones, 35,603 Nuwa stones, 35,600 were integrated into his body, which means that to fill the black hole, Ye Ye must sacrifice himself! It is permanent death! Instead of leaving energy to slowly revive like Nuwa did at the beginning.

And Ye Ye used one of the three extra stones to save the Yemen disciples, and the other two were directly given to Qin Feng and Huang Chen!

The black hole in the sky seemed to have spirituality and felt that it was about to be destroyed. The suction force became more violent, but Ye Ye's body was ignited with colorful flames, ignoring the suction force of the black hole. Moreover, after passing through a huge meteorite, he successfully entered the black hole.

Suddenly, the suction force stopped. Earthquakes, tsunamis, volcanic eruptions, and the spread of cracks all stopped. The sky suddenly burst into a dazzling light that surpassed the sun. Red, orange, red, green, blue, and purple, the seven colors kept changing colors.

Then, red landed on the ground first and calmed the volcano; orange also fell and healed the cracks; red followed closely and cooled the volcanic ash to form fertile soil; green revived plants; blue shone all over the sky, and the sky became purer; purple covered the entire earth, and everyone's face became calm under the illumination of purple light, and their hearts were settled!

After a long time, the colorful light dissipated. The black hole no longer existed. The earth was jubilant. The happiness of rebirth after the disaster filled the whole world! However, the Yemen disciples on Yemen Mountain looked gloomy. Perhaps only they knew that it was their leader Ye Ye who saved the whole world at the cost of his life!

A Yemen disciple walked forward and hugged Qin Feng and Huang Chen, who were sleeping quietly after the ghost energy dissipated. His face was very calm. He said: "Let's go! Take..." He wanted to say to take Xia Feng, but he didn't expect that Xia Feng had disappeared! Shaking his head, he led everyone slowly to the original back mountain location, and his whereabouts have been unknown since then!

Many years later, it is said that some people heard that there was a Taoist temple in a hidden mountain somewhere, and the deity enshrined there was not a deity or arhat, but a young man with a smiling face and colorful light all over his body; some people also said that countless treasures were found somewhere, and a sign was found that read: Huangdao League; some people also said that a woman, a cold beauty, often appeared in the middle of the night with countless cats, two of which were slightly larger, one black and one white. They appeared for a few seconds and then disappeared out of thin air.

Everything is a legend, everything is a cloud, submerged in the moment of history.

Also by Miko ML

The Billionaire's Unexpected Bride
The Billionaire's Unexpected Bride Season 1
The Billionaire's Unexpected Bride Season 2

The Gatekeeper of Night Spirits
The Gatekeeper of Night Spirits Vol One
The Gatekeeper of Night Spirits Vol Two
The Gatekeeper of Night Spirits Vol Three

Whispers of Jasmine
Whispers of Jasmine Season 1
Whispers of Jasmine Season 2

Standalone
The Enigmatic Banquet
◇◇◇◇◇ Desert Island in Malaysia

Milton Keynes UK
Ingram Content Group UK Ltd.
UKHW042004281024
450365UK00003B/169